continued . . .

Sun Kissed

"This smart, wholesome tale should appeal to any fan of traditional romance."
—*Publishers Weekly*

"Another heartwarming chapter in the Coulter family saga is on tap in the always wonderful Anderson's newest release. . . . Anderson is at her best when it comes to telling stories that are deeply emotional and heartfelt."
—*Romantic Times* (4½ Stars)

Summer Breeze

"Anderson understands the inner workings of the human soul so deeply that she's able to put intense emotion within a stunning romance in such a way that you'll believe in miracles. Add to this her beautiful writing style, memorable characters, and a timeless story, and you have an unmatched reading adventure."
—*Romantic Times* (4½ Stars)

"The kind of book that will snare you so completely, you'll not want to put it down. It engages the intellect and emotions; it'll make you care. It will also make you smile . . . a lot. And that's a guarantee."
—Romance Reviews Today

My Sunshine

"With the author's signature nurturing warmth and emotional depth, this beautifully written romance is a richly rewarding experience for any reader."
—*Booklist*

Blue Skies

"Readers may need to wipe away tears . . . since few will be able to resist the power of this beautifully emotional, wonderfully romantic love story."
—*Booklist*

"A keeper and a very strong contender for Best Contemporary Romance of the Year."
—Romance Reviews Today

Bright Eyes

"Offbeat family members and genuine familial love give a special lift to this marvelous story. An Anderson book is a guaranteed great read!"

—*Romantic Times* (4½ Stars, Top Pick)

Only by Your Touch

"Ben Longtree is a marvelous hero whose extraordinary gifts bring a unique and special magic to this warmhearted novel. No one can tug your heartstrings better than Catherine Anderson."

—*Romantic Times* (4½ Stars, Top Pick)

Always in My Heart

"Emotionally involving, family-centered, and relationship-oriented, this story is a rewarding read." —*Library Journal*

"[A] superbly written contemporary romance, which features just the kind of emotionally nourishing, comfortably compassionate type of love story this author is known for creating."

—*Booklist*

Sweet Nothings

"Pure reading magic."

—*Booklist*

Phantom Waltz

"Anderson departs from traditional romantic stereotypes in this poignant, contemporary tale of a love that transcends all boundaries . . . romantic through and through."

—*Publishers Weekly*

Catherine Anderson

Sun Kissed

and

Beautiful Gifts

A SIGNET BOOK

SIGNET
Published by New American Library, a division of
Penguin Group (USA) Inc., 375 Hudson Street,
New York, New York 10014, USA
Penguin Group (Canada), 90 Eglinton Avenue East, Suite 700, Toronto,
Ontario M4P 2Y3, Canada (a division of Pearson Penguin Canada Inc.)
Penguin Books Ltd., 80 Strand, London WC2R 0RL, England
Penguin Ireland, 25 St. Stephen's Green, Dublin 2,
Ireland (a division of Penguin Books Ltd.)
Penguin Group (Australia), 250 Camberwell Road, Camberwell, Victoria 3124,
Australia (a division of Pearson Australia Group Pty. Ltd.)
Penguin Books India Pvt. Ltd., 11 Community Centre, Panchsheel Park,
New Delhi - 110 017, India
Penguin Group (NZ), 67 Apollo Drive, Rosedale, North Shore 0632,
New Zealand (a division of Pearson New Zealand Ltd.)
Penguin Books (South Africa) (Pty.) Ltd., 24 Sturdee Avenue,
Rosebank, Johannesburg 2196, South Africa

Penguin Books Ltd., Registered Offices:
80 Strand, London WC2R 0RL, England

Published by Signet, an imprint of New American Library, a division of Penguin
Group (USA) Inc. *Sun Kissed* was previously published in a separate Signet edition.
"Beautiful Gifts" was originally published in *The True Love Wedding Dress*.

First Printing (Bonus Book), January 2011
10 9 8 7 6 5 4 3 2 1

Sun Kissed copyright © Adeline Catherine Anderson, 2007
"Beautiful Gifts" copyright © Adeline Catherine Anderson, 2005
All rights reserved

 REGISTERED TRADEMARK—MARCA REGISTRADA

Printed in the United States of America

Dear Readers:

New American Library is offering you a special treat in this reissue of *Sun Kissed* by including a bonus short story, "Beautiful Gifts," originally published in the anthology *The True Love Wedding Dress*. This new edition of *Sun Kissed,* with a beautiful new cover, will allow you to revisit Samantha Harrigan and Tucker Coulter's love story, or perhaps read it for the very first time. The additional story will allow you to take a lovely journey into the past to remind you of the families—the Keegans, Paxtons, and O'Shannessys—whose stories are linked to the modern-day Coulter series. This is, in a way, timely, because it is my plan to soon take you into the late 1800s with David Paxton's love story. Coming even sooner is *Here to Stay*, a contemporary Harrigan family novel featuring Zach Harrigan. You can read a preview of it in the back of this book.

I hope you greatly enjoy this special reissue of love stories that will bring you a magical blend of past and present.

Happy reading, my friends!

All the best,

Catherine Anderson

Joseph Simon Paxton, Sr. (1824–1866)

Dory Sue Jesperson Keegan (1831–1920)

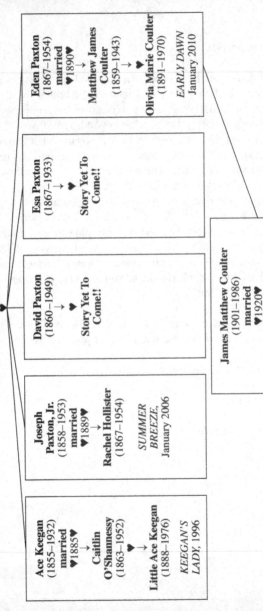

Ace Keegan
(1855–1932)
married ♥1885♥

Caitlin O'Shannessy
(1863–1952)

Little Ace Keegan
(1888–1976)

KEEGAN'S LADY, 1996

Joseph Paxton, Jr.
(1858–1953)
married ♥1889♥

Rachel Hollister
(1867–1954)

SUMMER BREEZE, January 2006

David Paxton
(1860–1949)

Story Yet To Come!!

Esa Paxton
(1867–1933)

Story Yet To Come!!

Eden Paxton
(1867–1954) married ♥1890♥

Matthew James Coulter
(1859–1943)

Olivia Marie Coulter
(1891–1970)

EARLY DAWN January 2010

James Matthew Coulter
(1901–1986)
married ♥1920♥

Sarah Beth Johnson
(1902–1989)

Harvey James Coulter
(1942–)
married
♥1967♥
→
Mary Ann McBride
(1946–)

Jake Coulter
(1969–)
married
♥2001♥
→
Molly Sterling
(1972–)
♥ →
Garrett Coulter
(2002–)
Cheyenne Coulter
(2005–)

SWEET NOTHINGS
January 2002

Zeke Coulter
(1970–)
married
♥2003♥
→
Natalie Patterson
(1973–)
→
Chad Coulter
(1992–)
Rose Coulter
(1999–)
(both adopted)

BRIGHT EYES
June 2004

Tucker Coulter
(1970–)
married
♥2006♥
→
Samantha Harrigan
(1977–)

SUN KISSED
January 2007

Isaiah Coulter
(1970–)
married
♥2005♥
→
Laura Townsend
(1973–)

MY SUNSHINE
January 2005

Hank Coulter
(1971–)
married
♥2003♥
→
Carly Adams
(1975–)
→
Hank Coulter, Jr.
(2004–)

BLUE SKIES
January 2004

Bethany Coulter
(1974–)
married
♥2000♥
→
Ryan Kendrick
(1970–)
→
Sylvester Kendrick
(2001–)
Chastity Kendrick
(2004–)

PHANTOM WALTZ
July 2001

Conor Patrick O'Shannessy (1839–1884)
Married
1859
♥

Hope Wilson (1841–1865)
♥

Caitlin O'Shannessy
(1853–1952)
married
♥1885♥
↓

Ace Keegan
(1855–1932)
♥
↓

Little Ace Keegan
(1888–1976)
Dory Sue Keegan
(1890–1979)

KEEGAN'S LADY,
1996

**Patrick Conor
O'Shannessy**
(1865–1954)
married
♥1887♥
♥
↓

**Faith Marie
Maxwell**
(1865–1947)
♥
↓

**Chastity Ann
O'Shannessy**
(1881–1952)

BEAUTIFUL GIFTS,
2005

Sun Kissed

This book is dedicated to my beloved niece, Robyn Antonucci, CVT, in deep appreciation for all her help with the technical aspects of equine care and treatment. Without her enthusiastic input and willingness to be on call whenever I needed information, this story might never have been written. Thank you so much for all your support, Robyn, and also the countless times you went to Dr. Heidi for her expert advice.

I also want to acknowledge all the wonderful horses that have crossed my path over my lifetime and remain in my memory. It is my hope that this book will increase public awareness of the abuse and neglect these magnificent animals must so often endure. If you see a skeleton horse, call your local humane society and the police. If you witness equine abuse, contact the authorities immediately. Too often when an animal is being abused, people look the other way. Please, don't! You may be that helpless creature's only hope.

Chapter One

For as long as Samantha Harrigan could remember, she had loved going to the rodeo. Now that she'd found the courage to come again, she could scarcely believe that she had deprived herself for so long of something she enjoyed so much. Thus far, she hadn't even glimpsed her ex-husband, a dyed-in-the-wool rodeo cowboy who had been her reason for staying away. He was probably too busy flirting with blond buckle bunnies to mingle with the masses. Early on in the marriage, his infidelities had broken Samantha's heart. Now she felt only relief that the divorce was final and Steve Fisher was out of her life.

As she worked her way through the crowd to reach the concession stand, the hot August sun beat down on the fairgrounds, creating a gigantic potpourri of scents within the circle of buildings. The sawdust underfoot sent up a woodsy musk that blended pleasantly with the pungent odors of livestock, a motley assortment of perfume and aftershave, and the mouthwatering aroma of junk food trailing on the breeze.

With each breath, Samantha was transported back to her childhood. Some of her earliest memories were of going to the rodeo with her dad and older brothers. Pictures flashed through her mind—of her father swinging her up to ride on his hip, of herself all decked out in brand-new rodeo finery, and of her brothers holding her up to see over the crowd while their dad competed in an event. To this day, she could remember the stickiness on her fingers from eating cotton candy, and how she'd hated having her face washed afterward with a spit-dampened handkerchief.

The memory made Samantha grin. Oh, how she had adored cotton candy—and still did, truth told. Being the ripe old age of twenty-nine didn't mean she no longer appreciated life's simple pleasures. Before she left the compound today, she would buy herself an extra-large cloud of cotton candy, and she would eat it just as she had years ago, pulling off big chunks and letting them melt in her mouth.

For now, though, she had a tall iced tea in mind, something cold and wet to soothe her throat, which was raw from yelling at the top of her lungs for her brothers, who had performed in some of the morning rounds. She mustn't be too hoarse to cheer when her stallion, Blue Blazes, and eldest brother, Clint, took first place in the cutting horse competition. Heck, no. She'd be in the front row, screaming for all she was worth. Her only regret would be that she wasn't in the arena herself. *Next year*, she thought determinedly. With another twelve months to distance herself from the painful memories of her marriage, she would be ready to compete again, without any fear that a glimpse of Steve's face in the crowd might make her freeze or hesitate, thus causing Blue to lose points.

It was in the cutting horse competition that the Harrigan line of quarter horses truly shone, for in that event, the quality, training, skill, and intelligence of an animal were put to the ultimate test. If her beloved Blue Blazes won—and there was no question in Samantha's mind that he would—her reputation as a breeder and trainer would get a huge boost, enabling her to name her price for Blue's stud fees. In her present financial situation, a good year would go a long way toward getting her ranch out of the red.

Samantha had nearly reached the concession stand when

she heard a horse scream. The sound of terror and pain tugged at her heart, and she whirled to locate its source. What she saw made her blood run hot. A stout, middle-aged man in flashy, Western-style clothing was trying to load a sorrel gelding into a transport trailer. The animal was balking, and its owner was beating it with the long handle of a lunge whip.

Samantha couldn't bear to see an animal mistreated. With purposeful strides, she advanced on the horse trailer, the heels of her riding boots digging deep into the sawdust. As she drew close, she realized the man was intoxicated. Each time he swung his arm, he staggered and almost fell from the loading ramp.

A group of onlookers had already gathered around the trailer. From the corner of her eye, Samantha saw several able-bodied men just standing there. *Why?* The poor horse needed help. Surely at least one of them had the gumption to intervene. But, no. The drunk swung viciously at the horse again, and no one in the crowd stepped forward. Sam's stomach lurched at the sound of leather-wrapped wood connecting with flesh.

"Hey!" she called out. "What do you think you're doing?"

The man didn't seem to hear her. Samantha saw blood glistening darkly above the horse's eye. There was another gash on its nose. Furious, she jerked her cell phone from her belt and started to dial 911 as she closed the remaining distance to the ramp. Before she could finish punching in the numbers, the device was swatted from her hand. Stunned, she looked up to find the drunk looming over her, his bloodshot brown eyes sparking with anger.

"You fixin' to call the cops, lady?" He jabbed a finger at her face. "Well, think again! This is *my* horse." He raised a massive fist to display the reins clasped in his thick fingers. "I'll beat some manners into him if I want. It's none of your damned business."

The sorrel tried to back away, but stopped short when the

reins pulled taut. That told Samantha that it wasn't the animal with a behavior problem. An adult quarter horse weighed anywhere from a thousand to thirteen hundred pounds, and had enough strength in its neck alone to lift a grown man off his feet. Instead of fighting back, this poor gelding stood obediently waiting to endure more blows. Samantha had no idea why the animal refused to enter the trailer, but judging from what she'd seen, she guessed that it was mostly the man's fault.

In that moment, Samantha felt a kinship with the horse that others might never understand. She circled the man to stand at the bottom of the ramp between him and the gelding. It wasn't a wise decision. Deep down, she knew that. But it was something she felt compelled to do: take a stand, face her demons, demand justice. There had been a time when she'd waited too long to do any of those things, and she'd learned the hard way that sometimes it was better to act rashly than do nothing at all.

The metallic taste of fear coated Samantha's tongue as she faced the drunk. He outweighed her by well over a hundred pounds, and there was a wild look in his eyes. In the not-so-distant past, she had faced another man with brutal fists and learned that she needed more than anger as an equalizer. Even so, she held her ground.

"The abuse of an animal is everyone's business," she managed to say evenly. "This horse is already cut and bleeding. He's had enough, and so have you."

"Are you sayin' I've had too much to drink?"

Samantha just stood there, meeting the man's gaze with fateful resolve, her heart pounding wildly and her body going clammy with sweat.

That was how Tucker Coulter first saw her—standing toe-to-toe with a man twice her size. While volunteering as an on-site rodeo veterinarian these last three days, he had seen so many women in skintight jeans, fringed shirts, and Stetsons that he'd long since lost count. But this woman didn't have the look of a weekend cowgirl. Her slender figure was showcased in snug, faded Wranglers worn thin at the knees and a simple blue plaid work shirt. Instead of a fancy Stetson, she wore a green ball cap with JOHN DEERE emblazed above the bill in bright yellow. Through the cap's rear opening, a cloud of ebony curls spilled down her slender back.

Normally Tucker didn't find fragile women all that attractive, but something about this one appealed to him in a way he couldn't define. Maybe it was the fear in her large brown eyes, which was completely at odds with her challenging stance. Courage was a trait he admired in anyone. As a kid, he'd loved the story of David and Goliath, an undersize warrior pitted against a giant. Only this lady didn't even have a slingshot to defend herself. She put him more in mind of Tinkerbell, sans the magical pixie dust, pitting herself against an evil Captain Hook.

Still pushing his way through the noisy crowd, Tucker couldn't make out the exchange between the man and woman. He'd been told by an excited, stammering young boy in the 4-H building a few minutes ago that a horse over here needed help. Tucker had taken that to mean that the animal was sick or hurt, so he'd brought his satchel. He hadn't realized until now that the horse was being beaten.

Not a good situation. As much as Tucker admired Tinkerbell for stepping in to defend the horse, it wasn't a smart move. When you witnessed a crime in progress, the best course of action was to call the police.

Toward the front of the crowd, Tucker paused to call fairground security, a number he had programmed into speed dial three days ago, when he'd begun his volunteer stint during Rodeo Days. The phone rang several times and was still ringing when the horse abuser let loose with a roar of anger and doubled his free hand into a fist. *Uh-oh.*

With a growing sense of urgency, Tucker broke the connection and punched in the speed-dial code again, thinking maybe he'd misdialed the first time. *Not.* The phone droned monotonously. While Tucker waited for an answer, he kept his gaze locked on the trio near the horse trailer. The man appeared to be intoxicated. Each time he wagged his fist in Tinkerbell's face, he swayed on his feet and nearly lost his balance.

"I'm not moving," Tucker heard the woman say. "If you mean to strike this animal again, you'll go through me to do it."

What? Tucker couldn't believe he'd heard her right. She didn't weigh much more than a hundred pounds soaking wet, and the drunk was built like a grizzly bear. The man responded with a shove that sent her staggering back against the gelding.

Decision time. This situation was fast getting out of hand. Tucker didn't believe in taking the law into his own hands; he truly didn't. But more deeply ingrained in him were the principles his father had taught him, including the steadfast rule that a man should never get physically aggressive with a woman. There were no exceptions, period, and it went against the Coulter creed to stand aside while another man transgressed.

"Here." Tucker thrust the phone at a stranger beside him. "Dial three for fairground security."

The man glanced stupidly at the apparatus in his hand. "Three?"

"For fairground security," Tucker repeated. "Get someone over here ASAP. If no one answers, dial nine-one-one, tell the dispatcher exactly where we are, and get a car here as fast as you can."

Turning sideways to avoid jostling a woman with an infant in her arms, Tucker shouldered his way through the remaining cluster of people. "Excuse me, excuse me." He squeezed past an elderly woman. "I'm a vet. Can you let me through, please?"

A collective gasp rose from the crowd, and Tucker heard

a woman cry out, "Oh, my *God*, he hit her! Somebody do something!"

Tucker strained to see over the bobbing heads in front of him. Icy disbelief coursed through him. Tinkerbell was bent forward at the waist, one hand cupping her cheek. Even as Tucker watched, the drunk jerked her hat off her head, taking some of her hair along with it.

Something in Tucker's brain short-circuited. One second, his thought processes were sequential and reasonable. The next, his head filled with white static, a haze of red filmed his vision, and he let loose with a snarl of outrage.

From that instant forward, everything seemed to happen in a blur. Dropping his satchel, he plowed through the remaining obstacles to reach the clearing. Then, with a flying leap, he covered the distance to the loading ramp and tackled the older man at the knees. The next thing Tucker knew, he was rolling in the sawdust with his adversary, the other man on top of him one second, under him the next.

The bastard was heavy. But Tucker, blessed with his father's tall stature and generous breadth of shoulder, was no featherweight himself. Working daily with large animals had also kept him fit. *No contest*, he thought grimly as he rolled to the top and quickly straddled his flabby, out-of-shape opponent. It was high time this guy learned, Coulter style, how *not* to treat a lady.

Only Tucker forgot the whip handle. From out of nowhere it came at his face. He heard a loud pop, similar to that of a champagne cork ejecting under pressure; then a burst of pain surged up his nose and exploded through his brain.

In a dizzying spin, the earth changed places with the sky. Tucker heard an odd sound, like air gushing from a balloon, and dimly realized the noise came from him. Stars, spots. He couldn't see anything.

Crossing his forearms over his face, he rolled onto his knees, ducked his head, and tried frantically to regain his senses so he might protect himself. Something sharp connected with his ribs, knocking the breath out of him, followed by another tearing pain, and then another. In some distant part of his mind, he realized the older man had regained his feet and was kicking him.

"Stop it!" he heard Tinkerbell scream. "Stop it! Oh, God, oh, God, somebody help me! He's going to kill him!"

Tucker tensed for another blow. *Sweet Christ.* He couldn't breathe, couldn't see. Where were his brothers when he needed them? This time the man's boot caught Tucker in the abs. He had to get up. Somehow he had to clear his head, regain his feet, and fight back.

Blinking, he managed to focus his vision enough to see splotches of sunlight and swirling expanses of sawdust. As he staggered erect, he realized he wasn't that badly hurt—*yet.* All he needed was to get in one solid punch. Then it would all be over.

In his spinning vision, Tucker saw Tinkerbell advancing on the other man. He wanted to yell at her to stay back, that he didn't need a half-pint female to rescue him, but his tongue wouldn't respond to the commands from his brain. To his horrified amazement, she lengthened her last three strides for momentum and followed through with the pointed toe of her riding boot, executing a dropkick that would have done any kickboxer proud. *Bull's-eye.* With a grunt of pain, the drunk crashed to his knees, cupped his hands over his crotch, and started retching.

The lady—stupidly, Tucker took measure of her height and confirmed that the top of her raven head barely reached his shoulder—dusted her hands on the legs of her jeans. "I asked you to stop," she told the drunk thinly. "It's your own fault I had to kick you. Why wouldn't you just *stop*?"

Dizziness sent Tucker staggering sideways. Small but surprisingly strong hands grasped his arm. He looked down. The pale oval of her face came clear and then went blurry again. Large, pretty brown eyes and a wild tangle of black curls swam in his vision.

"Are you all right?"

Tucker tried to answer, but his tongue still wouldn't work. *Damn.* He'd been rescued by a pixie. Now he was glad his brothers weren't there. They would never let him live this down. *Oh, man.* He wasn't feeling so good. His head hurt like a son of a bitch, and his stomach was lurching.

The horse chose that moment to wheel and run. People screamed, grabbed their children, and scattered to get out of the frightened animal's way. As the sound of retreating hooves faded, an eerie quiet blanketed the area.

"Are you okay?" the woman asked again.

To Tucker, the question seemed to come from a great distance, and it wasn't one he could readily answer. The whole front of his face throbbed, for one, and it felt as if his nose had been shoved into his brain.

Soft fingertips plucked at his wrist. "Move your hand so I can see."

Tucker hadn't realized he was holding his nose. He dropped his arm. She gently touched his cheek, making him wince.

"It's broken, I'm afraid. I am so sorry about this. I can't even think what to say."

Tucker could think of plenty, but nothing fit for mixed company. He couldn't *believe* this. His nose was broken? And even worse, a lady no bigger than a minute had felt it necessary to leap into the fray to save him. How humiliating was that? He stood six feet, four inches tall in his stocking feet, weighed in at two-twenty stark naked, and had taken first place in state wrestling bouts throughout high school and college. He should have rescued *her*, not the other way around.

His head was starting to clear, and he felt a little steadier on his feet. The throbbing had given way to a strange numbness, similar to when a dentist injected too much Novocain. Shock, he guessed—Mother Nature's remedy for pain. He saw it in his patients all the time.

He took stock of the woman's injuries. An angry red mark flagged her right cheekbone, and the delicate hollow under one eye was starting to swell. He shot the drunk a searing glare. The no-account bastard still huddled on his knees, his upper body convulsing each time he gagged. Tucker hoped he choked on his gonads.

He drew his gaze back to the woman. "I'm fine," he managed to say. "I'm more worried about you."

She gingerly prodded her cheekbone. "It's nothing an ice pack won't fix. Thank you for jumping in to help me. I was dialing nine-one-one when he knocked the phone from my hand." With a lift of one shoulder, she flashed a regretful smile and then began scanning the sawdust-strewn ground nearby. "Heaven knows where it landed."

Tucker felt a little better now, but he wasn't quite ready to sift through sawdust to help her look. He was checking out his nose when the stranger in possession of his cell phone approached.

Hand extended to return the device, the man said, "I never got through to fairground security, so I called the sheriff's department. Someone should be here shortly."

"Good." Tucker hooked a thumb toward the drunk as he took the phone. "He'll recover in a minute. I'd rather let a deputy deal with him."

"I hear you," the man replied. "Sorry I didn't help you out. I've got a bad back."

"It's good you stayed out of it then." Tucker scanned the crowd that had gathered to watch the excitement and saw several other men. In his opinion, there wasn't one of them worth the powder it would take to blow him to hell. "Thanks for calling the authorities for me."

"No problem. Least I could do."

Just then Tucker heard a low growl. He spun around to see the drunk lumbering to his feet. Before Tucker could move, the man charged at the woman, who'd turned her back on him in search of her phone. It took Tucker an instant to react, and in that instant the man tackled her from behind. She went down hard in a face-first sprawl, her lower legs manacled by strong, thick arms. When she tried to rise to her knees, she was knocked flat again by an elbow jab to her spine.

Tucker launched himself at the drunk again. Upon impact, they both went rolling, much as they had before, only this time momentum broke them apart before they came to a stop. The drunk staggered to his feet just as Tucker did, and they met halfway in a teeth-jarring body slam. He couldn't believe this guy had attacked a woman, not once but twice.

The whip handle was attached to the older man's wrist by several wraps of a leather thong, making it impossible for Tucker to dispense with the weapon. His only recourse was to duck his head against his opponent's beefy shoulder to protect his face and deliver uppercut jabs to the man's belly. With each punch, the drunk fell back a step, carrying Tucker along with him until they reached the horse trailer.

Having a barrier behind his adversary suited Tucker's purposes just fine. The stomach blows would have more impact against a solid surface. At some point the whip handle connected with Tucker's right ear. Pain momentarily paralyzed him, but he quickly regained his senses.

Finally the rain of blows to Tucker's shoulder stopped, and he felt the other man's body sliding toward the ground. Releasing his hold, Tucker stepped back. The drunk plopped rump-first on the sawdust, the whip handle lying uselessly beside him.

"You'll go to jail for this piece of work," he slurred.

"If I do, it'll be worth it," Tucker flung back. "Where I come from, manhandling a woman doesn't fly."

The drunk called the lady a filthy name. Tucker was tempted to knock his teeth down his throat. He settled for kicking sawdust in his face. Then he turned away to check on the woman.

She was sitting up but still looked dazed. Tucker hunkered beside her. "Are you all right?"

She blinked and swatted sawdust from her hair. "I think so. He knocked the breath out of me."

Tucker thrust out a hand to help her up. She studied his outstretched fingers for a moment. Then she glanced up to search his gaze before placing her hand in his. Tucker got the oddest feeling—like maybe she was afraid of him or something. And then the moment passed.

After allowing him to pull her to her feet, she laughed shakily and dusted off her jeans. "That'll teach me, I guess. Never kick a guy where it hurts and then turn your back on him."

Tucker couldn't see the humor. The arrival of a bubble top saved him from having to reply. He turned to watch a pencil-thin deputy in a khaki uniform push through the crowd. His pocket badge flashed in the sunlight. A pair of green aviator sunglasses and the shadow cast by the bill of his cap made it difficult to make out his features. He strode swiftly toward the older man and bent to help him up.

"Are you all right, sir? What in the Sam Hill happened here?"

"Hell, no, I'm not all right!" The drunk jerked his arm from the deputy's grasp. "They attacked me, and I'm pressing charges. I want them both arrested!"

The officer sent Tucker a questioning look. "Is that so, sir?"

Tucker opened his mouth to say the other man was lying, but that wasn't precisely true. "It's a little more complicated than that," he began.

The deputy raised a staying hand. "Before we get into explanations, just answer the question. Did you or did you not attack this gentleman?"

"The son of a bitch isn't a gentleman," Tucker shot back. Tucker's temper had always been his downfall. He couldn't remember exactly what he said after that, only that the woman jabbed him twice with her elbow, signaling him to shut up.

The next thing he knew, he was being read his Miranda rights and escorted to a patrol car.

Chapter Two

Cuffed and stuffed. In Tucker's profession, having a bad day was commonplace. He had been kicked by horses, waded through polluted ponds to reach mired patients, fallen face-first in fresh cow manure, gotten his arm stuck in the vaginal passage of a bovine, and had once even been trampled by panicked pigs. With over four years of veterinary practice behind him, he had experienced just about every pitfall of the profession and usually laughed about it later.

But *arrested*? He couldn't frigging believe it. With the help of two fellow officers who arrived shortly after he did, the skinny deputy had handcuffed both Tucker and the drunk, shoved them into the backseats of different patrol cars, and was now taking Tinkerbell's statement while his colleagues spoke with people in the crowd.

At least the woman was getting a chance to tell her side, Tucker reasoned. It was a cut-and-dried situation, the drunk clearly in the wrong. Once the deputy heard the story, he would apologize, turn Tucker loose, and haul the intoxicated instigator off to jail.

Not. Watching through the rear passenger window, Tucker saw the woman put her hands behind her back and turn to allow the deputy to handcuff her. Incredulous fury had Tucker's blood throbbing in his temples again. She was getting hauled in, too? Why? It made absolutely no sense. She'd tried to help a defenseless animal, and this was the treatment she received?

To Tucker's surprise, the woman was led toward the vehicle he sat in. The deputy opened the opposite rear door, cupped a hand over the top of her head, and pushed down as she swung onto the seat beside Tucker.

"I can't believe they're sticking you in here with me," he said. "Is this normal procedure?"

She shifted her hips to avoid getting bumped by the door as it was slammed closed. Even in his agitated state, Tucker couldn't help but notice the attractive curve of those hips and how they nipped in at her slender waist. Snug, faded jeans had never looked so good.

"I have no idea of normal procedure. I've never been arrested before." She leaned forward to get her arms positioned comfortably behind her, then settled back with a sigh. "I think it's more a matter of necessity. The third deputy has to go on another call, and that'll leave them with only two cars. From the sound of it, Rodeo Days has them hopping."

Tucker felt no sympathy for the law enforcement officers. "You shouldn't even be here. The bastard hit you first. Everything that happened afterward was completely his fault."

"True," she agreed, "but it's my word against his. My stars, what *is* that smell?"

"I think the last passenger got sick back here. They tried to clean up the mess, but it still stinks in this heat. What do you mean, it's your word against his? What about all the witnesses?"

She let her head fall back against the seat. "Not everyone in the crowd saw exactly the same thing."

Tucker peered out his side window at the deputy, now powwowing with his colleagues and taking notes in a little black book. Glancing back at her, Tucker asked, "How could they not see the same thing?"

"It's a phenomenon that often occurs with witnesses," she

explained. "One person says a perpetrator was tall, another that he was short. You see it all the time on television."

"That's fiction," Tucker bit out. "This is reality, and our bacon is on the plate."

"I don't blame you for being angry," she said softly. "If not for me, you never would have gotten mixed up in this."

Tucker strained his wrists against the metal bands. Popeye without his emergency can of spinach flashed through his mind. "I'm angry, yes, but not at you. I just can't believe this. The bastard belted you square in the face."

She cut him an apologetic glance. "I know, but some people didn't see that part."

"What *did* they see, for Pete's sake?"

"You tackling him from behind and me kicking him."

"Well, damn." Tucker wanted very badly to ram his fist into something. "If this isn't a hell of a mess."

A wan smile touched her mouth. "A few people told it straight. But overall, the deputies got conflicting stories. When they can't get to the truth, I guess the policy is to arrest everyone and sort it out later."

"Fantastic." Tucker's temper fizzled out, replaced with resigned acceptance. He'd been arrested only once before, when he was attending university—an underage-drinking charge that had ultimately been dropped when he'd proved he was twenty-one. Nevertheless, he could still remember how long it had taken for him to be released. When you dealt with law enforcement from the wrong side of a cell door, there was always tons of red tape. "I can think of better ways to spend my afternoon."

"Me, too. I'm sorry the situation got out of control, forcing you to step in."

Even handcuffed in the back of a police car, Tucker didn't regret his decision to help her. "No worries. You tried to call the cops. It's not your fault the guy went ballistic when he saw you with a phone."

"I could have walked away when he knocked it from my

hand." A dark, distant look filled her eyes. "Somehow that didn't seem like an option at the time. The horse was just standing there, waiting for more blows, too well trained to do otherwise." Her voice trailed off. Then she swallowed and went on. "People are like that sometimes, conditioned all their lives to follow the rules and expecting everyone else to do the same. When that isn't the way it happens, they don't know how to react."

Tucker had an uneasy feeling she might be talking about herself. Reacting to a situation had never been a problem for him. Reacting *appropriately* was his only challenge.

"You did what had to be done," he said. "And it took a lot of courage."

Her cheeks went pink with embarrassment. "Courage? I was scared to death."

"Isn't that what courage is all about? The guy who dashes into a burning building without fear isn't brave. He's just an idiot."

She laughed softly. Tucker decided he liked the sound, a melodic tinkling that lingered lightly in the air. He also enjoyed her smile, a hesitant curve of her lush mouth that tipped up the corners and then slowly blossomed.

For the second time since meeting her, he noted how pretty she was. Feature by feature, her face wasn't perfect. Her nose was a little too pronounced along the bridge, her cheekbones a bit too high, her mouth a shade too generous, but overall the effect was stunning. Lush black lashes lined her dark eyes, lending them depth a man could drown in if he wasn't careful. In the afternoon sunlight that slanted through the side window, her sun-kissed, ivory complexion put him in mind of peaches drizzled with cream, its flawless texture set off to perfection by her ebony hair, which wisped and curled in an untamed cloud.

Sitting with her spine arched to accommodate her cuffed hands had thrust her breasts forward like plump little melons beneath her blue plaid shirt. Not wanting to stare, he slid his gaze to the graceful slope of her neck, to the shell-like curve of her ear peeking out through the curls, and finally to her mouth. *Damn*. All his life his mother had preached that sometimes less was more. The saying had baffled him until now. This lady wasn't very big, but every inch of her packed a wallop. In retrospect, he wondered how he could have compared her to Tinkerbell. No pixie, real or imagined, could be so delightfully curvaceous.

Uneasiness washed over Samantha. He was staring at her as he might a strange bug pinned to velvet. Even worse, her skin warmed and tingled beneath his gaze.

Since her divorce, Samantha had maintained a bulletproof immunity to the opposite sex. Flirtatious grins left her cold. Suggestive innuendoes either revolted her or ticked her off, sometimes both. The only male company she really enjoyed anymore was that of her father, brothers, or ranch foreman, and she tried to maintain some emotional distance even with them. For that reason, it came as something of a shock that everything about this man appealed to her.

Even with his nose swollen and leaning sharply to one side, he was handsome in a rugged way—tall and lean yet broad-shouldered and muscular, with the look of someone who was no stranger to hard work. His tousled sable brown hair fell across his high forehead in lazy waves. His eyes, a clear sapphire blue, were almost startling in contrast to his skin, which had been burnished to teak by the sun. She especially liked the cut of his features, which were purely masculine, each line as sharp and hard as chiseled granite. He had a strong jaw, a square chin, and a firm yet sensual mouth. In addition to all of that, he was chivalrous, charming, and just impulsive enough to be interesting.

She would never forget how he had grumped at the deputy. Most people knew to keep their mouths shut in situations like that. But this man had spoken his mind, devil take the consequences. She liked that about him. She liked it a lot.

And that scared her to death. Instant attractions were dangerous. The little thrill she felt every time she looked into his eyes was a warning sign. She'd fallen fast and hard for a man once. It had been the worst mistake of her life.

"Are you okay?" he asked.

Samantha jerked her thoughts back to the moment, gathered her composure, and forced a smile. "I'm a lot more okay than you are. When we get this ironed out, you'll be spending the rest of the night in the ER getting your nose fixed. It's leaning over so far it's almost touching your cheek."

He crossed his eyes, trying to assess the damage. Then he shrugged. "In my line of work, getting my nose busted every once in a while is par for the course. Another knot will add character."

Samantha was about to inquire about his profession, but his complete lack of concern about his appearance made her lose the thought. When her ex-husband had gotten a pimple, he'd fretted over it for days, afraid it might leave a scar. It was refreshing to meet a man outside her immediate family who didn't obsess about his looks.

There had to be something about this guy she didn't like, she thought a little desperately. She had only to keep asking questions until she discovered what it was.

"My name's Samantha Harrigan," she blurted.

Mention of her last name rarely failed to weed out the jerks. Her father, Frank Harrigan, a self-made millionaire, was almost a legend in rodeo circles. Seven years ago Steve Fisher had been hugely impressed when he learned Samantha was Frank's daughter. Unfortunately she'd been so young and gullible back then that she'd failed to notice the dollar signs flashing in his eyes when he'd professed his undying love for her.

This man rolled her first name over his tongue as if savoring its flavor. Then he nodded. "Samantha. It suits you. I'm Tucker Coulter."

That was it? She'd expected more of a reaction, and stared at him, nonplussed. "Are you new to Crystal Falls?"

"No, born and raised here. Why do you ask?"

Samantha shifted her position, trying to regroup. Most rodeo enthusiasts knew the Harrigan name.

The deputy returned to the car just then. After slipping behind the steering wheel, he slammed the driver's door, started the engine, and turned up the air conditioner. "Sorry about the delay. It's a wonder you didn't suffocate in here."

As he nosed the vehicle through the throngs of milling people to reach the gravel road that led from the compound to the highway, he grabbed the radio mike. There followed an exchange between him and a female dispatcher that was mostly a bunch of number codes Samantha couldn't follow.

"Ten-twenty means your location," Tucker translated, as if sensing her confusion. "ETA means estimated time of arrival. Code four-A means no further assistance needed."

She sent him a wondering look. "And you know this because . . . ?"

"When I was a kid I wanted to be a cop, and memorized most of the codes." He inclined his head at the deputy. "A possible ten-one-zero-two means possible cruelty to an animal. UTL means unable to locate. I'm assuming he means the horse."

Samantha frowned. "Have they even bothered to look? That poor animal has some pretty nasty cuts. He needs veterinary care ASAP."

Tucker's eyes narrowed in thought. "The cuts were superficial. He'll be fine on that count. I'm more worried about him being at large and possibly injuring himself—or someone else." He returned his attention to the radio exchange and shook his head in disgust. "You didn't hit the drunk first. Damn. What's this guy been smoking?"

"He's just repeating what the witnesses told him."

"Right." Not bothering to lower his voice, he added, "Pardon me for pointing it out, but a good cop should have enough common sense to sort through the malarkey. What woman in her right mind would push an abusive, angry drunk into a physical confrontation?"

Samantha couldn't argue the point.

Hoping to calm him down, she said, "I'm amazed you can recall codes you memorized as a kid."

He shrugged. "I've always been good at remembering stuff."

As the county vehicle entered the stream of highway traffic and began picking up speed, Samantha's thoughts circled back to this man's total lack of reaction to her father's name. Given his sharp memory, he would surely remember if he'd ever heard of Frank Harrigan.

Curiosity piqued, she stared out the window at the passing buildings for a moment. Then she sent him a questioning look. "Are you new to the rodeo scene?"

He grinned good-naturedly. "I'm not part of the scene, period. Used to be years ago, but then a family tragedy made me lose interest. I only volunteer now because it's good for business."

He had the look of a horseman. Sam had teethed on saddle leather and knew a greenhorn when she saw one. Tucker Coulter didn't fit the bill. He even walked like a cowboy, his long legs slightly bowed, his hips moving with well-oiled ease. She'd first pegged him as a second- or third-generation rancher, someone who'd spent most of his life on a horse and remained in the family enterprise as an adult, much as she had. He wore the right clothing for it—well-worn Wrangler jeans, a wrinkled chambray shirt, and scuffed riding boots.

The car rocked to one side as it took a turn. With her arms cuffed behind her, Samantha had to lean sharply in the opposite direction to keep from toppling. "So you don't like horses and cows?"

"Didn't say that." Instead of struggling to stay erect, as she was, he pressed a shoulder against his door. "I love horses, and I like cows all right, although I have to say cows aren't the smartest animals on the planet. In my opinion, they're more appealing on a barbecue grill than on the hoof." Never missing a beat, he added, "Please don't tell me you're a vegetarian."

Samantha found herself wanting to smile again. Was it possible that he found her as attractive as she did him?

Not a good situation. Just looking at him made her pulse beat a little faster. "No, I'm not a vegetarian."

"Whew," he said, feigning relief. "You never know these days. I've dated four, no, five women over the last six months who got so pissed when I ordered a steak, they left the restaurant and called a cab."

Samantha wasn't surprised to learn that he dated a lot. A man with his dark good looks probably had a little black book as thick as a Bible. And there it was, a reason to dislike him.

"I'll bet you've never been married," she mused aloud.

"Nope. Here I am, almost thirty-six, and I haven't found the right lady yet." He gave her another long study. "Maybe I've just been looking in all the wrong places."

Samantha had heard that line before. She wanted to tell him not to waste his breath. But why waste hers?

"Count yourself lucky," the deputy interjected from the front seat. "I wish I was thirty-six and single. It beats the hell out of being forty-two and divorced with three kids to support."

Tucker winked at Samantha. "He's human, after all."

"Go ahead. Take your shots," the deputy said. "You think this job is a walk in the park? I've dealt with nothing but drunk troublemakers for two solid days." He jerked off his hat and tossed it onto the front passenger seat. "Long hours, pitiful pay, and"—he glowered at Tucker in the rearview mirror—"no respect. Do you think I *wanted* to arrest your lady friend? It's obvious as hell the drunk boxed her on the jaw. But guilt or innocence isn't for me to decide. I'm sworn to uphold the law. The other guy pressed charges. I can't let the two of you walk just because I think he's lying."

After a moment of silence, Tucker nodded. "I guess I owe you an apology."

"You guess?"

"All right, I *do* owe you an apology," Tucker amended. "I've given you a hard time for doing your job. I shouldn't have."

The deputy's sunglasses followed his hat onto the adjacent seat. "Thank you. And if I came off as unfeeling, I apologize, too. If it's any consolation, I think you'll be in and out pretty fast. That guy is so plastered he can't keep his name straight, let alone his story. It won't be difficult to trip him up and get to the bottom of what actually happened."

"So what went wrong with your marriage?" Tucker asked. "If you don't mind my asking, that is."

"You ever heard that song about the guy driving by his house and seeing some stranger living his life?" the deputy asked. "That's me. He's got my house, my wife and kids, even my dog. While I was working the night shift, trying to support my family, she was two-timing me. When all was said and done, the only thing I got was my pickup truck, and I owe payments on that."

Tucker lifted a dark eyebrow. "Surely you get to see your kids."

"Every other weekend, but it's getting so they don't want to come anymore. I don't have much to offer them for entertainment. I can't even afford a pizza." He huffed in disgust.

Samantha's heart hurt for the deputy. She knew how it felt to trust someone and be betrayed. At least she and Steve hadn't had children.

"Not all marriages end that way," Tucker said. "My parents have been together for forty years."

"They're lucky," the deputy replied. "Damn lucky. Nowadays marriages are like cars: not made to last."

Samantha agreed with that sentiment. The only way she would ever say "I do" again was with a gun pressed to her head.

The deputy braked to make a right turn into the sheriff's department parking lot.

"Well," she said, hoping to change the subject. "It looks like we're here."

Tucker gave her a sharp look. "Don't let them put you in a cell with anyone else," he said. "Chances are we won't be here very long, but just in case, it's better to be locked up alone."

"You think we have vacancies?" The deputy collected his hat and settled it back on his head. "I'll see what I can do, but don't count on it being much. The place is packed tighter than a can of sardines."

Samantha turned her gaze to the cinder-block building, painted icky government green. The only jails she'd ever seen had been in movies. "If they try to put you in with someone else, raise holy hell," Tucker stressed.

That was all he had time to say. The next second, another male deputy emerged from the building, the rear doors of the vehicle were jerked open, and she was seized by the elbow to be pulled unceremoniously from the car.

Chapter Three

The inside of the sheriff's department was a bustle of confused activity, with uniformed officers, both male and female, hurrying about, looking harried and exhausted. "Rodeo Days" was a muttered refrain in much the same tone as one might say, "Black plague." Tucker lost sight of Samantha Harrigan in the blur of moving bodies. He hoped she was having a better time of it than he was. He also hoped she remembered his warning and insisted on being given an unoccupied cell. As crowded as this place was, God only knew what kind of person she might get stuck with.

A few minutes later Tucker was led into an interior office, relieved of the handcuffs, and told to have a seat. "Aren't you going to lock me up?" he asked the stocky male deputy.

"No room." The man smoothed a hand over his gray hair. His uniform looked as if he'd slept in it. "All one hundred and forty-one cells are packed full. Never fails. Rodeo Days brings 'em crawling out of the woodwork." He sighed and shook his head. "We're working on getting the charges against you dropped. The drunk can't keep his story straight, and the woman is developing a shiner, corroborating her story that the man slugged her."

Sanity, at last. Tucker sat back on the chair, rubbing his wrists. "If she hadn't fallen against the horse, he would have decked her. What was I supposed to do, let him hit her again?"

"Between you, me, and a fence post, I would have jumped in, too." The deputy jabbed a thumb at a coffee machine along the wall. "Java's free. While you're waiting, help yourself. Just don't put your feet on the boss's desk. It really pisses him off."

Tucker took that to mean he was in the head honcho's office. After the deputy exited, taking care to lock the door behind him, Tucker pushed to his feet to circle the room. The walls were covered haphazardly with tattered papers—changes in procedure, work schedules, and scribbled notes.

A group of news clippings on a bulletin board drew Tucker's attention. He had just stepped over to check them out when the door clicked open behind him. He turned to see Samantha Harrigan entering, a middle-aged female deputy following at her heels.

"Since the two of you are friends, you can wait it out in here together," the deputy said. "Might make the time pass more quickly."

Speaking simultaneously, both Samantha and Tucker blurted, "We aren't really—" But then they both broke off before finishing the sentence. They weren't exactly friends, after all—or even what most people might term acquaintances. But the alternative—being stuffed into a cell crowded with strangers—wasn't appealing.

The deputy removed Samantha's handcuffs and gave her the same spiel Tucker had heard, that the drunk couldn't keep his story straight and she should be out of there and headed home within a couple of hours.

"Have you found the horse?" Samantha asked, rubbing her wrists where the cuffs had chafed her skin.

"We've called the Humane Society," the deputy assured her. "They've got people combing the fairgrounds trying to find him as we speak."

"He's hurt," Samantha stressed, "and probably frightened

as well. He shouldn't be wandering loose in a crowded compound. Horses are large, potentially dangerous animals, especially when they panic."

"We're on top of it," the older brunette insisted. "They'll find him."

"When they do, will they return him to his owner?" Samantha asked.

The deputy hooked the cuffs over her belt. "If what you've told us is true and the animal has been beaten, the owner will have to get a court order to reclaim his property." She flashed Samantha a saucy grin. "A more likely scenario is that the judge will slap him with a heavy fine and give him some jail time. In Oregon, the penalty for animal abuse is a maximum of five years in prison and one hundred and twenty-five grand. The horse will go to a shelter to be adopted out. If the guy owns any other animals, the same will go for them."

"I'm impressed," Samantha said. "I had no idea our laws on animal abuse were so strict."

"Legislators have concluded that there's a link between animal abuse and human abuse," the deputy explained. "By cracking down on criminal acts against animals, they hope to reduce the number of crimes against people as well."

Tucker folded his arms across his chest. "While on the subject, I need to fill out a report on this incident."

The deputy narrowed an eye at him. "Give us a break. okay? You'll be walking out of here shortly. By filing countercharges, all you'll do is create more red tape."

"I don't want to file charges, just a report," Tucker replied. "If I witness animal abuse of any kind, I'm required by law to file a report. If I fail to do so, I can be fined up to a thousand dollars, and it goes on my record."

"I don't remember any law like that," the deputy said dubiously.

Tucker shrugged. "Look it up. I'm a vet. Oregon statute 686.455."

The deputy's penciled brows lifted. Then she nodded. "I'll bring you the paperwork."

Samantha tucked in her shirt with short, expert jabs of her slender fingers as she followed the deputy to the door. "I need to contact my family. No one knows where I am, and they're going to be worried. Can I use this phone?"

"No, ma'am. We're so busy that all the lines have to be left open for official business only. When you're released, you can call out on your cell or use the public phone in the other room."

Samantha sighed as the door closed behind the departing officer. She turned to face Tucker. Except for the bruise on her cheek, which was still bright pink, and the slight swelling under her eye, she was to him absurdly beautiful for a woman who'd been through all that in one day. Her black hair fell to her shoulders in shimmering curls that looked artfully tousled rather than mussed, and her durable clothing showed few signs of the punishment it had taken.

"I thought the law guaranteed me one phone call," she complained. "That's not considered official business?"

"Guess not." Tucker cocked his head to listen to the cacophony of ringing phones, buzzers, office machines, and voices. "From their side, I suppose our contacting members of our families ranks pretty low on the importance chart right now. Business is pretty good today."

She puffed at a lock of hair that had fallen over her eye. "It's definitely crazy out there."

A few minutes later Tucker sat behind the desk filling out a form and trying to compose a concluding statement while Samantha paced from one side of the room to the other. Every few seconds she glanced at the wall clock. Blue's competition started at three, and it was already two forty. Even if she were released right then, she couldn't reach the fairgrounds in time. The realization brought a lump of disappointment to her throat. She and Blue had worked so hard to prepare for this day. Now she would miss seeing him win the championship.

"So you're a vet," she mused aloud to the top of Tucker's bent head. His hair was the rich color of homemade fudge that hadn't been whipped long enough to lose its gloss. "I'm surprised you didn't mention that."

He glanced up, his blue eyes twinkling above his swollen, discolored, and off-center nose. "At what point—before I hit the guy, or afterward?"

"I realize it wasn't exactly a great time to exchange personal information." Pivoting on her heel to change direction, she added, "It just seems strange, is all. When we were talking later, you mentioned volunteering at the rodeo because it was good for business, but you never said what your business was."

"I figured it went without saying."

"Why did you think that?"

"Because I showed up carrying a satchel, and I'm wearing a name badge that says Tucker Coulter, DVM?"

"I never saw a satchel, and you're not wearing a badge."

He glanced down and shoved a finger into a hole in his shirt above the right breast pocket. "I'll be damned. It was there earlier. The jerk ripped it off."

He looked so upset that Samantha said, "I'm sure they'll give you a new one."

"Not possible. It's irreplaceable."

"The name badge?"

"No," he replied, sounding exasperated, "my lucky shirt!"

Samantha examined the garment in question. It looked older than the hills and much the worse for wear. "Your *lucky* shirt?"

"Yes." He plucked at the hole again. "Good things always happen when I wear this shirt."

He'd done it again—made her smile. "I hate to point it out, but I don't think it brought you any luck today."

Frowning, he tugged at the rip again. Then he glanced up

at her and his expression cleared. "I don't know about that. I met you, didn't I?"

Samantha chose to ignore that. "So do you specialize in large animals?"

He signed the form, tossed down the pen, and rocked back on the chair. "I'm working my way into that, yes. My brother and I are partners at a clinic. He enjoys the small-animal end of it, and I love the fieldwork. I'm especially fond of working with horses."

Samantha gave him a thoughtful study. "Are you any good?"

His firm mouth tipped into a grin. "I'm the best. Unfortunately it takes a while to build a reputation, and I'm just getting started."

"No conceit in your family, because you have it all?"

He chuckled. "You asked, I gave you an honest answer. I'm not merely good; I'm phenomenal."

Samantha couldn't help but laugh. What was it about this man that she found so difficult to resist?

"What makes you so good?" she asked.

"My rapport with horses," he answered easily. "Runs in my family, along with conceit. You ever heard of my brother, Jake Coulter?"

Samantha thought for a moment. "The horse whisperer?"

Tucker let loose with another deep chuckle. "He isn't a whisperer. Is there such a thing?"

Samantha hugged her waist, a posture she recognized as being defensive even as she assumed it. As much as she liked this man, he frightened her on a deep and purely feminine level. She felt like a starvation dieter who'd stumbled into a room filled with chocolate cake.

"I don't know. You tell me," she challenged.

He rested his elbows on the arms of the chair and gazed at her over the tips of his steepled fingers. "To my knowledge, horse whisperers don't really exist. Rare individuals who have an instinctive understanding of horses are another story. My brother Jake is one of them. He calls himself an equine behavioral analyst."

"A sort of horse psychiatrist?"

"That pretty much sums it up. He takes in horses with serious behavior issues and patiently works with them to correct the problems. Then he sends them back to their owners so the problems can start all over again. He's a firm believer that the major problem with any horse is the person who owns it."

Samantha held to that belief herself. "And you? What do you think?"

"I absolutely agree. Which leads me straight back to why I'm so good with equines—because I have more respect for them than I do for most people."

Samantha nodded. "I know what you mean." And she did. In the stables with her horses was the only place she felt truly at peace. No lies, no subterfuge, no heartbreaking betrayals. Her animals loved her absolutely and unconditionally, and they were unfailingly steadfast. She couldn't say that about many of the humans she'd known over the course of her lifetime. "They're incredible creatures."

"Very large, powerful creatures," he elaborated. "Which is why a lot of vets prefer a small-animal practice. Going into a stall with a strange horse can be a dicey situation, especially if the animal is sick or in pain."

"But it doesn't bother you?"

"Didn't say that. I have a healthy respect for the kicking power of an equine. I don't waltz into a stall and start poking and prodding, I can tell you that."

Samantha had seen cautious vets in action. They came armed with hobbles and lip twitches. She had nothing against a vet using preventive measures with an ill-mannered horse, but she strongly objected when her own equines were victimized. Every animal on her ranch had been imprinted at birth and was easy to handle. "You take precautions, then?"

"I do," he confessed. "I start off by having a talk with the horse. Normally they'll let me know, right up front, if they'd like to kick my teeth down my throat." Amusement warmed his eyes. "Most times they wouldn't. They seem to realize I'm there to help and are glad to see me."

"I own a horse ranch," Samantha revealed.

A deep dimple she hadn't noticed before slashed his lean cheek. "You don't say? Never would have guessed."

She chose to let that pass. She knew her clothing marked her as a horsewoman, and she had no intention of changing that. As she retraced her steps across the room, she said, "This community can use another good horse vet. Doc Washburn, the vet we've used for as long as I can remember, is getting close to retirement age. My father worries that he may be the last of a dying breed."

The door swung open just then, and the female deputy entered with two plastic bags in her hands. "You folks are free to go," she chirped as she put their possessions on the desk. "Mr. Matlock finally admitted striking you," she said to Samantha. "Unapologetically, I might add. He says you interfered between him and his horse, and you had it coming for trying to call the cops on him." She picked up the report Tucker had filled out. "Very good. I'll make sure this goes on file. One more nail in his coffin when he goes before a judge."

Samantha emptied her things from one of the bags and quickly curled her fingers over the rosary beads, which she carried in her jeans pocket everywhere. "Any news about the horse at the fairgrounds yet?"

The deputy gave her a thumbs-up. "They found him. He's cut up pretty bad and has clearly been beaten. As sad as that is, it may be the horse's lucky day. He'll get a new home now and won't be mistreated again. The rescue folks screen applicants very carefully."

Samantha was glad to hear that. The gelding's passive acceptance of such cruel mistreatment had touched her heart.

An animal like that deserved to be loved and pampered just a little.

A quarter of an hour later, after they'd both tried to contact family members on the public phone without success, Tucker and Samantha stood in the parking lot, at a loss. Both their vehicles were at the fairgrounds.

"I can't believe my dad isn't answering his cell phone," she complained.

"My sister and brothers are all at the rodeo. Could be they've turned off their cells or just can't hear them over the crowd. Not my folks, though. I thought sure they'd be home. They never go to the rodeo anymore."

"Why is that? Is their health deteriorating?"

His mouth tightened. "No. My sister was badly injured in a barrel racing accident several years ago."

"Oh. I'm sorry."

"No need to be. She's happily married and has two kids. It was a sad time in our lives, but it's over now. For most of us, anyway. My mother and father still hate watching any kind of rodeo competition." Tucker gazed thoughtfully at the cell phone in his hand. "You want me to call you a cab?"

She shook her head. "I left messages on all their voice mails. One of them is bound to check his missed calls soon and come pick me up."

Tucker hated to leave her. He reached to rub his nose, but stopped just in time. "I need to visit the ER. If this schnozzle of mine swells any more, they won't be able to fix it tonight."

She tipped her head to study his face. "It's probably only the swelling, but it seems to be leaning sideways more than it was earlier."

Tucker had visited the men's room before leaving the building, and he'd gotten a shock when he looked in the mirror. His nose looked bad, no question about it. In the course of his work, he often got the cartilage broken. Most times he straightened it as best he could, shoved cotton balls up each nostril to hold it in place, and called it good. Treating the injury himself didn't strike him as being a wise idea this time.

"Do you have any money on you?" he asked. "I don't want to leave you stranded."

"Not enough for cab fare clear back to the fairgrounds." She held up a staying hand. "No, please. You've done enough."

He already had his wallet halfway out of his hip pocket. "Come on. A cab only costs a few bucks. I'll give you my address. You can send me a check to cover it."

"My dad or one of my brothers will show up any minute," she insisted. "I'll be fine. Really. Good luck at the hospital."

Tucker wanted very badly to ask her out. Considering the mess his face was in, the timing sucked, though. Instead, he dialed Information, got connected with Yellow Cab, and arranged for transportation to Saint Matthew's.

While waiting for his ride he stood beside Samantha, wishing he could think of something memorable to say. Nothing came to mind.

When the cab rolled into the parking lot, he turned and thrust out his hand. "It's been an experience."

She treated him to one of those slow, hesitant smiles that eventually made her face glow and her eyes sparkle. When she placed her slender fingers across Tucker's palm, he felt a zing he'd never experienced with any other woman, a promise of the magic that had been eluding him all his adult life. As he tightened his grip on her hand, he searched her beautiful brown eyes, wondering if she felt it, too.

"Can I call you?" he blurted, then immediately wanted to kick himself. Over the last twenty years he'd asked a fair thousand females out on dates and knew his lines by heart. "I'd like to see you again, get to know you better."

She nibbled her bottom lip, then shook her head. "I'm sorry. I really appreciate what you did for me today, but I'm very busy."

Normally Tucker countered that excuse with, "You have to eat, don't you? We'll go to dinner, talk, call it an early night. Nothing serious intended or expected." But somehow he couldn't say those words to her.

They would have been a lie.

He decided to leave it for another day. He knew her name. He could look her number up in the book. As he climbed into the cab, he sent her one of his failproof grins. "Can't blame a guy for trying."

She laughed. "Can't blame a gal for saying no, either."

Normally Tucker would have agreed, but something in her eyes told him that this time, *no* just might mean *maybe*. She wasn't as immune to him as she tried to pretend.

"Whoa! What the hell are you planning to do with that?" Eyes rolled back to see the doctor standing at the head of the gurney, Tucker glared at the rubber mallet the man held in his hand. "You hit my nose with that, partner, and we're going to tangle."

The lanky young physician with blond hair and a bobbing Adam's apple gave Tucker a reassuring smile. "I have to straighten the bridge, Dr. Coulter. Ever heard the expression 'Follow your nose'? You'll be walking in a circle the rest of your natural life if I leave it like this."

Tucker pushed at the sheet and tried to sit up. The ER physician placed a staying hand on his shoulder. "The injections for pain were the worst part of the treatment. Now that your nose is numb, you'll barely feel a thing."

Tucker didn't care if he felt it or not. "I'm out of here. Nobody is taking a hammer to my nose."

"It's a mallet, not a hammer."

"Mallet, then. It's still not coming anywhere near my nose."

"And what is all this fuss about?" a feminine voice asked.

Still propped partway up on one elbow, Tucker twisted to see his short, plump mother pushing through the striped privacy curtain. His father and his brother Jake trailed behind her, looking like sun-burnished, rough-and-tumble actors who'd just stepped off the set of an Old West movie. Their Stetsons, Wranglers, and riding boots, standard-issue in the Coulter family, looked incongruous in the sterile surroundings.

"This poor excuse for a doctor was about to pound on my nose with a hammer," Tucker grouched. "Nohow, no way. I'll fix it myself. That's what I've always done before."

"No wonder the bridge is so crooked," the doctor observed under his breath.

Mary Coulter, a matronly woman with curly brown hair and kindly blue eyes, clucked her tongue and came around the gurney to gently push Tucker onto his back again. After giving the mallet a worried study, she grasped Tucker's hand and smiled at the attending physician.

"A misunderstanding, I'm sure. Your poor nose has suffered enough abuse for one day. Right, Doctor?"

The young man blushed. "I only need to tap on it a few times. See that one big knot along the bridge? If I don't straighten it now, it'll be there forever." He gave Tucker a pointed look. "Is that what you want, to have a crooked nose the rest of your life?"

"I'm used to a crooked nose."

"Please, Tucker, don't try to sit up," Mary urged with another push on her son's shoulder. "That knot has been there a good long while," she informed the doctor. "He wouldn't look the same without it."

Jake came to stand at the opposite side of the table. Dark countenance creased in a frown, blue eyes glinting with mischief, he bent low to peer at his brother's face. "I have to side with the doctor. He'll be prettier without the knot, Mom. Let the doctor whomp it a time or two to straighten it out. Tucker's a big boy. He can handle it."

"Jackass," Tucker retorted. "Your nose isn't exactly straight enough to rule paper, either. Let him pound on yours for a while."

Jake grinned. "The reason my nose isn't straight is because you broke it with a bat once. Now it's my turn to get even."

"Nobody is going to hammer on my nose." Tucker sent the physician a warning look. "Just straighten it out as best you can and pack it. I don't plan on entering any beauty contests."

"Thank God for that," Tucker's father chimed in. He came to stand behind his wife, whose head barely cleared his shoulder. "They'd boo you off the stage with rotten eggs."

The young doctor sighed. "All right, then," he said to Tucker. "But don't come crying to me later when it heals crooked."

"I won't," Tucker assured him.

"How the hell did you manage to get in a fight at the fairgrounds?" Jake asked. "Just when I think you've sown all your wild oats, you go and do something totally crazy again."

As briefly as possible, Tucker recounted the afternoon's events.

"Samantha *Harrigan*?" Jake repeated incredulously. "*The* Samantha Harrigan?"

Tucker kept his gaze fixed on the doctor. "Why, she famous or something?"

"Her father, Frank Harrigan, is. Haven't you ever heard of him? The man is renowned."

"For what?"

"He raises the finest line of quarter horses I've ever seen," Jake replied. "I can't believe you haven't heard of him."

"I'm relatively new to the horse business," Tucker reminded him.

"Still." Jake sounded amazed. "His name and quarter horses are almost synonymous. People come from all over the country to an auction when one of his animals is for sale, and they pay him an arm and a leg for stud fees."

"His horses' stud fees, you mean," Tucker corrected.

Jake snorted. "Don't nitpick. I'd part with my favorite boots for a chance to talk to the man."

The doctor was laying out some wicked-looking steel instruments on a white towel. Tucker yearned for a belt of good whiskey, which, in his opinion, had Novocain beat, hands down. "I'll ask Samantha about getting you an introduction," he promised his brother.

"You got to know her that well?" Jake countered.

"No," Tucker admitted, "but I damned sure intend to." To the doctor, he said, "What're you going to do with that?"

The physician smiled. "You'd rather not know."

Harv placed a burly brown hand on his wife's arm. "What say we go up to the cafeteria and grab a cup of coffee while the doctor finishes up, sweetheart?"

Mary shook her head. "You and Jake go on, dear. I'll stay with Tucker."

Harv exchanged a long look with Jake. Then he glanced at the doctor, who gave an almost imperceptible shake of his head.

"It's crowded in here," Harv countered. "You'll be in the way. Better to step out for a few minutes and come back when Tucker's ready to leave."

Tucker realized his dad didn't want his mother to witness the procedure. "Pop is right, Mom. It's pretty tight quarters in here. Go have some coffee. By the time you're finished, I'll be all patched up and ready to go."

Mary tightened her hold on Tucker's hand. "I'd really rather not, in case you need me."

"I'll be fine." Tucker gave her a little push. "Go with Dad and Jake. I'll be in the waiting area when you come back downstairs."

"You're sure?"

"Positive." Tucker settled back on the gurney. "It's the doc who needs to worry. I may have a nose-jerk reaction if he whomps me with that hammer."

"*Mallet*," the physician corrected.

After his family left, Tucker closed his eyes and said, "Okay, Doc, get it finished."

"You want a bullet to bite?"

"I thought you said it wouldn't hurt."

"It won't. At least, not much. You just strike me as the bullet-biting type. Is your father a rancher?"

"Used to be. He's retired now. Two of my brothers are carrying on the tradition. They own the Lazy J."

"Do they raise cattle?" the doctor asked as he started to work.

Tucker winced. "Not anymore. They raise and train horses."

"Ah."

Two minutes later, Tucker hissed air through his clenched front teeth. "Jesus, *God*. You said it wouldn't hurt."

"I said it wouldn't hurt *much*."

It felt as if the rolls of cotton were being shoved into Tucker's brain. "Numb, you said." His voice was so nasal that the words weren't clear.

"You're as numb as I can get you without deadening your whole head." The doctor gave a final push at the cotton in Tucker's left nostril, then stood back and peeled off the surgical gloves. "All finished. I've always been told that doctors make the worst patients, but I didn't know the rule applied to vets."

Tucker got his discharge papers and spent the next ten minutes in the ER waiting room, leafing through magazines. When a pair of dusty riding boots appeared in his peripheral vision, he glanced up, expecting to see Jake or his father standing over him. Instead it was a stranger in ranch-issue Wranglers and a work shirt.

"Howdy," the wiry, dark-haired man began, tipping his brown Stetson to Tucker in a polite gesture of introduction. "I couldn't help but notice that your nose looks broke."

That struck Tucker as being an odd way to strike up a conversation. "That's right."

"Name's Frank Harrigan," the cowboy elaborated.

Tucker set aside the magazine. "Samantha's dad?" Pushing to his feet, Tucker extended his right hand. "Good to meet you, sir. Tucker Coulter here."

"I know your name," the smaller man replied. "My girl told me what happened, how you jumped in to stick up for her after that no-account bastard hit her. I owe you one, son."

"It was nothing."

Harrigan narrowed his gaze on Tucker's bandaged nose. "Pardon me for pointin' it out, but that doesn't look like nothing. Hit you with a whip handle, I understand."

Tucker felt a flush creeping up his neck. "I'm sure you heard the rest, then. It wasn't one of my most stellar moments. Instead of me saving your daughter, she saved me."

Frank Harrigan chuckled and rubbed his jaw. "She did mention that, yes. But it sounds like you redeemed yourself."

"I tried."

Harrigan nodded. "No shame in getting knocked on your ass, son. You got back up and showed him how the cow ate the cabbage. That's what counts."

Tucker glanced around the waiting area. "Did you bring Samantha in about her eye?"

The older man laughed again. "Hell, no. She's too stubborn to see a doctor for a bruise. Last I saw, her brother was putting a scraped spud over her eye, and she was telling him to go home and leave her alone." He sobered, and his brown eyes met Tucker's gaze with solemn intensity. "I came to thank you for what you did today. With the nose, I figured you'd be easy to spot, and it turns out I was right."

"You didn't need to drive all this way. A phone call would have done just as well."

"Not this time. The man could have seriously hurt my girl if you hadn't stepped in. Samantha tells me you're a vet and specialize in horses?"

"I'm getting there. My brother and I have a practice. I prefer working with large animals, especially equines."

"Got a card?"

Tucker reached for his wallet and withdrew a business card. After taking it, Harrigan studied the information for a moment. Then he tucked the paper into his shirt pocket. "One good turn deserves another. I'll see to it you get some business." He thrust out his hand again. "Good meeting you, Tucker. Could be I'll be calling you myself sometime."

As Tucker bade Harrigan farewell, he said, "I'll appreciate any business that comes my way, but please, don't feel obligated because of this afternoon. I only did what any man worth his salt would do."

"Exactly. That goes a lot farther with me than a character reference."

Frank Harrigan had just exited the building through the revolving door when Tucker's family entered the waiting room. Still feeling dazed by Harrigan's unexpected appearance, Tucker said to Jake, "You're not going to believe who I was just talking to."

"Who?"

"Frank Harrigan."

"You're shittin' me."

"No. It's true," Tucker insisted. "He drove out here to thank me for taking up for his daughter this afternoon. He's a totally nice guy."

Excitement lit Jake's blue eyes. "Did you mention me?"

"No. I never even thought to."

Jake's jaw muscle started to tic. "I just told you how much I'd like to meet the man, and you never even thought to?" When Tucker shrugged, Jake added, "I should have whomped your nose with that mallet when I had a chance. Some brother you are."

Chapter Four

Samantha's large ranch-style kitchen bustled with activity. Her four jet-haired brothers were determined to prepare her dinner to celebrate Blue Blazes's first-place win in the cutting horse competition that afternoon. Samantha wasn't fooled. Granted, they were as delighted over Blue's big win as she was, but the real reason for their presence was to look after her until their father returned.

And they meant to stay whether she wanted them to or not.

Seated at the table with a scraped potato pressed over her eye, she watched them with weary resignation. As dearly as she loved each of them, she needed some quiet time—an hour or two by herself to regroup and put the events of the afternoon behind her. She also yearned to visit Blue out in the stable. He was an indisputable champion now. That called for the equine version of a champagne toast, a blend of oatmeal and diced apples, fed to him by hand, with lots of petting and kudos in between bites. But oh, no, her brothers wouldn't hear of it. She needed to take care of herself first, they insisted. Congratulating Blue would have to wait.

Thanks to her dad, all of her brothers knew their way around a kitchen. They'd just never mastered the skill of tidy cooking. Clint, the oldest at thirty-six, stood at the stove, making his specialty, kielbasa-and-mashed-potato soup. The Viking range looked as if a shotgun blast of onions, cheese, and sausage had peppered its black surface. Quincy, two years Clint's junior, had been put in charge of making corn bread, and was managing to dust himself and that entire section of granite countertop with whole-wheat flour. Parker, a year younger than Quincy, had commandeered another work area to create a tossed green salad, and he seemed to think *tossed* meant lettuce thrown everywhere. Zach, who'd turned thirty-one three days ago on the ninth of August, had been assigned the duty of watching his sister to make sure she kept the potato pulp over her eye.

"I can't believe you guys are over here on a Saturday night, messing up my kitchen and fussing over me like this," she grumped. "It's only a little bruise. Don't you have lives?"

Clint broke off from whistling a cheerful ditty to wink at her over his well-muscled shoulder. With his wavy black hair, burnished skin, dreamy brown eyes, and perfectly toned body, he should have long since been married, but somehow he'd escaped that fate. "You want me to stop making soup and do what I really want to do?"

The kitchen went suddenly quiet, and Samantha, peering out at him from behind the spud, realized all her brothers were looking at her expectantly. With all their faces turned toward her, she was strongly reminded of the blood ties that bound the five of them together. They each had their father's curly, pitch-black hair, dark eyes, and irregular features, the only major difference being that the irregularities were a lot more attractive on their masculine visages than they were on hers. They also refused to wear sunscreen, despite all her lectures, and as a result, their skin had a bronzed, weathered texture that hers lacked.

"What is it, exactly, that you really want to do?" she asked cautiously.

"I've got a tire iron under the seat of my truck," Quincy replied.

Samantha narrowed her uncovered eye and thinned her lips. "Don't even *think* about it. The man hit me, it's over, and now he's in jail. End of story."

"Tire iron, hell," Clint said with a low growl in his voice. "My fists will serve me just fine. Just let me at him."

Zach, sitting across the custom-made alder table, slumped on the chair and thrust out both of his long, denim-clad legs to peruse his brown Tony Lama boots. "I'm wearin' my pointy-toed shit-kickers. Why bark my knuckles when a few swift kicks will do the job?"

Parker gave the lettuce an extra-hard toss that sent bits of green flying from the bowl again. "I'll let you boys have your fun. Then I want him to myself for a little finish work."

"Oh, please." Samantha propped both elbows on the table and groaned. She knew her brothers were absolutely serious. The Harrigan code was, "One for all and all for one," and her brothers had been fighting her battles most of her life. "That's just what I need, the four of you going off half-cocked and ending up in the pokey. Use your heads for something besides a Stetson rack."

"We are using our heads," Clint retorted. "That's why we're here, cooking you supper. We'd much rather be parked outside the sheriff's department, waiting for the asshole to make bail."

"To contemplate going there is beyond dumb," Samantha retorted. "You don't even know what he looks like."

"Mean, hungover, and butt-ugly is my guess," Zach said.

"And when we get done with him, he'll be even uglier," Parker added.

"When, in the entire history of the world, has physical violence ever solved anything?" Samantha demanded.

"Sometimes you are so *female* in your thinking, it totally blows my mind." Quincy turned from the mixing bowl. His black T-shirt had a hand smear across the chest. "Women think every damned problem can be solved by paying it a little lip service."

"Hello. Maybe, just *maybe*, we have it right. Did you ever think of that?"

Quincy wiped his hand on his T-shirt again. "Arguing with you is pointless. You have selective hearing, a one-track mind, and a stubborn streak a mile wide."

Samantha lowered the potato from her eye to smile sweetly at him. "If it's so pointless, why do you argue with me? Better to simply concede the point and admit you're wrong."

"Ha!" he retorted. "You're the one who's wrong. And I argue with you for two reasons, one being that Dad would think we were both sick if we suddenly stopped."

"And the second?"

Quincy smirked. "Because sooner or later you get pissed off and stop talking to me. The silence is music to my ears."

Samantha almost laughed. Sparring with Quincy was one of her favorite pastimes because neither of them ever took it seriously.

"Children, children!" Clint called from the stove. Pointing at each of them with his spoon, he added, "We're supposed to stick together at times like this, not squabble among ourselves. We all know you're right, Sam. Knocking the snot out of the guy would be a stupid move." Before turning back to the soup pot, he graced her with a burning glare. "Just understand that knowing you're right does nothing to make the idea any less appealing. The son of a bitch hit you. We have every reason to be royally pissed, so cut us a little slack."

Samantha drew the potato from her eye again to gesture with her hands. "You're all acting as if he walked away scot-free, and that wasn't the case at all. Before it was all over, I turned him into the human version of a bilateral cryptorchid."

Zach snorted at her use of the veterinary term for a male horse with both testicles undescended. "Good for you, sis. I never heard that part of the story. Used a little Harrigan judo on him, did you?"

Clint gave her a thumbs-up. "Yes!" he said with a burst

of enthusiasm. "All those hours I spent teaching you self-defense actually paid off."

"I only resorted to kicking him because I had no choice," she explained. "He nailed Tucker on the nose with a whip handle—one of those long, old-fashioned lunge-whip handles made of wood and wrapped with a leather thong. Tucker was blinded and couldn't defend himself. I bought him a few seconds to regain his senses."

"So physical violence is sometimes justified?" Quincy asked sarcastically.

"In self-defense, yes. It's different when you go looking for trouble."

"Enough on the pros and cons of physical violence," Clint interjected. "Tell us the rest of what happened."

"You've heard the rest. Once Tucker got back on his feet, he backed the guy against the horse trailer and pounded the devil out of him." Samantha chose to leave out the part about the drunk jumping her from behind. "That being the case, there's no score left for any of you to settle."

"I'd like to meet this Coulter fellow," Zach inserted. "He sounds like my kind of guy, a kick-ass good old boy."

Clint turned back to the stove to stir the kielbasa and bacon. "I'd like to shake his hand myself. Maybe I will someday. For now, we'll leave that to Dad while we hold down the fort."

Samantha sat straighter on the chair. "What do you mean, you'll leave that to Dad?" Silence. She quickly put two and two together. "Is that where he went—to see Tucker? I thought he had business in town."

"That's business, and the hospital's in town," Parker, the human SaladShooter, said over his shoulder. "Don't get your nose out of joint. When a stranger steps up to the plate and defends one of our own, we Harrigans owe him an official thank-you."

An image of Tucker's dark face flashed through Samantha's mind. When she'd said good-bye to him at the sheriff's department, she'd hoped to put the incident behind her and never see him again. "I thanked Mr. Coulter. What makes Dad think it's necessary to thank him again?"

Clint, always the self-appointed spokesman in Frank's absence, fielded her question with, "You can carry the independent-woman thing too far, Samantha Jane."

"What independent-woman thing?"

He waved the wooden spoon at her. "*That* independent-woman thing, the one where you get all huffy and bent out of shape over silly stuff."

In her estimation, her need to feel independent wasn't silly, but critical to her emotional health and well-being. She needed her father and brothers to respect her boundaries, and none of them even seemed to realize she had any. They meant well. They'd *always* meant well. But without intending to, they had a way of taking over her life.

In all fairness, she couldn't hold them totally to blame. She was the one who allowed it, after all. How difficult was it to say no? She frequently rehearsed exactly how she would handle the next infraction. *No, I think I'll do it this way.* Or, *I appreciate the advice, really I do, but I've already made my decision.* In her head, those responses sounded so reasonable, but even if she managed to say them, she had trouble making them stick.

Other women who found themselves being suffocated by a meddling family moved away, found a job, and cultivated friendships outside the familial circle. That was impossible for Samantha. Like her brothers, when she turned twenty-one, she had inherited from her father a two-hundred-acre share of the original Harrigan ranch and enough capital to start her own business. Out of respect for her dad, she couldn't just walk away, turning her back on everything he had sweated blood to build. It would break his heart.

"I need to be my own person," she said softly.

"So be your own person," Clint replied. "Who's stopping you?"

Who, indeed? Her father's place lay due west of hers, Clint's was directly to the north, and her other three brothers lived within shooting distance of her front porch. From anyplace on her property she could see the rooftops of their homes, and they all took frequent advantage of the short distance to visit her whenever they pleased. The only time in her life when she'd had any sense of separateness had been during the dark years of her marriage, when they'd all stayed away because they couldn't abide Steve.

"Forget it," she said wearily. "Just forget it. I could talk myself blue and never make you understand."

Clint made it clear he didn't care to understand by brusquely saying, "Get that spud back on your eye."

And there it was, the very essence of her problem with him and all the rest of her male relatives. They refused to treat her like an adult. In their minds she would always be Sammy, daughter and pesky baby sister. When she was eighty, they would still be telling her what to do.

"Do you have to be so bossy, Clint?" she asked. "It's my eye. If I have a shiner tomorrow, oh, well."

"Bossy?" Her eldest brother looked genuinely incredulous. "What in the Sam Hill are you talking about?" Before she could answer, he put the question up for a family vote. "Am I bossy, you guys?"

Quincy flashed a broad grin. "I'm not touching that one with a ten-foot prod."

"So you agree?" Clint shook his head. "You actually think I'm bossy?"

Parker chuckled. "Of course you're bossy, Clint. Helping Dad to raise all of us screwed you up."

"Yeah," Zach interjected with a lazy grin. "You think the power of persuasion is a size-eleven boot up somebody's ass."

"What is it with you and boots today?" Samantha asked Zach. "As for that, you can all clean up your mouths. This is my kitchen, not the barn."

"I haven't taken the Lord's name in vain," Zach protested. "Neither has anyone else."

"That soup is starting to smell mighty good," Quincy observed in an obvious attempt to change the subject. Boot heels tapping the slate tile, he crossed the kitchen and nudged Clint aside to put the bread in the oven. "I'm hungry enough to eat the south end of a northbound donkey without wiping its ass first." He slanted Samantha a glance. "Sorry, sis."

Samantha knew when to cut her losses. Her brothers would never break themselves of using colorful language. She picked up the potato to stare at the discolored pulp. "How long do I have to keep this stupid thing on my eye?"

Parker came to set the bowl of salad on the table. He stooped low to examine her bruise. "It's taken down the swelling some," he pronounced. "A few more minutes ought to do it."

The security system chimed just then, yet another sign of her family's devotion to her safety and well-being. The moment she'd kicked Steve out, the alarm system had been installed, and now, an entire year later, her dad still phoned her every evening at dark to make sure she remembered to set it.

The sound of the front door closing echoed through the house. A moment later Samantha heard her father's distinctive footsteps echoing on the hardwood floor.

When he appeared in the doorway, hat in hand, she said, "Mission accomplished?"

"Mostly," he replied, the expression on his burnished countenance unabashed. "And don't start," he warned. "I did what I needed to do, and whether you approve or not, there'll be no discussin' it."

It had been a long day, and Samantha was too weary to argue.

"What'd you think of Coulter?" Zach asked.

"I like him." Frank raked his fingers through his hair, trying to comb away the hat ring. Age had streaked the strands with silver at his temples, but they were otherwise as black as his children's. "I found him outside the ER, probably waitin' for a ride. He's a clean-cut, polite young fellow." He shot Samantha a sidelong glance. "Tall, sturdy. Good-lookin', too, in my estimation, even if he is sportin' two black eyes. I figure the other guy probably feels worse than he does."

"We can only hope. Sammy laid down the law." Quincy grinned at his sister. "If we go anywhere near the jail, she's gonna kick our butts."

"I think Coulter took care of the paybacks for us," Frank said, patting his shirt pocket. "And one good turn deserves another. I got his card. Reckon I'll steer a little business his way, maybe even some of my own."

"That's a good idea, Dad," Clint remarked. "Old Doc Washburn will be retiring soon. Having a young vet on line who knows his stuff can't hurt."

"Just because he took up for me doesn't mean he knows his stuff," Samantha pointed out.

Hooking his Stetson over the finial of a tall-backed chair, Frank sat down next to her. Even at sixty-one, he was as fit and trim as a thirty-year-old, testimony to a lifetime of hard work. Though semiretired now, he could still run circles around men half his age.

"You're absolutely right, Samantha Jane. And you know me: I don't let just any vet touch one of my horses."

"So why consider recommending him to others or giving him business yourself?" she asked.

"On the way home, I did some callin' around to check him out," Frank replied. "Thought the name Coulter sounded familiar. Now I know why. He's that new fellow old Jim Ralston has been braggin' about. I trust Jim's opinion. He claims the boy is flat amazing with horses."

"How so?" Parker asked.

"Not afraid of 'em, for starters. That's important in a vet." A rumble of general agreement urged Frank to continue. "More important, Jim says the boy has a gift."

Samantha recalled Tucker's talking about his rapport with equines. "How do you mean?"

Frank's brow furrowed in thought. "Jim says the young man can calm a frightened horse like nobody he's ever seen, as if he communicates with the animal in a way most folks can't."

Samantha knew firsthand how charming Tucker Coulter could be.

"Jim had a filly go lame on him," Frank went on. "Thought she had real promise as a cuttin' horse, and he'd hoped to put her with a professional trainer. But all of a sudden she developed a limp. He took her to a couple of other vets. They prescribed confinement and inactivity to let the foreleg heal. But she kept goin' lame again as soon as Jim let her resume normal activity. He finally took her to Tucker Coulter, and now that filly is fit as a fiddle."

"What'd Coulter do to fix her up?" Clint asked.

"Come to find out," Frank continued, "there was nothin' wrong with her foreleg. Coulter X-rayed it and discovered Jim's farrier was trimming her hoof wrong. Too much inward slope. It was puttin' a strain on the tendon, and every time she got the least bit active, the swelling and tenderness returned."

"And the other two vets didn't find that?"

"Never bothered to X-ray the hoof and leg." Frank chuckled and shook his head. "Can't find somethin' if you don't look for it, now, can you?"

The conversation turned to veterinarians—stories about good ones and bad ones and all the mediocre ones in between. When supper was finally on the table, all talking came to a halt. Frank began the blessing by making the sign of the cross, and the six of them quickly recited the prayer that they'd been saying before meals for as long as Samantha could remember.

"Boy howdy, Clint, you've surpassed yourself. This soup is superb," Frank observed after taking a bite. "You got any wine, sweetheart? We're celebrating Blue's big win tonight. An occasion like this calls for a toast."

Samantha left the table to get wineglasses and a bottle of merlot. As she set the bottle on the table and started to open it, Parker snatched the corkscrew from her hands. "Here, let me."

"I do know how to open a bottle of wine," Samantha reminded him.

If Parker heard her, he gave no sign of it. She circled the table to resume her seat. The wine was soon poured, and Frank passed her a glass.

"To the finest breeder and trainer this side of the Mississippi," her dad said with a lift of his goblet. "Congratulations, sweetheart. Blue Blazes is a horse to be proud of."

"Hear, hear!" her brothers said, and each took a swallow of merlot.

"Present company excluded, of course," Zach said with a grin. "About you being the finest breeder and trainer, I mean. On that count, I think we all run neck and neck."

Another toast was made to Blue, the finest cutting horse this side of the Mississippi, which prompted Zach to once again say, "Present company excluded, of course."

There followed hoots of laughter when Parker said, "Speak for yourself. I'm not a horse."

Clint seconded that with, "Me, neither."

When the laughter abated, Clint was complimented yet again on the soup.

"It's all that cheese he puts in it," Quincy, the health nut, complained. "You can make anything taste good if you put in enough cheese."

"You ever stop to think that God gave us cheese?" Zach protested.

"Not to mention our taste buds," Parker tacked on. "They regenerate every four days. Seems to me we're supposed to enjoy the taste of our food."

"You can enjoy your food without clogging all your arteries," Quincy countered. "Do you have any inkling how much fat is in just one of those sausages?"

And so it went, the members of her family arguing good-naturedly back and forth as they enjoyed the meal. The tension eased from Samantha's shoulders, and a slight smile touched her lips as she attended the conversation. There would be time enough later to worry about her difficulties with them. Tonight she wanted only to relax and enjoy being together.

Chapter Five

The log walls of Jake's living room shimmered in the light like polished amber. Tucker, replete after a fabulous steak dinner, relaxed from being pampered, and kicked back in a leather recliner with an ice pack on his nose, was considering the possibility of a short nap. With half his face covered and still partly numb from the Novocain injections, he couldn't comfortably engage in the after-supper conversation taking place between his dad and elder brother, so he stared at the open rafters above him instead, only half listening to the debate on all the possible causes of mad cow disease. Occasionally when Harv and Jake were both dead wrong, he thought about putting in his two cents' worth, but the wine he'd had with his meal was making him feel too sleepy.

That was one of the things he liked about Jake's log house: its relaxed atmosphere. Shortly after Jake's marriage to Molly, a cute, whiskey-haired woman no taller than Tucker's mother and almost as round, the original structure had burned to the ground. Tucker had expected the identical new house to take on a different character with Molly in charge of decorating. But somehow she'd managed to put her stamp on every room without altering the rustic theme. Handmade furniture, an array of Western paintings by local artists, and a collection of antique farming and ranching implements worked together with more feminine accents to create an appealing space where a man could sprawl in a comfortable, oversize chair and not worry about his boots soiling the upholstery.

Tucker liked his own house, a two-story Victorian surrounded by English gardens and a white picket fence. He'd had the spacious interior professionally decorated, and every room was the antithesis of what he'd known as a kid. The furniture had fine upholstery and lots of curlicues in the wood, the dishes were dainty, patterned with tea roses and trimmed in gold, and almost every room sported an imported area rug that had cost the earth. He'd loved it all at first and determinedly ignored the ceaseless ribbing from his brothers, who were all men's men with rugged tastes. Tucker loved fine things, and he was confident enough in his masculinity to surround himself with them.

Only now that the newness had worn off, he wondered sometimes if he'd made the right choices for long-term living. Yes, crystal decanters and fine bone china appealed to him, but practically speaking, they weren't things he wanted to use on a daily or even monthly basis. His finger wouldn't fit through the handles of the teacups. The decanters dribbled out booze when he preferred a generous slosh, and when he wanted a mixed drink in the evening, he always sought out a sturdy tumbler. For his library, he'd also broken down and bought a comfortable chair, which looked blockish and far too massive for the room, rather like Tucker himself.

In short, he was a bull living in a dollhouse with a huge, graceless rottweiler named Max as a roommate. Max chewed knucklebones on the fine area rugs, his black fur constantly drifted on the currents of circulating air, and the teacups on the rack in the formal dining room performed the singular purpose of collecting dust. It wasn't a wholly practical situation, and Tucker had been toying with the idea of making a change, the only problem being all the merciless teasing by his brothers that he would have to endure if he sold his Victorian home and bought a place on a larger acreage better suited to his lifestyle.

"The mad cow threat makes a man afraid to eat beef," Tucker's father said. "I wish we still raised our own. Buying meat at the supermarket, I could wake up some mornin' mad as a hatter and drooling at the mouth."

"Just don't eat the brains, spinal tissue, or vital organs," Tucker muttered. It wasn't easy to speak clearly around an ice pack, especially with a numb upper lip. "Not much danger otherwise."

"I'm still not talking to you," Jake said, his voice laced with teasing gruffness. "My one big chance to meet Frank Harrigan, and you didn't even think to introduce me. You knew I was right upstairs in the cafeteria."

"I'm sorry," Tucker said, not for the first time. "I don't know where my head was."

And that was the truth. Tucker hadn't felt so nervous since going to pick up a girl on his first date. What had her name been? His head was too foggy to remember. He recalled only being so tense that he stuttered and tripped over his own feet.

Until this afternoon, he'd believed himself to be over that awkward stage. But meeting Frank Harrigan had plunged him back into it, leaving him uncertain what to say and worrying about the impression he'd made. How crazy was that?

Tucker wondered if his numb lip had wandered all over his face when he smiled. And had he gripped Harrigan's hand firmly enough? Ranchers judged a man by his handshake. And—*oh, damn*—had he really been leafing through a fashion article, looking at the best- and worst-dressed people of the year, when Samantha's father approached?

Why Tucker cared, he didn't know. Then he decided he was lying to himself. He was taken with Samantha, and it was important that her father approved of him. How else could he hope to make any headway with the woman?

Cheyenne Lee, Jake's fifteen-month-old daughter, let

loose with a shriek from somewhere upstairs, followed by the sound of running footsteps. "Young lady, you get back here!" Molly cried.

The next thing Tucker knew, his baby niece stood on the landing overlooking the living room, her plump, naked body rosy from her bath, damp chocolate curls framing her cherubic face. Peering down at him through the log railing, which had been constructed for toddler safety, she grinned broadly, flashing eight new pearly whites.

"Hey, gorgeous," Tucker called up to her.

She jabbered something and then giggled as if she'd just told a joke. The punch line was yet to come. She assumed a suddenly intent expression and started to pee, the stream running down her chubby thighs to puddle on the floor.

"Jake!" Tucker called, exercising a childless uncle's prerogative to call on the parent when accidents occurred. "She's taking a leak without a diaper."

But the call came too late. The puddle cascaded over the edge of the landing to rain on Tucker, the recliner, and the floor. The ice pack went in one direction and Tucker in another as he scrambled to escape the downpour, wondering how a quarter cup of urine could sprinkle such a large area.

He cursed under his breath and swatted at his jeans. A chortle of delight came from above, and Cheyenne stomped her chubby feet, clearly pleased with the ruckus she had caused.

Tucker growled, doing an imitation of an angry bear, and charged up the stairs. His intended victim screeched in delight and launched a counterattack, running toward him instead of away, making him increase speed considerably to reach the unlatched safety gate at the top of the staircase before she did.

"Gotcha!" he yelled. "You wet on your uncle Tucker. Now you gotta pay."

Cheyenne giggled as Tucker snatched her up, growled again, and pretended to devour her, paying special attention to her most ticklish spots. He made sure to avoid nibbling on any part of her from the knees down, however, namely her ankles or toes, which were transferring their wetness onto his shirt.

The tiny girl suddenly went quiet and still. Tucker stopped tickling her and raised his head. Solemnly, she reached out a pink, dimpled hand to touch the bandage over his nose.

"Owee," she said.

"Yes, a big owee," Tucker agreed, "but the doctor made it feel all better."

Molly appeared behind her daughter, holding aloft a cream-colored bath towel. Short, generously curvaceous, and almost as cute as her little girl, she flashed Tucker a radiant smile as she enveloped the baby in terry cloth and scooped her out of his arms.

"She had an accident." Tucker pointed to the wetness. "It spilled over and got the floor, me, and the recliner downstairs."

Molly followed his gaze. "Uh-oh. Another bath for you, young lady." Leaning over the railing, she called, "Daddy, cleanup time."

Jake had already gone to the downstairs bathroom for a damp towel and a spray bottle of disinfectant. Looking like the Marlboro Man on a mission, he gave his wife a mock salute as he advanced on the target area. "Yes, ma'am, got it covered."

Molly grinned. "I love it when he calls me ma'am. It's so sexy."

Jake chuckled as he crouched to clean up the mess. "I'll remember that."

"Say, 'Bye-bye, Uncle Tucker,'" Molly instructed her daughter, grabbing the baby's pudgy wrist to show her how to wave.

Tucker wiggled his fingers in farewell. Gazing after Molly as she disappeared through a doorway along the hall, he felt funny inside, sort of hollow and lost. He wanted what all his brothers had found, one special woman with whom he could build a life. His youngest brother had a second child on the way, and Tucker wasn't even married yet. Even worse, he had no prospects and wasn't sure he ever would.

It wasn't for lack of trying. He dated regularly. Hell, he'd even traveled to Colorado in June, thinking he might get lucky if he returned to the place where this branch of the Coulter clan had first begun. Sadly, he'd found no magic in No Name, Colorado, only some weathered headstones and a handful of bewildered distant relatives who could never quite grasp why he'd gone to such lengths to find them.

In retrospect, Tucker wasn't sure, either, and felt a little foolish. Love wasn't like gold or buried treasure, something tangible that you could search for and unearth. And you weren't more likely to find it simply because you traveled to a different place. If you were fortunate, love just happened, most times when you least expected it, according to his mother.

His thoughts circled back to the afternoon and that first moment when he'd seen Samantha Harrigan. He'd felt something when he was with her today—an expectant feeling he'd never experienced before. Had she felt it, too? Or was it just wishful thinking? She was a pretty lady, and he'd found a lot in her to admire during their short acquaintance. But chances were he'd never see her again.

The stable phone started to ring just as Samantha offered Blue the last of his apples and oatmeal. She allowed the stallion to nibble her palm clean before leaving the stall to answer the call.

"Hi, Dad," she said without waiting to find out who it was. "No, I haven't set the alarm yet. Yes, I'm out in the stable after dark. I'll be going in and battening down the hatches in about ten minutes."

Her father said nothing for a long moment. Then he cleared his throat and replied, "I'll give you a call back in ten minutes, then."

Samantha gritted her teeth. As much as she appreciated her father's concern for her safety, his habit of constantly checking in with her was a pain in the neck. If she decided to have a long soak in the bathtub after calling it a day, she had to make sure she took the portable phone into the bathroom with her. If she needed something from the store and made an evening grocery run, God forbid that she forgot to let him know.

"I'll be all right, Dad. Jerome is right upstairs in the stable apartment if I need him, and Steve hasn't shown his face around here in over a year."

Frank said, "I know that, Sammy, and chances are good that he never will again. But there's still no harm in playing it safe."

Samantha mouthed the words, *An ounce of prevention is worth a pound of cure,* while her father recited the familiar refrain in her ear. When he finished speaking, she said, "I love you, Dad."

"I love you, too. Make sure you lock up tight when you go in the house."

"I will," she promised.

"And if you hear any odd noises, don't hesitate to call me."

"I won't."

"There's my good girl."

As she broke the connection, Samantha said, "That's me, Daddy's good girl." Replacing the phone in its cradle, she returned to Blue's stall. Looping her arms around the stallion's neck, she pressed her face against his salt-and-pepper coat and soothed herself by breathing in his smell.

"Am I horrible, Blue?" She sighed wearily, wishing the horse could respond. He was her best friend, after all, and that was what friends were for, to give advice. "I just want a little privacy once in a while. Is that so wrong?"

Blue nudged her with his nose, bumping her off balance. She laughed and patted his shoulder. "I know, I know. I'm an ungrateful brat. The ranch, the house, and the very dirt I'm standing on were gifts from him. He even lent me the money to pay Steve off so I wouldn't lose this place, and he never says a word about me paying him back. I should be more appreciative."

The stallion snorted and dipped his head as if he were nodding. Maybe, Samantha decided, he could impart some advice after all. As she left the stall and closed the gate, she glanced at the telephone, tempted to call her father back. But, no. He'd be calling again in precisely—she glanced at her watch—six minutes. She'd just make it a point to be nice when she answered.

As she crossed the indoor arena, she called good-night to Oregano and Nutmeg, promising to bring them treats in the morning. At the personnel door she stopped to look back at the forty spacious stalls that lined the riding area before she turned out the light. A gift, her early inheritance, a dream come true. If her last name weren't Harrigan, she would have none of it. She needed to remember that and try to be more patient with her father.

Once outside the building, Samantha stopped for a moment to enjoy the beautiful evening. The moon hung in the sky like a curved quarter shard of a broken supper plate, and stars twinkled around it like sequins that had been tossed willy-nilly onto dark blue velvet. When she breathed deeply she could smell alfalfa, freshly cut grass hay left to dry in the fields, and the faint perfume of wild clover.

She took a slow turn, keeping her gaze fixed on the sky. *I wish I may, I wish I might . . .* The verse carried her back through the years to her childhood and brought a sad smile to her lips. No matter how many times Clint had warned her, she'd never been able to resist telling him what she had wished for. How different things were now, with her most secret wishes held close to her heart.

When a sound came from behind her, Samantha assumed it was one of the wild creatures that frequented the property after dark and didn't pause in her circling to look over her shoulder. The front window of her ranch foreman's second-story apartment was just above her, and even though the lights were out, she knew he was home. Jerome, only a few years younger than her dad, went to bed with the chickens, but he was a light sleeper and would surely hear her if she called for help.

Not that it would ever be necessary. Unlike her father and brothers, she didn't live in fear of Steve Fisher any-more. She'd put that demon to rest. Only five of the original kitchen chairs that went with her custom-made table still existed. The sixth had met its waterloo when she brought it down on top of Steve's head and then proceeded to whale the tar out of him with the broken pieces.

It wasn't one of her fondest memories, and she would never feel proud of the person she'd become that night. But the altercation had served two good purposes: teaching her that size, weight, and muscle didn't always determine the outcome of a physical confrontation, and teaching Steve that the dictatorship he'd called a marriage was finally over.

He'd left that night and never returned, sending a friend in his stead to collect his belongings. He was a coward and a bully who pushed people around only when he felt confident they wouldn't push back. He would never step foot on this property again. She felt confident of that.

Chapter Six

The following morning after her customary three-mile run and a quick shower, Samantha left the house at precisely six o'clock. On Sundays, especially, it was important that she began her work early so she could break free shortly after eleven to attend noon Mass.

En route to the stables, she carried five one-gallon freezer bags filled with treats for her horses—quartered apples, fresh baby carrots, and their favorite, oatmeal and diced fruit. A granola bar rode in her shirt pocket—her version of a human breakfast, which she liked to eat over coffee with her foreman before she began morning rounds.

After entering the arena via the personnel door, she hung a sharp left and ascended the wooden stairs to Jerome's on-site living quarters. Rapping sharply on the door, she turned the knob and leaned in to yell, "You decent?"

"When am I ever not decent at this time of day?" the fifty-four-year-old foreman answered. "Come on in, honey. Coffee's made."

Samantha stepped inside, closed the door, and hooked her straw hat over the knob, making a mental note to search through her closets for another ball cap as soon as she found the time. "Thank goodness. I need a cup of your black mud to get my blood pumping this morning."

His graying brown hair still damp from the shower, Jerome flashed a welcoming smile, his brown eyes sharpening on her bruised cheek. "I figured you might need a jump start. How you feeling?"

"Better than I look."

The compact apartment, originally intended to be used as foaling quarters, featured a tiny living room area divided from the kitchen by a breakfast bar. A closet-size bathroom and bedroom lay at the back. Jerome had moved in eight years ago, right after the stables and arena were built. Prior to that, he'd worked twenty-two years as a ranch hand for Frank Harrigan.

Though technically their relationship was that of employer and employee, Samantha never thought of Jerome as her subordinate or treated him as such. She'd known him all her life, trusted him immensely, and couldn't have loved him more if he'd actually been a blood relative. His knowledge of horses was second only to her father's, and she picked his brain at least a dozen times a day.

She swung a leg over an oak barstool, plopped the equine treats on the counter, and accepted the mug of steaming coffee that he slid toward her.

"Ah," she said appreciatively after taking a careful sip. "Nobody but you makes coffee quite as good as Dad's. What's the secret?"

"Right before we set the pot on to boil, we spit in the grounds basket."

"Liar." Samantha wrinkled her nose but confidently took another sip. "No wonder you never got married. No woman in her right mind would put up with you."

Jerome laughed. He was still a good-looking man, his medium frame trim and superbly fit. "The ladies like me just fine. And it's not my old-fashioned boiled coffee that attracts them, either."

Samantha had no difficulty believing that. Jerome had a lazy, relaxed manner that put everyone at ease.

"It's a little after six on a Sunday morning," she popped back. "You can't tell me you had a hot date last night."

"That Friday- and Saturday-night nonsense is for you young people. I do my socializing on weeknights. Over the weekends I hang around here to do early feedings so all of you can party at the honky-tonks until the wee hours."

"Not me."

"More's the pity," Jerome replied. "You could do with a little fun for a change. How long has it been since you went dancing?"

"Not long enough." Samantha lifted her cup to her lips and smiled at him over the rim. "My dance-floor career was an abysmal failure. I was born with two left feet."

"You dance pretty enough when you're working with a horse," he pointed out.

Samantha let that pass. "Who came in yesterday to work a half shift?"

"Carrie and Kyle. I let both of them leave an hour early so they could go to the fairgrounds and watch Blue win the cutting horse competition."

"And he didn't disappoint them!" Samantha said proudly. "I'll bet afterward Kyle told everybody who would listen that he trained Blue himself."

Jerome chuckled. "You're probably right. That boy has an incredible talent with horses, but it's mostly on the tip of his tongue."

They passed a few minutes recalling comical moments in Kyle's horse training career, the most notable the time he accidentally stepped inside the loop of a lasso when the other end of the rope was tied to the saddle of a green cow pony. Fortunately for Kyle, Jerome had been close at hand to prevent disaster, and Kyle hadn't been badly hurt.

When their mirth subsided, Samantha asked, "How's Carrie seem to be doing?"

"Well enough, I reckon. Doing her work, anyway, and she seems to enjoy the horses. Why do you ask?"

In the process of peeling the wrapper off her granola bar, Samantha shrugged. Carrie was a relatively new employee who'd been cheerful and friendly when she'd first hired on. "She hasn't been very talkative lately. I'm concerned that the job may be all that she hoped. I know her wages could be better."

"You explained before you hired her that things would be tight for another year. She knows you'll give her a raise as soon as you're able."

"Yeah." Samantha took a small bite of the bar, then chewed and swallowed. "Promises don't pay the bills, though. I know she's pulled a couple of extra shifts recently for that nursing agency she used to work for. That tells me her check must not be stretching from one payday to the next. Maybe she's upset because I haven't put her on full-time yet."

"I don't think that's the problem."

"So you've noticed it, too?"

Jerome nodded as he lifted the lid of the cookie jar to grab a handful of Oreo cookies. After popping one in his mouth and chewing industriously, he said, "I think she may be having boyfriend trouble."

"A boyfriend?" Samantha considered the possibility. "I didn't think she was seeing anyone. I know she wasn't at the beginning. We used to joke around about our not-so-exciting plans for Saturday night."

"Could be she met someone," Jerome said. "Relationships can be rough on girls like Carrie. She's not very pretty, and she's always struck me as being a little too eager to please."

Envisioning the thirty-one-year-old, Samantha decided Jerome was right. Carrie had lovely hazel eyes and golden brown hair, but her facial features were masculine, and her tall frame was a little too muscular to be attractive.

"You'd think some good fellow would look beneath the surface and realize what a nice person she is."

"It's a woman's looks that usually attract a man first," Jerome replied. "He doesn't worry about things like personality and character until later."

That was one of the many reasons Samantha never intended to have another relationship. She *did* place a high value on personality and character, and very few men in her acquaintance, the members of her family and Jerome excluded, measured up to her expectations.

"Why the long face?" Jerome asked.

Samantha brightened her expression. "Nothing. Woolgathering, I guess." She took another bite of granola. "Sorry for spacing out on you."

He treated her to a penetrating study. "If you're honest with yourself, Samantha Jane, it's a man's looks that first attract you, too."

"No, it's not."

"Honey, you're either lying or kidding yourself." He popped another cookie into his mouth. Cheek bulging, he added, "If you like what you see, you trouble yourself to learn more about him. If you don't, he never gets to first base. What makes you think it's so different with men?"

"Because most men don't bother to learn more about a woman until after their trousers have hung on her bedpost."

"Ouch!"

"Well, it's true. As much as I love and admire you, Jerome, you aren't looking for a long-term relationship every time you sleep with a woman."

He didn't bother to deny it. "And every woman I sleep with understands that *before* I hang my britches on her bedpost. Don't blame every man you meet for the actions of one, or you'll end up a lonely old woman."

"A fine one you are to talk. The single life seems to suit you well enough."

"Women aren't the only ones who can get taken in by sneaky sidewinders. I just wasn't lucky enough to get an earful of good advice after it happened to me."

Samantha's heart caught. Jerome had never before hinted

that he had remained a bachelor because he'd been badly hurt. "You were in love once?"

"Of course I was in love once. Isn't everybody?" He finished off the last Oreo and dusted his hands clean of crumbs. "Unfortunately, the experience was so awful that once was enough to last me. Looking back on it now, I wish I'd given love another chance. But I didn't, and now I'll grow old alone. Be a smart girl and don't let the same thing happen to you."

"I'm sorry you got hurt."

He arched a silver-tipped eyebrow. "And I'm sorry you did. But that's how real life goes, honey. Greenhorns step in horseshit. They have to scrape their boots clean a few times before they learn to avoid the piles."

Samantha sighed and looked out the window. "What a serious conversation for such a beautiful morning." She glanced back at him. "How did we get off on the pitfalls of relationships?"

"Carrie, being so quiet," he reminded her.

"Oh, right." Samantha considered the problem again. "What makes you think she's got boyfriend trouble?"

"All the signs are there. When you first hired her she never even put on lipstick, and her hair was always slicked back in a braid. About two months ago she started wearing makeup and doing her hair different." He flapped his fingers near his temple. "All curly and soft around her face."

"You're right. I never registered the changes, but she has been fixing herself up."

"At first I thought maybe she had her eye on Kyle."

"Oh, *dear*." Kyle Jorge was a good stableman, but he was otherwise everything Samantha abhorred in the opposite sex: flirtatious, preoccupied with the female anatomy, shallow, and so full of testosterone, it seemed to ooze from his pores. "I hope not. He'd break her heart, for sure."

"It's not him," Jerome assured her. "I've watched, and he doesn't know she's alive."

"That doesn't mean she isn't attracted to him."

"No, but I've seen her talking on her cell phone a lot. The first couple of months after you hired her, she seemed totally devoted to the horses, and I never caught her hiding out in the tack room to talk on the phone. That suddenly changed—right about the time her hairdo did. She met someone. I'd go to the bank on it. And chances are, she's been quiet the last couple of weeks because the relationship is going south."

Samantha hoped not. Carrie was a kind person with a big heart. She didn't deserve to be hurt.

Making morning rounds was Samantha's favorite task of the day. She always began with stall number one. "Hello, Cherry," she said to the three-year-old sorrel filly, whose registered name was Cherry Cream. "How's my pretty little girl this morning?"

The young horse eagerly nudged the bags in Samantha's hands. Samantha dropped four of the cumbersome treat containers to the ground and opened the fifth. Cherry eagerly went after the proffered baby carrots, taking three and four at a time from Samantha's palm and greedily munching them. While the filly enjoyed her snack, Samantha stroked her with a free hand.

The next stall held Oregano, a four-year-old dun with a grayish brown coat and a black mane and tail. Samantha entered the enclosure to feed him, taking measure of his conformation as she ran her hand over his shoulder and back. He was filling out beautifully and showing great promise in training. He wasn't quite so quick as Blue Blazes, but Samantha believed he had it in him to become a champion, nevertheless.

Next in line for treats was Cilantro, an eleven-year-old blue roan mare who held the honor of being Blue Blazes's dam. That spring she'd thrown another blue roan colt who was now five months old, brimming with boundless energy, and needing a name. He also needed to learn some manners, Samantha decided as he pushed ahead of his mother for treats. Samantha allowed him to take one carrot before firmly pushing him aside to give the queen of the stable proper deference.

Cilantro batted her black lashes as she nibbled her velvety lips over Samantha's palm to select a treat. With gentle elegance, the mare took the plumpest carrot and nodded as she made fast work of eating it.

"Ah, yes," Samantha murmured as she petted the horse and colt. "My beautiful babies. Yes, you are."

It was her habit to talk softly to all her animals. Over the years she'd determined that it didn't matter what she said, only how she said it. The horses responded to the sound of her voice. As she doled out carrots to the mare and colt, Samantha considered possible names for the baby.

Stroking the foal's nose, she said, "You need a memorable handle, don't you? You're going to be a champion someday, and all great champions need catchy titles."

The double doors to the paddock swung open just then. Jerome entered from outside, wielding a shovel to muck out the stall. As he set to work, he said, "You back on that again? Why don't you choose a normal name for a change? Greased Lightning, maybe."

"Greased Lightning is so trite. I'm sure it's been used."

"Hell on Wheels, then."

She laughed. "That would be perfect, but I can't picture us calling him Hell for short, and it doesn't fit in with my theme."

"Forget your theme. Just because Sage Creek flows across your land and you named the ranch after it doesn't mean every damned horse from your stable has to be christened with the name of a spice, flavor, or food."

"How silly would it sound if I suddenly changed direction? I have big plans for the Sage Creek Ranch. Someday I hope to see my line of quarter horses renowned nationwide as some of the finest ever bred."

"It'll happen. You're off to a grand start, anyway."

"I *know* it'll happen," Samantha assured him. "And when it does, I want my horses to be recognized as being mine when people hear their names. Besides, it's not easy to come up with original names for the AQHA. You know that. I hate when I fall in love with a name, and they kick it back at me, saying it's already on the registry."

"You've definitely got a corner on the kitchen cupboard," he remarked. "The stall roster reads like a damned grocery list."

"No, sir." Samantha chuckled and waved him away. "You just love to give me a hard time." She thought for a moment. "I went through my cupboards one night last week, looking for ideas. What do you think of calling him Hickory Smoke?"

Jerome leaned on the handle of the shovel and repeated the name softly. "That's not bad. He's sort of smoke gray, and Hickory or Smoke would be cute for a nickname."

Samantha bent at the knees to look the colt in the eye. "What's your vote, little guy? When you win a huge purse someday, will you prance around the arena with pride when they yell, 'Hickory Smoke!' over the loudspeaker?"

Jerome resumed shoveling. "I swear, girl. You talk to these horses like they might talk back. He'll be happy with any name you give him."

"Hickory?" Samantha called softly. The colt flicked his ears forward. "He likes it, Jerome."

"Well, then, that settles it. We can add a new grocery item to our list."

The colt kicked out with his rear hooves, making Jerome leap to one side. He sent Samantha a meaningful look. "You'd best watch your p's and q's with him, Samantha Jane. One of these times he's gonna kick out like that and cut you up good."

"Oh, pshaw." Samantha imprinted all her foals at birth and worked with them continually after that into adulthood.

There wasn't a grown horse in her stables that wasn't gentle and well mannered. The foals were just more energetic and unpredictable. "I'm always careful."

"Like just then?"

She chuckled. "It was you in his line of fire, not me."

"How much would you say he's consumed?" Tucker asked a woman over the phone who'd just called the clinic in a panic because her gelding had been eating dirt.

"Bucketfuls," she cried. "When I go out there he glares at me and gobbles up more. I've never seen anything like it. Mud dripping in globs out each side of his mouth. I don't know what's gotten into him."

Tucker signaled his on-call assistant, Marsha Lattimer, that he'd just vacated an examining room and needed it sterilized for the next patient. *Sundays.* Every single time Tucker was on call over the weekend, he stupidly hoped to see very few patients, but instead it was always one emergency after another. Fortunately, his brother Isaiah would be relieving him at noon, allowing Tucker to put in his last volunteer stint at the fairgrounds that afternoon.

"My guess is he's craving a trace mineral of some kind," he told the woman. "Sometimes horses eat dirt because something's lacking in their diet." Tucker reached to pinch the bridge of his nose, a habit when he grew thoughtful. Luckily, he caught himself in the nick of time and rubbed his temple instead. His poor nose was sore as all get-out today. "Would you like me to come out and have a look at the animal? I might be able to fit in a short visit in the early afternoon."

Tucker grabbed his appointment book to make sure he had a few minutes available before he went to the fairgrounds. The two hours he'd hoped to have free for a break and some lunch were filling up fast. After arranging a time to make the field call, he dropped the phone back into its cradle and headed for examining room two.

"You ready for some excitement?" he asked his assistant. "Daisy, the Saint Bernard, swallowed a stick, and it's caught in her throat."

Marsha groaned. "Is that the dog with the inch-long fangs and the personality disorder?"

"That's the one."

"Why'd she swallow a stick today? Why not wait until tomorrow, when Noreen will be here?"

"You don't like Noreen?"

Marsha grinned. "She's uppity. Long fingernails and oh, so fancy." She wiggled her hips and flapped her wrists. "All us gals have decided she needs to be taken down a couple of notches."

Tucker lowered his voice as he drew closer to the room. "Daisy'd be the dog to do it. No argument there."

Tucker was flashing his professional smile as he opened the door to greet the Potters and a snarling Daisy, who lunged against the leash and almost jerked her master off his feet.

Cujo, reincarnated.

"Dang, that *stinks*!" Jerome pressed his shirtsleeve over his nose. "Lord Almighty, I've never in all my days smelled anything so foul."

Samantha was far more concerned about Tabasco, her four-year-old sorrel stallion. She'd seen many a horse with diarrhea, but never a case as severe as this. Tabasco was a gorgeous animal, and she had great hopes for him, but more important, she loved him.

"There's blood in the excrement," she said as she examined the fecal spray on the wall. "Do you think he ingested some of that bad hay before you noticed all the foxtails in it and sent it back?"

Jerome shook his head. "None of that hay ever reached the stables. I checked it the same day it was delivered and called the supplier to come get it immediately. Something sure as hell gave him diarrhea, though."

And a bad case, at that. The entire stall had been splattered, and Jerome was right: It had a terrible, incredibly foul odor. "I'm calling the vet. I don't like the looks of this."

"Can't say I blame you," Jerome replied. "He's a valuable animal, and if it's something contagious we need to protect the other horses."

Samantha left the enclosure to use one of the arena phones. Seconds later she was speaking to the receptionist at the Loyal Companion Veterinary Clinic. "Doc Washburn is in Europe? But I need a vet out here today, Pam."

"No worries. His new partner, Darrin Black, is handling everything in his absence. Shall I send him out?"

Samantha didn't care to use a strange vet, but she couldn't see that she had a choice. "Yes, please, as soon as possible. I may have a very sick horse on my hands." She broke the connection and returned to the stall. "Washburn is in Europe on vacation for a month," she told Jerome. "Can you believe it? He never even notified us that he'd be out of town."

"Maybe he let Frank know, and your dad just forgot to tell you."

"No. Dad doesn't forget things like that." Concerned about her horse, Samantha stepped over to rub Tabasco's forehead. "Poor baby. You must feel awful."

"He's mighty fidgety for a sick horse," Jerome observed as he tossed shovelfuls of the foul-smelling hay and watery manure into the adjoining paddock for removal by tractor later. "Means he's hurting something fierce."

The horse did seem fidgety, Samantha realized. He kept lifting his hooves and sidestepping even as she petted him. "He acts like it hurts even to stand."

"More likely his belly aches, and it hurts more when he's still. Who's coming out to look at him?"

"Washburn's new partner, Darrin Black. He'd better be good, that's all I know." Samantha rolled back Tabasco's lip. "His gums look a little pale to me."

Jerome came over to have a look. After pressing the stallion's gum tissue, he said, "Maybe a little, but his capillary refill is still pretty good." He patted Samantha's shoulder. "Stop fretting. Horses' systems can get out of whack sometimes, just like ours."

"I've never seen a case of diarrhea to equal this."

"It's bad, I'll grant you that. I'll be interested to hear what the vet has to say."

Two hours later the vet finally arrived, a count against him right there. Samantha expected prompt responses to her emergency calls. Darrin Black was a tall, skinny redhead with countless freckles and a receding chin. He didn't look old enough to have gone through veterinary school, let alone to have had much experience treating equines. She ushered him into Tabasco's stall and watched anxiously as Black examined the horse, checking his gums and eyes, palpating his belly, and then taking his temperature.

"Nothing's jumping out at me," he finally said. "My guess is that he got ahold of something that gave him diarrhea, and it'll just pass."

Samantha wasn't surprised that nothing was jumping out at the man. Every vet she'd ever known always listened to a horse's belly first thing. No gut noises were a sure sign of colic, and colic was the number one killer of equines.

"My horses don't get ahold of things without my knowledge, Dr. Black. We follow a very strict feeding regimen, the paddocks and pastures are checked weekly for any poisonous plants that may pop up, and if an animal's diet is changed, we introduce the new food slowly."

The young vet glanced up. "I saw some plastic bags filled with goodies outside the stall. It appears you allow them to have treats. A few too many here and there can give a horse the runs."

"I'm the only person who gives the horses treats, and they get the same stuff and the same amount every third day. I rotate with carrots, apples, and oatmeal mixed with apples. All of them are used to those *goodies*."

"Hmm." Black scratched his head. "I'm sorry, but there's just nothing that jumps out at me. Watch him for the next few hours. See how he does. If he has another bout of diarrhea, give me a call."

Samantha realized he was about to leave. "Shouldn't you take blood and fecal samples?"

He pushed his glasses higher on his nose and gave her a long study. Finally he asked, "For what reason?"

Samantha couldn't believe her ears. Doc Washburn always took a blood sample. She'd come to believe it was standard procedure. "I keep a number of very expensive animals in this stable, Doctor. If this is a contagion of some sort, the other horses may catch it. Normally when a horse gets sick, Dr. Washburn at least runs blood tests, and if it looks like something serious, he checks the feces, too. He wants to make sure nothing potentially deadly is afoot."

"It's my determination that this horse isn't sick with anything serious *or* contagious."

"Pardon me? How can you know that without doing any diagnostics?"

"I'm all but certain it's nothing catching," the redhead insisted as he patted Tabasco's shoulder. "He just has diarrhea, Ms. Harrigan. That happens sometimes."

He spoke to her as if she knew next to nothing about horses. Samantha regretted now that Jerome had cleaned the stall and removed all the evidence. "I've been around horses all my life, Dr. Black. This was no ordinary case of diarrhea. It had an extremely bad odor, was very watery, and there was some blood."

"Horse manure stinks," he replied. "As for the blood, that isn't all that uncommon with a bad case of diarrhea. Keep a close eye on him, make sure he has plenty of fresh water. I'll call tomorrow to see how he's doing."

Samantha was too furious to escort the vet out. She drew the stall gate closed after he left and then leaned against it, her hands knotted into fists at her sides. She had been there for several minutes, watching her horse, when Jerome stopped working on the tractor to come in out of the hot sun for a break.

"What did the vet have to say?" he called as he entered the arena by a rear personnel door.

"That horse manure stinks!"

"Say what?"

Samantha turned to rest her folded arms atop the gate rail. "You heard me," she told the bewildered foreman. "He informed me that horse manure stinks."

Jerome drew off his hat and smoothed his sweat-dampened hair. "Well, now, there's a news flash for you."

"I'm so frustrated I could spit. What an arrogant toad! He refused to do anything more than shove a thermometer up his butt. Washburn always takes a blood sample, and most times more than that." She lifted her hands. "Maybe it's unnecessary, and he runs tests only to make me feel better. But at least I always feel that he's checking out every possibility."

"A good vet normally does, especially with valuable animals like these. Sounds to me like your father had better find another vet. Washburn is out of town on vacation a lot these days. If he's not going to arrange for a qualified partner to take over his practice, what other choice is there?"

Samantha recalled the kitchen conversation with her father and brothers yesterday evening, and she knew exactly which veterinarian her dad would try first. She'd hoped not to see Tucker again, but if it came to a choice between that and the well-being of her horses, she'd be the first to pick up the phone.

Jerome checked his watch. "You can still make it to church if you shake a leg. I can keep an eye on Tabasco while you're gone."

Samantha shook her head. "Thanks for the offer, but I want to stay close, just in case. Regardless of what Dr. Black thinks, I don't believe this is a little intestinal upset. I want to watch the horse to see how he acts."

"Trust your gut feeling," the foreman told her. "In my experience, it's seldom wrong."

"And you, Jerome? What's your gut feeling?"

The foreman frowned. "I'm with you. If it's nothing more than a little upset stomach, it's the worst I've ever seen. Best to watch him, I think."

After giving Max his nightly knucklebone, Tucker mixed himself a drink and settled at the dining room table with the phone book in hand. *Harrigan.* He leafed through the white pages until he found the Hs, then ran a finger down the row. *Bingo.* There were eight Harrigans listed, beginning with Clinton Harrigan and ending with Zachary Harrigan, but Tucker found no Samantha or S. Harrigan in the lineup.

Disappointed, he ran through the first names again—Clinton, Frank, Hugh, Mark, Parker, Paul, Quincy, and Zachary. No matter how long he stared, he could conjure up no Samantha. He had looked forward to calling her all day.

Not a man to give up so easily, he dialed Information, hoping against hope that he might get her number from an operator. Dead end. The woman who took his call said in a nasal, singsong voice, "I'm sorry, sir. There is no listing for a Samantha Harrigan."

Tucker broke the connection, sighed, and looked down at Max. "What d'ya think, partner? Should I call her father to get her number?"

The rottweiler stopped gnawing the bone to give Tucker a bewildered look.

"I hear you. Not classy." He considered the situation for a moment. Then he brightened. "There's nothing wrong with calling him to see how she's doing, though. How does that idea strike you?"

Max growled low in his throat and then went, "Woof!" The sound was so deep and vibrant, Tucker could have sworn the glass doors of the china cabinet rattled.

"Could you be more explicit? Is that a yes, a no, or a maybe?" Tucker switched his gaze to the portable phone. An image of Samantha's lovely face flashed through his mind. Was he going to allow a little thing like an unlisted telephone number to stop him from seeing her again? *Hell, no.* "That fellow roughed her up pretty good," he explained to the rottweiler. "She didn't appear to be seriously hurt yesterday, but sometimes injuries aren't apparent until the following day, when soreness sets in. A gentleman would call to make sure she's all right."

Max growled again.

"What's that supposed to mean? I'm a gentleman. You think I'm not a gentleman?"

"Grrr! Woof!"

"Some friend you are. Who asked for your opinion, anyway? You're just a dog. What do you know?"

Tucker dialed Frank Harrigan's number. The phone rang three times. Then a man picked up and said, "Hello?"

Tucker replied, "Mr. Harrigan, this is Tucker Coulter."

"Tucker! How's the nose doing today?"

"Fine, just fine." Tucker settled back in the chair, trying to convince himself he wasn't nervous. "I, um, just called to see how Samantha's doing. Aside from the bruise on her cheek she seemed fine yesterday, but sometimes injuries aren't apparent until you wake up the next morning."

"So far as I know she's doing nicely. I haven't actually spoken with her today. She had a little horse problem and couldn't make it to church. When me and the boys got home, I was busy all afternoon spreading gravel on my road."

"Oh, I see." Tucker could feel this conversation fading away to an abrupt end. "I, um—" He broke off and swallowed hard. Why was he saying "um"? It made him sound brainless. "I'm sorry for bothering you. I would have called Samantha directly, but her number isn't in the book." *Hint, hint.* "I guess it's unlisted."

"She had some trouble with prank calls a while back. Her

ranch number is listed, but she only gives out her personal number to a select few people."

And Tucker wasn't one of them. "I see. Well, that's certainly understandable. When you see her, please tell her I called, and give her my regards."

"Would you like it?"

Tucker snapped erect on the chair. "Her number? Yes, sir. You bet." He hurried to the kitchen as Frank Harrigan rattled off the digits. Jerking open the junk drawer, he found a pen but no paper. "Hold on." He ran to the library, hoping to find a piece of mail on his desk. The cleaning woman had been there. *Damn.* He hated when she put everything away. How was he supposed to find stuff? His hand. He could just write the number on his hand. "Okay, I'm ready. Can you give it to me again?"

Less than a minute later, Tucker was listening to Samantha's personal line ring. He almost parted company with his skin when she said, "Hello!"

"Hi. This is Tucker."

"I'm not in right now," she went on. "But your call is very important to me. Please leave your name and number, and I'll be in touch as soon as I can."

The answering machine beeped, and Tucker hung up. Then he immediately wished he hadn't. How dumb was it to hang up without saying anything? He redialed the number, listened to the brief message again, and waited for the beep. Then he said, "Hi, Samantha. This is Tucker Coulter. I just thought I'd call and see how you're doing. Call me back if you have a minute."

He'd already hung up before he realized he hadn't left his phone number. *Stupid, stupid.* What was it about the woman that turned his brains to mush? Exasperated with himself, he called back.

"Sorry. I don't know where my head is tonight. I forgot to give you my number." He recited the digits; then he said good-bye and broke the connection. The moment he pressed the button, he realized he hadn't repeated his name the second time around. "Shit."

Max growled and went, "Woof."

"She'll know the second message was from me. She'll hear them back-to-back and recognize my voice."

Max made an O with his mouth and let loose a mournful howl.

"Shut up!" he told the dog. "You're supposed to pump me up, build my confidence. Some friend you are. And what makes you think you're such an expert? On your first date, you humped the lady's head. How slick is that?"

Samantha got in just before dark, locked all the doors, set the security alarm, and then went to the kitchen to find something to eat. As she whipped up a sandwich and green salad, she listened to the messages on her home phone. Her dad had called just to say hi. Clint had phoned to ask how her eye was doing. The third message was blank, with only the sound of heavy breathing.

She paused in slicing a tomato to stare at the phone. A prank? No, Steve no longer knew her number, and only he had ever called and breathed heavily into the phone, hoping to unnerve her. The machine moved on to the next message.

"Hi, Samantha. This is Tucker Coulter."

Samantha smiled slightly at the sound of his voice. He spoke rapidly and in fits and starts, as if he were nervous. She found that charming, but immediately clamped down on the thought. Of *course* he came off as being charming. Men like him practiced in front of a mirror for just that effect.

She had his number, she assured herself, and she wasn't thinking of his phone number. That boyish charm was surely an act. Given his education, he undoubtedly came from an upper-middle-class family and had never wanted for anything, except perhaps a dash of humility. Not that she had any room to point fingers, having been born with a proverbial silver spoon in her mouth. It had been different for her, though. Her father was the salt of the earth and didn't have a fancy bone in his body. He'd raised her to appreciate the value of a dollar, to have a good work ethic, and to judge others by their character, not by their bank balances.

Most people who had privileged childhoods thought they were special. Samantha knew better. She was just lucky. If the dice had fallen differently for her dad when he gambled on success, she could have grown up poor as a church mouse.

Tucker Coulter, on the other hand, had probably had everything handed to him all his life: good grades, lots of friends, popularity with the girls. She finished making her sandwich, wiped her hands, and stepped over to erase his messages.

Chapter Seven

Samantha rose the next morning at four, grabbed a quick shower, got dressed, confined her wildly curly hair into a French braid, and went directly to the stables without going for her daily run. Even though Jerome had promised to check on Tabasco periodically throughout the night and call her if there were any changes, she had barely slept for worrying about the young stallion. He'd had no more bouts with diarrhea yesterday afternoon, but he'd seemed listless and had eaten very little of his evening measure of hay. She couldn't shake the suspicion that something was seriously wrong.

She was pleased beyond measure when Tabasco met her at the gate of his stall and nudged her shirt pocket, searching for treats. "Ah, you're feeling better, are you?"

She ran her fingertips through the horse's forelock as she checked to make sure his eyes were clear and bright. No sign of jaundice. She pushed up the stallion's lip to have a look at his gums. They were still a bit pale, in her estimation, but not alarmingly so.

When the horse bumped her half off her feet, she laughed and said, "I think a day without treats is in order, Tabasco. I don't want anything to upset your stomach again."

The horse whickered and gave her another push.

"I know, dear heart. But let's stick with small portions of

hay and lots of fresh water for the next several hours. If you seem okay, maybe I'll bring you something this afternoon."

"Is he sick?"

Samantha jumped at the unexpected question. Pressing a hand to the base of her throat, she turned to see Carrie standing a few feet away. "My goodness, you startled me out of ten years' growth. I didn't think anyone but Jerome and I were here."

Carrie shrugged and kicked at the powdery dirt of the arena floor. "I came in really early so I can get some of the heavier work done before it turns hot."

Samantha glanced at her watch. It was only a quarter to five. "Sleepless night?"

Carrie gave her an intent look, and two bright spots of color flagged her pale cheeks. "Why do you ask that?"

"It's so early, it's still almost yesterday," Samantha replied, quoting one of her father's favorite sayings. "Jerome's out loading hay to start feeding. Care to join me in his apartment for a cup of coffee and some Oreo cookies while we're waiting?"

"I'm dieting," Carrie replied. "Oreo cookies aren't on the menu."

Samantha sighed. "They aren't on mine either, but I still like to cheat every once in a while."

"You're on a diet? Why, for heaven's sake?" Carrie moved into Tabasco's stall to give him fresh water. As she turned on the spigot, she said, "You're already skinny as a rail."

Samantha's ex-husband had used precisely that expression to describe her figure, and the memory still stung. Shaking it off, Samantha replied, "I think it's easier on the horses if I keep my weight down. I work them pretty hard when they're training."

Using her palm, Carrie scrubbed the sides of the rubber trough and gave it a quick rinse. "Your brothers are a lot heavier than you are, and they don't seem concerned about their weight."

"True," Samantha conceded. "I'm a worrywart, I guess."

Watching her employee refill the trough, Samantha concluded that Jerome was right: Carrie's appearance had changed drastically. The young woman wore makeup this morning, a shade too much for Samantha's taste, and had also curled her shoulder-length hair. Sadly, the garish red lipstick and heavy eyeliner only enhanced the masculine cut of her features.

Hoping to draw her employee into a more personal conversation, Samantha rested her arms on the stall gate. "So how did your weekend go?"

"Okay," Carrie replied noncommittally. "I went to the rodeo Saturday afternoon and worked a shift for the nursing agency on Sunday."

"Bummer," Samantha said. "I'm sorry it's necessary for you to work a second job on your days off. As soon as I'm able, I'll increase your hours and give you a raise. I know you're not making very much."

"It's enough for now." Carrie smiled stiffly. "I live with my mom, so I don't have to pay rent or anything. I only work the second job for spending money, not necessities. If my diet continues to work, I'll be wanting to buy some new clothes."

"What kind of diet are you on?" Samantha asked. Her brother Quincy, the family nutritional expert, lectured constantly against the popular high-protein regimens.

"I'm just not eating."

Samantha didn't like the sound of that. Carrie worked hard in the stables and needed sustenance to keep up her energy. "My brother says starving is bad for you, that it's better to eat small, frequent meals so your metabolism doesn't shut down."

Carrie turned off the water. "He's probably right. But I need to lose weight fast, and hopefully I won't have to do this for very long. I have a salad at night. During the day I only drink water or iced tea. It's working. I've already lost five pounds."

Samantha wondered why Carrie felt it necessary to lose weight so quickly. Maybe Jerome was right, and the young woman was involved in a rocky relationship, possibly with a man who found fault with her figure. The thought saddened Samantha. No one knew better than she how miserable it was to love a man who constantly criticized. A strong urge came over her to dole out advice, but she bit her tongue. Carrie was her employee, not a close friend, and her personal life was none of Samantha's business.

Jerome entered the arena just then, effectively ending the conversation. Samantha was nevertheless troubled as she resumed her morning chores. Carrie was a sweet, caring individual. If she was involved with a man who didn't love her exactly as she was, she was bound to get her heart broken many times before the relationship ran its course.

Samantha had other concerns to take her mind off Carrie's love life over the next few days. Though Tabasco had no more bouts of diarrhea and his appetite had improved a little, he wasn't bouncing back as quickly as Samantha would have liked. She spent an inordinate amount of time standing at his stall gate, watching him.

"I think he's going to be fine," Jerome told her three mornings later. "He's eating and drinking, and his feces look normal now."

"But he isn't back to his old self."

"True. Whatever it was hit him hard and took a lot out of him. I had food poisoning that did me that way once. Took me damned near a week to get my strength back."

"This couldn't have been food poisoning. It was like that, though, wasn't it? Almost as if some kind of contaminant got into his feed." Samantha looked to Jerome for confirmation. "I know it's silly, but I've got a bad feeling, and it just won't go away. I've never seen anything quite like this."

"A bad feeling about what?" Nan Branson, a slender blonde who'd been working at Sage Creek Ranch for just under a year, joined them at the gate. Her pretty blue eyes were filled with concern. "Tabasco's going to be okay, isn't he?"

"Sure he is." Jerome clasped Samantha's shoulder. "Sam's just doing her mother-hen thing."

The foreman left the two women to continue the conversation without him. Nan joined Samantha in her study of the sorrel. "You don't think somebody poisoned him, do you?"

The question startled Samantha. "Good grief, no. What makes you think that?"

Nan shrugged her thin shoulders. As Samantha often did, Nan wore her shoulder-length blond hair drawn into a ponytail that poked out through the back of her green baseball cap. "I just heard you talking to Jerome about a contaminant getting into his feed. Seems to me the only way that could happen is if someone deliberately put it there."

The suggestion sent a cold shiver over Samantha's skin. "Don't even talk that way. Who'd want to poison one of my horses?"

Even as Samantha asked the question, she knew the answer. *Steve.* The morning their divorce had been finalized, he'd waited for her outside the courthouse. Not even the presence of her father and brothers had prevented him from spewing his venom.

The memory made Samantha feel shaky and nauseated. She pushed it away and took a deep, calming breath. Glancing at Nan, she said, "I'm sorry. I didn't mean to snap at you."

"No problem." Nan tugged up the strap of her tank top, which kept slipping from her shoulder. "I'd probably react the same way if someone suggested that my horse had been poisoned. Not that I think Tabasco was, mind you." She shrugged again. "I don't know why I even said it."

Samantha wished she hadn't. Now that the thought had been planted in her mind, she wasn't at all sure she'd be able to banish it.

A shrill wolf whistle brought both women's heads around.

Kyle waved as he crossed the arena to join them. He was a handsome man, of medium height, with a stocky, muscular build, wavy black hair, and dark blue eyes. Unfortunately, in the half decade that he'd worked for Samantha, she'd learned that the thirty-four-year-old stableman was his own most devoted admirer.

"Oh, *bother*," Nan whispered. "Here comes living proof that the male of our species thinks about sex every three seconds."

Samantha tried to stifle a startled laugh and snorted air up her nostrils, which set both her and Nan to giggling.

"What's so funny?" Kyle asked as he drew up behind them.

"Nothing," Nan said innocently.

In his supreme self-confidence, Kyle never would entertain the notion that they might be laughing at him. He rubbed his chest, squeezing and massaging one well-toned pectoral through his white undershirt. Samantha had noticed he did that a lot. She didn't know if it was a suggestive gesture or merely a preoccupation with his own anatomy. She only knew that watching him fondle himself made her uneasy.

The undershirt displayed an excess of darkly suntanned skin, showcasing the powerful muscles of his broad shoulders and arms. His blue jeans were so tight, he looked poured into them. Nan had once suggested that he stuffed a sock behind his fly to create the impressive bulge. Samantha suspected the fullness was real, yet another reason for Kyle to be so stuck on himself.

Samantha envied him that, in a way. How nice it would be to have no complexes. On the other hand, though, Kyle's high opinion of his looks had the perverse effect of making others search for defects. His neck was too thick for her taste; he was built more like a brick than a triangular wedge, which she found far more attractive; and his facial features were too pretty-boy perfect for a man. The package was attractively wrapped, but there wasn't much inside.

"Anything I can do for you ladies this morning?" he asked.

It was a question he posed to Samantha nearly every day. Did he really think she was that desperate? Just to see the look on his face, one of these times she wanted to say, "Oh, Kyle, please, make passionate love to me." Only she was half-afraid he might take her seriously.

Nan, three years Samantha's junior, apparently had no such concern. "The batteries went dead in my electric boyfriend a week ago, and I'm about to die. You want to have sex with me in the tack room?"

For an instant Kyle looked as if he believed her. Then he rolled his eyes and laughed. "Sorry, honey. I had a late night. Give me a few hours to recuperate."

"It figures. All talk and no do."

Kyle's black lashes swept low as he gave Nan's slender body an appreciative once-over. "Trust me, sweetheart, there's a lot more to me than talk. When you're serious, you just let me know."

Samantha held up her hands. "I'm out of here."

Nan laughed. "You don't have to go. I'll behave."

Samantha waved as she walked away. "Unlike some people I know, I have work to do."

Soon it had been a week since Tabasco's bout with diarrhea. Samantha's black eye had completely healed, but the stallion still wasn't back to normal. That evening Samantha and Jerome once again stood outside Tabasco's stall, watching the stallion in silent contemplation.

"I think I've got to agree with you," Jerome finally said. "He's not bouncing back like he should. He's lost weight, and I noticed this afternoon that the whites of his eyes look a little yellow. Bright and early in the morning, we need to call a vet."

Tears burned at the backs of Samantha's eyes. She'd noticed the jaundice, too. "I'm afraid he's going to die," she confessed.

"Nah." Jerome looped an arm around her shoulders and gave her a comforting jostle. "He's not himself, I'll grant you that, but he's not at death's door, either." Jerome's arm fell away. "He's going to snap out of it. If we get a decent vet out here, he'll figure out what the problem is. Maybe it's a virus. Horses can catch airborne diseases just like people."

"Then why haven't the other horses gotten sick?" she asked.

"We've kept him away from them, for one thing. Hell, I don't know. There's not much point in our trying to figure it out. We'll let the vet do that." Jerome glanced at his watch. "You need to be heading for the house. You know how riled your dad gets when you're out here after dark."

"Dad worries too much. I have a yard light. On a dark night, it's bright as day out there." But even as Samantha protested, she also accepted. There were some things she couldn't change, and her father was one of them. "But I'll head that way, all the same. It's easier to be there when he calls than to argue with him."

Jerome chuckled. When Samantha went up on her toes to hug his neck, he tightened his arms around her.

"Do you think I should call a vet tonight?" she asked against his gray shirt.

"Nah. It's Sunday and getting late. It'd cost you double, and to what end? Tabasco will be fine until morning."

Samantha gave the foreman a quick peck on the cheek. "Good night, then. I'll see you again before the rooster crows."

Jerome gave her a swat on the rump. "You just concentrate on getting some rest. You've put in a long day."

As Samantha crossed the arena, she turned to walk backward. "If there's any change, do you promise to call me?"

"Only if you'll promise to call me when you get to the house."

She laughed and threw up her hands. "What is it, a hundred yards to my door? Who's going to get me, the bogeyman?"

"Just humor an old worrywart."

"All right, all right." She opened the door to step outside. "Jeesh! It's not even fully dark yet."

A few minutes later, after arriving home, locking up, and calling Jerome, Samantha answered the phone to reassure her father that she was safely inside the house with the alarm set. Instead of giving him her usual lip, she confided to him her concern for Tabasco.

"He's still not perking back up?" Frank asked.

"No." Samantha sighed. "I don't know, Dad. Maybe I'm making a mountain out of a molehill. He's eating fairly well, just not enthusiastically. I've taken his temp, and he's never feverish. All indications are that he should be fine. But he just isn't acting right."

"Go with your gut," her father told her. "Nobody knows your horses like you do."

"So you don't think I'm overreacting?"

"Nope. I had a mare once that looked fine to everybody but me. I had the vet out to look at her. He ran a few tests. Some of her blood counts were a little off, but nothing really alarmed him. Come to find out she had cancer."

Samantha sank onto a chair. "Jeez, thanks, Dad. I feel so much better."

He chuckled. "Tabasco doesn't have cancer. My point is, you need to trust your instincts. Get the vet out there to look at him."

"I will." Samantha closed her eyes. "Washburn still isn't back from Europe, though, and I wasn't impressed with the fellow who's handling his patient load."

"Call Tucker Coulter."

Samantha had known that was coming. "I don't even know the name of his clinic."

"I do. I got his card, remember?" A rustle of paper came over the line. "Got a pen and paper?"

Samantha rose to get both. "Okay, I'm ready." Her stomach knotted with dread as she jotted down Tucker's name and number. "If he's a lousy vet, it's on your head."

"What is it about the man that you don't like?" Frank asked.

"I didn't say I don't like him." Just the opposite was true. She'd liked Tucker Coulter too well.

"Let me rephrase the question. What's your problem with him, then?"

Samantha had lied to her father more times than she cared to recall during her marriage. She wasn't about to resume that bad habit now by denying there was a problem. Instead she said, "I don't really know. He just . . . I don't know, Dad. He makes me uneasy."

"You know what I think?"

Samantha had a feeling she was about to find out.

"I think he makes you uneasy because you can't find anything about him to dislike. That's what I think."

Her dad knew her too well. "Maybe so," she conceded. "Whatever the reason, I can't help how I feel."

"You can't live the rest of your life running scared every time you meet a man you like, either."

"Why not? It only seems smart to me. As you know, I'm a lousy judge of character."

"One bad call doesn't make you a lousy judge of character."

"One *abysmally* bad call." A dull throbbing took up residence in Samantha's temples. "Can we have this conversation later? I'm really bushed."

"Sure." Her father sighed. "I love you, honey."

"I love you, too, Dad." And Samantha did love him—so very much. It was just that he swallowed her, somehow, making her feel like Jonah trying to escape the belly of the whale.

"Keep that number where you'll be able to find it in case Tabasco takes a bad turn during the night."

"Done." Samantha affixed the sheet of paper to the front of the fridge with a magnet that read, NO HORSING AROUND IN MY KITCHEN. "I'll give you a ring tomorrow. Hopefully I'll know something by then."

"If Coulter's as good a vet as Jim claims he is, you'll know a good deal more by this time tomorrow," her father assured her.

Samantha had just drifted off to sleep when the treble ring of the phone on her nightstand jarred her back to wakefulness. Her first thought was for Tabasco. She grabbed the portable unit from its base, punched the TALK button, and said, "This is Sam," as she sat up in bed.

"We got trouble," Jerome barked over the line. "Get a vet out here, ASAP."

"Oh, God. Is it Tabasco?"

"Jesus, Lord, no. It's Blue. He's gone plumb loco."

Samantha disconnected, dropped the phone, and scrambled into her clothes. Then she raced downstairs, slapped on the kitchen lights, and grabbed the paper she'd left on the front of the refrigerator. Her hands were shaking so badly that she misdialed the number twice. When she finally got it right, an answering service took her call.

"This is Samantha Harrigan at the Sage Creek Ranch. I need Tucker Coulter out here on the double."

"What seems to be the problem, ma'am?"

Samantha bunched a fist in her hair. "I don't know what the problem is. I haven't seen the horse myself. My foreman just called from the stable. He says my prize stallion has gone loco."

"I'll forward your message to the veterinarian on call," the woman said pleasantly.

"No, *no*. I want Tucker Coulter, nobody else."

"I'm sorry. It's the other Dr. Coulter who's on call this evening."

The other Dr. Coulter? Samantha was so upset, the response

made no sense to her. "I don't care who's on call. I want Tucker Coulter."

"It's the middle of the night. My instructions are to contact only the vet on call."

Samantha could still hear the raw panic in Jerome's voice. Normally the foreman had nerves of steel. "You listen to me, lady." When the woman started to protest, Samantha raised her voice and said, "Shut up for a minute and just listen. This is a *very* valuable horse we're talking about. He's in a bad way. If you don't call Tucker Coulter and that horse dies, I will have your job. Do I make myself perfectly clear?"

"Yes. That's clear. We do have a certain protocol we have to observe, though."

"What's your name?"

"Abigail Spence."

"Screw the protocol, Ms. Spence. You get Tucker Coulter out here to this ranch on the double."

Samantha disconnected, slammed the phone down on the counter, and took off for the stable at a dead run. Halfway there she could hear Blue's screams. It seemed to her as if that last fifty yards to the building were a hundred miles, and she knew she would never forget those sounds for the rest of her life.

Inside the arena the noise was deafening. The stallion had indeed gone loco. He was rearing and thrashing the walls of his stall with his front hooves. His usually liquid brown eyes had a crazed look in them, and the irises were completely ringed with white. When Samantha reached the gate, Jerome grabbed her arm to keep her from going into the stall.

"No, honey. He'll kill you."

Samantha jerked her arm free. "Not Blue. Never!"

"Look at me!" Jerome yelled, pointing at his forehead.

Samantha finally focused on him, and when she did, her legs nearly buckled. One half of his face was covered with blood, the source a gash four inches long above his right eye. "Oh, my God. Oh, my God."

Jerome grasped her shoulder, his fingers digging in hard. "He can't see you; he can't hear you. He's striking out in a blind fury. I know you love him, honey, but he'll kill you, sure as the world. We have to wait for the vet, and pray to God he brings a sedative. But getting a needle into that horse is going to be tricky."

Samantha looked over the gate at her stallion and could barely see him through her tears. *Blue.* Her beautiful, gentle, amazing Blue had turned into a deadly killer. She couldn't believe this was happening.

"What's wrong with him?" she cried. "Oh, *God.*" She put her hands to her ears, unable to bear the sound of his screams. "Oh, Jerome. What'll we do? I'm not even sure the answering service will send Tucker Coulter out. We may get someone else."

Jerome stroked her arm. "We have to wait for a vet. That's all I know. He damned near killed me."

Samantha stared stupidly at her foreman's forehead. "You need a doctor yourself. I'll call Daddy. He can take you to the ER."

"Like hell. I'm not going anywhere. But call your father all the same." Just as Jerome spoke, Blue lashed out at the gate with such force that one of the hinges snapped. "Tell him to get over here, fast. If that horse escapes, we're going to need all the help we can get."

There were four phone stations within the arena. Samantha ran the twenty yards to the nearest one, frantically dialed her father's number, and then paced until he answered.

"Daddy? Get over here fast. It's Blue. He's gone nuts."

Her father said, "I'm on my way."

That was all, just those four words, and then he broke the connection. Samantha stood there, clinging to the phone, Blue's shrieks and the cacophony of his lashing hooves pummeling her eardrums. Her whole body was trembling.

"Get hold of yourself," she told herself sternly. "Jerome's all right. Blue's only a horse. Get a grip."

Only Blue wasn't just a horse. Still clinging to the phone, Samantha turned to look at him. Her beautiful, wonderful Blue Blazes. She'd raised him from birth. She loved him almost as much as she might a child. He was her pride and her joy, her friend and her confidant. And he was also her future.

If Blue died, all her dreams would die with him.

Chapter Eight

Tucker overshot the turn and slammed on the brakes. After shifting the Dodge into reverse, he backed up until the headlights washed over the archway again. A hand-carved wooden sign hung from the uppermost log that spanned the distance between the two side columns. It read, SAGE CREEK QUARTER HORSE RANCH.

This is it, he thought, and silently thanked God that he'd spotted the entrance. In the darkness he might have driven several miles before realizing he'd missed the turn. According to the woman at the answering service, the life of a very expensive equine was in peril.

Tucker couldn't be cavalier about this particular horse belonging to Samantha Harrigan. He'd almost given up hope of ever seeing her again, and now, out of the blue, she had called him out to her ranch on an emergency. Tucker wasn't sure which possibilities he found most exciting, the professional or personal ones.

He nosed the truck off the main road and onto the gravel lane. About a half mile up ahead, pine trees were etched in black against the moonlit sky, their graceful branches underscored by rectangles of golden light. Pleased that the road was fairly smooth, he increased his speed. The private byways he usually encountered on farms and ranches were rough and pitted with chuckholes, forcing him to creep along to protect the equipment he carried under the truck's canopy. The portable video endoscope alone had cost him a small fortune. He also leased a battery-powered ultrasound system and a portable EKG machine that would be costly to repair.

When he reached the cluster of buildings, he saw that they comprised the ranch proper. Porch lights illuminated the front of a two-story cedar home. About a hundred yards off to the left was a huge structure with plank siding that Tucker guessed to be a stable and indoor riding arena, a common setup around Crystal Falls because of the snow in winter.

Five pickups were parked willy-nilly in front of the immense building, their colors difficult to determine in the bluish white glow of a sodium-mercury yard light. He parked near the other vehicles, cut the engine, and grabbed his satchel before exiting the cab.

Almost before Tucker's feet touched the ground, a man rushed from the building. Tucker momentarily mistook the fellow for Frank Harrigan. Only as they hurried toward each other did Tucker realize this man was much younger. One of Frank's sons, possibly? Even in the eerie light, Tucker could see a strong resemblance.

"You Tucker Coulter?" the man asked, raising his voice to be heard over the screaming of a horse inside the building. "I'm Zach Harrigan, the one you called for directions. The horse is this way."

Zach's urgent manner told Tucker that the situation was dire indeed. Due to the cyclic nature of their professions, most ranchers and farmers developed a deceptively laid-back mien, the common motto being, "Why hurry up to wait?" It took a catastrophic event to make a cowboy shift out of slow gear into fast-forward.

Tucker followed Zack Harrigan into the building. Once they were inside, the noise level was deafening. At the far end of the huge riding arena, Tucker saw a knot of people, including Samantha Harrigan, gathered in front of a stall.

Within the enclosure was a crazed blue roan. Tucker had never been particularly fond of roans, blues least of all. The best way he could think of to describe their color was salt-and-pepper. Even at a distance, though, he could tell that this blue roan was exceptional, its silvered body offset by a pitch-black face, mane, legs, and tail.

Tucker lengthened his stride, drawing slightly ahead of Zach Harrigan to close the distance more quickly. As he jogged, his attention became fixed on Samantha. Despite the tangled, pillow-tossed state of her hair, she was just as pretty as he remembered, her tidy figure temptingly round in all the right places, her delicately molded countenance slightly irregular in profile, yet absolutely lovely.

She turned at his approach. In that instant of eye contact, Tucker registered her panic. Her oval face was deathly pale, and she held herself with an almost brittle rigidity that told him more than she could know. Her anguish was almost palpable. Tucker fleetingly wished he could reassure her, but he'd learned never to make promises as a vet that he might not be able to keep.

Just then the horse screamed and pummeled the inside of his stall with such force that one of the boards snapped, the sound as loud as a rifle shot. Vaguely registering the presence of Frank Harrigan and five other men, Tucker pushed forward to look over the gate.

What Tucker saw made his blood run cold. Now he understood why Samantha looked so stricken. He had seen more than a few horses go berserk, but never anything to equal this. The animal had a blind, wild look in his eyes and had worked himself to a point beyond exhaustion, sides heaving, nostrils flared, and lather flecking his body like shaving foam.

Doing a quick visual exam, Tucker saw that the horse's legs were already covered with lacerations, some deep, others superficial, but the cuts were nothing compared to the injuries the horse might sustain if he was allowed to continue on this course. Something had to be done, and quickly; otherwise this episode could very well end with a euthanasia injection. Just the thought made Tucker's stomach roll.

"What brought this on?" Tucker yelled over his shoulder to no one in particular.

"No idea!" a man yelled back.

"Any other horses acting up?"

"Nope, only this one," the same man yelled back. "It came on fast. At six, when I gave him his hay out in the paddock, he seemed just fine. It wasn't until I let him into his stall around ten and gave him his nightly ration of grain that he started going crazy."

"What kind of grain?" Tucker demanded.

"Wet cob, actually, not grain. It's the same stuff he gets every night right before lights-out. After giving each horse a measure, I went upstairs. I wasn't inside more than twenty or thirty minutes before I heard Blue screaming."

Tucker's brain had begun to race. *Wet cob*—ground corn-cobs with a little molasses mixed in. Horses and ruminants loved it. People in rural settings mixed wet cob with dry and fed it to herds of deer. It had a pleasurably sweet taste and was nourishing but harmless. Tucker felt certain wet cob had not caused this kind of behavior in the stallion.

Only what had? He needed to get in close to examine the horse.

"We'll have to cross-rope him so I can sedate him," he called out. "Two men out in the paddock and two in here."

Tucker had to say no more. Zach raced for the tack room to get the ropes.

Frank Harrigan sauntered over to where Tucker crouched over his open satchel. "Even with lines to hold him, son, it won't be easy to get a needle into that horse."

Tucker glanced up. "I'll have to do it intramuscularly. Normally we prefer to inject sedatives directly into a vein. They're faster-acting that way. But it won't be possible with him."

"That's for sure," Frank agreed. "I've given a fair number of shots in my day, but never to a horse that loco."

Neither had Tucker, and that made him wonder yet again what had brought this on. That was a question he couldn't possibly answer until he got a close look at the horse. *Damn.* He hated to administer a sedative before he knew what the problem was. He couldn't be sure how it might affect the equine. But in this situation he had no choice.

Zach returned with four coils of rope on his shoulder. Without a word he began handing the lassos out to the other men.

Tucker bent back over his satchel to prepare the sedative. He estimated the stallion to be in the top weight bracket for his breed and decided to mix a xylazine-and-Dormosedan cocktail. Both drugs were fairly quick to take effect, even given intramuscularly, and the doses could be manipulated to have a short duration of action with few adverse side effects.

As Tucker filled a syringe, the other men set themselves to the task of cross-roping the stallion. Tucker heard a lasso sing above his head, the sound unmistakable and one that he'd often heard as a boy. The next instant, all hell broke loose.

"Son of a *bitch*!"

A jet-haired young man flew past Tucker as if he'd just sprouted wings. Fortunately the fellow had wrapped the rope around his wrist. When he collided with the stall gate in a jarring body slam, he lost only his hat, not his grip on the lasso.

Tucker half expected the man to crumple to the ground, holding his ribs, but this fellow was made of sturdy stuff. He bounced off the gate rails, regained his balance, and planted a boot against a cross-buck for leverage, thus managing to hold the stallion by himself until Frank could leap forward to help.

"Get another loop over his head!" the younger man yelled

to whoever had taken up position in the paddock. "Dad and I can't hold him alone!"

Tucker blocked out all the confusion and concentrated on doing his part. After filling the syringe with the appropriate mixture of drugs, he would need to swing up onto the gate and be ready to jump inside the stall the instant the horse was anchored in one spot. The window of opportunity to give the injection might be brief, possibly only a matter of seconds, depending upon the men's ability to hold the lines.

"I'll do it," a feminine voice said just as Tucker pushed to his feet.

He'd almost forgotten Samantha's presence. When he turned and saw her drawn, pale face, his heart caught.

"Please," she said tautly. "He's my horse. As crazy as he is right now, I know he won't hurt me."

Tucker shook his head. "He's beyond being able to differentiate between one person and another," he informed her. "And it isn't as easy as it looks to give an injection to an animal that won't hold still." When she parted her lips to protest, Tucker quickly added, "If you keep too firm a grip on the syringe, the needle can bend or break. The goal is to get the sedative into the horse on the first try. Right?"

For an instant she stared worriedly at the stallion. Then her lashes fluttered closed, and she nodded. "Right," she murmured.

Tucker slipped the loaded syringe into his shirt pocket. *Showtime.* Ducking between the ropes, he sprinted to the gate, grasped the top rail, and swung up to straddle it. Once in position, he locked his knees to keep his seat and waited for all four lassos to be thrown.

The instant each of the loops snapped taut around the stallion's muscular neck, Tucker pushed off into the stall. "Easy, boy, easy." Taking care to avoid the horse's back hooves, which could be lethal even with the animal unable to rear up and strike, Tucker moved in. "Easy, easy." The stallion's entire body jerked when Tucker touched his neck. "It's nothing bad, just a little stick to make you feel better."

For a fleeting instant Tucker thought giving the injection was going to be a piece of cake, after all. The horse responded to his voice and whickered plaintively, almost as if pleading for help. But then he went crazy again, kicking, jumping, and twisting in midair, frantically trying to escape the ropes. Tucker wasted no time. He picked his target, stepped in as close as he dared, and quickly inserted the needle. With one smooth push he depressed the plunger.

"Nice job," Frank said as Tucker landed on his feet outside the stall gate again. "Damned nice. Couldn't have done better myself."

Tucker's heart was pounding, and he was breathing as if he'd just run a mile. He put the capped syringe back in his pocket and wiped sweat from his brow. "He'll calm down in a bit so I can have a look at him. Should work in about ten minutes."

Frank didn't look happy to hear that, and Tucker understood why. Ten minutes of crazy horse were ten too many.

As it happened, though, the men were able to hold pressure on the ropes until the chemical restraint began to take effect. In those final seconds before Tucker could enter the stall, Frank took advantage of the lull to make hurried introductions.

"Tucker, this is my oldest boy, Clint."

Tucker inclined his head at the fellow who'd collided with the gate. "Good to meet you, Clint."

Clint, still holding tension on one of the lines, nodded and flashed a white-toothed grin. "Good to meet you, too!" he replied with undisguised enthusiasm. "Not many vets I know would've gone into that stall. Before you leave, be sure to give me one of your cards. I'll definitely be in touch."

Tucker returned the man's friendly smile. "I'll appreciate any business you bring my way."

Zach, who was still holding the other rope, broke in with, "We can help with that." He sent his father an amused look. "Dad isn't merely a good contact; he's *the* contact in quarter horse circles."

Frank gestured to the three men in the paddock. "Out yonder's my other two boys, Parker and Quincy, and Sammy's ranch foreman, Jerome."

Just as Tucker acknowledged the men outdoors with a wave, Samantha came to stand at his elbow. "What do you think's wrong with my horse?" she asked shakily.

Tucker wished there were an easy answer, but in veterinary medicine there seldom was. "Hard to say until I examine him."

Tucker watched the stallion closely. The moment the horse began to hang his head and look a little wobbly, he collected his satchel, opened the stall gate, and went inside.

When Tucker realized that Samantha was at his heels, he stopped dead in his tracks. "It might be safer if you stayed out of here," he informed her. "The sedative will probably keep him calm, but there's no guarantee."

"Blue won't hurt me," she insisted. "I never for a moment thought he might."

Tucker had no doubt that Samantha had a very special relationship with the stallion. As a general rule, horses were incredibly devoted and faithful creatures who responded reciprocally to love and gentleness. "I'm sure he wouldn't intend to hurt you," he compromised. "Right now, however, he may not be able to stop himself."

Despite the warning, Samantha remained at Tucker's elbow. He decided to let it go. She'd been raised around horses, just as he had, and surely understood the risks. It wasn't his place to lecture her.

Blue was swaying on his feet now. When Tucker touched the stallion's neck, the animal showed no sign of agitation. Taking care not to move too quickly, Tucker deposited his satchel on the floor of the stall.

"Good boy," he intoned softly. To the men holding the ropes, he called out, "You can cut him some slack now!" The instant the lines relaxed, Tucker drew them off over the horse's head. "Now let's see if we can figure out what's wrong with you, fella."

The first thing Tucker always did when he examined a sick horse was check for colic. After withdrawing the stethoscope from the satchel, he pressed the chest piece to the animal's belly. In cases of severe colic, all intestinal activity often ceased, the result being an ominous and deadly silence.

Acutely aware of Samantha's anxious gaze following his every movement, he said, "The belly sounds good."

He stepped around to the horse's head. The stallion's pupils were dilated, but given the sedation, that was to be expected. Tucker folded back the equine's lip. "Good capillary refill response. Two seconds on the dot."

Tucker placed the stethoscope on the right side of the stallion's chest to get a pulse reading. "That's odd," he murmured, and then immediately wished he'd kept the thought to himself when Samantha asked, "What's odd?"

"His pulse rate is forty. With all the sedatives in his system, I expected it to be a little slow, not at the high end of normal."

"Is that a bad sign?" Her voice trembled as she posed the question.

Tucker frowned as he checked the stallion's respiratory rate, which was also normal. Then he bent to riffle through his bag for a large animal thermometer. "I don't think it's a bad sign, necessarily," he told Samantha as he took the equine's temperature. "The normal range is from thirty-six to forty-two. It's just unusual for it to be that fast under sedation."

The stallion's temp proved to be normal as well. After returning the thermometer to the satchel, Tucker moved to the corner of the stall where a black rubber dish sat. "Is this the grain dish?"

"Yes." An older man with graying brown hair and dark eyes entered the stall from the paddock where he'd been manning one of the ropes. He was a good-looking fellow for his age, trim yet well muscled, as most ranchers and horsemen tended to be. "If you're wanting to see what he ate, I can fetch you a little of the cob."

"There are traces still in the dish." As Tucker bent to collect the bowl, he noticed a deep gash on the older man's forehead. "Ouch. The horse do that to you?"

"Did it to myself by staying when I should've went," the man replied with a humorless smile. "Can't blame the horse for my own stupidity." He thrust out a hand. "Name's Jerome Hudson. I'm the ranch foreman."

While shaking the foreman's hand, Tucker said, "Looks to me like a trip to the ER is in order. You'll be needing a few stitches."

The older man nodded. "I'll drive to town and get it taken care of in a bit."

"Hell you will," Frank said from the gate. "I'll take you in."

Tucker returned his attention to the bowl and what remained of the wet cob. A white, barely visible powdery substance clung to the corn particles. "Do you mix vitamins in with his cob?"

"We give vitamin powder in the morning with the bran and grain," the foreman replied.

"Do you rinse out the dishes between feedings?" Tucker asked, thinking some of the powder might have clung to the bowl.

"Rinse and dry them both," Jerome assured him.

Tucker moistened his fingertip to collect a bit of the powder. "There's something on this cob."

The foreman stepped over to have a look. "That's not vitamin powder. Ours is yellowish brown."

"Did you notice any powder on the cob when you measured it out?" Tucker asked.

"I didn't measure it. We have the day-shift people do that before they leave. The filled dishes are put on a shelf, which is numbered according to stall order. Saves me work late at night." The foreman shook his head and glanced apologetically at Samantha. "I didn't notice any white powder on Blue's cob, but I didn't really examine it, either."

Samantha pressed close to examine the dish's contents. Then she lifted a frightened gaze to Tucker's. "What do you think it is?"

"I'm not sure." Tucker handed the dish to Hudson. "Can you put this someplace safe? We may need to have that powder analyzed."

"Analyzed?" Samantha echoed.

Tucker avoided her worried gaze as he returned to the horse and drew a blood sample. The situation baffled him, and he didn't want to do too much of his thinking out loud. The traces of powder on the cob indicated possible poisoning, but the horse exhibited none of the usual symptoms.

When the vial of blood had been filled and marked, Tucker deposited the sample in his bag and went back to studying the horse. "Has he had any diarrhea?" he asked, directing the question to no one in particular.

"Nope," Jerome replied, stepping over to the gate to hand off the dish to Clint for safekeeping. "Far as I know, he's been fit as a fiddle until tonight."

"Another horse did have diarrhea, though," Samantha interjected. "Tabasco, a four-year-old stallion. It was the worst case I've ever seen, and we called out a vet." She glanced at Jerome. "What was it, a week ago?"

"Last Sunday morning. He hasn't perked back up the way we'd like to see, either, and we've been worried." The foreman met Tucker's gaze. "We planned to call someone out in the morning to give us a second opinion."

"What was the first opinion?" Tucker asked.

"That it was nothing more than a little stomach upset," Samantha replied, her soft mouth thinning with disgust.

"The vet was Doc Washburn's new partner. Maybe you've heard of him?"

Tucker had heard stories about the new veterinarian, and none thus far had been favorable.

Samantha gestured limply with a hand. "I wasn't impressed, and needless to say, I won't use him again."

"I'd like to have a look at Tabasco later," Tucker told her. "First, though, I need to treat this stallion's lacerations."

Blue suddenly threw up his head and looked at them with white-ringed eyes. Only a little time had passed since the sedative had been administered, and Tucker was taken by surprise.

"The sedative's wearing off," he noted out loud.

"So soon?" Samantha sent him a bewildered look. "Doesn't it normally last longer than this?"

Tucker was too busy filling another syringe to reply. But he wasn't quick enough. The stallion shrieked and wheeled. Frank slapped the gate closed so the animal couldn't escape, and Tucker looped an arm around Samantha's waist to swing her out of the way.

"Get out of here," he ordered as he released his hold on her.

Jerome grabbed Samantha's arm to propel her toward the gate.

"Whoa, boy, whoa," Tucker soothed.

The stallion quieted, and the moment he did Tucker stepped in close to give him another injection. Then he, too, vacated the stall.

This time the horse didn't get quite so excited, and the injection worked a little more quickly because there was still some sedative in his system. Tucker's brain had begun to race with all the possible causes of excitement that could be controlled with sedatives for only short periods of time. One of those possibilities truly alarmed him.

When the stallion was standing calmly again, Tucker left

the stall to find some privacy and whipped his cell phone from his belt to call Isaiah, his twin brother and partner.

Isaiah answered in a hoarse, sleep-slurred voice. "Coulter residence."

"Hey, bro," Tucker said. "I need your help."

"Tucker?" Isaiah yawned loudly. Tucker heard his sister-in-law Laura murmur sleepily in the background. "What do you mean, my help? It's . . . what . . . midnight?"

"A few minutes after. I'm sorry for waking you up, but this is an emergency. I've got a loco horse on my hands."

Tucker began relating the particulars, only to have his brother say, "Whoa, slow down. Give me a minute, here. I'm still half-asleep." Isaiah sighed and yawned again. Then, "Okay, all right. What kind of cocktail did you say you mixed?"

"Xylazine and Dormosedan. It only kept him calm for a little over twenty minutes. Then he started going ape again."

"That soon?" Isaiah was starting to sound more alert. "Xylazine is short-action, but with the Dormosedan on board, it should have worked longer than that."

"What if the horse has ingested an opiate?" Tucker suggested.

"An *opiate*?"

"You heard me. That's all that makes sense. A sedative might only counteract the effects of an opiate for twenty minutes or less. That's essentially what I'm seeing, a horse that's chemically restrained, but not reacting normally to the sedative. His pulse is forty, at the high end of normal range, and his respiration is normal as well. By all rights, both should be a little slow—unless there's a stimulant in his system to counteract the sedatives."

"An *opiate*?" Isaiah repeated. "Who in his right mind would give a horse an opiate? I know they used to dope racehorses with opiates to make them win at the track, but that was outlawed years ago. If you don't know exactly how much to give, you can overdose an equine and make it go completely berserk."

"I need some blood panels done, stat," Tucker informed his brother. "If this horse ingested an opiate, it won't wear off for four to six hours. To keep him calm, I'll have to inject him with xylazine and Dormosedan every twenty minutes or so. I hate like hell doing that. With the opiate breaking through like this, I'll be guessing each time on how much is safe to give him. I don't want to kill him with an accidental overdose."

"Where the hell can you get blood panels done at this time of night?"

"The hospital," Tucker replied. "They have a twenty-four-hour lab."

"They don't do equine panels."

"I don't need any norms. We know what those are. All I need are the blood workups, just like they'd do for a human. I'll make sense of the results myself."

"They'll think I'm nuts."

"Call Ann Kendrick. She used to be a nurse at Saint Matthew's. She may still have some connections."

"You want me to call Ann Kendrick at a quarter past twelve in the morning?"

"Yes." Their sister, Bethany, was married to Ryan Kendrick, Ann's son. Tucker didn't think Ann would mind being awakened in the middle of the night by her daughter-in-law's brother. "Tell her I think someone deliberately overdosed a horse with morphine."

"Sweet Christ, Tucker. Do you realize what you're saying? There are only two reasons I can think of that someone would do that."

Tucker knew exactly what reasons had popped into his brother's mind. A horse overdosed with an opiate was bound to do one of two things—injure himself and die a brutal death, or kill a human being.

"Call me crazy for thinking it. Just do this for me, Isaiah. Please."

"Like I'd ever say no?"

In the background Tucker heard the rustle of clothing and pictured his brother getting dressed. He gave Isaiah directions to the Sage Creek Ranch. "Get here as fast as you can," he urged. "If I'm dealing with an opiate, I need to know it. Otherwise this horse could go berserk when I least expect it and kill someone."

"I'll be there in twenty," Isaiah promised.

"I really appreciate this."

Isaiah made a snorting sound. "Not a problem. You know that."

Tucker returned to the stall and set to work treating the stallion's injuries. Some would leave scars, he knew. He doubted Samantha was happy about that. He could tell by looking that this horse was a very expensive animal with champion bloodlines.

Only as they worked together, cleaning and bandaging the cuts, all Tucker saw in Samantha's lovely eyes was pain—a pain that ran so deep it couldn't be expressed with words. She loved this horse. It wasn't about the value of the animal, not to her.

By the time they'd finished treating the stallion's cuts, the sedatives were wearing off again. Tucker quickly gave the horse a third injection, praying as he did that he wouldn't overlap the amounts and accidentally kill his patient.

After giving the shot, he knew he would have only about twenty minutes before the drug began to wear off. "I'd like to cross-tie him," he informed Samantha. "Also, I need some leg pads if you have them."

Impressing Tucker with her agility, Samantha vaulted over the stall gate as easily as any man he'd ever seen. She was back in a couple of minutes with leg wraps, the quality of which was almost as impressive as her gate-jumping ability. Everything at this stable was first-rate, Tucker realized, including the woman who owned it.

The men entered the stall to help cross-tie the stallion, a

method Tucker hated to use, because he couldn't imagine it being very comfortable for the horse. But a little discomfort was better than a life-threatening injury if the animal suddenly went loco again.

When Tucker had finished doctoring the stallion's legs, Samantha hurriedly applied the wraps, which were actually braces that covered a goodly length of leg and were hinged at the elbows and points of each hock. They would help to shield the stallion's already lacerated appendages from further harm.

When they had finished with the horse, Tucker turned to Samantha and asked, "Where's the four-year-old that had the diarrhea?"

In only a few minutes Tucker was drawing more blood samples, a lump of dread swelling in his chest. Unlike Blue Blazes, Tabasco exhibited clinical evidence of poisoning. He was lethargic. His pulse was weak. The whites of his eyes were mildly jaundiced and bloodshot, the last hinting at compromised vascular integrity. The young stallion's capillary refill was also slow. Tucker didn't like the looks of this. He didn't like it at all.

"When he had the diarrhea, was there any blood in the feces?" he asked.

"Yes," Samantha replied. "Quite a lot of blood."

"Was it particularly watery and foul?"

"Yes," she confirmed. "I've never smelled anything like it."

Though the evidence indicated a deliberate attempt on someone's part to harm Samantha's horses, Tucker kept rejecting the possibility. As a vet, he occasionally treated poisoned animals, but he would never understand the mentality of an individual who could do something so cruel.

Rather than upset Samantha unnecessarily, he decided to wait until he could study the blood panels before voicing his suspicions aloud.

Chapter Nine

Samantha felt oddly numb as she watched Tucker Coulter join two pieces of aluminum conduit and drive one end of the tubing into the earthen floor of the stall. His confident manner should have soothed her, but the events of the night had rubbed her nerves raw. Even now, as she tried to focus all her concern on Tabasco, a part of her listened for Blue, who might go berserk again without warning.

As though he sensed her thoughts, Tucker glanced over his shoulder at her. "We'll hear if he starts to act up."

Samantha nodded and tried to smile, but in a way no one else could really understand, her whole world had come under siege. Earlier, when she'd gone to bed for what she'd believed to be the night, her concerns had all been focused on Tabasco. Now two stallions were gravely ill. Other women her age had husbands and children to consume their lives, but she had only her horses.

Desperate for anything that might distract her from the ache of worry that had centered in her chest, Samantha inclined her head at the conduit the vet was piecing together. "What's that you're assembling?" she asked.

"My version of a portable IV-fluid tree," he explained as he worked. "I learned to make these a couple of years ago when I volunteered at some relay races upstate, and I've kept one or two in my truck ever since. They do the job just about anywhere, come apart in a snap, and can be stored under the seat of my truck until I need them."

"So you think Tabasco needs IV fluids?"

"In cases of severe diarrhea, hydrating the patient is pretty much standard procedure."

Samantha wasn't fooled by his noncommittal tone. He clearly had an idea what was wrong with her horse. He just hadn't chosen to share his suspicions with her yet.

"You know, Dr. Coulter, I—"

"Tucker, please." He flashed her a quick smile.

At any other time, or in any other place, Samantha might have been impressed by how darkly handsome he looked in the bright illumination of the overhead lights. His hair lay over his forehead in glistening chocolate waves, and his skin had the rich, deep tones of melted caramel, striking such a contrast to his eyes that they looked electric blue.

"Tucker, then." Samantha moistened her lips, temporarily at a loss as to what she'd meant to say. "I, um, can understand your reluctance to tell me very much at this point. It has to be difficult to make diagnoses without any test results or data. But I'm dying here. These horses are more to me than just business inventory. You know? They're my babies."

He riffled through a pile of stuff that he'd brought in from his truck. When he straightened with a clip in his hand, his blue eyes flicked toward her, the expression in them so intense that her heart missed a beat.

"I've noticed you're very fond of your animals." He stepped over to attach the clip to the top of the aluminum pole, the muscles that roped each side of his spine bunching and rippling under his green shirt with every flex of his arms. "And it's certainly not my aim to keep you in an agony of suspense. I just hate shooting my mouth off before I know all the facts."

Samantha hugged her waist and realized she was trembling. "I understand; really I do. But from a purely personal standpoint, I'd rather hear your best guess, even if it's wrong, than be left in limbo, imagining the worst."

"I'll second that," her father said from behind her.

At the sound of her dad's voice Samantha nearly jumped out of her skin. Why, she didn't know. She'd heard Frank and Jerome arrive at the stall gate moments before and shouldn't have been startled.

"I'll cast my vote with theirs," Jerome inserted. When Samantha sent him a grateful look, he smiled reassuringly. "Your brothers are watching Blue Blazes. If he starts getting twitchy, they'll holler."

Tucker moved to Tabasco's head to insert an IV catheter into the stallion's jugular vein. "Before I answer any of your questions, I have a couple more of my own."

"Fire away," Samantha replied. "If I can't answer them, I'm sure Jerome can."

"Can you clearly remember the day this horse first got sick?" Tucker asked.

Samantha thought back. "I think so. Is there something particular you're curious about?"

Tucker rested a large hand on the stallion's shoulder. "I'm just wondering if Tabasco was put out to pasture that day—or possibly the day before."

Samantha couldn't recall, and sent her foreman an imploring look.

"He came down sick last Sunday morning," Jerome supplied. "I know it was Sunday because Samantha stayed home from Mass that morning to watch after him and speak to the vet." The older man cleared his throat. "With so many horses, we pasture them on a rotating schedule according to their stall numbers. Tabasco is put out to graze on Sunday afternoons and on Tuesday and Thursday mornings. When he came down sick that morning, he hadn't been put out to graze yet."

"So for nearly three days prior to falling ill, he wasn't outside at all?" Tucker paraphrased.

"He was outside, just never out to graze," Jerome corrected. "On nonpasture days, we put the horses on the walker for at least an hour, and we also let them out into their paddocks for fresh air."

Tucker nodded as if he were filing away each tidbit of information. "When you took Tabasco out to put him on the walker, is it possible he might have been tethered for a few minutes before or after, maybe next to a building, where he could have grazed on weeds or clumps of grass along the foundation?"

"I suppose that's possible," the foreman agreed. "There's lots of times when I take a horse off the walker that I'll tether it for a few minutes while I finish doing something else."

"Do you spray weeds and unwanted grass around the foundations of the outbuildings with any herbicides or pesticides?" Tucker asked.

"Never," Jerome answered unequivocally. "We just cut the weeds back. If I saw anyone spraying any kind of chemical anywhere on this ranch, I'd fire him or her on the spot."

"How about pigs?" Tucker flicked a look at Samantha. "Have you ever raised any on this ranch?"

Bewildered by the question, Samantha shook her head. "No, why do you ask?"

"I was just wondering if there might be an outdated bag of swine feed tucked away and forgotten near the horses' grain."

Samantha's father folded his arms atop the gate and broke into the conversation again. "You thinkin' these horses got into some arsenic? I've never heard of arsenic makin' a horse go berserk."

Tucker taped the large-bore catheter to Tabasco's neck. "I don't think Blue got into arsenic. His symptoms have my mind going in another direction entirely. But Tabasco here, I believe he's gotten into a poison of some kind."

"Arsenic?" Samantha's thoughts immediately turned to the Cary Grant film *Arsenic and Old Lace,* and how quickly the old ladies' victims had perished. "But Tabasco fell ill over a week ago."

"Small amounts of arsenic aren't always instantly fatal," Tucker told her. "That isn't to say small amounts can't do plenty of damage, but they aren't necessarily an immediate death sentence, either."

Samantha pressed a hand over her pounding heart. "Are you sure Blue Blazes didn't get poisoned, too?"

"His symptoms are different. In my professional opinion, for what it's worth without lab reports to back it up, I don't think he ingested a poison, per se. I do believe there's a possibility that this horse has, though."

"How could that happen?" Samantha looked to Jerome. "We're so careful."

Tucker suspended a bag of IV fluids from the pole and adjusted the drip. "Even if you're extremely careful, it does happen," he assured her. "Is it possible that any of the wood in these buildings or any of your fence posts were treated with CCA?"

"No," Jerome said. "This place is only eight years old, and we knew the dangers of CCA when we poured the foundations. We went out of our way to make sure all the wood for the buildings and fences was arsenic free."

Tucker patted Tabasco's shoulder. "He's a great horse. I love his temperament."

Samantha was too shocked to appreciate the compliment. "There's no way this horse could have eaten or drunk anything containing arsenic."

Tucker examined the horse's eyes again. "Could be I'm wrong, then. He's a little jaundiced, and his eyes are bloodshot. His cap refill is a little slow as well, and he's dehydrated. But a lot of different conditions can produce the same symptoms. I won't know for sure what's going on with him until I see his blood panels."

He crouched down to sort through his satchel, then sighed and pushed erect. "That said, with your permission, I'd like to start treating this horse for arsenic poisoning. The drugs I'll use shouldn't hurt him if I'm wrong, and they'll help a great deal if I'm right."

Samantha was relieved to finally have a vet on board who recognized a problem and was willing to act. "You definitely have my permission."

"Good." A hint of a smile warmed Tucker's eyes as he met her gaze. "Would one of you mind coming out to my truck and holding a flashlight for me? I need to get some medicines out of my fridge."

"You have a fridge in your truck?" Jerome asked with surprise.

"AC/DC. I try to keep a broad range of medications on hand, and a few need to be refrigerated. It saves me from having to drive back to the clinic every time I need something out of the ordinary."

Samantha turned to follow him from Tabasco's stall. Just as they exited and closed the gate, Blue Blazes screamed. Tucker hurried back for his satchel, and together they ran the length of the arena, her father and Jerome jogging behind them.

As Tucker prepared another injection for Blue, Samantha stepped close to the cross-tied stallion and spoke softly, trying to calm him down. For the first time since Blue's birth, her voice failed to soothe him. The realization brought tears to her eyes. Of all her horses he was her most beloved, maybe because he had been her very first Sage Creek foal. Others had been born on her ranch before Blue, but their dams had belonged to her father and had been pregnant when Samantha bought them. Without any advice from anyone, she had handpicked Blue's dam and sire, using her knowledge of horses and genetics to produce not only a gorgeous blue roan, but also a champion.

In some way she couldn't explain and might never completely understand herself, this stallion defined her as an individual. He represented everything that she'd worked so hard to become—a world-class breeder of exquisite quarter horses.

"Is it safe to give him so many of these shots?" she asked Tucker. "The sedative doesn't seem to be working very well."

"Xylazine is a short-action drug, so normally it only lasts for about twenty minutes." A vial in one hand, a syringe in the other, Tucker glanced up at her from where he crouched over his bag. "The Dormosedan usually gives it more wallop, but it doesn't seem to be doing the job effectively with him."

Samantha picked up on what he hadn't said. "I asked if the shots are safe, and you haven't answered my question."

His jaw muscle ticked. "Relatively safe."

"Meaning?"

"Meaning that I'm guessing each time I load the syringe. The drugs aren't working like they normally do. To keep him calm, I'm having to give more frequent injections and at stronger doses than I'd usually expect for a horse this size. I can only hope I don't screw up and give him too much."

Samantha didn't like the sound of that. "You can only hope? I'm sorry, but that doesn't inspire much confidence."

"Until I have some test results to look at, my hunches are all I've got," he told her flatly. "Any vet who tells you different is lying through his teeth."

No one knew better than Samantha how important sound intuition was when it came to working with horses. In the not so distant past, before the advent of computer databases, Internet searches, telecommunication, and high-tech diagnostic equipment, much if not most of animal medicine was a guessing game, and out in the field it probably still was. Time and again she'd seen her father visually examine a horse, make a call, and save the animal's life by taking the right action in the nick of time.

"I know that doesn't sound very scientific," Tucker went on, his tone apologetic, "but there you have it. Veterinary medicine has come a long way over the last twenty years, but much of the diagnostic equipment is stationary, primarily because most vets can't afford the portable versions. I carry more equipment with me than the average vet, but even so, every time I go out on a call, it's still mostly guesswork. It's only later, after I've returned to the clinical environment and can review the results of the tests, that I know for sure if I guessed right."

Looking into his unwavering blue eyes, Samantha felt no need to ask how often Tucker Coulter guessed wrong. She ran a trembling hand along her stallion's neck. "What are your instincts telling you about Blue?"

He gave her a sharp look. "Truthfully?"

"Of course, truthfully. If I didn't want an honest answer, I wouldn't have asked."

He searched her gaze for a long moment and then nodded. "If he were my horse, I'd try another drug, one that's a complete long shot. I have absolutely no data to justify my reasoning, but if my suspicions are correct and my instincts are sound, it would work a hell of a lot better than these sedatives and would also be much safer."

"Are you asking for my authorization?"

He hesitated, then nodded. "Yes, I suppose I am."

For a moment, Samantha stood frozen. Then, with a soft release of breath, she said, "My father believes in you. His opinion counts for a lot with me. What is this drug you'd like to use?"

He sat back on his boot heel. "It's an opiate antagonist called naloxone."

"An opiate antagonist? My ignorance is showing, I'm afraid. I've no idea what that is."

"An antagonist is any drug capable of counteracting the effects of another drug, in this case possibly an opiate. I'm guessing morphine."

"Morphine?" Samantha felt her eyes widen. "Wasn't it used at the tracks years ago to fix horse races?"

"Until it was outlawed, yes, doping horses to excite them

and make them run faster was a common practice. Sadly, if the animal was given too large a dose, the doping often back-fired, making the animals go totally berserk or pushing them beyond endurance. Either way, the result was either dead or ruined horses, and eventually laws were passed to prohibit the use of morphine."

A long-forgotten memory of her ex-husband, Steve, popped into Samantha's mind. She distinctly remembered his once telling her about doping a rodeo bronco to make it impossible for an opponent to win a competition. The ground felt as if it shifted beneath her feet, and she reached out a hand to steady herself against the wall. For an awful moment she thought she might faint.

Blue, her sweet, beautiful, loyal Blue, might be in grave danger. If the morphine broke through again, there was no guarantee that the ropes would hold the horse and protect him from injury.

"What makes you think it's morphine?" she asked.

"The symptoms, mainly. The sedative combination I'm giving him should keep him calm for at least a half hour, with lingering effects after the drugs start to wear off. But that isn't happening. I'd also expect a reduced pulse rate and slower breathing, but I'm not seeing either. It's as if something else in his system is counteracting the sedatives. Answer—morphine. It's the first agent that comes to mind because it's so renowned for exciting equines."

"And you're certain naloxone will counteract it?"

He nodded.

"Let's try it, then."

"It's purely an opiate antagonist," he warned. "It has al-most no analgesic effect."

"In other words, it will do essentially nothing unless Blue has ingested an opiate?"

"Precisely. He could go totally berserk again."

Samantha envisioned the white powder on Blue's wet cob. Though it sickened her to consider the possibility, she believed a chemical analysis might prove that substance to be morphine.

She stroked the stallion's neck one final time. Then she turned toward Tucker. "Give him the naloxone," she said thinly.

He bent back over his satchel and withdrew another vial. Giving her a questioning look, he said, "Are you sure? Like I said, it's a long shot."

"I'm sure," she whispered.

Within seconds, he was giving the agitated stallion an injection straight into the jugular. "It's a rapid-onset drug," he explained to Samantha as he depressed the plunger. "If my guess is right and he ingested morphine powder, we'll know in one to two minutes."

Samantha leaned against the wall to wait. As if with a bone-deep chill, she was trembling from head to toe. She could feel her father's gaze on her. A part of her wanted to run to him and feel his strong arms around her, but another part of her held fast and avoided looking at him. *Shame*. That was what she felt, only instead of burning through her, it felt cold as death.

During those endless seconds—each a small eternity of waiting—Samantha remembered all the other times that she'd caused her father pain. In each and every instance Steve Fisher, the one grave mistake of her lifetime, had been the cause. He was like an inoperable cancer. Over the last year she had convinced herself that Steve had finally been removed from her life. And then when she least expected it, he had infected it again.

"It's working," Tucker said softly.

Samantha brought her head up to stare at her horse. Even cross-tied, the stallion looked like his old self again. He held his head as high as the ropes would allow, his eyes were clear and bright, and for the first time since this nightmare had begun, he looked at her with recognition.

"Ah, Blue." Samantha pushed away from the wall and

went to hug her horse's neck. He chuffed and whickered softly, almost as if he were apologizing for his bad behavior. "It wasn't your fault, baby. It wasn't any of it your fault. We all know that." She breathed into his nostrils to give him her scent. Then she pressed closer to bury her face against his neck. "Can the ropes come off now?"

"Naloxone's duration of action only persists from forty-five to ninety minutes," Tucker explained. "If we remove the ropes, accidentally drift off to sleep, and don't get another injection into him when he begins to get agitated, the opiate could break through again."

"I won't fall asleep," Samantha assured him, and looking into her horse's eyes, she knew it was a promise she would keep. "I hate seeing him tied up like this. He's a wonderful, gentle horse and deserves to be treated with dignity."

When the ropes fell away, Blue Blazes walked directly to the stall gate to nudge Jerome's shoulder with his nose. Jerome scratched behind the horse's ears. "I know, son. You remember hurting me. But I don't hold it against you."

"He's sayin' he's sorry, clearer than words," Samantha's father said with a faint smile. "Poor fellow. Must be terrible to eat something that makes you crazy and not be able to stop yourself."

"I've been crazy drunk a few times," Jerome replied, still fondling the horse's ears. "Said and did things that made me ashamed later. I reckon maybe that's how he feels."

Tears stung Samantha's eyes. Without thinking of the consequences or how Tucker might interpret the gesture, she turned and gave him a fierce hug. "Thank you. Thank you so very much."

For just an instant he seemed uncertain how to react, but then he curled an arm around her waist and returned the embrace. "I'm just glad it worked. I was sweating bullets, I'll tell you."

"Me, too," she confessed with a wet laugh.

When she went to pull away, he quickly released his hold

on her. As she stepped back their gazes locked, and some-thing—a feeling Samantha had never felt before—passed between them. It lasted for only an instant, but during that brief expanse of time, the impact was stunning. Even more alarming, he felt it, too. Samantha saw it in his eyes.

The realization filled her with a sudden need to escape. Glancing at her watch, she decided to go check on Tabasco. As she left the enclosure, she saw her brothers sitting on the arena floor with their backs braced against the gate of the adjacent stall. Brown Stetson tipped low over his eyes, Clint sat in a slump, long legs extended and crossed at the ankle, the pointed toes of his boots forming a lopsided V. Beside him Quincy sat with both knees bent, heels planted in the dirt, arms crossed over his chest. Parker and Zach had each taken end positions and looked like two perfectly matched bookends.

"Blue is doing better," she informed them. "We took a gamble, and he responded to the antagonist."

"We heard." Clint thumbed up his hat to settle a chocolate brown gaze on her. "I'm fixing to respond to an antagonist, too," he drawled. "Only not in a favorable way."

The anger in her eldest brother's voice was unmistakable, and Samantha held up a hand to stop him from saying any-thing more. "I can't go there right now, Clint. Let me get Blue and Tabasco through this first. Then we'll talk."

"You know who did this," he replied in that same throb-bing tone. "It's written all over your face."

Samantha had no doubt that Clint could read her expres-sion. He'd been doing so all her life. "What I do or don't know isn't the issue right now."

"What is?"

"Saving my horses!" Samantha heard the shrill edge in her voice and swallowed hard to regain her composure. "I can't deal with anything more right now."

"I'm not asking you to deal with it. All I want is a go-ahead from you, and I'll do the rest."

"A go-ahead?" she repeated incredulously.

"Somebody's got to take him to task," Clint retorted, his voice vibrating with leashed rage. "Time after time we let it go, and now look where that's landed us. He has no boundaries, Samantha. He won't stop with this. If you're thinking he might, you're dreaming."

She shook her head. "Please, Clint, not right now. Let me get my horses well, and then I'll decide what to do."

"Like you decided before?" His eyes had gone so black with anger, they glittered in his dark face. "Let me handle him this time."

"No. I can't have my brother acting like some half-cocked vigilante. There are laws in place, Clint. If Steve did this, he'll pay, but it won't be at your hands."

"The law only works when a perpetrator is caught and proved to be guilty. Steve is smarter than that. He did this. You know it, I know it, and everybody else knows it, too. But mark my words, you'll never be able to prove it. Is that what you want, to let him do something this vicious and just walk away scot-free?"

Samantha had started to shake again. "Talking to you is like talking to a rock. Why do you never listen to me? *I cannot deal with anything more right now.* What about that do you fail to understand?"

Spinning away, she headed for Tabasco's stall. Every step of the way she felt Clint's gaze burning a hole in her back. She loved her brother, she truly did, but sometimes he made her so furious she wanted to wring his neck.

She was breathless by the time she entered Tabasco's enclosure. To keep from bursting into tears, she grabbed his brush and set to work grooming him, her strokes brisk and short at first, then settling into longer, gentler sweeps. The horse chuffed and bumped her with his nose. Samantha sighed and stopped brushing him to comb her fingers through his forelock and scratch under his halter straps.

She heard someone enter the stall behind her. That someone deposited some things in a corner and then stepped over to the IV pole. Tucker, she guessed.

"The first bag is almost gone," she said needlessly. "I can't believe how fast it went."

"I'm hitting him pretty hard with fluids. If he ingested arsenic, the more fluids, the better. That, along with the medicines I just added to the IV, will help cleanse his body of the chemical."

"Have you treated a lot of animals with arsenic poisoning?"

"None, actually."

"How can you know for certain what medicines to use then?"

"Good question," another masculine voice very like Tucker's said from behind them.

Samantha glanced over her shoulder and thought for just an instant she was seeing double. Tucker Coulter—or someone who looked exactly like him—stood just inside the stall gate.

"Your eyesight's fine," he assured her with a crooked grin. "I'm Isaiah, Tucker's twin."

Over her lifetime, Samantha had known several sets of twins who claimed to be identical, but upon close inspection she'd always been able to see slight differences. Not so with the Coulter brothers. Except for their clothing, they were mirror images of each other—tall, bronzed, and dark-haired, with eyes as blue as laser beams.

"Unfortunately for me, he got the photographic memory," Isaiah went on, "and I didn't." He sent his brother a laughing glance. "He probably read about arsenic poisoning when we were cramming for a final at vet school, and now the symptoms and treatments are chiseled on his brain."

"You're a vet, too?" Samantha said incredulously.

Isaiah's lean cheek creased in a teasing grin. "Our mother dressed us alike and warped our personalities. I've never had an original thought in my entire life."

"That is so not true," Tucker retorted. "You got married, didn't you?"

Even as drained as Samantha felt, she couldn't help but smile at the Coulter brothers' verbal sparring. It reminded her of the exchanges that took place among her own brothers on a daily basis.

"Okay, I'll give you that one," Isaiah conceded. "But marrying Laura was my only individual act."

Tucker shook his head and winked at Samantha. "Don't listen to him. Next he'll be telling you about our symbiotic relationship and his theories on emotionally conjoined twins."

"They exist," Isaiah insisted. "Tucker and I are a perfect example. To look at us, we're exact duplicates, but under the surface that is absolutely untrue. Instead we're two halves of a whole, neither of us complete without the other."

Samantha was fascinated in spite of herself. "Really?"

"No, not really." Tucker sent his twin a disgusted look. "You're here for the blood samples, right?"

"Nah. I was just out for a middle-of-the-night drive and happened to see the lights."

"Smart-ass," Tucker muttered as he crouched over his satchel.

"Ask a stupid question . . ."

"And get a stupid answer," Tucker finished. "You got in touch with Ann, I take it."

"I did," Isaiah replied. "She made a few phone calls and did some schmoozing at Saint Matthew's. The hospital lab has agreed to do the blood panels. They figure they can have them finished in about an hour."

Tucker grinned. "There, you see? Knowing the right people, anything's possible." He withdrew the marked vials of blood from his bag. Before handing them to Isaiah, he said, "I need a chemical and heavy-metal panel on Tabasco, and also a kidney and liver function."

Isaiah accepted the first two vials and tucked them into a pocket of his lightweight jacket. "Got it."

As Tucker handed over the third vial, he said, "All I need on this one is a drug panel."

"You're still thinking morphine?" Isaiah asked.

"I'm convinced of it now." Tucker related the success of the experimental dose of naloxone. "Worked like a charm." He gestured toward Blue's stall across the arena. "He's calm as can be now, and the sedative has long since worn off."

Isaiah frowned and shook his head. "Why would anyone want to dope a horse with an opiate? That's brutal."

Samantha remembered how Steve had laughed while telling her the story of the doped rodeo bronco. It had been a turning point in their marriage, a moment of revelation and clarity that had harshly exposed Steve's complete lack of compassion for other living things. From that moment forward, she'd been forced to accept that she'd fallen in love with an illusion. The man she'd believed Steve Fisher to be had never existed except in her mind.

At the time, Samantha had honestly believed that nothing else she learned about Steve could ever hurt her more. How very young and pathetically naive she'd been back then. Now she understood that the heartbreak of her marriage had only just begun with that discovery and still hadn't stopped, even now.

Her father's greatest fear had come to pass, she realized with a shiver of apprehension. Steve Fisher had sneaked back onto the ranch to do her harm, just as her dad had always predicted, only instead of targeting Samantha, he'd taken aim at her horses. That was so like Steve. He had a mean streak a mile wide, unmitigated by any measure of empathy for anyone or anything. Inflicting pain on defenseless animals was just his style.

"You okay?"

The question brought Samantha's head up. With a blink and a slight jerk of her shoulders, she found Tucker gazing worriedly down at her. "Yes. I'm . . . fine. I'm sorry. My mind wandered off for a moment, I guess."

He searched her expression. Then he nodded. "I'm going to see Isaiah out. Be right back."

"Good meeting you," Isaiah said from where he stood at the gate. He lifted a large brown hand in farewell. "If all goes well I'll be back with the test results before my dust completely settles."

Samantha forced a smile. "I hope so. Thank you for being our gofer. I really appreciate it."

After Tucker and Isaiah left, Samantha returned to Blue's stall, settled herself on the hay, and pressed her back to the wall, prepared to divide her time between the two sick horses for the remainder of the night.

She'd been alone in the enclosure for only a couple of minutes when her father came in to crouch beside her. "I spoke to Clint. He's sorry for mouthin' off at you earlier."

"He's always sorry," she said hollowly. "Why does he always talk *at* me, Dad, and never *to* me?"

Her father shook his head. The sadness in his eyes told Samantha how deeply it pained him to have two of his children on the outs. "I don't have answers, honey. I only know he loves you, maybe more than you'll ever know."

Love. In Samantha's experience, people all too often used the emotion as an excuse to inflict pain. Almost before the thought took root in her mind, she felt guilty for entertaining it. Clint was many things—arrogant, infuriating, and domineering, to name only a few—but no one who knew him well would ever accuse him of being deliberately cruel. "I know he means well," she settled for saying. That was the entire problem with Clint, wasn't it? He always meant well.

"For all his faults, darlin', he's loyal to the marrow of his bones. Instead of goin' home, he's beddin' down in an empty stall to grab some shut-eye so he can spell you and Tucker later."

A knot of resentment formed at the base of Samantha's throat. That was another problem with Clint. No matter how badly he behaved, he always managed to redeem himself in everyone's eyes. "That's good of him," she pushed out. "I honestly doubt I'll be able to rest, though."

Her father nodded. "I know your heart's hurtin', honey. It's a terrible thing Steve's done."

A chill moved through her. There it was, the acknowledgment they'd both been avoiding. Steve had done this. Mentally, she kept circling the truth of it, much as she might a coiled rattlesnake. Steve, her monstrous nemesis, had reared his ugly head again.

"Maybe it's a mistake somehow," she said softly.

"A mistake?"

"Yes. You know, an accident." She turned aching eyes on her sire, wanting him to lie to her, yet knowing he wouldn't. "Like Tucker mentioned earlier. Arsenic leaching from the wood, stuff like that. There's no proof of a deliberate poisoning yet. Maybe we're jumping to conclusions."

Her father just stared at her, his look inexpressibly sad. "You know better than that, Samantha Jane."

It was true; she did know better. She had nothing more to say. Quite simply, there were no words. The person she'd once believed she loved more than anyone else in the world was taking another stab at her, and this time, the blade had hit home in a way she'd never thought possible. Her horses. *Oh, God.* That was the trouble with intimate relationships: You revealed too much and made yourself vulnerable. Steve knew she'd rather cut off an arm than see harm come to one of her animals.

"The other boys are headin' home to stretch out and sleep on a proper bed," her father informed her softly. "Come mornin', you and Jerome will be wiped out. The three of them will help keep things under control over here while you snooze for a few hours."

"But they have their own ranches to run."

"And they'll run 'em," her father assured her. "Between the three of 'em, they'll also run things over here for a bit. It's not that big a deal." He pushed clumsily at her hair and then patted her shoulder. "I love you, honey," he said gruffly. "I'm sorry it's come to this. If I could change it for you, I would."

Tears sprang to Samantha's eyes. She blinked them away and tried to smile. "I love you, too, Dad."

"You want me to go find the bastard and kill him for you? I'm an old fart. If they put me in jail and throw away the key, I've already had a damned good life."

"It's a tempting thought," she said shakily. "But he isn't worth it." She lifted her shoulders in a shrug. "I can't talk about it right now. I know we'll have to discuss what should be done very soon. Just not right now."

"I understand," he whispered.

Only he didn't, not really. Samantha doubted anyone could understand the myriad emotions that were at war within her right then, anger and regret struggling for supremacy, with a host of other feelings tangled inside her like a skein of yarn that had been batted about by a pair of kittens. She needed some quiet time—some thinking time. That was a luxury to be denied until Blue got through this crisis and she felt confident Tabasco was going to survive.

"I'm taking off," her father whispered. He gestured with a swing of his head. "Jerome needs stitches. I'm taking him to the ER."

Until that instant Samantha had forgotten all about the gash on her foreman's forehead. "Oh, God," she said faintly. "Where's my mind at?"

"On important matters," her dad replied. He gave her shoulder a hard squeeze as he pushed to his feet. "Jerome understands that. Go easy on yourself for once."

Eighty-three minutes after the first injection of naloxone, Blue Blazes began to get fidgety. Tucker noted the time on a small tablet, which he carried in his shirt pocket, and prepared a second shot. He heard rather than saw Samantha stir from her trancelike vigil.

"It's working even better than I hoped," he told her. "Naloxone's period of action lasts anywhere from forty-five to ninety minutes. He's gone almost a full ninety." He administered the second dose of the drug, patted the stallion's shoulder, and then sent the horse's worried mistress a reassuring smile. "He'll be fine now. Come morning there'll be only the cuts on his legs to remind you it ever happened."

She hugged her knees. Gazing down at her diminutive form, Tucker decided he'd never seen anyone more beautiful. He'd dated more striking women, to be sure, but by comparison, all of them had been fussy and artificial, all acrylic fingernails, artfully styled hair, and expensive clothes, with nothing natural about them. Samantha had bits of straw in her wildly curly hair, her clothing was wrinkled, and, God forgive him for noticing, she wore no bra. Without support, her breasts were more softly rounded under her shirt and jiggled just a bit when she moved, and her nipples were more readily visible when they hardened and jutted against the cotton.

"I am so grateful to you for saving him," she said softly. "I don't know how I'll ever repay you."

Tucker could think of a few ways she could settle the debt, but those were the kinds of thoughts a gentleman never shared with a lady. Not that he'd ever worried overmuch about being a gentleman. Maybe, he realized now, that had been because he'd always kept company with women who'd never expected that of him.

"Trust me," he said, "you'll feel the debt has been settled in full when you pay my bill."

She smiled wanly. "I'd forgotten about that. You have a way about you that makes people think you do it all simply because you care. That's a rare gift in a vet."

"I do care," he replied. "In a perfect world, I'd treat my patients for free, but in the real world, I have to eat and pay off a mortgage."

Tucker plucked the tablet from his pocket again to jot down another note.

"You write in that a lot."

He depressed the button on the pen to retract the tip before putting it back in his pocket along with the tablet. "I'm anal."

She rewarded him with a laugh. He had almost forgotten how much he enjoyed the sound.

"Seriously. I'm a record keeper. When I return to the clinic, I'll enter all this information into my computer. If you ever call me out to look at Blue or Tabasco again, I'll have an accurate account of my last visit—all the drug info, what worked and what didn't. Isaiah thinks I have a compulsive filing disorder."

She laughed softly again. "Do you?"

"Depends on how you look at it, I guess. He's totally disorganized. If he doesn't have his nose in a thick tome, researching a disease, he's treating animals."

"Ah, the conjoined-twin syndrome again."

He rolled his eyes. "Isaiah's idea of filing something is to throw it in a drawer. That's no syndrome; it's laziness." He winced and made a gesture as if to erase the words. "Strike that. It isn't laziness, not really. More that he hyperfocuses. He's a fabulous vet, the best I've ever seen, next to myself."

"There's that phenomenal conceit again."

Tucker grinned. "Guilty as charged. When it comes to my ability as a vet, I'm pretty high on myself." He hunkered down to reorganize his satchel. "Only I like to think of it as confidence, not conceit." He sent her a questioning look. "When it comes to breeding and training horses, don't you feel absolutely confident? I only ask because I think you should. Your horses are incredibly well mannered, and they've got fabulous temperaments. Tabasco is a pretty sick boy right now. If ever a horse had reason to be crabby and difficult, it's him. But he's a big old baby. That's impressive."

Her small chin came up a notch. "I don't feel absolutely confident," she said thoughtfully, "but I do feel extremely proud. Breeding blue roans isn't easy, and I'm beginning to make real strides in that. Training any horse to be unfailingly gentle takes a lot of hard work, too."

Sensing that breeding horses might be one of her favorite topics, Tucker cocked his head. "What's difficult about breeding blue roans?"

She loosened her arms from around her knees and settled back against the wall, treating him to another look at those soft, perfectly shaped breasts that he'd been trying so hard to ignore. Clearly enamored of the subject, she said, "A lot of people might tell you it isn't difficult." She puffed at the curls that lay in wild disarray over her forehead. "They're the ones who don't know what they're doing, and as a result they sell supposed blue roans to others for outlandish prices, and the buyers eventually end up with grays or some other color. Some of them never realize they've been gypped and perpetuate the mistake by breeding their horse to another supposedly true blue roan."

She began citing genetic codes, which Tucker suspected made most people's eyes roll back in their heads, but he found it interesting. The lady not only understood equine genetics, but could also recite all the various combinations that produced different colors of horses.

"To an untrained eye, a lot of horses look like blue roans," she told him.

Biting back a smile, Tucker sat down and settled his back against the opposite wall. It was good to see her like this. Despite the exhaustion that had underscored her eyes with dark smudges and leached her face of color, her expression suddenly burned with passion. "How's that?"

"Trust me, some grays look very much like blue roans. It takes an expert eye to see the difference. In a gray, the roaning extends up onto the head and down the legs and often into the tail. *That* is not a blue roan. It's a gray."

"I'll be damned. I think I've been mistaking grays for blue roans, then." He flashed her a sheepish grin. "When I got here tonight, my first thought when I saw Blue was how gorgeous he is, which kind of surprised me, because blue roans don't normally appeal to me."

She looked affronted. "Blue roans are beautiful animals."

"*True* blue roans." He winked at her. "You should name one of your colts True Blue."

She smiled but shook her head. "I name all my horses after things in my cupboards. Blue is named after a spicy brand of smoke-flavored barbecue sauce. The others are pretty self-explanatory. True Blue is a cute name, though. Maybe my dad will use it."

Tucker watched her push easily to her feet. That was another thing about her that he found attractive: She was in superb physical shape. Not the working-out-every-day-at-the-gym kind of good shape so common in his age group, but the kind of physical conditioning that came only from hard work. She was lean, toned, and able to move with surprising speed.

"I'm going to check on Tabasco," she informed him.

Tucker regretted seeing her go. They'd just found some common ground and, he hoped, were becoming friends. Now she was off, aborting the conversation before it could delve any deeper into more personal subjects.

Watching the swing of her nicely rounded hips, he wondered if that wasn't exactly her aim—to keep him at arm's length.

Chapter Ten

At just a little past three in the morning, Isaiah Coulter returned with the blood panel results. When Samantha caught movement and glanced up at the stall gate, she was surprised it wasn't Clint rousing himself to spell her for a while, or her father returning from his emergency run to the hospital. Instead she saw Isaiah's dark, handsome face. Despite his resemblance to Tucker, she recognized him by the jacket he wore.

He waved a handful of documents. "Where's Tucker?"

"Over with the other horse." Slipping her rosary back into her pocket, Samantha pushed to her feet, her gaze shifting to the papers in Isaiah's hand, which he'd rested atop the gate. Tucker's guess about the morphine had already been proved correct by the successful effects of the naloxone, but she was still hoping he might be wrong about the arsenic. "What do Tabasco's test results show?"

Isaiah shook his head. "Sorry. It's Tucker's place to tell you that. Just know you've landed yourself one fine vet."

That told Samantha more than she wanted to know, namely that Tabasco had indeed been poisoned. Blue had almost a half hour left to go before he would need another injection, so she walked with Isaiah to Tabasco's stall. Tucker was adjusting the IV drip on a fresh bag of fluids. When he saw his brother, the first words from his mouth were, "Is it arsenic?"

After they entered the stall, Isaiah closed the gate behind them and thrust out the paperwork. "I'll let you make the call on that."

Tucker took the reports, his forehead furrowing in a frown as he scanned each page. Samantha craned her neck, trying to read the results herself, even though she wouldn't know good numbers from bad.

Finally Tucker nodded. "Definitely arsenic, then." He flipped to another page, scanned it, and said, "Damn, it's playing hell with his liver and kidneys. Let's just pray I'm not too late, and that the D-penicillamine works."

"D-penicillamine?" Isaiah echoed. "For what, an arsenic chelator?"

"It's been used with good success in humans," Tucker replied, "and it has a wide margin of safety for use in animals. For a horse this size they recommend fifty milligrams three to four times a day. I've already given him the first injection."

"All joking aside about the photographic memory, how the hell do you remember all this stuff?" Isaiah asked. "Do you have your laptop out in the truck so you can look it up?"

Tucker gave his brother a vaguely irritated look. "I don't know how I remember stuff. I just do."

Samantha's stomach twisted into a painful knot. She gazed past Tucker at Tabasco. "Is he going to die, then?"

"I hope not," Tucker replied. "His liver and kidney counts don't look good. I'm not going to lie to you about that, Samantha, or make promises just to ease your mind. He's a very sick horse."

She gulped and nodded. "What are his chances, do you think?"

Tucker pushed a big hand through his sable hair. "I don't know. The poison has been in his system for over a week, with no chelating agent to get it out of his body."

Samantha closed her eyes. If Tabasco died, she would

be partly responsible. When she'd learned Doc Washburn was away on vacation she should have called Tucker immediately. Instead, because she'd dreaded seeing Tucker again, she had settled for negligent care from a second-rate veterinarian.

"How does a chelator work?" she managed to ask.

"It's an agent that helps remove heavy metals from the bloodstream. Arsenic lingers in the blood and tissues, and in large enough amounts it continues to do damage long after it's ingested. A chelating agent acts sort of like a magnet. It bonds with heavy metals and minerals such as arsenic, allowing them to be flushed from the body."

"Think of it as a body wash," Isaiah inserted, "only on the inside."

"So it *is* arsenic poisoning," Clint said.

Samantha jumped with a start and turned to find her brother standing just inside the gate, which he'd left yawning open behind him. His face was clenched in anger, his jaw muscle ticking. Bits of straw clung to his blue chambray work shirt.

"That day at the courthouse," he said evenly, directing his gaze at her, "I swore I'd make that son of a bitch regret the day he was born if he ever hurt you again. It wasn't an empty threat. It was a vow."

Samantha shook her head, silently pleading with Clint not to air her dirty laundry in front of two strangers. But he was too furious to notice.

"I stayed away from this ranch when the marriage went south," he went on, his voice vibrant with rage. "I looked away when I saw the bruises, telling myself you'd gotten hurt working with the horses. I lied to myself because I knew you didn't want me to interfere. He was your husband, and it was between you and him, so I tried my damnedest to stay out of it." He leaned closer to get nose-to-nose with her. "But that's not the case now. The marriage is over, and he's going to pay for this. I'm going to hunt him down like the worthless dog he is, and I'm going to stomp the living hell out of him."

"Clint, that's enough," she tried.

"No, not nearly," he shot back. "He gave Blue a shitload of morphine for it to have affected him that way. Have you even stopped to wonder why?"

Samantha shook her head. "We don't know for certain it was Steve. You need to calm down."

"Like hell I'll calm down. He knows how much you love Blue Blazes, and killing Blue with arsenic wouldn't have been horrible enough to suit him. So instead he set out to make him die the most awful, goriest death possible, while you watched. Either that or he was hoping you'd be foolish enough to enter the stall so the horse could kill you. He's a mean, rotten, lying, low-down bastard, and right now he's probably kicked back in a recliner, drunk as a lord, laughing his ass off."

"Clint, *please*."

"If I don't stop him he'll try again," her brother warned. "He won't be happy when he finds out Blue isn't dead. And he'll find a way to sneak back in here and do it again."

Samantha whipped away from her brother, only to see Tucker and Isaiah staring at her with shock and pity in their expressions. She was so humiliated she wanted to crawl into a hole. She shoved past Clint to escape the stall and ran from the building.

Tucker gazed after Samantha until she reached the personnel door and disappeared outside. Then he turned to look at Clint. The man stood with his boots braced wide apart, all his anger seemingly gone, replaced by what now appeared to be hopeless regret. He was pinching the bridge of his nose. His eyes were closed. An ashen pallor tinted his sun-bronzed face.

"Damn it," he whispered. "Why is it I can never get it right with her?"

Tucker glanced uneasily at his brother. Isaiah met his gaze for a moment and then bent his head to dig at the straw with his boot heel.

"Judging by what you just said, you think Samantha's ex-husband did this to her horses?" Tucker was hoping for clarification and possibly Clint's reasons for suspecting the man.

Clint lowered his hand from his eyes, curled his thumbs over his belt, and nodded. "I don't think; I *know*." He gestured with his head. "And so does she."

Tucker rechecked the IV drip and patted Tabasco on the rump. "By law I have to report this, Clint. It appears that two horses have been deliberately poisoned. If you've got sound reasons for thinking it was her ex-husband, I'd like to hear them."

"She divorced him a little over a year ago, and there was a bitter court battle over the assets. Steve married her for her money, and when she finally wised up and sent him packing, he went after half of everything she had."

Tucker nodded to indicate that he was following.

"Normally that's fair," Clint continued. "Two people get hitched, and they acquire assets together. But Samantha already had her inheritance when Steve came into the picture. That was what attracted the bastard to her in the first place."

Tucker could think of many other things about Samantha that would attract a man, but he held his tongue.

Clint swung a hand to indicate the ranch. "When each of us kids turned twenty-one, our father gave us an equal share of his land and a hefty sum of money to start our own horse-breeding businesses."

"And this guy Steve wanted half of Samantha's share?" Isaiah asked.

"He damned near got half." Clint's jaw muscles bunched. "I talked myself blue trying to get her to make him sign a prenup agreement. But would she listen? Hell, no. She was young and in love, with stars in her eyes. The way she saw it, asking him to sign an agreement would have been a slap in his face and a betrayal of their love for each other. So when the marriage went bust, he got half of almost everything. The only thing the judge refused to split down the middle was the inventory. Samantha's horses, in other words. They were hers before the marriage, and they were the backbone of her business. Steve had his rodeo stints to bring in an income. The judge felt it was only fair to leave Samantha with some way to support herself, too.

"Steve was so pissed he couldn't see straight," Clint went on. "These horses are worth more than you can imagine, hundreds of thousands. One of Sammy's regular foals can't be touched for less than sixty grand, and that was *before* Blue Blazes won the cutting horse competition a couple of weeks ago.

"Right after the hearing, Steve waited for her on the court-house steps," Clint said, his voice quavering at the memory. "He was so fit to be tied by the judge's mandate that he for-got himself and got in her face, swearing on all that was holy to make her regret leaving him. I had a lot of pent-up anger." Clint shrugged. "If you don't have a baby sister, you just can't know how I hated the rotten bastard. But there I go, justifying my actions. I decked him, plain and simple. He wasn't going to bully my sister again, not on my watch, so I tore into him. My dad and brothers had to pull me off."

Tucker nodded. "I hope you whaled the snot out of him." Just the thought of someone bullying Samantha, and pos-sibly even striking her, made Tucker's blood pressure go up several points. "It sounds like he had it coming."

Clint studied the sick stallion through narrowed, glitter-ing eyes. "Evidently I didn't whale on him quite enough, not if he worked up the gumption to do this. Spineless, sneaky, backstabbing asshole. I'm gonna take him apart."

Tucker could only imagine how deep and hot Clint's an-ger ran. "We aren't sure Steve Fisher did it yet," he tried.

Clint cut him a disgusted look. "Maybe you aren't. I know him. I know how he thinks. In his mind, Samantha cheated him out of what was rightfully his, so now he means to kill her horses. It doesn't matter that he walked away with more than his fair share, or that my sister had to borrow over a million dollars from our father to settle up with him instead of selling this place. All he cares about is what he didn't get. So he figures she won't have it, either."

"You need to keep a clear head, partner."

It was Isaiah who spoke, and the unexpected comment brought Clint's head around and some sanity back into his dark eyes.

"Tucker and I have a sister, too," Isaiah elaborated, "and we're a close-knit family. If anybody ever hit her or hurt her like this, we'd want to beat the hell out of him, no question about it."

Clint nodded his approval, and Isaiah's face broke into one of his famous grins. "But wanting to do something is different from actually *doing* it. You know? If you lay a hand on the guy, he'll file charges against you."

"Not if he's dead, he won't."

Isaiah shook his head. "You're not a killer. You'd just mess him up real bad and leave him to lick his wounds. And the first thing you'd know, the cops would be hauling you away to the hoosegow. It's better to keep a clear head and go after him through the appropriate channels. If he did this, the police will find evidence to prove it."

"He covered his ass," Clint insisted. "Trust me on that. He's a saddle tramp, but he's a smart saddle tramp. They won't find anything that points to him."

Samantha huddled in the corner of an outdoor stall where the fading moonlight didn't reach her. It was dark, and it was quiet, and she needed the privacy as much as she needed the air to breathe. She couldn't believe that her brother had said all that in front of two strangers, particularly Tucker. She didn't want him to know she'd remained in an abusive marriage for five years. On a scale of one to ten, the shame of it went clear off the chart.

She'd watched all the talk-show debates about battered women. She knew how cruelly they were stereotyped and had heard the clinical experts wax poetic on their theories. Women like that were sick. They were game players. They were trying to satisfy a deep, quirky, psychotic need to be punished. They fell in love with men like their abusive fathers, trying to reenact their childhoods and finally come out winners. They were helplessly attracted to brutal, bullish individuals because being knocked around turned them on.

Only where did she fit into all their hypotheses? She'd never been abused as a child. Just the opposite. She'd been well loved by her father and adored by her brothers. At bedtime almost every night her dad had knelt with her to say her prayers before he tucked her in, and then he'd read to her until she fell asleep. On those rare occasions when he'd been too busy, her brothers had filled in for him. She could still remember Zachary, only two years her senior, trying to read her *The Night Before Christmas* when he'd been barely old enough to make out the words. She'd been loved, damn it. She'd been cherished. There was nothing within her that had ever gone looking for punishment because she had some irrational, perverted need to suffer.

Why couldn't the experts understand that nothing was ever as simple as they wanted to paint it? Marriage, for instance. Where in their theories did they allow for deep religious convictions that forbade divorce? Where in their theories did they explore habits and beliefs and behaviors and doctrines that had been drilled into a woman all her life? And where in their theories did they allow for the possibility that some women were simply too proud to quit or too humiliated to admit to the world that they'd made a stupid mistake?

In her case, all of those things had applied, with an additional dash of pure terror that Steve would follow through with his threat to take half of everything her father had worked and sweated all his life to give her. Yes, she'd remained in the marriage. In the beginning she'd honestly believed Steve's need for other women was due to something lacking in her, and she'd tried exhaustively to please him. Cooking. Dressing up for him at night. Never contradicting him in front of others when he made a poor business decision.

She'd known he was an alcoholic. Right after he got a ring on her finger and consummated their marriage, the booze had come out of the closet. Some evenings he would pick a fight with her just to have an excuse to storm from the house, and then he'd come back in the wee hours of the morning, reeking of whiskey and another woman, so drunk he could barely walk.

Toward the end, the physical abuse had begun. Just a light slap across her mouth when they argued. Just a push to set her off balance when he got mad. It hadn't been serious at first. But then he had escalated, sometimes breaking dishes, sometimes dragging her up the stairs when he wanted sex and she was too furious or hurt by his constant infidelities to sleep with him. And finally the beatings.

Samantha lifted her face to the sky and let the breeze cool her hot cheeks as she remembered those times. She hadn't remained in the marriage for very long after the violence began, but looking back, she realized now that even a day would have been too long. It had done something to her way deep inside, snuffed out something that had once been clear and bright. Innocence, she guessed. She'd gone into the marriage believing in love, marriage, commitment, and forever.

And why not? Her father had taught her by example to believe in all those things. To this day, nearly thirty years after her mother had died giving birth to her, he still never looked at another woman. He'd found his one true love—his sweet, precious Emily—and he'd told Samantha more than once that he could never settle for anything less. Her mother had been his everything, and if he looked for fifty years, he'd never find anyone else quite like her.

"Samantha?"

At the sound of her name, she gave a violent jerk. *Tucker.* The yard light shining behind her limned him in shimmering brightness, defining his sharply chiseled features with shadows and frosting his hair with silver. He stood at the opposite side of the rail gate, looking in at her. There were twelve outdoor holding areas. How on earth had he found her?

"You startled me."

He nodded and folded his arms over the gate, one knee bent, his other leg stretched out behind him. "I'm sorry. I need to talk to you."

"About?"

"Tabasco. Come morning, I'd like to take him to my clinic. I'll be able to monitor his kidney and liver functions more closely there. I want to make arrangements with Isaiah before he leaves to come back with our trailer in the morning."

"I have a trailer. I can transport him."

"I'm sure you have a top-notch trailer, but ours is sort of special."

From somewhere out in the stable yard, Isaiah hollered, "Tucker's version of a horse ambulance! The only thing it lacks is a siren and lights."

Tucker huffed and sighed. "Brothers. Don't you love 'em? I've spent half my life pretending he isn't related to me."

Samantha giggled. The sound burst from her, as unexpected as it was inappropriate, but somehow it felt wonderfully good.

"You're hearing me," he said.

"Oh, yes, I'm hearing you *exactly*. It's pretty awful, isn't it, with the family resemblance to contend with?"

"Family resemblance?" Isaiah yelled something else that was indecipherable. Tucker grunted and swore under his breath. "Try having a twin. Then you've got *real* resemblance issues."

In the darkness, a poor imitation of a siren's wail rose toward the moon. Tucker listened for a moment and then shook his head. "Do you have a gun? I'll put him out of his misery."

She laughed again. "Only a shotgun for rattlesnakes. It'd be messy."

"True." He shifted his weight and threaded his fingers through his hair. "And if his conjoined-twin theory holds water, I'd probably be lost without him."

Samantha could empathize with that sentiment, too. For all her grumping about Clint, she loved him dearly and wouldn't know what to do without him in her life. She sighed softly, allowing some of her anger to slip away.

"So what's the real story on the horse ambulance?" she asked.

"I just have our trailer set up to transport sick equines. Took the divider out, for one thing, to create one wide stall. Tabasco's weak. If he goes down, there's room for him to rest comfortably. I also installed hooks and clips so I can keep him on the IV."

Samantha pushed erect. Her feet had gone numb, and needles pricked her heels as she walked toward him. "Sounds pretty high-tech to me. All right, sure, let's use your trailer. That will be better for him."

Tucker motioned the okay to Isaiah, and a moment later she heard a truck door slam closed, followed by the rumbling ignition of a diesel engine. Tucker drew open the gate for her; then they walked together back toward the arena. In the distance, she could hear Isaiah's pickup going *thump-ka-chunk*, his headlights sending bobbing flashes of yellow light into the sky behind the buildings.

"Beautiful night, isn't it?" Tucker said.

Samantha hadn't really noticed. "Yes, gorgeous."

He opened the personnel door and stood back for her to enter. After stepping in behind her, he said, "Blue is doing great. If he consumed the morphine around ten, like Jerome figures, I think he's through the worst of it. He shouldn't need any more naloxone."

"It may have been more like eleven when he actually got the cob," she informed him. "Jerome was working alone, there are a lot of horses, and Blue's stall is at the back."

Tucker fell into step beside her. "I still think he's through the worst. Morphine wears off after four to six hours. He's going to be fine now. If you'd like to grab some sleep, no worries. I'll be here until Isaiah comes back with the trailer in a few hours."

Samantha had no intention of leaving Tabasco, and despite what Tucker said, she didn't feel comfortable leaving Blue yet, either. "I'm fine. Raising horses, you get used to going without sleep." She rubbed her palms dry on the legs of her jeans. "Tucker?"

He tipped his dark head to regard her. "Yes?"

"I'm sorry about the scene with my brother. I'm sure it was as uncomfortable for you and Isaiah as it was for me."

His blue eyes twinkled warmly down at her. "That was a scene? You should be around my family."

She shook her head. "Oh, no. I have it on good authority that we Harrigans hold the all-time record for creating scenes."

"Not true. Enter the Coulter clan. Six kids, five of us married, and of those five, most of them starting to have kids. My older brother, Zeke, married a singer and nightclub owner with two kids and a zany extended family whose sister, Valerie, once arrived at a family gathering wearing a handkerchief skirt over a thong with a rhinestone in her navel." At Samantha's amazed look, he lifted his hands. "Would I lie to you? Then there's Jake, six-foot-four in his stocking feet, who married Molly, a plump, whiskey-haired munchkin who now controls the financial portfolios of practically everyone in the family and isn't shy about critiquing our spending habits during family dinners. Normally that might only make for interesting conversation, except for the fact that she's got this amazing talent for ferreting out secrets and exposing them over the crème brûlée, like the time Zeke's wife, Natalie, paid almost a thousand dollars to have his name tattooed inside a heart on the left cheek of her butt, and the tattoo artist got the spelling wrong."

Samantha gulped back a startled laugh. "You're kidding."

"Who'd kid about something like that? Zeke was so upset he wanted to sue. It cost him another thousand bucks to get the first letter removed and redone. And I can't forget my baby brother, Hank, whose wife has congenital cataracts and lattice dystrophy. She's early on in her second pregnancy, which could make her go temporarily blind again, so Hank is constantly blending algae-green protein shakes for her to drink and killing everyone's houseplants."

She cocked her head. "Their houseplants?"

He nodded. "Carly pours the shakes in a flowerpot every time Hank turns his back, and he blends the shakes at all of our houses. Not that I blame her. They smell like putrid seaweed. But he's convinced Carly's corneas will remain healthy if only she'll drink the stuff four times a day. When he catches her dumping a drink into a planter, the fight is on, and in my family, any upheaval draws in at least half the people present. Trust me, the Coulter clan's familial altercations are far more entertaining than anything the Harrigans could come up with."

Samantha momentarily wondered if he was stretching the truth to make her feel better, but then she decided the profiles were too outlandish to be fabricated on such short notice. Some of the tension eased from her shoulders.

"It sounds as if you have a very interesting family."

"Interesting isn't the word. You can't imagine what it's like when twelve to fourteen adults and X number of kids are all talking at once about how much it will cost to remove a D from my sister-in-law's butt and replace it with a Z—or how pissed Zeke got when our mother, God bless her frugal soul, suggested they just leave the wrong man's name on

Natalie's posterior because no one but Zeke would ever see it, anyway."

"I concede," Samantha said with a laugh. She took a deep breath and slowly released it. "Your family definitely has mine beat, hands down. But please accept my apology. It was rude of both Clint and me to quarrel in front of you."

"Apology accepted. But I still maintain that you have nothing to apologize for. It's been one hell of a night. Everyone's tense. Tempers flare. It's no big deal."

Tucker continued to move back and forth between the two horses for the remainder of the night, keeping a close eye on both animals' vital signs. Staying awake gave him plenty of time to mull over all that Clint Harrigan had told him about Samantha's past. No wonder the lady was so reluctant to let down her guard. She'd been hurt—very badly hurt, and in the worst possible way—by her husband.

The knowledge made Tucker even more determined to save Tabasco. She'd suffered enough pain and disappointment in her young life. He didn't want to see her endure anything more, especially not at Steve Fisher's hands.

As the night deepened to black just before dawn, the ambient temperature inside the stalls grew chilly. Tucker was freezing and hadn't thought to bring a coat. As he entered Tabasco's stall for another listen to the horse's heart and respiration, he chafed his arms through his shirtsleeves.

"Damn, there's a bite in the air," he said to Samantha.

She had draped Tabasco with a blanket, but she sat without cover on the straw, her slender shoulders pressed to the wall. In the yellow glow of the stall night-light, she looked frighteningly pale and fragile, and he worried that staying up with the horses had exhausted her to the point of illness. She looked dazed, and when she met his gaze full-on, she had a hollowed-out appearance. Rosary beads were twined through the slender fingers of her right hand, yet another thing about her that was different from any other woman who'd ever interested him. Samantha Harrigan was devoutly religious.

Tucker had admired the lady's courage from the first moment he'd seen her, standing toe-to-toe with a ham-fisted drunk twice her size. But now his respect for her deepened even more. Except for the silent tears he'd glimpsed on her colorless cheeks a few times over the course of the night, she hadn't wept. Instead she'd worked tirelessly to make her horses more comfortable and had helped him in any way she possibly could. He'd lost track of how many times she'd cleaned Tabasco's stall. Every time the young stallion urinated, which he was doing frequently because of all the fluids that were being pumped into him, she forked up the soiled straw and brought in fresh. When there was no task for her to perform, she sat and kept a constant vigil.

If love and prayer could perform miracles, and Tucker believed they could, Tabasco would beat all the odds and survive.

As the sky lightened to a steel blue streaked with rose, Tucker's own exhaustion got the better of him, and he nodded off. He had no idea how long he dozed, only that the soft, choked sounds of muffled sobs jerked him awake. He blinked and brought his bleary vision into focus. Samantha stood with her arms wrapped around her stallion's neck, her face pressed against his mane. She was weeping as if her heart might break.

Tucker tried not to move or reveal in any other way that he was awake. Years ago, when his sister, Bethany, had been paralyzed in a barrel racing accident, he had wept just that way, and he understood her need to grieve in privacy. A lump rose in his throat as he watched her through lowered lashes. Her pain was so intense, he could almost feel it. He wanted to go to her—if only to press a comforting hand to her shoulder. But he instinctively knew she would reject any such overtures, just as he would in the same situation.

Sometimes the hurting ran so deep, it wasn't for display.

Somehow she sensed his gaze on her. Tucker didn't know if he inadvertently moved, or if she simply noted a change in his breathing, but she suddenly gulped, grabbed for breath, and hurriedly wiped her cheeks. Her expression once again became deadpan. Her effort to project stoic strength touched him even more than her tears had.

She began stroking the horse with a trembling hand, making no attempt to explain her temporary lapse of composure. She loved her animals and was devoted to each of them in a way most people reserved for mates, parents, or children.

Just after dawn, Frank Harrigan returned, Jerome trailing behind him. The foreman's forehead was swathed in bandages. Samantha stirred from her stuporlike vigil to meet the two men at the gate. "How did it go?"

"They just stitched me up and gave me a lollipop," Jerome replied. "I reckon I'll live."

Frank shook his head. "Ornery, I guess," he said with a smile. Then he settled a concerned gaze on his daughter. "Honey, you look like you were dragged through a knothole backward. Why don't you go to the house and get some sleep?"

"No. Tabasco is going to be transported to Tucker's clinic in a bit. I want to go with him."

That was news to Tucker. "That's really not necessary," he interjected. "I'll ride in the trailer with him. And I'll keep you posted by phone on how he's doing."

Samantha sent him a burning look. "I'm going with my horse," she said, her tone brooking no argument.

"Sweetheart." Frank rubbed his mouth. "You need to get some rest. Then you can drive to the clinic later."

"No. I was with Tabasco when he was born. I've been with him through every illness and sprain and little cut. I'm going to be with him now. I'm not coming home until Tabasco does." She looked at Jerome. "I need you to look after things here. Parker, Quincy, and Zach will be coming over soon to take care of the chores. Once you get some rest, I want you to make as much use of the security system as possible and watch these horses constantly. Will you do that for me?"

Tucker approached the gate. "You know, Samantha, I don't really have accommodations for owners at my equine center. The only cot in the whole place is used by the night tech, who stays to monitor the animals."

"I don't need accommodations, just a blanket, pillow, a few changes of clothes, and some toiletry items. It'll only take me a few minutes to throw everything I'll need into a duffel bag."

Frank lifted his eyebrows at Tucker, his expression conveying more clearly than words that there was no point in arguing. Taking his cue from the man who probably knew Samantha better than anyone, Tucker shrugged and said, "Fine, then. Just don't expect Best Western. You aren't going to be very comfortable there."

"Good. It's settled, then." To Jerome, Samantha said, "The lab work came back. Tabasco has been poisoned with arsenic, Blue with morphine. Whoever did this may try again. Lock the paddock doors at night so no one can enter any of the stalls from outside. Make sure all the other doors are locked as well. And set the security alarm."

"No problem," Jerome assured her. He shifted his gaze to Tucker. "What do I watch for in the horses—for early signs of arsenic or morphine poisoning, I mean?"

Tucker quickly listed the symptoms, and Jerome nodded his understanding.

Frank said, "The boys will be over soon. We'll divide the stable into sections and examine every horse in here. If any others have been poisoned, it'll help to catch it early."

Tucker wished he'd thought to examine the other horses himself. His only excuse was that he'd been so busy caring for the two sick animals that he simply hadn't had time.

At eight o'clock, Isaiah showed up. He backed the trailer into Tabasco's paddock, extended the ramp, and waved hello to Tucker. "You need a shave, bro. You've bypassed five-o'clock shadow and moved up to half-inch stubble."

Tucker didn't doubt that he looked like hell. "Unlike some people, I haven't had the luxury of a hot shower."

Tucker tossed Samantha's duffel bag at his brother, smiling when the overstuffed satchel struck Isaiah's chest, then plopped at his feet. When he turned to collect his patient, he was surprised to see that Samantha already held the stallion's lead rope.

"I'll load him," she said. "All I need is for you to carry the fluid bag."

Tucker wasn't inclined to argue. He had a feeling she could lead the horse through fire. He pulled the aluminum tubing free of the earth, unhooked the IV pack, and followed behind her and the horse as they exited the stall.

Tabasco needed three starts to make it up the ramp, even though the trailer was low to the ground and the grade slight. Samantha stood patiently at her horse's head each time he needed to rest, and then she encouraged him to go a few more steps, her urgings soft and gentle, until the sick stallion finally made it inside the trailer.

Tucker remained outdoors to speak with Isaiah. Then he gave Frank the keys to his Dodge. "If somebody can drive it to the clinic, I'd appreciate it," he said. "I'll give whoever it is a ride back."

Frank looked into the trailer at his daughter. "I wish you'd turn loose of this idea, honey. Tabasco will be fine without you there to fuss over him every minute."

She shook her head, black curls dancing over her slender shoulders. "I'm staying with him. That's final."

Frank shrugged and shook his head. "You remind me so much of your mother sometimes."

"That's a fine compliment if ever I've heard one," she replied.

Frank shrugged and nodded.

Regardless of the difficulties, Tucker decided not to point

any of them out until a better moment presented itself. He had a mom and sister. Experience had taught him that when a woman set her mind on something, arguing with her only made her more stubborn. He collected his medical bag and paraphernalia, stowing the latter in the bed of Isaiah's truck. Then he climbed into the trailer, joining Samantha at the front. He set his bag at his feet.

"You don't need to ride in here with us," she protested.

Tucker braced his shoulder against the reinforced aluminum wall. "Isaiah has the driving end of it covered. Why not?"

In truth, Tucker was afraid to leave her back there alone. Tabasco was none too steady on his feet. If he went down, Tucker wanted to be there to look after not only the stallion, but Samantha as well. He estimated Tabasco to weigh approximately eleven hundred pounds. That was no small amount of horseflesh, plenty enough to crush a human femur or shatter several ribs if the stallion fell.

The trailer rocked forward just then, forcing all three of its occupants to struggle for balance. Tucker never rode in a horse trailer that his respect for equines didn't go up a notch. How they managed to remain standing during long rides without bracing themselves against a wall totally amazed him. Maybe having four legs gave them better balance.

An instant later the whole trailer bounced, telling Tucker that Isaiah wasn't watching for potholes and that the fun had just begun.

"Hold tight," he warned Samantha. "My brother's a fabulous vet, but his mind is seldom on what he's doing unless he happens to be treating a patient."

Her mouth twitched. "Are we going to get to your clinic in one piece?"

"We will if he doesn't forget we're back here."

"I want to thank you," she surprised him by saying.

"For what?"

"For not arguing about my coming. If you had, my father would have jumped on it."

Tucker thought about that for a moment. "Truthfully, I think you're going to be very uncomfortable staying at my equine center. But you're a big girl. That's your choice to make."

Her mouth twitch became a full-blown grin. "Thank you *again.* In my family, it's not often anyone gives me credit for being a big girl. Clint thinks I'm still a three-year-old."

Tucker wanted to ask questions so she might elaborate, but he was quickly coming to learn that Samantha Harrigan was a lady with closely guarded secrets. If he pushed her to reveal them before she was ready, she would just get that wary look in her eyes again and shut him out.

Chapter Eleven

By that afternoon Samantha was settled in at the equine clinic with her horse. Her father had brought her a snack basket filled with fruit, crackers, cheese, and a bottle of sparkling cider, and he'd promised to replenish the supplies if she stayed longer than expected. Clint stopped by with a six-pack of her favorite carbonated water, a bag of red licorice ropes, and two small boxes of jelly beans, which he handed over with a hangdog, apologetic look that earned him a hug and the forgiveness he was seeking, whether he could bring himself to ask for it or not. Her other three brothers also made brief appearances, mostly just to stand in Tabasco's stall for a few minutes, looking uneasy and out of place, but Samantha appreciated their show of support nonetheless.

"You sure you won't see reason and come home for the night?" Parker asked. "You aren't going to be comfortable here."

Samantha couldn't disagree. Just like at home, the stall had a dirt floor and was lined with clean straw for her to sit on, but there all similarities ended. Monitors decorated the walls of this enclosure, and Tabasco's body now sported shaved spots, onto which were affixed electrodes with protruding wires that carried electrical pulses to the machines.

Just outside the chamber, people bustled back and forth in the hallway and came into the stall on a regular basis. It was either time for another injection, another blood draw, or a urine output check. And every once in a while, the monitors buzzed a warning, which brought the techs running. Even though it always seemed to be a false alarm, Samantha's heart rate accelerated each time.

"I need to stay," she told Parker, the words to explain eluding her. "It's just something I have to do."

Parker sighed but didn't argue. He and her other two brothers remained for a few more minutes, and then they shuffled away, promising to drop by again the following day to see if she needed anything. Samantha wasn't worried on that score. Up the highway within walking distance was a McDonald's. She could get breakfast, lunch, and dinner there, if necessary. She'd also seen a pizza parlor and a full-scale restaurant nearby.

As the hours mounted, Samantha's brain became too fuzzy with exhaustion to remember just how long she'd gone without rest. She only knew that every part of her body ached and felt heavy. To pass the time, she said her rosary. Whispering the prayers over and over comforted her in a way that nothing else could.

At some point she grew so weary that she fell asleep with her eyes open. When a sound suddenly wakened her, she discovered that her eyeballs had grown so dry it was difficult to blink.

"Are you all right?"

She was so tired that not even the unexpected sound of Tucker's voice jangled her nerves. "I'm sorry?" She rubbed her eyes closed with knotted fists and then batted her lashes back open. "What did you ask me?"

As he slowly came into focus, she saw that he wore a blue lab jacket. From the hem down, faded denim jeans and scuffed Tony Lama boots preserved his cowboy image.

"At least I went home and crashed for a few hours last

night," he informed her. "If you don't get some rest, you're going to get sick."

She glanced at her watch. "I thought it was evening."

"No, ma'am, six o'clock in the morning. You've gone two days and nights without sleep. Why don't you take a break and try out the cot down the hall? Housekeeping changes the linen every morning, and no tech will need to use it again until tonight."

Samantha had set out to stay with her horse, just as she had once set out to stay with Steve, and exhaustion wasn't going to push her off course. "I'm fine right here."

"Like hell. You're a zombie."

She worked to bring his face into focus again. Even as exhausted as she felt, she thought he was deliciously handsome. "I'm fine."

"No, you're not fine." He came to crouch in front of her, all worried blue eyes, bronzed skin, and broad shoulders. "You need to sleep. Just for a while. I promise to wake you up in four to six hours. How's that? In the meantime, Tabasco will be okay. I'm doing everything possible to help him get well."

"I know." And Samantha meant that with all her heart. If anyone could save her stallion, she believed it would be this man. She pushed at her hair. "Do you have a shower here?"

"Cleaning up isn't what you need, honey."

Samantha's heart skipped a beat. *Honey?* When had they moved from a first-name basis to endearments? "Pardon me?"

He sighed, and his shoulders went lax. "Has anyone ever told you you're more stubborn than a Missouri mule?"

Missouri. She tried to picture where the state was located on a map. All she needed was to get her brain working again. "Not all mules are stubborn," she settled for saying. "It's a myth."

"Okay," he said with a ring of determination. "If you won't go to the cot, the cot will come to you."

In what seemed like mere seconds, Tucker reappeared with a metal-framed bed. A stocky man in a green lab coat helped to carry the contraption. They settled it at the end of the stall opposite the gate, and the next thing Samantha knew, Tucker had grasped her wrist and was pulling her to her feet.

"Lie down," he said.

"Excuse me?"

"Don't argue. If you don't get some rest, I'll call your father to come get you."

Indignation tried to break through the haze of unreality that surrounded her, but the foggy layer had grown so thick, not even anger could penetrate it. "He may come to get me," she managed to grump. "Doesn't mean I'll go."

"You'll go if I kick your butt out of here. My clinic, my rules. You have to lie down and get some sleep."

He gave her a gentle push, and she found herself lying on the mattress. "But what about the night tech? Where will he sleep?"

"It's morning. I'll send Riley to town for another cot. Don't worry. Just rest."

Moments later a wonderfully soft pillow appeared under her head. Shortly thereafter a light blanket fluttered down over her.

"How is Tabasco?" she asked.

"Better than you are, sweetheart. Just go to sleep. I promise to keep an eye on him for you."

Samantha groped with her hand. She wasn't sure for what. She found his warm, hard fingers, and drew comfort from his strong grip. "I don't want him to die. If I go to sleep, I'm afraid he'll die. I need to keep saying rosaries for him."

A gentle hand brushed lightly over her hair. "You've said enough rosaries. Just go to sleep."

"But I—"

"Just go to sleep. I'll pray for him. I don't know how to say a rosary, but I do know how to say a Hail Mary. I'll just keep saying them, one after another, until you wake up."

Samantha decided that sounded really good. Almost as good as a rosary. Her eyes drifted shut. Blackness enveloped her. And somewhere in the shifting shadows, she heard Tucker's voice.

"I'll take care of him, honey. Trust me."

Tucker couldn't remember how the hell to say a Hail Mary. His mom had taught him the words in strict Irish Catholic fashion when he was just a little tyke, but his dad had never been much for organized worship, and over the years Tucker had taken Harv Coulter's cue. He knew only the first few words of the prayer: "Hail Mary, full of grace." And he knew the last few words: "Pray for us sinners, now and at the hour of our death. Amen." The middle had gotten lost somewhere, and that irritated the hell out of him, because he never forgot anything.

He settled for saying the parts of the prayer that he could remember. A promise was a promise, after all. He muttered the words over and over. "Hail Mary, full of grace," as he went over lab reports. "Pray for us sinners," as he drew blood from an equine possibly infected with the West Nile virus. "Now and at the hour of our death," as he settled back in his desk chair with a much-needed cup of coffee. "Amen," when Max lifted his massive head from his paws and went, "Woof!"

"No barking in the clinic," Tucker reminded the rottweiler. "You might scare the horses. You know the rules. If you can't follow them, you'll have to stay home next time."

Max groaned, lowered his head back to his paws, and sighed.

Tucker sighed with him. Even with some sleep under his belt, he still felt fried. He took another sip of coffee and pushed at the papers on his desk. Then he muttered the prayer again, which earned him another bewildered look from his dog.

"I'm not talking to myself. I'm praying. It's a totally normal thing to do. Lots of people pray." He tossed the canine a piece of chicken jerky from the treat canister to shut him up.

A heavy weight anchored Samantha to the mattress, and someone was snoring to rattle the walls. As she came slowly awake, hot breath wafted over her cheek. It smelled faintly of halitosis and chicken, not a pleasant combination. She eased her head around and cracked open one eye to find a massive black head on the pillow next to hers. Struggling to focus, she made out floppy, rust-colored jowls and a lolling tongue flecked with dry drool. With a start, she realized she was nose to nose with a rottweiler.

"Oh!" She jerked upright, gaping at the dog. "Where did you come from?"

The huge beast merely yawned, licked his chops, and stretched out to take up the section of mattress she had just vacated.

"Max!" Samantha turned to see Tucker standing just inside the stall entrance, a glower on his face. "You aren't supposed to be in here." He snapped his fingers at the canine. "Come on. Get down from there. What were you thinking?"

The dog yawned again and groaned as he crawled slowly off the mattress, and then stuck one leg out behind him in a delicious stretch.

"I'm sorry," Tucker told her. "He knows better than to enter any of the stalls. I don't know what got into him."

"It's all right." Tucker looked so discomfited that Samantha struggled not to smile. "My brother Quincy has two Australian shepherds. Tabasco is used to dogs."

"That doesn't mean you are. I can't believe he got in bed with you." Tucker shoved the gate wide. "Out. Shame on you."

"Really, it wasn't a problem." Samantha pushed at her hair, almost smiling again when the rottweiler tried to tuck under a tail he didn't possess to make a shamefaced exit. "How long have I been asleep?"

"About six hours. Your entire family filed through here at different times this morning. It's after noon." He stepped over to place a stethoscope on Tabasco's neck. After listening for a moment, he moved the chest piece to take the horse's pulse. "Good news. He seems a little better."

"Do you think?" Samantha asked hopefully. She got up and stepped over to look at her horse. "Steadier on his feet, maybe."

"And he actually seemed hungry for his grain this morning," Tucker added. His blue eyes met hers. "Honestly, it's too early to tell much, one way or the other. After this crisis is over, it'll be another two weeks, possibly three, before his blood panels will reveal anything conclusive, good or bad."

Samantha's heart caught. "And if they're bad?"

He scowled. "We'll cross that bridge if we come to it." Then, after hesitating for a moment, he added, "But my gut tells me we aren't going to cross that bridge. I think he's going to make it."

"Oh, I hope so. He's a wonderful horse."

"I have nothing on which to base my optimism," he reminded her.

"Will he have to stay here the entire two to three weeks?" she asked.

"That depends greatly on you. When I think he's strong enough to be taken off the IV drip, he'll need IV injections throughout the day. I'll leave the catheter in, so they'll be easy enough to give. If you're comfortable doing that, I see no reason why he can't go home. I can drive out to the ranch to draw blood so I can monitor how he's coming along."

"I don't have a problem giving IV injections."

"He may be ready to go home in a week or so then." He stroked the stallion's mane. "I prayed for him while you were asleep."

"You did?" A rush of pleasure moved through her. It touched her beyond measure to imagine a busy veterinarian saying prayers for her horse as he administered to other patients. It also filled her with hope. In her opinion, it wasn't always possible for man or beast to be cured by science alone. "I appreciate that, Tucker. I truly do."

He grinned at her. "I can't remember all of a Hail Mary, but I said the parts I know."

Samantha was fascinated in spite of herself. "Are you Catholic, then?"

"My mother is. She didn't practice for a long time, although I believe she may be now. But she made sure all of us kids were baptized, and when we were little, she did her best to give us a rudimentary knowledge of her Irish Catholic faith."

Samantha studied him for a moment. "We're Irish, too."

He glanced at her over Tabasco's shoulder, his blue eyes dancing with mischief. "I ne'er would ha' thought it," he said with just enough of an Irish brogue to tell her someone in his family had spoken Gaelic. "In our family, the Irish runs strong on both sides. My grandpa McBride was born in the old country. When Isaiah and I were little, Grandpa would plant us, squirming and kicking, on his knees, hug us up close, and tell us stories about the wee folk."

"My dad's parents were both born in Oregon, but they were Irish all the same, and raised in the Irish tradition."

He checked Tabasco's IV. "The Irish are good, solid stock. Hardworking, and sometimes hard drinking, but I've never met an Irishman yet with a cold heart."

That was true in Samantha's experience as well. Her grandpa Harrigan had loved his Irish whiskey, but even in his cups, he'd always had a gentle hand and a ready hug for his grandchildren.

"I'm sorry about Max crawling in bed with you," Tucker said, jerking her from her reverie. "I took him to dog obedience school, believe it or not."

He left that revelation hanging.

"And did he learn a lot?" she couldn't resist asking.

Tucker's dark face flushed slightly. "Yes, how to count. He totally ignores me until I say something three times."

The honest discomfiture in his expression made Samantha burst out laughing, a great, huge guffaw that came so hard and fast it embarrassed her. She liked this man. From the start, he'd had a way of working past her defenses, and the better she came to know him, the less inclined she felt to resist his relaxed, effortless charm.

That made him ever so dangerous to her still-wounded heart, and she would do well to remember it.

Over the next several days, Samantha came to realize there were certain things in life against which she was nearly incapable of defending herself: kindness offered without any strings attached, dollops of humor tossed in to lighten her heart when she least expected it, and quiet strength when she needed support.

Tucker Coulter offered her all three.

He brought her fresh coffee whenever he was at the clinic, made strong, just the way she liked it. He ordered takeout for her, morning, noon, and night, refusing recompense even when she insisted on paying the tabs. He also made sure the clinic bathroom was kept stocked with fresh towels and washcloths so she could take regular showers. And during the rocky stages of Tabasco's recovery, when Samantha felt sure the stallion might die and wanted only some privacy to cry, Tucker was there with a joke to make her laugh or a heartening prediction to rekindle her hope.

"He *can't* die," he said one evening when a blood panel showed no improvement in the stallion's kidney and liver counts. "I've worked too hard and said too many prayers, damn it. He just can't die."

With that proclamation, he promptly began changing the horse's medications, muttering the names of drugs Samantha had never heard of as he mixed what he called "a surefire cocktail" and gave it to her horse intravenously.

"He *isn't* going to die," he told her again. "Trust me. It's not happening."

And Samantha believed him, even though common sense told her that there were some things this side of heaven that all the medicine on earth couldn't cure. Perhaps her confidence was inspired by her growing belief that Tucker Coulter was no ordinary vet. Each time he studied her horse, his eyes burned with determination, and she couldn't count the times he brought thick tomes into the stall, sat on the straw, and pored over sections of text, trying to devise new treatment strategies. His dedication was truly amazing.

"What is it you're trying now?" she asked.

He glanced up from the book he was scanning. "I've used all the tried-and-true chelating agents, so I decided it was time to start rolling the dice. I'm trying a drug that has been used on humans to good effect. I can't find any documented findings on its success with horses, but I'm still looking, and either way, I think it's worth a shot."

Her throat felt tight and itchy. "So the one you were using wasn't working?"

A deep line appeared between his thick, dark brows. "I can't say it wasn't working, just not as quickly as I'd like. I want to experiment. Are you game?"

Samantha took a while to answer. What if this new drug wasn't as effective as the one they'd been using up until now? She'd never been much of a gambler, and she was especially reluctant with Tabasco's life hanging in the balance. But she'd come to believe in Tucker Coulter and in what he'd told her early on in their acquaintance: that he was a phenomenal equine specialist. If he thought a different drug might work better, she could be signing Tabasco's death warrant if she withheld permission.

"My horse is in your hands," she managed to say. "If you think it's time to roll the dice, then continue to roll them."

He held her gaze for a long moment. Then he nodded decisively. "I think it's time."

Instead of going home that night, Tucker stayed at the clinic, grabbing catnaps on his reclining desk chair, but awakening every two hours on the dot to check Tabasco's vitals or give him another dose of what Samantha prayed was a lifesaving concoction.

Sometime the next afternoon, he sent samples of Tabasco's blood off to a lab for analysis.

"Yes!" she heard him yell at about seven that night. "Thank you, God!"

Before Samantha could leave the stall to see what on earth Tucker was shouting about, he appeared at the gate. "I just got off the phone with a gal at Saint Matthew's lab." He gave her a thumbs-up. "His levels have improved. Not by much, but it's been less than twenty-four hours since I started using the new drug."

Samantha's heart lifted with joy. "Oh, how wonderful! That's the best news I've had in a week!"

"It's a little early to celebrate too much," he cautioned. "I can't guarantee anything yet. But it's a very good sign."

During the long, exhausting hours that followed, Samantha lost track of night and day. She dozed off and on, but never for long stretches at a time, and at some point she moved past exhausted numbness into survival mode, no longer noticing that her body ached and cried out for sleep. What she did notice was Tucker Coulter, veterinarian extraordinaire, who had taken to spending almost as much time at the clinic as she was, going home only to shower and change clothes.

As a result, Max, the friendly rottweiler, who couldn't be left at home unattended for so many hours, was always at the clinic with his master and took to sneaking into the stall to snooze on Samantha's cot every chance he got. When she wanted to lie down herself, she had to make Max move over. He was a huge, sweet, and absurdly lovable animal whose only major fault was chicken breath, after all. So why not share?

As three days mounted into four, and four became five, Samantha realized that she'd come to trust Tucker Coulter as much as she'd ever trusted anyone, including her father. The feeling frightened her and made her wonder if she'd lost her mind. But when she tried to steel her heart against him, she found it to be impossible. Even when he wasn't physically present in the stall, she could hear his voice as he spoke to the other animals he treated, his tone always gentle and comforting, much as it was when he spoke to her.

Several days after she'd taken up squatting rights at the clinic, Tucker appeared in the stall wearing riding boots, Wrangler jeans, a green plaid short-sleeved shirt, and a brown Stetson tipped low over his sky blue eyes. Accustomed to seeing him in a lab jacket, Samantha had almost forgotten how devastatingly sexy he looked in regular clothes.

"You're due for an outing," he announced, his deep voice as rich and warm as fine Irish whiskey.

"I am?"

"You are." He leaned a shoulder against the wall, crossed his ankles, and folded his arms, his relaxed posture at odds with the stubborn gleam in his eyes. "It's been so long since you've been outdoors, you're developing a case of prison pallor. You need a little sun and some fresh air—doctor's orders."

Samantha knew an outing would do her a world of good, but she didn't want to leave Tabasco. "You're not a people doctor."

"True, but I own this joint. That gives me special license. You're going for a ride with me and Max. The horse will be fine. Riley has promised to keep a close eye on him while we're gone, no worries."

When she hesitated, he added, "Please? I just got a call from a very special client. He's an old guy with five acres of patchy sod, two cows, three pigs, a flock of chickens, and an ancient gelding named Old Doc. The horse is eating dirt, and if my guess is right, he's probably ingested foxtails like three other horses I've treated recently. If the foxtails have caused abscesses in his mouth or throat, I'll have to anesthetize him to swab them out. John Sorenson is too old and feeble to be of much help, and I'm going to need assistance."

Samantha knew Tucker seldom required an extra pair of hands. Besides, if he truly needed help, which she doubted, he would ask one of his techs to go along. This was only a trumped-up excuse to get her outdoors for a while, nothing more. Nevertheless, how could she say no? He'd been there for Tabasco, and by extension for her, day after day and night after night, never complaining.

A few minutes later Samantha was in Tucker's Dodge, sandwiched between her chauffeur and Max, who crooked his front feet over the bottom edge of the open passenger window to enjoy the wind in his face. Every time Samantha looked in the dog's direction, all she saw was the rust-colored heart shape on his butt.

"Max has no modesty," Tucker informed her. "If he farts—and he does that a lot—bury your nose in my shirt, or you'll expire from the smell."

Samantha laughed in spite of herself. "With a vet as his owner, I'm surprised he's flatulent. Have you tried putting him on a special diet?"

Tucker flashed a mischievous grin at her. "Absolutely. Pizza, burritos, steaks, hamburgers, and fries. You name it; he gets it. I'm very good at lecturing my clients on proper diets for their pets, but I can't quite bring myself to practice what I preach. Max has the pleading, abused-puppy-dog look perfected to a fine art."

Samantha almost laughed again. Tucker Coulter made her want to forget that she was a jaded divorcée who'd vowed never to trust another handsome man. She was enjoying the ride. The breeze coming in through the open windows created a fresh and clean whirlwind inside the cab that moved over her scalp and face in cool gusts and made her feel more alive than she had in days.

Once at the north end of town, Tucker headed for the rural outskirts, where ranch and farmland replaced businesses and residential areas. Here the air smelled even cleaner, and Samantha drew in a huge breath, savoring the scents of alfalfa and grass hay.

"Good?" Tucker asked.

"Fabulous," she admitted. "Thank you for inviting me."

A moment later Tucker slowed the Dodge and turned onto a long graveled driveway that led to a blue ranch rambler badly in need of fresh paint. Neglected flower beds overgrown with weeds told Samantha the gardening enthusiast who'd once tended the plants had either fallen ill or was no longer in residence.

"Mae Sorenson passed away two years ago," Tucker explained. "This was a showplace when she was alive. She grew the most gorgeous irises on record, and, oh, man, you should have seen her geraniums. Mine are pretty, but they're nothing compared to hers."

Samantha glanced up in surprise. "You grow geraniums?"

"Oh, yeah, and just about every other kind of flower you can name. I have a gorgeous English garden in my backyard, complete with white trellises and wrought-iron benches. Do you like clematis?"

She had no idea what a clematis was. It sounded like a kinky sexual act. "I'm totally ignorant about flowers, I'm afraid. Are they pretty?"

"Breathtaking. I'll take you over to see my garden some afternoon. I hire landscapers to maintain it because I work such long hours, but I still spend a lot of my leisure time puttering in the dirt." He killed the truck engine, threw open his door, and then turned to help her out. "Max, you stay put."

An elderly man in blue overalls, a threadbare red shirt, and a limp straw hat met them at the end of the drive. His kindly blue eyes warmed with friendliness as he shook Samantha's hand. Then he led the way around to the pastures and outbuildings in back.

Old Doc, the buckskin gelding with the sudden passion for dirt, stood motionless with his head hanging dejectedly as they approached his pen. His elderly owner unfastened the chain on the gate and preceded them into the enclosure.

"I'm sorry to bring you out on a Sunday, Tucker, especially when it's not your weekend to take calls. But he's in a bad way, and I don't trust anyone else. I've never seen anything like this. He's eating dirt like there's no tomorrow. Downright strange, I tell you."

Tucker spoke softly to the horse, then asked, "Is he off his feed?"

"It bein' summer, I'm mostly only givin' him hay. He ate a little this mornin', but not much." Sorenson gestured to a pile on the ground nearby. "You can see for yourself he didn't eat a lot."

Samantha crouched beside the mound to more closely inspect the hay. "You guessed right, Tucker. This stuff is loaded with foxtails." Glancing up at Sorenson, she added, "I'll bet you got it from Crystal Falls Feed and Tack."

"Yep." The old man lumbered over to squint at the pile. "Foxtails, you say? My eyes aren't what they used to be. I never noticed."

"Lots of foxtails," she replied. "They delivered a truckload of bad hay to my place, too, but my foreman caught it right away and sent it back."

Tucker ran a hand along the ridge of the gelding's neck. Then, murmuring reassurances, he drew back the animal's lip. Standing at his elbow, Samantha saw pus oozing out over the horse's bottom gum. Further exploration revealed two large abscesses under Old Doc's tongue.

"It's foxtails, all right," Tucker told the retired farmer. "This is the third case I've had." He glanced over his shoulder at Samantha. "Somebody needs to raise hell with the owner of that feed store. I can't be the only vet who's seeing this. Sooner or later somebody's going to lose a horse to colic or internal abscesses."

"Is Old Doc gonna be all right?" Sorenson asked.

"I hope so."

Samantha saw regret in Tucker's expression that he couldn't offer John Sorenson more reassurance. But telling white lies, even to ease a client's mind, simply wasn't Tucker's way. The realization had come to Samantha the night Blue Blazes had gone crazy from the overdose of morphine, and she'd been mentally circling it ever since. If a man was unfailingly honest in every other aspect of his life, didn't it follow that he would never be deceptive in a personal relationship?

A tight, breathless feeling squeezed her chest, and once again she allowed her thoughts to scatter rather than reach the only possible conclusion: that Tucker Coulter, despite his charm and good looks, could be trusted absolutely and unconditionally in any situation. She didn't know why it panicked her to think along those lines, but it did. It was like standing at the edge of a high cliff and feeling the earth giving way beneath her feet.

"Well," Sorenson said, "do what you have to do, Tucker. I know it'll cost a pretty penny, but me and Old Doc go back a long ways. I can't bear to lose him."

Tucker gave Old Doc a measuring look to estimate his weight and then prepared an injection. "I'm erring on the side of caution," he explained as he administered the shot, "by going light with the sedative just in case Old Doc has a weak ticker. His heart sounds strong, but I'd rather be safe than sorry." Patting the horse's neck, he said, "That should do the trick, but he won't be out for long. Once he goes down, I'll have to work fast."

Three minutes later the elderly horse began swaying on his feet. Tucker looped a nylon strap around the horse's neck, then handed one to John, instructing him to put it around Old Doc's belly. "We're going to pull him toward us. All right? That way, when he goes down, he'll go in the direction I want him to."

Sorenson sent Tucker an incredulous look. "I'm not as spry as I used to be, son. I may not be able to get out of the way."

Tucker chuckled. "He won't fall toward us, but just in case, let Samantha hold the strap."

Samantha hurried over to take John Sorenson's place. Unlike the farmer, she had no fear that Old Doc would fall toward her. To stay on their feet, horses had a natural inclination to shift their weight against the pull of the straps. When she and Tucker suddenly eased the pressure, the drugged gelding would topple in the direction he was leaning, away from them.

"Okay," Tucker said. "He's pulling hard against us. Let loose on the count of three."

When they released their hold on the straps, Old Doc went down, falling away from them just as Tucker had predicted.

"Damn, son," Sorenson said. "That was slick."

"Just a trick of the trade," Tucker assured him. "When you're dealing with animals that outweigh you by over a thousand pounds, you learn quick."

He drew a towel from his satchel and slipped it under the straps of Old Doc's halter to protect the side of his head that lay on the ground. "He'll be totally out in a second."

The moment the horse lost consciousness, Tucker went to work, calling upon Samantha to hand him pieces of sterile gauze and antibiotic ointment as he lanced and swabbed the abscesses. She enjoyed assisting him, even though she knew he could have managed just as well without her. It felt good to be outdoors in the late-summer sunshine, and helping the old horse to feel better when he woke up filled her with a sense of accomplishment.

As Tucker cleaned the last abscess, he gave John Sorenson instructions on follow-up care, stressing that the hay should be returned to the feed store and that the owner should be forced not only to refund the purchase price but also to pay Old Doc's vet bill.

"Don't settle for anything less," Tucker insisted. "And whatever you do, don't buy any more of his hay when you're not wearing your glasses."

Sorenson chuckled and patted his shirt pocket. "I hate the dad-blamed things, but I'll wear 'em to buy hay from now on, rest assured."

While Old Doc was coming back around, Samantha followed Tucker into Sorenson's shop, where they washed their hands at a utility sink.

"Thank you," Tucker said as he handed her a paper towel from the roll above the faucet. "Just for the record, I think you chose the wrong profession. You'd make a damned good veterinarian."

A half hour later they were back in the truck, Samantha once again sitting between Tucker and Max. Even with the windows rolled down, the interior of the cab was uncomfortably warm. Tucker poured his dog a drink from the cooler jug he kept on the floorboard. When the dog had finished lapping from the plastic bowl, Tucker leaned across Samantha to riffle through the glove compartment for a bag of jerky. His shoulder grazed her breasts, each contact sending shivers of sensation coursing into her belly. She was glad when he finally straightened. Or so she told herself.

"Ladies first," he said as he handed her a portion. "You have to love veterinary work. Some fancy lunch, huh?"

Max wolfed down his portion of dried meat without even chewing, licked his drool-flecked chops, and looked expectantly for more.

"Oh, no. *One* for you, *one* for me, and *one* for Samantha. Just because you finish first doesn't mean you get more." When the rottweiler barked, Tucker said, "You are so spoiled, you're rotten." He tossed the dog another piece, leaned across Samantha again to return the bag to the glove compartment, and then started the truck. "That's it, you glutton. You won't have room for dinner if you fill up on jerky."

After backing the truck from the drive onto the road, Tucker plucked his cell phone from his belt to order a giant pizza to go, half sausage and black olive, and half Canadian bacon and pineapple, Samantha's favorite. It wasn't lost on her that he remembered. A funny, warm feeling moved through her at his thoughtfulness.

As the truck picked up speed, Max hooked his front paws over the lower edge of the window. Seconds later, face to the wind, ears inside out and flattened against the sides of his broad head, the rottweiler was the very picture of contented bliss. Samantha kept having to wipe flecks of wind-borne drool from her cheeks, and so did Tucker.

"Hey," he said. "A dog is man's best friend, remember? You have to take the good with the bad."

Just then the Dodge listed into a left-hand turn. Max, straining to keep his balance on only his hind legs, let loose with a loud and very odoriferous fart.

"Nasty!" Tucker waved a hand in front of his face. "Damn it, Max. We're in mixed company. It smells like something crawled up inside of you and died."

"It smells like a rotten bean burrito to me," Samantha corrected with a choked laugh, then took his earlier advice, burying her nose against his shirtsleeve until the wind dispersed the odor.

She thought that they would eat at the clinic as they usually did, but after picking up the pizza, Tucker drove toward the river. Samantha hadn't bargained for an impromptu picnic. She wanted to get back to Tabasco as quickly as possible.

As if he sensed her concern, Tucker called the clinic to check on the horse. After disconnecting, he smiled down at her. "Riley says Tabasco is doing just fine, and there's no reason for us to hurry back. Stop worrying and enjoy yourself for a while."

"Where are we going?" she asked.

"To a special place I know. You'll love it."

Five minutes later, Tucker parked at a bend of the stream where huge ponderosa pines with cinnamon trunks cast deep shade over the grassy riverbank. He spread a wool lap blanket on the ground, deposited the pizza box at its center, and then produced a bottle of merlot, a corkscrew, and two crystal goblets.

"You planned this," she accused.

"Guilty as charged," he admitted, his eyes warming on hers. "And I went to a lot of trouble, so please don't ruin it by worrying."

Max plunged into the water, sending up a spray that nearly reached the blanket. Dunking his head below the surface, the rottweiler pushed against the current, sending up a wake behind him that rivaled that of a speedboat.

"What on earth is he after?" she asked.

"Minnows. It's one of his favorite pastimes—that and trying to catch frogs. He never gets anything, but he doesn't let that discourage him." Tucker sat cross-legged in one easy motion, uncorked the bottle of wine, and then handed her a filled goblet. After pouring a measure of merlot for himself, he touched the rim of his glass to hers.

"To good friends," he said.

"To good friends," she repeated, but the feeling that moved through her when she looked into his eyes felt much stronger than mere friendship.

That worried Samantha, but not nearly as much now as it had when she first met him. Tucker was devastatingly handsome and charming, yes, but there all similarity to Steve Fisher ended.

"It's lovely here," she said softly.

Taking a sip of wine, she gazed across the river at a meadow carpeted with yellow dandelion blossoms. Never in her memory had she seen anything so pretty. The sentiment made her wonder if she was losing her mind. How could she grow almost breathless over a bunch of weeds? Maybe it wasn't the scenery that she found so extraordinary, but the man who sat beside her.

"Beautiful," he agreed, only when she turned to look at him, he was gazing at her, not the meadow.

Tension stiffened Samantha's spine and crawled up the

back of her neck. Friendship between them was one thing, but the thought of anything more scared her half to death.

As if he sensed her unease, he opened the pizza box and said, "I don't know about you, but I'm starving. That jerky was only an appetizer."

Always at hand during mealtime, Max lunged from the water onto the bank, braced his feet, and began to shake. Tucker slapped the pizza box closed in the nick of time, then threw up an arm to protect his face from the deluge that followed. Samantha managed only to cup a hand over her goblet and took the spray on her cheeks.

"Damn it, Max! How many times do I have to tell you not to shake right next to people?"

Still drippy and sporting a happy grin, the huge canine lumbered closer and plopped his wet rump on the edge of the blanket. Tucker shook his head as he reopened the pizza box. "Did I mention that I took him to dog obedience school?"

"Yes."

"Did I also mention that he flunked?"

"He what?"

"We had to go three times before he finally earned his 'attaboy' certificate. The lady who taught the class almost gave up on us." As they dug in to the pizza, he entertained her with hilarious accounts of the stunts that Max had pulled during training, last but not least the dog's love affair with a female cocker named Lady. "It was ugly. Lady's owner didn't realize her dog was coming into heat and brought her to the very last class of our third session. Max had been doing great, sitting when I said sit and dropping when I said drop and staying even when I walked away. I honestly thought he was going to graduate with honors that last time around."

Grabbing a napkin, Samantha wiped pizza sauce from the corner of her mouth. "Only he didn't?"

"Let's put it this way: An amorous male rottweiler doesn't sit, drop, or stay, no matter how loud you yell, and it's really

hard to untangle the leashes when two dogs are doing a canine version of the bedroom tango."

She smiled at the picture taking shape in her mind.

"Max got his certificate, but only by the skin of his teeth. I
think the woman passed him in desperation, not wanting him
in one of her classes again."

Samantha thought it was far more likely that the woman
had kept flunking Max so she could continue to enjoy Tucker's company. "Is she married?"

"Who, Lady?"

Samantha let loose with an undignified snort of laughter.
"No, not Lady, the *teacher.*"

He frowned. "I don't know. I never thought to ask. Why?"

"Just wondering." She gave the dog a piece of the pizza.
Max devoured it whole, pineapple and all. "I think it's odd
that she flunked Max twice. He's very well behaved, in my
opinion."

"And the teacher's marital status is important because . . . ?"

Thinking quickly, Samantha replied, "Maybe she fought
a lot with her husband and flunked poor Max twice in a row
because she was in a terrible mood."

"Trust me, that wasn't it. *Max* put her in the bad mood.
The first time he met her, he sniffed her jeans and peed on
her leg."

Samantha shrieked, laughing so hard and for so long she
felt weak. "No more," she pleaded. "I can't eat and laugh at
the same time."

"It's a *giant* pizza. You have to eat."

Max whined pathetically for another offering, his liquid
brown eyes fixed on the pizza box. Samantha grinned and
gave him a second serving.

After they finished eating, they took a walk along a trail
that followed the river. At another bend in the stream Tucker
grasped her hand and helped her up onto an outcropping of
rock.

"Have you ever seen water so clear?"

Samantha was so distracted by the warmth of his fingers curled around hers that she only dimly registered their surroundings.

"Look at that trout! Isn't he a whopper?"

She gave herself a hard mental shake and leaned forward to see. Just then Max gamboled up onto the boulder, bumping against the backs of her legs. Just like that, off she went. Still holding her hand, Tucker made a gallant attempt to save her from falling, but his riding boots slipped on the rock, he lost his footing, and both of them plunged willy-nilly into the water, Samantha doing a belly flop, Tucker landing butt-first.

Water went up Samantha's nose and down her throat. She shot to the surface, coughing, sputtering, and gasping for breath. About three feet away, Tucker, minus his Stetson, treaded water, his hair flattened like a skullcap and droplets glistening on his dark eyelashes. Max barked excitedly from the rocks, clearly delighted that his human companions had finally decided to have a little fun.

"Are you all right?" Tucker asked.

Just then catching her breath, Samantha managed to croak, "Fine, I think, except that I'm sinking."

Her boots were full of water and pulled at her feet like cement blocks. Thrashing with her arms, she tried to swim toward the bank, but she'd never been a strong swimmer and felt herself going under despite all her efforts. Just as the water reached her mouth, Tucker hooked a strong arm around her waist, lifted her up, and swam with her toward shore.

When he could finally touch bottom, he said, "No worries, honey. I've got you."

Still in over her head, Samantha clung to his neck as he pushed closer to shore. Moments later he deposited her on the bank, his arm still clenched around her waist. For a moment that seemed to last an eternity, she stood pressed full-length against him, unable to drag her gaze from his. She felt his heat and the hard planes of his body. Everything within her felt as if it were melting. Her heart pounded like a trip-hammer, and her breath came in shallow, jagged bursts. She was sure he meant to kiss her, and if he did, she would be in big trouble. He filled her with physical yearning that she'd never experienced with Steve. It was madness. She knew it was madness. But right then clear thinking eluded her.

Tucker broke the spell by releasing her. Running his palms over his hair to rid it of water, he blinked as if he'd been poleaxed. He looked downstream for a long moment, then directed a burning glare at his barking dog. "Dang it, Max, that hat cost me almost two hundred dollars. Now it'll end up in the Pacific Ocean! One of these days I'm going to wring your damned fool neck."

Still shaken by the near occasion of intimacy, Samantha released a tremulous laugh. "Oh, now, he didn't mean to do it. He's just big and clumsy."

"And dumb."

She sat on a rock to tug off her boots and pour out the water. "He isn't dumb. I remember reading somewhere that rottweilers, border collies, and Australian shepherds are the three smartest breeds." She stuffed her feet back into her boots and looked up at him. "Don't be mad. How did you end up with a rottweiler, anyway? Most vets I know have herd dogs."

"Max is a herd dog. He just herded us straight off that rock into the river, didn't he?"

Samantha burst out laughing again, the sensual tension that had sprung up between them moments before almost forgotten. Because they were already wet, they spent the remainder of their respite at the river romping with Max in the shallows, throwing sticks for him to fetch, and trying to help him catch minnows. They were no more successful at fishing than the canine had been.

When they were finally back in the truck, Samantha said, "Thank you, Tucker. This has been fun."

He flashed her a dazzling grin. "It was my pleasure."

*   *   *

A few mornings later Tucker brought in a giant breakfast burrito for their first meal of the day, which he divided with a scalpel and served up on paper towels. Samantha had grown accustomed to joining him for takeout meals at his desk and sat across from him without invitation. As they chewed food and sipped steaming mugs of coffee, they each broke off pieces of burrito for Max, who clearly considered himself deserving of his share.

When the meal was almost finished, Tucker looked Samantha dead in the eye, assumed a solemn expression, and said, "You can take Tabasco home today."

Samantha almost choked on a bit of ham. "What?"

His firm mouth twitched at one corner. "His levels have dropped again. He's not out of the woods yet. I won't say that. But he's come far enough to be off the fluids and monitors. You can take your baby home."

The news filled Samantha with gladness but also with a strange, inexplicable sense of loss. Her time with Tucker was almost over. Despite all her efforts not to, she'd come to enjoy being with him, maybe even to need being with him. Sharing simple meals like this one. Watching him as he pored over medical tomes. Working beside him as he treated Tabasco. Once she returned to the ranch, she'd see him only briefly when he came out to check on her horse. She wasn't sure why that made her so sad, only that it did, and the realization made her feel all mixed-up inside.

She carefully set down her cup of coffee, removed the paper napkin from her lap, and pushed to her feet. She couldn't speak past the huge lump that had come into her throat. Before she embarrassed herself, she fled the office and ran to the bathroom, the only place in the clinic where she could hide behind a locked door.

Once there, she sat on the commode, still struggling against tears, her emotions in such a tangle that she couldn't make sense of them. She was delighted that Tabasco had improved enough to go home. She was absolutely *overjoyed*, in fact. For days on end she'd spent nearly every moment frantically praying he wouldn't die. So why did she feel this overpowering urge to cry? It was silly. No, more than silly, it was *stupid*.

Tucker tried to concentrate on his work. Tabasco wasn't the only sick horse in his clinic, after all. He had a mare with colic and had to periodically put her on a stomach pump to infuse her belly with special fluids in an attempt to break up the blockage in her upper intestine. He also had two post-ops, one who'd needed a tendon repair and another who'd gotten tangled in barbed wire, cutting up its legs.

As Tucker paced the hall, he told himself he couldn't, absolutely *couldn't,* linger outside the restroom, wondering if Samantha was all right. But she'd been in there for thirty minutes. He wondered if she was crying and could only shake his head at the thought. He'd delivered good news. He had expected her to jump up and down with joy. Instead she'd turned white as a sheet.

Females. He would never understand them. His mother, his sister, and all his brothers' wives occasionally baffled him to the point where he could only scratch his head. They didn't see the world the way men did; that was for damned sure.

As Tucker worked with the colicky mare, he wondered who'd come up with the phrase "the war between the sexes." It wasn't a battle to be waged, but a mystery to be solved, and he had a feeling few men succeeded at the task.

Maybe that was a good thing. If the world were made up of only left-brain thinkers, there might be no poetry or great pieces of art or delicate china, and Tucker needed beautiful things in his life almost as much as he did the analytical and scientific.

Riley, the senior tech, came into the stall where Tucker

was working. He hemmed and hawed for a moment, and then he finally said, "Ms. Harrigan has been in the john for over half an hour. I need to take a leak."

Tucker looked up from where he was crouched near the mare. "You've got the same equipment I do, Riley. Step out behind the building."

"What if someone sees me?"

"If you're not smart enough to make sure no one sees you, what are you doing working as a tech in my clinic?"

Riley rolled his eyes but nevertheless exited the building, leaving Tucker to regret almost snapping the man's head off. Still, it was no big deal that the restroom had been occupied for thirty minutes. No female techs were working a shift, and Samantha surely deserved the same consideration that she'd so readily shown to others.

Tucker couldn't count the times he'd heard her ask everyone in the building if they needed to use the facility before she grabbed a quick shower. He'd also heard her offer to help the technicians with the more menial tasks. She'd cleaned stalls, forked hay, washed out water troughs, assisted with feedings, and all but taken over the coffee counter, making sure a fresh pot of java was always available and sometimes even making the rounds with cups filled to the brim, fixed just as each technician liked it.

If she wanted to hog the restroom for a few minutes, she'd earned the privilege.

Tucker finished what he was doing and descended on the john. But when he stood in front of the door, he couldn't bring himself to knock. She would come out when she was ready. All she needed was a little time away from prying eyes, and he respected that.

Some news flash that was. He'd come to respect almost everything about her.

He remembered coming upon her in the middle of the night as she knelt in the straw by her cot, saying a rosary. He recalled walking in another time to find her sharing that same narrow cot with Max, her slender body curled around the dog's massive shape to make room for two. He thought of the many times over the last few days that she'd shared her food with the silly dog as well, one bite for herself, one bite for Max, each offering followed by a light pat on the rottweiler's broad head.

She was a gentle creature, his Samantha, and as sweet as they came. She loved animals with a depth and constancy that made him almost jealous, because he'd developed a yearning to have her look at him that way.

I'm in love with her. It hit him like a brick between the eyes. After all these years it had finally happened. For the life of him, he couldn't say how, exactly. It sure as hell hadn't gone according to his plan, which involved months of dating and lots of romantic evenings so he could try a woman on for size. He'd never even kissed Samantha, let alone been intimate with her. And they'd never had a long conversation, sharing their thoughts on life, either. He'd always considered that to be an absolute must. You had to know a person before you could love her, right?

Only he'd fallen for her anyway. The soft curve of her lips right before she smiled. The pain in her lovely brown eyes when her heart was breaking. The way she counted off Hail Marys on her fingertips when she was too busy to sit in the corner with her beads. The light, gentle way she patted Max's head and the soft murmur of her voice.

He supposed he did know her, in a way, perhaps better than he might have come to know her in a dating situation. He'd seen her in good moments and in bad, and probably at her worst a few times as well. He knew she looked just as pretty with straw in her hair as she did coming fresh from the clinic shower with her clothes stuck to her damp skin and long curls hanging in wet ribbons over her shoulders. He had also come to understand on a purely emotional level that had nothing to do with reason or logic that she was everything he'd ever wanted in a woman.

Only where was the magic? Tucker had watched all his brothers fall in love, and to a man, they'd gone around in happy dazes with goofy grins on their faces, barely hearing when they were spoken to and replying in fits and starts, their minds clearly elsewhere. Tucker didn't have an urge to grin. Instead he felt as if his stomach were a wet rag being wrung out by brutal fists.

She didn't love him back. That was the bottom line. Sometimes he wasn't even sure if she saw him as a man. He was just Tucker Coulter, the vet. And whenever he dared to step over that invisible line, trying to take their relationship to a deeper level, she withdrew from him. That day by the river when he'd almost kissed her, she'd gone as tense as a coiled spring.

When forty-five minutes had passed, Tucker returned to the restroom door and rapped his knuckles on the wood.

"Samantha, are you all right?"

To his surprise, the door swung open, and the next thing he knew his arms were full of delicious feminine softness that smelled faintly of dog because she'd shared her bed with Max again last night.

"Thank you, Tucker," she whispered fiercely against his collarbone. "Thank you so much for all that you've done."

At the back of Tucker's mind, he knew and accepted that she clung to him only out of gratitude. But another part of him grabbed hold of the moment, and he gathered her close against him, acutely aware of how she felt in his arms. *Right, absolutely right.* He wanted the seconds to last forever. He wanted to believe that she felt some small measure of affection for him.

Then she drew away, and the moment was gone. Rubbing beneath tear-swollen eyes with quivering fingertips, she smiled tremulously up at him. "I'm sorry. I feel like an idiot. I don't know what's wrong with me."

There was nothing wrong with her, not as far as he could see, but that was a thought better left unspoken.

"Tabasco isn't completely out of the woods," he reminded her. "I just think he's strong enough to go home now."

She nodded that she understood, but Tucker wasn't sure she heard him. He could only hope that she wasn't setting herself up for a devastating disappointment.

He hoped he wasn't, either.

Chapter Twelve

By late afternoon Samantha and Tabasco were back at Sage Creek Ranch and settled in. The first thing she did after seeing to her sick stallion's comfort was make her rounds of the stable, greeting every horse, and then staying for a bit to make each animal feel special.

"When you run out of horses," Kyle said to her over a gate, "I'll take one of those hugs. I've missed you, too."

For once Kyle's manner failed to make Samantha bristle. As was often the case, it wasn't so much what the man said, but how he said it that bothered her. But she was far too distracted right then by mixed emotions to pay him any mind. She was delighted to have Tabasco home again, but also sad because her time with Tucker had ended.

"And I just might give you one," she popped back. "I've missed you, too. Thanks for helping Jerome hold down the fort while I was gone."

When Samantha reached Blue Blazes's stall, her heart went still and quiet. She opened the gate and stepped inside, her gaze immediately shifting to the scabbed-over lacerations on his black legs. The stallion whickered and bobbed his noble head as he moved toward her. Samantha stepped in to hug the horse's neck.

"Oh, Blue," was all she said. It was enough. Anything else

that needed saying came from her heart, and Blue heard the message.

"Close call, huh?"

Samantha glanced over her shoulder. Carrie stood outside the gate. In addition to wearing her hair curled and loose, the stable hand had frosted the honey brown strands with blond since Samantha had last seen her. On the right woman it would have been becoming, but on Carrie it only looked brassy and pathetically feminine in contrast to her masculine visage.

"Yes, it was a very close call." Samantha left her stallion to join Carrie at the barrier. "And even though Tucker Coulter is a fabulous vet, Tabasco could still die. I'm praying not, but we're taking it day by day."

"Do you have any idea how it happened? I heard—" Carrie broke off and shrugged. "Well, what I heard didn't make a whole lot of sense. The police said Blue was given morphine and Tabasco arsenic."

"The police?" Samantha hadn't been told that the police had been notified. But of course they would have been. Her father had probably called them. Thinking back, she could only wonder why she hadn't thought to do it herself. Her only excuse was that she'd been so worried about Tabasco that she'd been able to think of little else.

"Yeah, they came out the next morning," Carrie told her. "It was kind of creepy, actually. They made all of us feel like criminals."

Samantha patted Carrie's hand where it rested atop the gate. "I'm sorry. I'm sure they didn't intend to make you feel that way."

"Feel what way?"

Both women turned to look at Kyle, who was walking toward them. "Carrie was just saying that the cops made all of you feel like criminals when they came out to investigate the poisonings."

"I didn't feel like a criminal," Kyle said, drawing to a stop at Carrie's side. "I think their hunch is absolutely right, that teenagers did it."

"Teenagers?" Samantha repeated. "What makes them think that?"

"An adult would have done a better job of it," Kyle replied. "Two different substances, neither in large enough quantity to be deadly. Sounds like kids to me. They took some herbicide from Dad's gardening supplies and a few morphine tablets from Grandma's medicine cabinet, being careful not to take so much that anyone would notice." Kyle shrugged. "It smacks of teenagers out to do mischief."

Samantha hadn't considered the possibility. The theory made sense, she supposed. Maybe she'd been totally off base to suspect Steve.

"I'm sure the authorities will do their best to get to the bottom of it," she finally said. "We just have to make sure it doesn't happen again. During the day, keep a close eye out for anything suspicious."

Kyle held up a hand. "We've already been through the drill a dozen times with Jerome and your dad. Examine the feed as we measure it out. Check the hay for any kind of powder, and smell a handful to make sure it hasn't been sprayed. And above all, yell to high heaven if we see a stranger skulking around the stables."

Samantha nodded her approval. "Exactly. We're also locking up tight in the evening and arming the security system. If anyone tries to enter the building or a stall from outside, the siren will go off."

"It won't happen again," Kyle said confidently. He winked at Samantha. "School has started back up. The long, boring days of late August have come to an end, and most kids are busy now at night doing homework, not going out after dark to look for trouble."

"School has started?" Samantha hadn't realized so many days had passed. "Labor Day already came and went?"

"Yeah," Kyle said with a laugh. "And with you gone, none

of us got Monday off, let alone the weekend. Hello? Earth to Samantha. It's Thursday, September seventh."

Samantha felt awful about depriving all her employees of the holiday off with their families. Even worse, she felt guilty about Tucker, who had worked both days and nights over Labor Day weekend.

She tried to tell herself that it would be just as he had predicted, a debt she would handsomely repay when she wrote out the check to cover his bill. But deep in her heart she knew Tucker hadn't done it for the money. He'd done it because he cared, not only about Tabasco but about her as well.

"You okay?" Kyle asked.

Samantha jerked and refocused. "Yes. I'm fine. Just very sorry that this mess has been such a burden on all of you."

Kyle laughed again. "Not a problem. I, for one, kind of like having you in my debt."

Carrie gazed sadly at Blue, then straightened her shoulders. "I was glad to be here when you most needed me," she said. Then, glancing at her watch, she added, "I'd better get cracking if I hope to finish up before quitting time."

Kyle stared after Carrie as she left to resume her work. "Isn't she a sight?"

Samantha turned to watch Carrie walk away. "I'm sorry?"

He flapped a hand near his head. "All the goop on her face and now the blond hair. She looks like a linebacker in drag."

It was a fairly accurate description, and for that reason it galled Samantha all the more to hear it said aloud.

At five o'clock that afternoon, Samantha's father and eldest brother stopped in to say good-bye. They were headed out for tomorrow's horse auction at the outskirts of Bend, an annual event on the second Friday of each September that Samantha had totally forgotten. Not only would they sell some of their horses, but they'd also be on the lookout for new mares, a constant necessity in their business.

"I hate to leave you," her father confessed as he hugged Samantha tight.

"Don't be silly," she said, looping both arms around his neck. "It's only forty miles away, and you have no choice but to go. A good share of your annual gross comes to you at that auction, and you need some new blood in your stables as well." She leaned back within the circle of his embrace to grin up at him. "Keep your eyes open for me, too. I'd love to get my hands on a nice black mare."

"It's just such a bad time." Frank pressed his cheek to the top of her head. "With all that's happened, I hate being gone overnight."

"I'll have Jerome," she reminded him. "And if, by chance, I need you, you'll only be a half hour away. I've got your cell phone number memorized."

"Mine, too, I hope."

"Of course, yours," she said, giving Clint a hug. "Not that I'll need to call either one of you. Tabasco is on the mend. Tucker will be out tomorrow morning, bright and early, to get another blood sample. Jerome and I will arm the security system before lights-out and be safe as two bugs in a rug."

"You'll be stayin' here with Jerome, then?" her father asked hopefully.

For just an instant Samantha resented the question. She was perfectly capable of spending a night alone in her own house when her father was away on business. But she saw the genuine concern in his eyes, and she swallowed her pride.

"Absolutely. My bedroll is already on his couch. I won't even be going home to eat. A pot of his famous Blue Buzzard Ranch chili is simmering on the stove."

"Blue Buzzard chili?" Frank's eyebrows rose. "Well, hell, that settles it then. I ain't leavin'."

Samantha laughed. "Sucks to be you. I'm going to have two heaping bowlfuls and hot corn bread slathered with butter."

"You'd better have plenty of antacids on hand," Clint cautioned.

Samantha had not been cursed with a sensitive stomach. She'd loved Jerome's Blue Buzzard chili since she was knee-high to a tall grasshopper. "I'll devour it and sleep like a baby after I beat the pants off of him at canasta."

In truth Samantha planned to fall into an exhaustion-induced coma the moment she went upstairs, but she didn't think it necessary to tell her father that.

"Well, then," Frank said, rubbing a hand over his mouth. A twinkle crept into his dark eyes. "After eatin' two bowls of Blue Buzzard chili, you'll have a built-in weapon if Steve comes around. You can just breathe on the bastard and knock him flat."

Samantha was still smiling when she stood outside the stable to wave her father and brother off. Quincy, Parker, and Zach would also be gone for the night. The horse auction was always a family affair. Samantha knew that employees would be on shift around the clock at each of the other ranches, but it was still a lonely feeling, knowing that all her family would be gone until sometime late tomorrow. She rubbed her arms, chilled despite the warmth of the late-summer evening.

As always, Samantha thoroughly relished every bite of Jerome's famous chili. He guarded the recipe as jealously as a leprechaun a treasure of gold, and she couldn't rightly blame him. Big, tender chunks of beef, infused with homemade sauce, all but melted on her tongue. Jerome sat beside her at the counter, his elbow almost touching hers.

"I love this stuff," Samantha finally said to break a silence that didn't really need to be broken. She turned to regard his face, which had grown a little more wrinkled and ever dearer with each passing year. "One of these days I'm going to hog-tie you and jab you with pins until you give me the recipe."

"Maybe I'll leave it to you in my will," he drawled between slurps.

"Yeah, right. It isn't written down anywhere."

"How do you know?"

She sent him a sidelong glance. "Because I looked in your recipe box. You'll get old and die, and all I'll have to go on is memory."

"You went through my recipe box?"

"Yes. Who's Moony?"

Samantha had come across the name in a letter Jerome had stuffed into the soup section. She'd skimmed only a few lines before she realized it was a love letter and stopped reading.

"You little whippersnapper." His eyebrows slowly arched. "You got no business snooping in my recipe box."

Samantha struggled not to smile. "I wasn't snooping, Jerome. I was looking for your chili recipe." She lost the battle and grinned broadly. "I never expected to find a love letter tucked behind a split-pea-soup recipe."

"I don't have a recipe for split-pea soup. I hate the stuff."

"Oh. Well." Samantha frowned. "Must have been a bean recipe then. The point remains. I never expected to come across anything personal."

"My point stands, too. You got no business poking through my recipe box."

"True," she conceded. "I just couldn't help myself, that's all. It's what you get for having such a good recipe and keeping the ingredients a secret."

"You start with prime chunks of beef," he said, leading her to believe that he finally meant to give her the details. "Then you marinate it for several hours in two cups of nosiness."

Samantha almost fell off the barstool from laughing. Jerome nearly helped her on her way with a jab of his elbow. "You stay out of my personal effects, young lady. You're liable to get an education."

She pressed a palm to her forehead. "Lands, don't shock

me. I am, after all, still innocent as a babe and wet behind the ears."

Jerome's weathered face went suddenly solemn. "That you are, darlin', and just don't know it."

Samantha's mirth faded as quickly as his had. A quick flash went through her mind of Steve dragging her to the bedroom by the hair of her head. "Trust me, Jerome, I kissed innocence good-bye long ago."

As a general rule, everything in Samantha's stables ran as punctually as a Swiss watch. At ten every night, the horses got their last bit of nourishment for the day, three cups of wet cob.

In all the years Jerome had worked for her, he'd never once complained about the extra hour of work that this particular foible of Samantha's caused him. She suspected it was because Jerome settled back with a bowl of ice cream before he went to bed every night, and he figured the horses deserved the same.

At precisely ten o'clock they went downstairs and began to make the rounds, dividing the stalls equally between them. Samantha was pleased to note that her foreman took as long with each horse as she did.

Samantha couldn't help herself. She particularly loved Blue Blazes, so she began her half of the stable at the rear for once, giving him his measure of wet cob first. She checked every grain, the memory of her last night with him still fresh in her mind. The mixture of ground cob was dark and pure. She even ate some herself to be certain. Nothing but sweetness melted over her tongue.

Blue, her sweet boy. She loved him in a special way that posed no slight to the others. There was just something precious between her and the stallion, something she couldn't explain or define, and she didn't try. She loved all the others just as much in their own way, but she adored the blue roan stallion particularly, and had ever since she'd held him, still wet from birth, in her arms.

She spent a few extra minutes with him, which she felt was natural. She'd come so very close to losing him, and would have if it hadn't been for Tucker. As she stroked the stallion and fed him, she tried to think of ways, beyond paying her bill, to tell the vet how greatly she appreciated all that he had done. Because of him, Blue gobbled his cob eagerly and looked at her for more.

"Oh, no," she said with a laugh. "Do you want to get fat? This is it, sweetheart."

The stallion nudged her with his nose, nearly knocking her off her feet. A love push, that was all. Samantha knew these huge, powerful, and undeniably wonderful creatures better than she knew the lines on her palm.

It wasn't easy to leave Blue's stall, but others were waiting. She marked off each stall with offerings of food and affection. As she fell into the pace, which had long since become second nature to her, she could hear Jerome's low voice across the way as he performed the same tasks.

Samantha was tired, oh, so very tired, and looked forward to a night's sound sleep. Even so, when she reached Tabasco's stall, she stayed longer to check his respiration and pulse. All seemed fine. Even the yellowish color of his eyes was beginning to fade, a very good sign.

When she was satisfied that Tabasco was okay, she moved to the next stall to say good-night to Cilantro and her colt. The smell hit her full in the face before she actually saw the horses. Blood, feces. The walls of the enclosure were covered. Disbelieving, Samantha threw the gate wide, ran inside, and stood over her horses, who had already gone down. She looked at them, and then she screamed.

Jerome came running. When he braked to a stop inside the stall, he cried, "Oh, sweet Jesus!"

Everything after that was a blur. Samantha went to her knees, turning to first one horse and then the other. They were still alive, but just barely.

"Call Tucker!" she cried. "Hurry, Jerome! Oh, my God, oh, my *God.*"

Tucker arrived twenty minutes after he received Jerome's call. No matter that he'd broken all the speed limits in excess of thirty miles an hour. When he stepped into Cilantro's stall, the smell of imminent death surrounded him. He did his thing—all that he'd been trained to do, checking for and finding clinical evidence of damaged microvascular integrity, severe colic, hypovolemic shock, dehydration, and cardiovascular collapse. Working like a dervish, he started IV fluids, gave injections, ran stomach tubes down the horses' throats to flood their stomachs with GI protectants, and prayed that something, anything, might work. But in the end, there were no miracles in his black satchel, only useless concoctions that were no defense against huge doses of poison.

Emptying himself as most humans and animals did at the last, the colt died first. As death claimed him, Samantha started to wail as if she were demented. Cilantro raised her head to sniff her dead baby, and then, despite the injections Tucker frantically pumped into her bloodstream, the mare lay down her head and expelled her final breath.

For Tucker, Cilantro's passing marked the end of a battle barely fought. If only Samantha or Jerome had noticed the sick horses earlier. If only he'd had a little more time, he might have been able to save them. It was such a horrible thing to stand over them now, knowing his medicines had failed them.

That was the way of it for a vet, he reminded himself. Sometimes he won the battle, and sometimes he didn't. He couldn't give up the fight simply because the failures were so devastating.

"Noooo!" Samantha cried when she realized Cilantro was dead. "Noooooo!"

Tucker had never heard such pain in a scream, and he

prayed he never would again. It went on and on. She knelt over the dead horses with her head thrown back, her neck muscles distended, her hands knotted into fists. Tucker actually feared for her, the noise was so awful, bouncing off the interior walls of the huge arena like an echo in a canyon.

When she stopped screaming, the expression on her small face went absolutely blank. She had lost all her color. Her eyes were as lifeless as the animals that lay in front of her. She pushed jerkily to her feet.

"Jerome," she whispered. "I have to go to the house. Arm the system the moment I've left the building. Don't go upstairs. Don't sleep. Watch the others until I come back. If one of them even starts to act sick, call Tucker."

It was then that Tucker realized she had gone completely over the edge. He was standing right in front of her.

"Samantha?"

She left the stall as if she didn't hear him. He looked questioningly at Jerome. "Where's she going?"

In a choked voice, the old foreman said, "I don't rightly know, son." And then he went back to staring at the horses, his shoulders jerking with sobs he refused to release.

The horses were indeed a terrible sight. Tucker didn't need lab reports this time to tell him that the animals had been poisoned, but dimly he realized he would need blood and tissue samples nevertheless. The cops had laid the last poisonings off on kids, but there would be no shrugging these deaths off as a prank. A serious crime had been committed. Very valuable horses had perished. Insurance companies would be involved. Tucker would have to file a detailed report, and he would need clinical evidence to back it up.

He bent to his task, thankful, at least, that Samantha wasn't there to watch. As he worked, he heard Jerome outside the stall, gagging. Tucker had long since learned to distance himself, to see yet not see. He did what he had to do as quickly and neatly as possible, then put the samples into marked plastic bags, covered the mutilated horses with saddle blankets, and hurried into the arena restroom to wash his hands before he went after Samantha.

As he left the stable, a killing rage welled within him. Now he understood Clint Harrigan's furious outburst the night Blue Blazes had been doped with morphine. Tucker wanted to kill the son of a bitch who'd done this. *Arsenic.* The smell of death followed him out into the summer night, making him want to vomit.

Samantha drew the shotgun from her kitchen broom closet. She kept the weapon loaded and near at hand for snakes, and tonight she planned to kill the biggest of them all. Her hands shook as she worked the lever action and heard the satisfying click of a cartridge being shoved home. She didn't know where Steve Fisher was, but she meant to find him. And when she did, the walls of his hidey-hole would be as bright with blood as Cilantro's stall.

It wasn't about the law, or right and wrong anymore. Not to her. It was about protecting her own. Yes, they were only horses. But damn it, they were so much more than that. Did he think they had no feelings, that they were incapable of suffering? He was going to pay for this—oh, yes, he was going to pay. She imagined how he might look when he realized he was facing death, and in her mind, she grinned and pulled the trigger.

She was startled to meet Tucker on the porch. He loomed like a tree in her path, his chiseled face and broad shoulders limned in gold by the porch lights behind her. His stance was reminiscent of when he'd gone toe-to-toe with the drunk. She knew by the determined set of his jaw that he meant to block her path and relieve her of the gun.

"Get out of my way," she bit out. "I mean it, Tucker."

"Sammy, you're not thinking straight right now."

She blinked at the nickname, something only her father and brothers ever called her. "Get out of my way, Tucker. I don't want to hurt you, but I will if I have to. Get out of my way."

"I know how you're feeling," he said.

"*No*, you *don't* know how I feel!" she cried. "Cilantro was Blue Blazes's dam. I was going to name her colt Hickory Smoke. You don't know how I'm feeling. You can't *possibly* know. He killed them! With no thought for the pain they would suffer, without an instant's remorse, he coldheartedly murdered them to get back at me."

In that instant Tucker accepted that maybe he couldn't know how she felt. No one he'd loved had ever died a violent, agonizing death at the hands of a sadistic maniac. The closest he'd ever come to experiencing what Samantha felt now was when he stood over the crumpled form of his sister after her riding accident. In those endless minutes when he hadn't known if Bethany would live or die, he'd turned his hatred on the horse she'd been riding when she fell. If it hadn't been for his elder brother Jake's intervention, Tucker would have helped their dad put a bullet in the mare's brain.

"Samantha, stop and think."

To her credit she didn't point the gun at him. Instead she charged, one slender shoulder dropped to ram him in the belly and knock him off his feet. Problem. He outweighed her by over a hundred pounds, and even though she was well toned and in superb condition, she was no match for a man. Tucker held his ground and caught her hard in his arms. The gun clattered to the porch, the ring of cold steel striking the wood planks with a hollow finality.

"Let go of me!" she cried. Doubling her fists, she swung futilely at his chest. "Let *go* of me. He has to pay. Don't you see? If I don't go after him, Clint will!"

So that was it. Tucker caught her wrists to stop her wild swinging. "You can't protect Clint by going after Steve. Clint's a big boy and responsible for his own actions. Give him a little more credit."

"Steve Fisher was *my* mistake," she insisted. "Mine, only

mine. My family has suffered enough. If Clint goes after Steve, he'll end up in prison."

Tucker curled his palms over her fists and pressed them firmly to his chest. Then he hunched his shoulders around her and buried his face in her hair.

"Sweetheart, focus," he whispered. "Clint hates Steve Fisher. I don't argue the point. But your brother is also an intelligent, levelheaded man. He talks mean. We all do in situations like this. But he's mostly just blowing off steam. He may want to go after Steve. Hell, I'd like a piece of the bastard myself. But if push comes to shove, Clint's good sense will carry the day."

He felt some of the rigidity leave her slender body. "You think?"

"I know," Tucker assured her. "Clint is no dummy."

She started to sob. Tucker slipped his arms around her. He hadn't cried since his sister's accident, but tears filled his eyes now. Oh, how he wished that he'd been able to save her horses. It hardly seemed fair that the two worst failures of his career had occurred tonight and brought this particular woman so much pain. She was the last person on earth he would set out to hurt.

"I'm so sorry," he said. "I am so sorry."

All reservations gone in her grief, she pressed fully against him, giving him a taste of how it might feel to hold her in his arms when no tears came between them. Sadly, that wasn't possible tonight or anytime in the near future. Arsenic wasn't the only poison Steve Fisher had doled out. Samantha wouldn't trust easily a second time, if ever at all.

Tucker bent at the knees and scooped her up into his arms. She fit easily against him. Shouldering his way through the partially open doorway, he entered a brightly lit kitchen with a slate floor, gorgeous granite countertops, and ash cabinetry. An archway led from the kitchen into a shadowy dining room and then to an even darker living room.

Feeling his way through the dimness, Tucker finally

bumped against a leather sofa with his shins. Turning, he sank onto the soft cushions, then shifted the sobbing woman in his arms to lie curled against his chest. Half choking on a relentless flood of tears, she spoke unintelligibly against his shirt, the only words he could clearly make out being an occasional "Steve," or the names of her dead horses. Tucker wished with all his heart for a magic potion to ease her pain, but lacking that, all he could do was hold her tight and hope that his nearness might somehow help.

When at last the worst of the storm had passed, she took a ragged breath, stirred slightly against him, and whispered, "I loved her so much."

"I know," was all he could say.

Her voice went thin with another rush of tears. "Steve knows it, too. Next to Blue, she's always been my favorite, and he knows it."

What could he possibly say to dispel the horror of that? A man to whom she'd once entrusted her heart had deliberately and coldheartedly destroyed two gorgeous, living and breathing creatures to settle a score. No matter how many times Tucker circled that in his mind, he couldn't accept that any sane person could do such a thing.

"She was so special," Samantha murmured. "Truly a gentle soul."

In that moment as never before, Tucker understood exactly how much Samantha's horses meant to her. They had never been mere stepping-stones in a pathway to glory and blue ribbons. To her, each and every horse in her stable was a cherished friend.

"I know, sweetheart," he whispered. "I'm so sorry I couldn't save her. I'm so sorry."

She turned her face against his shirt and began to weep again. Tucker rocked her and stroked her hair, experiencing her pain as he'd never done with another human being. When she finally quieted, he slumped against the cushions and just held her close.

Eventually exhaustion won the war, and she slept. Even though Tucker knew other serious matters awaited his attention, he sat there and held her awhile, savoring the feeling of having her in his arms. Finally, when he could put off the unpleasantness no longer, he gently shifted her off his lap to lie on the cushions. As his arms slipped from beneath her, she sobbed softly, still weeping even in her dreams.

He hated to leave her, but like it or not, he had business to take care of, first and foremost to get in touch with Frank and let him know what had happened. Jerome obviously hadn't thought to call him. Otherwise the place would already be crawling with Samantha's family members.

Tucker returned to the kitchen. After a cursory search of the cabinet drawers that turned up no phone book, he fiddled for several seconds with the portable phone, trying to find Samantha's speed-dial list. No luck. Irritated, Tucker slapped the communication device back down on the counter and spun on his heel to exit the house.

Once outside on the lighted front porch, he bent to retrieve the shotgun. Murderous anger ran cold through his heart as he checked to make sure Samantha had jacked a cartridge into the chamber. *Just in case*, he thought as he descended the steps. If Steve Fisher was still on the property and meant to perpetrate any more mischief tonight, he might meet with a little more opposition than he expected.

After a hurried walk to the stables, Tucker found Jerome still inside Cilantro's stall. The older man sat beside the horses, his head bowed, his shoulders hunched. He didn't move when Tucker entered the enclosure.

"I'm sorry, Jerome," Tucker said hoarsely. "I know you're grieving and need this time alone. But I need to get in touch with Samantha's family, and I don't know any of their numbers."

Jerome settled a trembling hand on the mare's neck. "Of all of them, I've always loved her the best," he said hollowly. "She was my special girl." He lifted a tear-streaked, age-lined face, looking a decade older than he had the last time Tucker had seen him. When he spotted the shotgun, he didn't so much as blink. "You going after the son of a bitch?"

"No," Tucker pushed out. "We both know that isn't the way."

Jerome nodded and wiped his weathered cheeks. "I want to go after him. But in the doing, I'd only hurt Sammy more. That girl has suffered enough at Steve Fisher's hands." He sighed raggedly and visibly struggled to collect himself. "I don't understand this, Tucker. I've watched these stables like a hawk for days on end, and tonight we locked up well before dark and armed the security system. How could the bastard have gotten in?"

Tucker glanced at his watch. He'd noted the exact time of each horse's death and was amazed to see that only a little over thirty minutes had passed. Shifting the shotgun into the crook of one arm, he crouched down to meet Jerome's gaze. "We can figure out the how of it later. Right now I need you to listen up, Jerome. For Sammy's sake."

The foreman swallowed hard. "Where is she?"

"At the house. She needs her family. I have to get in touch with them. I think she should have her father here before we call the police. Can you give me their numbers?"

Jerome sighed again. "No one's home. They're all at the auction."

"What auction? Damn. They must have cell phones with them. I have to get them home."

Jerome recited a number. Frank Harrigan answered on the first ring.

Tucker was about to return to the house to check on Samantha when she reentered the arena. He quickly crossed to the back of the building, scanned the office for interlopers, set the shotgun just inside, and turned the lock before shutting the door. If that bastard Steve Fisher was lurking in the darkness, Tucker sure as hell didn't want him to get hold of a gun.

Samantha looked like a disaster survivor, her arms hanging limply at her sides, her face so drawn that her delicate bones stood out in sharp relief beneath her pale skin. Instead of heading for Cilantro's stall, she began making rounds, checking all the feed bowls for residue and examining each horse for any sign of poisoning. Glad to see her recover her equilibrium so quickly and also relieved to have something to do, Tucker grabbed his satchel and joined her. Soon Jerome was trailing behind them.

"How could he have gotten in?" the foreman kept asking, his voice faint, his expression dazed. "There isn't a door or gate in the whole place that isn't secure after we set the alarm."

Tucker knew the window of time for a large dose of arsenic to do its damage ranged anywhere from a few to several hours. The horses had died at eleven o'clock. It was entirely possible that someone had slipped Cilantro and Hickory the poison long before the stable had been locked up around seven. It was equally possible that the arsenic had been ingested later, as little as two or three hours ago. In short, he had no answers.

"Was the security system installed when Steve used to live here?" Tucker asked.

"No," Samantha informed him. "Dad had it installed right after I kicked Steve out."

"Do you arm the house system during the day?"

She gave him a bewildered look. "Not normally. I'm in and out too often to bother."

"Is there a special place you keep important papers that Steve knows about?" Tucker quizzed.

She nodded. "There's a safe in the downstairs office."

"Does Steve know the combination?"

"Yes, but I'm not following why that's important. He was given any important documents that were his when the marriage was dissolved."

Tucker glanced up from checking Nutmeg's gums. "I

was thinking you might have the security code written down somewhere, and if so, it only makes sense that you'd keep it under lock and key."

She shook her head. "It isn't written down. I used my baptismal date, three/eleven/'seventy-seven. Jerome and everyone in my family know it by heart."

"Isn't it possible Steve knows it, too?"

Her face, already pale, went absolutely white. "He might. He always made light of my religion, so I didn't think—" She broke off and swallowed. "He might know it. If not, it's on my baptismal certificate in the safe."

"Oh, sweet Jesus," Jerome whispered. "How the hell do we change the code?"

"I can't remember the exact procedure," Samantha said. "We'll need the alarm manual. I'll run over to the house and get it."

"No," Tucker quickly inserted. "Tell Jerome where it is and let him go."

"It'll be quicker if I do," she argued.

Tucker shook his head. "No way, honey. Call it an overreaction, but I don't want you wandering around out there alone. He could still be somewhere on the property. I don't think he'll confront Jerome, but he might you."

"He's right," Jerome said. "A man who does something like this isn't right in the head. He hates you. Why, I'll never understand, but there you have it."

Samantha scanned the arena, her gaze filled with fright. "If he could still be on the property, we need to check the building."

Tucker realized she was right. "We'll do that while Jerome goes over to the house for the alarm manual."

"It's in the kitchen drawer under the microwave," she told the foreman.

When Jerome had left, Tucker initiated a search of the stables. He considered retrieving the shotgun from the locked office but decided against it. Weapons had their uses, and

Tucker supported the rights of law-abiding citizens to possess firearms. But he didn't feel comfortable carrying a gun
with murder in his heart. His fists were weapon enough, and
it was highly unlikely that he might kill someone with them.

As if she read his mind, Samantha asked, "Where'd you
put the shotgun? If Steve's anywhere around, I don't want
him to find it."

"It's in a safe place," he assured her. "I locked it up in the
office."

She walked at his side as they covered the stables. Each
time Tucker opened a door he felt her tension, yet she didn't
always hang back, allowing him to enter first. On the one
hand, he wasn't sure that was wise, but on the other, he had
to admire her nerve.

When every nook and cranny had been investigated, she
said, "All clear."

Tucker nodded, and in unspoken agreement they resumed
their rounds of the stalls to check on all the horses.

As they worked, Samantha said, "I'm sorry about my behavior earlier, Tucker. Out on my porch, I mean. When I said
I'd shoot if you didn't move out of my way, I truly didn't
mean it. It was only an empty threat."

Tucker had nearly forgotten the incident. Recalling it
now made him want to smile. If he'd been asked to name
one particular trait that defined her as a person, her inherent
kindness toward all living things would have been the first to
come to mind.

"I knew it was only a threat," he assured her.

"You did?"

She looked so incredulous that he lost the struggle and
grinned at her. "You don't have it in you to harm anyone,
Samantha. I'd bet my life on that."

A troubled look entered her eyes. "I wish I were as certain
of that."

"Trust me. I'm an excellent judge of character." He ran
a hand along Nutmeg's spine, checking for fever by touch.

"I've worked with horses nearly all my life, and one thing I've noticed about all of yours is their sweet, loving personalities. That doesn't happen by accident. These horses have never experienced cruelty, only patience and kindness, and it shows in their manner."

Two bright spots of color flagged her pale cheeks. "I like horses far better than I do most people. Maybe that explains it."

He chuckled. "I feel pretty much the same way. Horses don't lie, they don't cheat, they're eager to please those they love, and if they happen to kick you in the teeth, you were either careless or had it coming. I always know where I stand with a horse. I can't say the same about a lot of humans."

She pushed at her hair, then spent a moment nibbling her bottom lip, which was puffy from crying. "I still need to apologize. My behavior was inexcusable. I went a little crazy, I guess." She shrugged and sent him a helplessly bewildered look. "I've never killed anything. Why I thought I could go after Steve with a shotgun, I'll never know."

"You're under a lot of pressure," he reminded her. "I've seen Clint with his dander up. He loves his sister, and seeing you hurt, directly or indirectly, pisses him off so bad he can barely see straight. I know it must be frightening for you to think he may go off half-cocked and do something stupid."

Her lashes drifted low, then fluttered up again.

"But that isn't the way," Tucker said softly. "We can't stoop to Steve Fisher's level. Not you, not Clint, not me, as much as the thought appeals right now. If we allow him to push us into that, he wins. It's as simple as that."

Tears filled her eyes. "You're right," she whispered, "and I'm grateful you were there to make me remember that." She stared off for a moment. Then she blinked. "From the start, all Steve ever brought into my life was ugliness. That changed me in ways I'm not even sure I realize. You think I'm incapable of hurting someone. But you don't know. You just don't know."

Tucker waited, hoping she might say more. She checked Nutmeg's pulse and then continued. "That last night—when I finally worked up the courage to kick Steve out—I tried my best to kill him," she confessed. "Not with a knife or gun or anything like that. He was hitting me, and when I fell, he grabbed me by the throat to drag me back to my feet." She touched the hollow of her collarbone. "He wouldn't let go. He just kept squeezing harder and harder, and I couldn't breathe. I thought he was going to strangle me."

Tucker clenched his teeth against a rush of rage and pretended to concentrate on Nutmeg's respiration.

"I can't remember how I got loose," she acknowledged thinly. "All I remember is beating him over the head with one of the kitchen chairs. After he went down, I kept on hitting him, fortunately all over his body, not only on his head. Something inside of me snapped, I guess. I couldn't make myself stop until the chair was in pieces and he was unconscious on the floor."

His voice taut, Tucker asked, "Then what'd you do?"

"I dragged him out of the house, dropped him on the dirt, and spit on him." A lost, puzzled look entered her eyes. "I didn't call for an ambulance. I didn't check to see if he was breathing. I just went back in the house and locked all the doors, hoping he was dead."

"Remind me never to get on your bad side."

A startled laugh escaped her, and then suddenly they were both snorting with mirth. She laughed until she was holding her sides. Tucker laughed until his legs went weak and he had to lean on the horse to stay standing.

It wasn't really funny. It was, in fact, the most awful story Tucker had ever heard. But the laughter provided them both with release, and they gave themselves up to it. When they were so weak they could no longer remain erect, they sank onto the straw and braced their backs against the plank wall.

After a long silence, she whispered shakily, "I saw hell that night."

Tucker glanced over at her suddenly solemn countenance, and all desire to laugh abandoned him. She truly had seen hell; he could see the truth of that in her eyes.

"It's not anything to do with being punished by fire," she informed him softly. "Hell is when everything good within you is snuffed out—just gone as if it never existed—and all that's left is pure evil."

Tucker drew up a knee to rest his arm. "You aren't evil, Samantha."

Her gaze clung to his, the expression in her eyes revealing hope so faint it barely shone through the shadowy veils of shame.

"How can you think it's evil to fight to save your own life?" he asked gently. "You were being brutally attacked, and your survival instinct kicked in."

She shook her head. Fresh tears welled in her eyes. "You don't understand. I committed murder in my heart. I didn't call an ambulance. I never even looked out a window to see if he was still alive. Instead I went upstairs to the bedroom and locked the door."

"The very fact that you went upstairs and locked yourself in tells me all I need to know." He paused to lend that emphasis. "You were probably in shock. That happens when a person comes within an inch of losing her life. As for beating the man with a chair, that was a pure adrenal rush coming to your rescue. He'd almost killed you. Somewhere in your panic you knew he'd finish the job if you gave him the chance. It was him or you, an inarguable case of self-defense. Instead of feeling guilty, you should be grateful God gave you the strength to break away from him and the presence of mind to grab a chair as a weapon."

She wiped her cheeks with quivering fingertips. "You think?"

"I know," he assured her. "If you'd really meant to kill him, you would have. You certainly had the chance. Instead you dragged him outside and left him to regain his senses.

I'm not saying you didn't whale the tar out of him, only that you didn't inflict a mortal wound when you easily could have. As for not calling an ambulance, deep down you knew he would be all right."

"I did?"

Tucker managed to dredge up another smile. "Of course you did. Why else would you have locked all the doors and barricaded yourself in the bedroom?"

Frowning thoughtfully, she looped her slender arms around her knees. "I suppose you're right. I guess, deep down, I did know. There'd be little point in locking the doors against a dead man." She glanced over at him. "Thank you for making me see that. I feel as if a thousand pounds have been lifted from my shoulders."

Tucker shifted on the straw. "I'm happy to be of service." He waited a moment and then added, "As for the rest . . ." His voice trailed away. "I know it must be a disturbing memory. You just have to keep it in its proper perspective. You're not evil, Samantha. You weren't that night, and you aren't now. Never think it."

He heard a slight catch in her breathing and glanced over to find that she'd closed her eyes again. "You okay?"

She nodded and made an inarticulate sound low in her throat. "You know the worst part? All this time later, after regretting what I did that night at least a hundred times, now I find myself wishing I'd killed him."

Tucker completely understood why. "Yeah, well, you didn't," he pointed out. "What's more, you aren't going to, and neither am I. When Steve Fisher goes to hell, neither one of us is going along to keep him company."

She sent him a searching look. "You're the first person I've ever told about that night," she whispered. "Not my dad, not anyone."

Tucker suspected she'd kept that night a secret for fear of what her protective male relatives might do if they learned of Steve's attack on her. In a strange way, it helped him to understand his sister, Bethany, a little better. There'd been a time when she had struggled with the problems that came with protective older brothers, and Tucker had committed as many offenses in his efforts to shelter her as anyone had. "I'm honored you chose me."

She searched his gaze. "I can't believe you're not shocked about me beating him up."

Despite the seriousness of the topic, Tucker chuckled. "Why would I be shocked? I think you should have strung him up over a high beam and castrated him." At her incredulous look, he added, "Hey, I'm sorry, but that's how I feel. In my family men don't knock women around. It's a capital offense."

She smiled slightly, albeit tremulously. "If it helps any, I did drag him facedown out of the house."

"Kudos! Details, lady. I'd really like to pound his face in right now."

She grinned and the tension eased from her slender body. "No need. I made him pay. Facedown across the rough slate, over the threshold, clear across the plank porch, and then down the steps. He used to fret every time he got a pimple, afraid it would leave a scar." She raised both eyebrows. "When last I saw him on the courthouse steps, he wasn't quite such a pretty boy anymore, and that was *before* Clint bashed him in the face."

Tucker chuckled again. "Thank you. That relieves my feelings of frustrated anger immensely. It's not quite as satisfying as messing him up myself, but almost."

Jerome returned just then. "What's there to be smiling about, I'd like to know?"

Samantha looked up at the foreman. "I was just telling Tucker about the night I whaled the tar out of Steve Fisher and left him for dead in the front yard."

Jerome sent his boss an accusing glare as he handed her the manual. "You never told me that story. Right now, I could do with hearing it. I want to take him apart with my bare hands."

So Samantha repeated the tale, this time sharing even more of the details. When she had finished, Jerome's jaw muscle was ticking and his eyes glittered with hatred. "I didn't know," he said shakily. "Why didn't you tell me, Samantha Jane? I would have had a talk with him."

"A talk?" She shook her head. "You would have killed him, Jerome. Or you would have called my father, and he would have. It was better the way it happened. It didn't go on for very long, and in the end I handled it myself, said good riddance, and no one ended up in prison."

Tucker wasn't entirely sure that was an accurate statement. Samantha had erected walls around her heart. If that wasn't a form of imprisonment, he didn't know what was.

Frank and Samantha's brothers showed up just as Tucker was reprogramming the security system. Blue Blazes's birth date had been chosen as the new code, six/five/two thousand.

"Chances are, he won't think of that," Clint approved. "He'll try Sammy's personal numbers first, birth date, Social Security number, stuff like that."

Frank looped an arm around his daughter's shoulders. Expression grim, he studied the security panel. "I don't like the idea that there's any chance under the sun he can come up with the code. He knows Blue is Sammy's favorite. How can we be sure he won't try his birth date?"

Tucker stopped programming. "Maybe we shouldn't use a date then."

"How about a number he'll never think of?" Quincy suggested. "Blue's weight, maybe. What do you guess him to weigh, Tucker?"

Tucker cleared the panel screen. "I estimate his weight at the top for his breed, thirteen hundred pounds, plus." He perused the keyboard. "I can enter a plus sign. Should I go for it?"

"What do you think, honey?" Frank asked his daughter. "Can you remember Blue's weight?"

"It works for me," Samantha agreed.

As Tucker set himself to the task of reprogramming the security code, Samantha led the way to Cilantro's stall. Tucker didn't go with them. She had her father and brothers to comfort her now. He was only the vet and, whether he wanted to accept it or not, an outsider.

Chapter Thirteen

A fter only two hours' sleep, Tucker was back at the clinic, treating his patients. Though he'd cut back on small-animal appointments, he still had a few, and today was no exception. After removing the claws of a feline, he carried his unconscious patient to a recovery cage, covered her with warm towels, and stepped to the sink for a tall glass of water.

"Tucker," Isaiah said from behind him, "we need to talk."

Tucker downed the last bit of water, set aside the tumbler, and turned to his brother. They'd spoken briefly upon arrival at the clinic earlier, and Tucker had related the events that had taken place at the Sage Creek Ranch during the night.

"I'm listening." Tucker grabbed a container of yogurt from the fridge, which Isaiah's wife, Laura, kept well stocked. "What's on your mind?"

"Can you come to my office?"

Tucker set down the yogurt and followed his brother through an examining room to the north wing. When they were behind the closed door, Isaiah sank onto his desk chair, propped his arms on the blotter, and gave Tucker a penetrating look.

"I'm worried."

"What about?"

Isaiah rubbed a hand over his face. "I'm afraid you're in trouble up to your eyebrows and don't realize it."

Tucker took a seat in the opposite chair. "Can you just spit it out, Isaiah? I've got two spays and a neuter yet this morning. Then I need to check on a colicky mare."

Isaiah released a taut breath. "Okay, no beating around the bush. Did you fill out an official report on the first two equine poisonings at Samantha's ranch?"

"Of course. I'm obligated to do that."

"In that report, what did you divulge?"

Tucker sensed where this was going. His brother knew him too well. A knot formed in the pit of his stomach. "The horses lived. The cops determined it was a teenage prank. No big deal."

"The horses last night weren't so lucky, and they were very expensive animals," Isaiah retorted. "Have you stopped to consider the possibilities? More important, have you made the cops aware of them?"

"What possibilities?" Tucker asked evenly.

Isaiah steepled his fingers. "Is Samantha in any kind of financial trouble?"

"Damn it, Isaiah. What are you implying?"

"That she must have large insurance policies on most of those horses. Who stands to gain if any of them die? The owner. You should have made that clear to the police the first time around, and definitely have to now. Kids didn't give that blue roan stallion morphine. You know it and I know it. A teenager would have no idea of the effect of opiates on equines. I think it's fair to say most adults wouldn't either."

Tucker slumped in the chair.

"You *know* I'm talking good sense," Isaiah went on. "Anyone who understands the effect of opiates on a horse would have to be someone who's been around horses for years, either a vet or a lifelong equine enthusiast. They haven't doped racehorses at the tracks for a long time, so it's not as if the general public has read about it in the news recently. So how would a dumb kid or an adult unfamiliar with horses come by the knowledge?"

"Samantha didn't dope Blue Blazes. She adores that stallion." Tucker suddenly felt so angry that he wanted to grab the front of Isaiah's shirt and give him a hard shake. He surged forward on the chair and glared the threat. "And she didn't poison the other horses, either."

"You don't *know* that." Isaiah held up his hands. "And stop with the threatening posture. We haven't tied it up in years, and we aren't going to start now. Especially not over a woman you barely know."

Tucker realized the inappropriateness of his behavior and sat back. "I'm sorry. It just gets my temper up, that's all. If you knew Samantha better, you'd never suggest such a thing." Tucker recalled the first time he'd ever seen Samantha, and recounted the incident to his brother. "She put her own safety at risk to defend that poor horse. She'd never do something like this."

Isaiah lifted his hands. "Hey, I like the lady, too. Don't get me wrong. But you aren't that well acquainted with her, and people can do some surprising things when they get in a financial jam. You can bet she's going to receive a very tidy sum of money for the deaths of that mare and colt."

"If you want to discuss this, Isaiah, don't cast the blame in her direction. Samantha is a sweet, wonderful, caring person. She didn't kill those horses."

Isaiah rocked back on his chair, making the reclining mechanism creak under his weight. "I haven't said one damn thing you haven't thought of yourself."

That was true, but there was a whole lot more to take into account. Financial gain wasn't the only possible motive for someone to have poisoned those horses. A sick need for revenge could be just as compelling, and who besides Steve Fisher had a score to settle with Samantha? Tucker had felt her pain last night in every convulsive shudder of her body as she lay sobbing in his arms, and he *knew* she'd had nothing to do with it.

"You heard Clint Harrigan's take, that her ex is the culprit. Why are you suddenly so suspicious of Samantha?"

Isaiah considered the question for a moment. Finally he replied, "The honest truth is, I'm not. In my opinion it probably was her ex, trying to get even. Crazier things have happened, certainly. I just don't see the cops buying into that theory, not without rock-hard evidence to implicate the guy. They're going to follow the money trail, and the money trail will lead directly to Samantha." He gave Tucker an intent study. "You're really getting hung up on her, aren't you?"

Pushing to his feet, Tucker took a turn around the office. "Yeah," was all he could get out. Then anger helped him to go on. "And you're asking me to sic the dogs on her."

Isaiah shook his head. "No, I'm reminding you of the law and your duty as a vet. Now that two horses have died, insurance companies are involved, and the situation could turn nasty, fast. When the cops realize they may be dealing with equine mortality insurance fraud, it won't be long before they note the fact that the veterinarian on call during the first incident failed to divulge all the pertinent facts, namely that the perpetrator couldn't possibly have been a kid. If you fart around this time and don't file an unbiased report *immediately*, you could lose your license. All those years of school and everything you've invested in this practice will go down the drain. There's no woman on earth worth that."

"Not even Laura?" Tucker flung back.

A red flush crept up Isaiah's neck. "That isn't a fair question. Are you actually putting a woman you barely know on the same plane as my *wife*?"

Tucker thought about it. "I guess maybe I am. I'm in love with her, Isaiah. You can say what you want about me not knowing her well enough. It'll fall on deaf ears. I know everything I need to know."

Isaiah rocked back in his chair again, this time almost tipping it over. "Well, hell."

Tucker braced his hands on the edge of the desk to look his brother in the eye. "I'm convinced her ex-husband poisoned all four horses." He related his reasons for believing that. "It all stacks up. You saw how Clint hates the bastard. Well, let me tell you, he's got reason. It was worse than he related to us, possibly because Samantha, bless her heart, never told him the half of it. The bastard knocked her around more than once. At the last, he nearly choked her to death. What kind of man does that?"

Isaiah said nothing for several seconds. "You don't have to convince me that she's innocent. I've just been playing devil's advocate, trying to make you see how it's bound to go with the cops. You *have* to file a completely unbiased report. The cops are going to suspect Samantha anyway. In a situation like this, with big money involved, that's inevitable. It's not a betrayal to do your job. If she can't understand that, then she's not the right woman for you."

"Oh, she's the right woman. Trust me on that."

"Then have a little faith in her. If she's half as wonderful as you say she is, she won't want you to lie by omission to protect her, and she sure as hell won't want you to jeopardize your career. You have to draw a line between your job and your personal life." Isaiah slapped a hand on the desk. "I don't want you to be caught in the cross fire. It's not only you who will pay the price. As your partner, it will affect me as well."

Late afternoon sunlight slanted over the roof of the outdoor holding pens, warming Samantha's shoulder and the right side of her face as she stood beside her father and watched Jerome finish digging a massive grave for Cilantro and her foal with the ranch backhoe. When the last shovel of dirt had been removed, the foreman backed up the piece of heavy equipment and turned it toward the stables. Samantha kept her gaze fixed on the fresh excavation, not wishing to see the mare or colt lifted onto the rear tines of the machine and carried back to the burial site.

"You picked a nice spot," her dad said thickly.

"I think they'll like being next to the pasture." As she spoke, she remembered how Hickory had run about inside the enclosure only weeks ago, frolicking and kicking up his back hooves. "Cilantro loved it here."

"She had a wonderful life," Frank reminded her. "Lots of love and attention every day, the very best of care. Few horses are so lucky."

Samantha knew her father was only trying to make her feel better, so she refrained from pointing out that Hickory had barely lived at all. "How could anyone do this, Daddy?"

Frank looped a muscular arm around her shoulders and hugged her close. "That's a question I can't rightly answer, honey. Some people are just born with a part missin', that's all, and they don't have feelings like the rest of us. Psychiatrists have a bunch of fancy names for it, but the bottom line is, some folks just don't have a heart."

A scalding sensation washed over Samantha's eyes. "What's missing in me that I failed to see what kind of person Steve is?" She sent her father a helpless look. "You saw it; Clint saw it. Both of you tried to warn me. How could I have loved someone who has it in him to be this cruel?"

Frank dipped his head to kiss her brow, the brim of his Stetson nudging her hair. "You gotta mix with polecats occasionally to recognize one. You were so young when you met him, and I'd kept you wrapped in cotton most all your life. I should have been less strict with you, should have made your brothers back off and let you learn your own lessons the hard way. You weren't prepared for the likes of Steve. I doubt you even knew his kind of people existed."

Samantha had thought all the same things, laying much of the blame for her naive stupidity on the man who even now hugged her so protectively. "You were a wonderful father," she murmured. "If you were guilty of anything, Daddy, it was loving me too much. I know it can't have been easy, raising a girl all alone."

His dark gaze trailed slowly over her upturned face. "Raisin' you was the greatest joy of my life. I love my boys, don't get me wrong, but they're a reflection of me. You, on the other hand, remind me so much of your mama. Every time I looked at you, I saw her sweet face. Every time I heard your laughter, I heard hers. Maybe that's why I was always so driven to keep you safe. I failed to protect her, and she died far too young. In you, I got a second chance."

Her father had never before attempted to explain why he'd always been so protective of her. That he'd done so now, and with such eloquence, brought a lump to Samantha's throat. "Oh, Daddy. It wasn't your fault Mama died in childbirth."

"Sure it was. We were tickled pink when she got in the family way with you. But the truth was, we needed another child like we needed a hole in the head. We already had four boys. Bein' Catholic and forbidden to use birth control doesn't mean a woman has to have babies every year. We were usin' the rhythm method at the time." His firm mouth twisted. "For all the attention I paid to her charts and safe times, I reckon I thought that meant doin' it to music."

Samantha gave a startled laugh. "I can't believe you just said that."

Frank chuckled and gave her a jostle. "Neither can I. And there's another count against me, I reckon, never talkin' to you enough about the birds and the bees. Never bothered me with your brothers, but every danged time I tried with you, I broke out in a sweat and felt like a boot sock had been shoved down my throat."

Samantha heard the backhoe returning. In a way, she almost resented the intrusion. This was the first time her dad had ever spoken so openly with her, and she didn't want the moment to end.

"Anyhow," he said with brisk finality, "your mistake in

marryin' Steve wasn't all your doin', honey." He raised his voice to be heard over the increasing noise of the heavy equipment that approached them from behind. "It was mostly my fault. I don't think I've changed much. I still try to shelter you."

"You don't need to change, Dad."

"Sure I do. I fuss over you way too much, and I know there are times you wish you lived a hundred miles away and had your own life. I promise myself I won't call you a half dozen times that day or drop by to check on you, but the first thing I know, I'm pickin' up the phone or buzzin' over here on the four-wheeler."

He gazed off across the pasture. "Bottom line is, you'll always be my baby girl, the only part of your mama that I have left, and the thought of any harm comin' to you makes me a little crazy."

Tears filled Samantha's eyes. As she watched Jerome put the backhoe into reverse and approach the grave with her beautiful Cilantro's dead body draped over the steel tines, she found herself wondering how she could feel such grief and bittersweet joy both at once. "Thank you for explaining, Dad." She brushed at her cheeks. "It helps me understand. From now on, I won't mind your checking up on me so much. I've always thought you did it because you felt I was incapable of taking care of myself."

"Why the hell did you think that?" he asked with honest surprise.

"Look at the mess I made of things the one time in my life I made a decision on my own."

Frank frowned. "You've made hundreds of decisions on your own." He swung his arm. "Just look at the success you've made of this ranch. I'm so proud of you, I could bust."

"I haven't done it alone." She nodded at Jerome. "You cut him free so he could be over here, monitoring my every move and advising me in your place."

"The hell I did," Frank protested. "I cut Jerome free because he's the best damned horseman I've ever known. Do you think I got my start in this business with no help? No, sir. Jerome Hudson taught me half of all I know about quarter horses. I wanted you to have the same advantage."

"Jerome didn't go with any of the boys," she pointed out.

"No, but other horse-smart employees did. Clint got Hooter, Parker got Toby, Quincy got Pauline, and Zachary got Cookie. There wasn't a one of you kids who started up your ranch alone. I made sure each of you had a good adviser and friend to show you the ropes."

Samantha had always known that her brothers had each acquired one of their father's most trusted employees when they started up their own ranches, but for some reason, she'd never put that on the same plane as her acquiring Jerome. She watched the ranch hand operate the backhoe, his every movement expert. "I got the best of the lot, then. Jerome wasn't just an employee, but your foreman, and he'd been with you for twenty-two years."

Frank nodded. "No argument. You did get the best of the lot." He joined her in watching Jerome work. "You're my only girl. I'll always watch out for you more than I do the boys. Jerome loves you like a daughter. He's known you all your life. Helped me raise you, truth told. I knew he'd watch after you and lay down his life to protect you, if it ever came down to it."

Through breaks between the outbuildings, Samantha glimpsed a dark green sedan pulling up in front of her house. "Great. Who is that, do you suppose?" Two men in gray suits emerged from the vehicle. She sent a bewildered look at her father and drew in a bracing breath. "Do you think they're plainclothesmen?"

Frank drew off his Stetson and slapped it against his leg. "Cops, you mean?" He signaled Jerome with a slashing motion across his throat. "We got company," he shouted. When Jerome cut the diesel engine, Frank added at a lower pitch, "Cops, by the looks of them."

Turning to look backward, Jerome straightened on the seat to study the newcomers. "What now? I thought we answered all their questions this morning."

Samantha stared with an aching heart at the mare she'd loved so dearly, hanging like an oversize rag doll from the cruel metal prongs of the lift. There was something so awful about the angle of Cilantro's beautiful neck that she couldn't bear it. She sprang forward to cradle the horse's head in her arms.

"We did answer their questions. Now is Cilantro's time." Samantha sent her father an imploring look. "No more right now, Dad. I can't leave her hanging here like this. They can either wait or come back later."

"I know it's a bad time, honey, but—"

Samantha was shaking. The smell of death rolled off the mare in heavy waves. "No buts. I'm going to bury my horses."

Frank nodded, settled the hat back on his head, and set off to meet the two men. Samantha watched for only a moment, then sought the gaze of her foreman, who hadn't yet abandoned the backhoe seat.

"We'll finish it," she told him.

Rimmed with red, Jerome's eyes held the dry, aching look that came only with deep grief. He restarted the equipment and motioned for Samantha to stand aside. Gaze fixed on her horse, hands folded around her rosary, she whispered Hail Marys as the tines bucked low and dropped the massive weight of her longtime friend into the hole. At the sound of cold flesh hitting bottom, Samantha jerked and felt as if she might vomit. No more tears. Like Jerome, she'd already cried herself empty. But the pain was still there, an awful, horrible torment, perhaps worse now in the light of day than it had been last night.

She collected Cilantro's blanket and jumped down into the hole. After tenderly covering the mare, she said a heartfelt prayer. Then she pushed wearily to her feet, thrust up an arm, and allowed Jerome to pull her up to ground level again. Even as he crawled back onto the backhoe, she felt his questioning gaze on her.

"We'll finish," she said again. "If they insist on talking to me today, they're going to have to wait."

Jerome shifted into forward, expertly wheeled the large piece of equipment around, and headed back to the stable. Samantha watched him for a moment, and then she returned her gaze to the horse.

"I'm sorry, honey," she heard her father say as he retraced his steps to her side. "These gents are detectives. Seems they're here to ask a few more questions, and their schedule's tight. They don't have time to wait."

"Then they'll have to come back," she said, the firmness in her voice edged with an awful trembling she couldn't control.

She felt rather than saw her father return to the men, who stood a few feet away. In only a few moments Jerome arrived with Cilantro's baby, who hadn't lived long enough to be officially christened. As Samantha watched the foal being lowered into the grave with his mother, she remembered him as he'd been such a short time ago, a little guy with unbridled enthusiasm and limitless energy. Seeing his limp form now nearly broke her heart.

She refused to allow the presence of two strangers to interfere with the ceremony she'd planned. Back into the hole she went to cover Hickory with a blanket. Maybe it was silly, but she couldn't bear the thought of them being cold.

Once topside again, she resolutely ignored the watchful eyes of the two strangers. Her father and Jerome flanked her and bowed their heads as she said a prayer aloud and then recited a heartfelt eulogy. When she'd finished praising Cilantro for a lifetime of loyal service and unfailing devotion, she spoke briefly of Hickory Smoke, who would surely have become a champion if only he had lived. At the last, the tears she'd believed she didn't have left to cry sprang to the surface, and she shed them with jerking sobs, unable to finish her speech.

Her father clamped a hard arm around her waist and finished for her. "God, our Father, we commend these two wonderful horses into your loving hands. They were very special friends of ours and deserve a special place in your heavenly kingdom."

"Amen," Jerome said. "If there's no place for them, I'm canceling my reservation."

"There's a place for them," Frank countered. "You've only to look in a horse's eyes to know that. Any creature that loves like they do has to have some kind of soul."

Samantha bent to gather two handfuls of dirt and tossed them into the grave. Then she nodded to Jerome that it was okay to cover the remains. Her father stayed at her side while Jerome manned the backhoe.

When it was finished, and Jerome was driving back to the equipment shed, Samantha stood at the grave for several seconds, groping for her composure. It didn't come easily, but with determination she finally found that zone where she could set her feelings aside, compose her face, and turn to confront the detectives.

Walking toward them, she said, "Good afternoon, gentlemen."

The older man, a surly-looking individual with sharp features and a steel gray crew cut the same color as his jacket, drew back his sleeve to check his watch. "Almost evening, actually."

"I'm sorry for the delay. As you can see, you came at a bad time."

The younger man was blond, looked to be around thirty, and possessed a kindly face. His stance was relaxed compared to the rigid posture of his partner.

"Our timing is never good," he said.

Samantha introduced herself to the older man first.

"Detective Galloway," he replied as he shook hands with her. "This is my partner, Detective James."

"Sorry we're here under such unpleasant circumstances," the younger fellow said, motioning toward the grave. "Our condolences."

"There are a few loose ends we need to clear up, Ms. Harrigan," the senior detective said. "Is there someplace a bit more comfortable where we can chat?"

Even though it was now early September, the waning afternoon sunlight was still warm, and Samantha imagined the detectives were sweating in their suits and ties. "Certainly," she assured them. "Come over to the house. I'll get you something cool to drink."

The cops grunted their assent, and accompanied by her father, Samantha led the way to her home. Once in the kitchen she played hostess, providing coffee for the blond, ice water for the stern older man, and then sitting beside her dad at the table.

"We answered a lot of questions this morning," she began. "Did the officers forget something?"

"No, no." The older man took a sip of water, relaxed on the chair, and actually smiled slightly. "Some more information came to light after they spoke with you, and the case has been assigned to us."

Samantha decided to take this as positive news. Detectives were surely better trained to investigate crimes. Perhaps with their involvement, everything would be resolved more quickly and her horses would be safe again.

The elder detective pushed forward on the chair and withdrew a notepad from an inside pocket of his suit jacket. "I'll apologize in advance if we cover the same ground twice. I've got notes from the officers who talked to you earlier, but I need clarification on a few things." He depressed the button of his ballpoint pen and jotted something on the tablet, underlining it with a bold slash. "As I understand it, you have reason to believe your ex-husband, Steve Fisher, may be responsible for the deaths of your horses?"

Samantha thought carefully before she replied. "It would be more accurate to say that my ex-husband is the only person I'm aware of who might want to hurt me. I've no proof of his involvement, only strong suspicions."

"Can you explain why you have those suspicions?"

Haltingly, Samantha recounted the details of her divorce settlement and Steve's rage over the fact that the judge hadn't ordered a liquidation of all her stable inventory and granted him half of the proceeds. "After the hearing, he waited outside on the courthouse steps. He was very angry and threatened to make me regret cheating him out of what he felt was rightfully his."

The detective nodded. "And that was it, just a vague threat to make you sorry?"

"It was more than a vague threat. Steve is very"—Samantha searched for a word—"volatile."

Her father broke in with, "The man's a violent alcoholic, Detective. During the last weeks of the marriage, he physically abused my daughter."

"How badly?" Galloway asked.

Beneath the table, Frank grasped Samantha's hand. "My daughter has kept the details about those incidents pretty close to her chest. I can't say how far it went, only that I saw evidence of the abuse several different times. Samantha was still tryin' to save the marriage, so she made excuses, sayin' she'd fallen or been bumped by a horse."

Galloway cut Samantha a hard, relentless look. "The time for keeping the details 'close to your chest' is over. Did Fisher seriously harm you?"

"No," Samantha answered. "Never any broken bones or anything like that. I ended the marriage before it got that bad."

"Did you ever fear for your life?"

Samantha's response became lodged in her throat like a large piece of meat she'd tried to swallow without chewing.

She clenched her father's hard fingers, wishing with all her heart that he weren't present to hear this.

"The last night my ex-husband spent under this roof, he got crazy drunk and almost killed me," she said thinly. She quickly recited the sequence of events as she recalled them. She felt her dad stiffen beside her, but to his credit, he didn't interrupt. "Somehow I got away from him before he choked me to death. I grabbed a chair, hit him, and he went down." Samantha chose to skip the part about how she'd continued to hit Steve. That was something she'd never shared with anyone but Tucker and Jerome. "When I felt sure he was unconscious, I dragged him out in the yard, then ran back inside and locked all the doors."

The detective gave her a measuring look. "You're not a very large woman, Ms. Harrigan. Are you saying you hit the man once with a chair and knocked him out cold?"

"He was drunk," she reminded him. "He was already well on his way to passing out."

"So you struck him only once?"

Samantha struggled to swallow again and seriously considered lying. But in the end, the tenets of her faith, which had been drilled into her head since childhood, forestalled her. "No, not only once. I hit him several times, so many times, in fact, that I lost count. I was scared, and my adrenaline was high. I went a little crazy." Remembering something Tucker had said, she added, "I'm not proud of what I did that night, but to my credit, I aimed most of the blows at his body, not his head. I wanted to keep him down, not kill him."

The older man jotted a note. Then he sat back on the chair again, slipping the notepad and pen back inside his jacket. "Did Fisher file charges against you for assault?"

Samantha shook her head. "I was covered with bruises. For two weeks after, I wore turtlenecks under my work shirts to hide the marks on my throat. If he'd filed charges against me, they wouldn't have held up in court. There was too much evidence to prove that he attacked me first."

"As yet we haven't had time to follow up on the Fisher angle. We'll try to put out some feelers tomorrow or maybe Monday to see where he was last night." The detective smiled again, although humorlessly. "If he did this terrible thing, we'll do our best to bring him to justice. Anyone who'd senselessly poison defenseless creatures and cause them to die an agonizing death should pay dearly for the crime."

Samantha thought she glimpsed a flash of warning in the man's eyes as he made that statement, but it vanished almost as quickly as it came, and she couldn't be certain she'd seen it at all. "I agree," she said, "and I'll thank you in advance for all your efforts to get to the bottom of this. Cilantro was a very special mare, and her colt, Hickory, showed great promise. It's a frightening thing for me, not knowing when it may happen again."

"As I understand, you set the security system at the stable around seven?"

"Yes."

"Does your ex-husband know the pass code?"

"No, but I foolishly chose a special date for the code that Steve might know. It's entirely possible he made a wild guess and got lucky—or sneaked in during the day when the system was off to play with the console until he entered the right sequence of numbers."

"Is it your practice to use special dates for passwords?"

"Yes," she admitted. "Special dates are easy to remember."

"Is Fisher aware of that habit of yours?"

"We were married five years. I'm sure he is."

Galloway tipped his head in question. "Am I correct in assuming that the horses that died last night were extremely valuable animals?"

"Yes, especially the mare."

"How much would you say she was worth?"

"Two hundred thousand?" Samantha couldn't readily recall. "Maybe more than that. I'd have to look at my records to be sure."

"Is that how much you insured her for?" he asked. "Two hundred grand?"

"Somewhere in that neighborhood. I can't remember the exact figures on Cilantro. I have a lot of horses out there, and many of them are insured."

Galloway's jaw muscle rippled in his cheek. "I'll refresh your memory then. The mare is insured for three hundred thousand."

At that moment, Samantha realized Galloway already knew the answers to many of the questions he was asking. He was either trying to verify information or catch her in a lie, and she strongly suspected it was the latter.

"Can you explain how it happens that a mare worth two hundred grand, in your opinion, is insured for three hundred? Is there a blue book on horses, like there is on cars, or do you just pluck a figure that suits you out of thin air and insure the horse for that amount?"

Samantha shifted on her seat. Sweat had begun to trickle from her armpits down her ribs. "When I insure a horse, I sit down with the agent, and we determine the animal's value together, using the purchase price and the cumulative costs of training, veterinary care, and boarding. We also do comps, looking at the value of horses of the same breed and of comparable quality and reputation. In addition to that, we figure in replacement costs should something happen to the horse. For example, now that I will no longer have Cilantro in my stable to bear foals, my profits will decrease until I can find a mare to replace her. In the event that I can't find an equivalent mare, I may have to raise a filly to take her place, and in the interim I will lose money every year. I insure a horse to cover not only the loss of the horse but also to offset my estimated losses if the horse is no longer a productive piece of inventory in my stable.

"In short, no, I don't just pluck a figure from thin air. Insuring a horse is costly; the higher the estimated value, the higher the premium. It's only good business to make sure I don't take a huge loss if a horse dies, just as it's bad business to overinsure. In the event that I were ever foolish enough to do the latter, there'd be every chance that the insurance adjuster might investigate the actual value of the dead horse and advise his company against reimbursing me for the inflated amount, so I would have made all those higher insurance payments for nothing."

"So if your claim is accepted, you'll be getting a hefty amount of cash from the insurance company soon. That should be of some consolation in your grief."

"It isn't only about money, Detective Galloway. I loved Cilantro very much, and I've lost a cherished friend."

He nodded. "I understand." He hesitated a moment, holding her gaze. "But putting all sentiment aside, you insured both horses and surely intend to collect on the policies if you can."

A cold feeling moved up Samantha's spine and lingered there. "I haven't had time to contact the insurance company yet or think that far ahead. But, yes, both horses are insured, and I'll definitely file claims. As you say, putting all sentiment aside, I'm running a business here, and I've invested a lot of money in both animals. The policies will barely cover my losses."

"Really?" Galloway raised his eyebrows and chuckled dryly. "I'm sorry, but this is all foreign to me. It's difficult to conceive how a horse could be worth more than my house."

"Cilantro had champion bloodlines. She wasn't an ordinary horse."

"Ah," he said. "That helps to explain it then."

"Explain what?"

"Why you have the colt insured for so much. A hundred thousand dollars, isn't it?"

Samantha had taken out the policy on Hickory just recently, and his estimated value was still fresh in her mind, allowing her to respond to the question with a positive, "Yes."

"Is his value due to his mother's bloodlines?"

"His dam's," she corrected. "And, yes, it's due to the bloodlines of both dam and sire." Samantha squeezed her father's hand more tightly. She didn't like the way this conversation was going. Galloway exhibited only polite curiosity, but the sharp intensity of his azure gaze told her he never wasted time on unimportant chitchat. There was a reason behind every question. "Just in case you're wondering, it's common practice to insure all the foals in a high-end stable."

"Really?" Galloway frowned. "How many foals are in your stable right now?"

"Eight, counting Hickory, the foal we just buried."

"Eight. I see." His frown deepened. "Perhaps I missed something when I spoke with your insurance agent. I thought he told me that you had only one foal covered by an equine mortality rider. Is that correct?"

"Yes, only Hickory."

"But didn't you just tell me it's common practice in a high-end stable to insure all the foals? Yet out of eight you insured only one, the foal that died last night."

"I misspoke," Samantha explained. "I should have said all *valuable* foals."

"So your other foals aren't valuable?"

"Yes, quite valuable. All of my horses are fine animals. But Hickory was a blue roan with the homozygous roan gene."

"Stick to English, please."

"Homozygous essentially means a double roan or lethal roan gene, coming from both his sire and dam. That made him quite rare. Hickory's sire, Gorgonzola, commands ninety thousand a pop in stud fees, and his dam, Cilantro, dropped gorgeous foals, many of which became champions, making her extraordinarily valuable as well. In addition to that, I had genetic testing done on Hickory to verify his bloodlines."

"I've seen lots of blue roans. It doesn't seem to me they can be all that rare."

"No," Samantha corrected. "You *think* you've seen blue

roans. They aren't that common. Grays are often mistaken
for blue roans by amateurs. True blue roans aren't easy to
breed, and blues like Hickory with the homozygous roan
gene are particularly rare because until recently breeders believed that the fetus always died in utero. Only a few exceptions existed, and people were reluctant to try for a double
roan for fear of losing their stud fee or possibly losing their
mare to complications. For small-time breeders, there was
also the financial blow of a missed season."

"A missed season?"

"People with only one or two good broodmares often count on their foals for income. Mares carrying a foal
with the lethal roan gene normally abort approximately five
months into gestation, making it difficult, if not impossible,
to get her with foal again that year." Samantha lifted her
hands. "That equates to no issue from the mare and no income until she goes into estrus again."

"But you've been breeding foals with the lethal gene?
I can only assume you're more adventurous than most
breeders?"

It was obvious to Samantha that this man had no idea
who her father was and knew zip about horse breeding. "I've
built my business around producing fine quarter horses, but
my real success comes from my beautiful blue roans. In answer to your question, yes, I have been more adventurous
than most, I suppose. My father taught me all I know about
horses, and to achieve any acclaim, sometimes you have to
gamble."

"At the expense of your mares? What if Hickory had died
in utero? Wasn't there a chance that . . . Cilantro—was that
her name?—might have had complications and died with
him?"

"In Hickory's case, the in-utero fatality theory had already
been disproved when Cilantro was bred to Gorgonzola. A
wonderful doctor, the late Ann Bowling of the University of
California at Davis, did a study just shortly before her death

that proved that an equine fetus with the homozygous roan gene isn't doomed to die in utero."

"So you felt safe breeding two blue roans together?" At Samantha's nod, the detective asked, "And how about before the theory was proven to be false? Did you breed any other blue roans to have the lethal roan gene before you knew it wasn't lethal?"

Samantha glanced at her father. "Yes."

"What about your mares' health?"

Frank Harrigan suddenly sat forward on his chair. "Where the hell is this goin'?"

The blond jerked at the sudden outburst and slopped coffee on his suit.

"If you're accusin' my daughter of somethin'," Frank went on, "you'd best spit it out, because I'm fast runnin' out of patience."

"Dad," Samantha whispered. To Galloway she said, "It's difficult for my father to comprehend that the general public has no idea of the equine genetics that produce different colors—or the procedures that take place behind the scenes in top-notch stables. You asked a fair question, and I'll try to answer it."

"Please do."

"Before the theory was disproved, the risk to Cilantro when bred to another blue roan was no greater than if she'd been bred to a black. Most of the time when a foal dies in utero, the mare simply aborts. That's no harder on a mare and possibly even easier on her than if she dropped a healthy foal. Second, we aren't backyard breeders. When we still believed a double roan foal might die in utero, we took every precaution with Cilantro's health. During her pregnancies she was regularly examined to be sure her foal's heartbeat was still strong. If the vet suspected at any time that the fetus had died, he would have induced labor, and Cilantro would have been fine."

"Ah. So it was fairly safe all along."

"Apart from unrelated complications that may occur during any equine gestation, it was absolutely safe except for the foal. Fortunately we never had an in-utero death. Long before the double roan theory was disproved, we suspected it was false because we'd had such success in our breeding programs."

Galloway took a long swallow of ice water and then cleared his throat. In that instant his hard-edged expression softened, and he smiled genuinely for the first time. "I hope you'll accept my apology, Mr. Harrigan. I meant no offense. It's my job to ask questions, and half the time they're stupid ones."

Frank sat back on his chair. "Apology accepted."

Galloway directed his gaze at Samantha again. "Speaking of vets, yours is named Coulter, correct?"

"Yes, Tucker Coulter."

Galloway nodded. "We received a fax from him this afternoon—the official report on the deaths of your horses. We found it very interesting. Didn't we, Detective James?"

The blond looked up from blotting his jacket. "Yeah, interesting. And informational." He tossed down the napkin. "I never realized there were horses in Crystal Falls as valuable as yours—or that people actually insure horses for so much money. Famous racehorses, maybe, but not plain old quarter horses."

"There is nothing *plain* about my quarter horses," Samantha reminded him.

"Right. I'm starting to get that." He pulled a folded piece of paper from within his jacket, put it on the table, and slid it toward her. "That's a copy of the vet's report. You may want to go over it later."

"I'm sure Tucker will supply me with my own copy."

"Take it all the same. Maybe you'll find it as illuminating as we did. This is my first case involving equine mortality insurance fraud."

"Excuse me?" Samantha's heart went still in her chest. "Did you say insurance fraud?"

The blond inclined his head at the report. "It clearly wasn't a random act, Ms. Harrigan, and it definitely wasn't perpetrated by teenagers. Coulter makes references to the first incident, involving two other horses, one doped with morphine, another with arsenic. He clearly states in the report that the guilty party has to know about horses and how they react to opiates. It's also his opinion that the arsenic used to kill the horses last night had to be highly concentrated. Where does the average Joe get his hands on arsenic? Coulter speculates that the most likely source would be outdated swine or poultry feed, both of which were laced with arsenic to promote weight gain and growth. The practice has been outlawed here in the States, so far as he knows." He pushed up from his chair. "Have you ever raised pigs on this ranch?"

Samantha's father shoved up so suddenly from his seat that the chair went skidding backward. "All right, I've heard enough. I'll kindly ask you gents to take your leave. The next time you want to speak to my daughter, call for an appointment. She'll want to have her attorney present."

"We're finished questioning her for the moment," Galloway replied. "Now we'd like permission to search the property."

"For what?" her father demanded.

"Traces of arsenic," the detective replied. "The vet clearly states in the report that the horses may have been fed outdated swine or poultry feed. We'll be looking for that, or arsenic residue in the storage areas. We will also be taking grass samples in case the pastures were sprayed with an herbicide or insecticide containing arsenicals."

"You can go straight to hell," Frank bit out. "Not without a search warrant, you won't."

"Dad," Samantha cried softly as she pushed up from the

chair. "I have nothing to hide. If the detectives wish to search the property, why not let them?"

"Because it only stands to reason that they *will* find traces of arsenic somewhere," Frank shot back. "Your horses were poisoned with the damned stuff."

"We can drive back to town, ask a judge to sign a warrant, and be back here before dark," Galloway inserted. To Frank he added, "You can delay the search, but you can't stop it."

Frank retorted, "True, but a warrant will specify where you can search and what you can search for, providing my daughter with at least some protection."

"I don't need protection," Samantha insisted. "I'm not guilty of anything." She moved to stand beside her father. "Someone killed my horses, Dad. I want to get to the bottom of this every bit as much as they do, and the faster, the better. Until the person's caught, my horses will remain in danger."

Frank sighed and passed a hand over his eyes. "All right," he finally agreed. "But you aren't executing a search alone. I'm going with you."

Samantha stood in the doorway. At the steps, her father turned to look at her. "This won't take long."

From the yard Galloway said, "It isn't necessary for you to accompany us, Mr. Harrigan."

"Damned if it ain't." Frank's boots echoed on the planks as he descended the porch steps. "You think I don't watch the news? All you cops care about is pinnin' the crime on someone and makin' yourselves look good. There'll be no plantin' of evidence on this property, I can guaran-ass-tee you that."

Samantha felt weak at the knees. Turning back to the table, she resumed her seat and picked up the copy of Tucker's report. Tears burned in her eyes as she scanned the paperwork. Time of death, probable cause of death, a list of the clinical evidence. Reading the information sharply reminded her of the horror she'd seen last night. As she went over Tucker's concluding statements, her heart squeezed with regret that he'd been put into such an awful position, obligated to state the facts, even if they implicated a friend. She knew it must have pained him to type every word.

With trembling fingertips she touched the letters, imagining him at his computer and then sending the fax, his forehead creased in a frown, his jaw muscle ticking. A sad smile touched her mouth, for even in a report, he was honest to a fault.

Chapter Fourteen

By five o'clock that same afternoon, at her father's be-
hest, Samantha had hurriedly interviewed three local
security companies via telephone and hired Hawkeye Security Services to patrol her ranch, starting immediately. It
was Frank's feeling that the entire property, including its perimeters, needed to be under constant surveillance until the
individual who'd poisoned the horses had been caught. They
couldn't take the chance that someone might sneak onto Samantha's land to spray the grazing pastures with arsenicals
or contaminate the hay storage.

Samantha wasn't sure how she felt about her place being protected by armed guards. Out of necessity, she had
employees coming and going throughout the day, and she
was reluctant to interrupt the horses' normal routines. On the
other hand, she and Jerome couldn't possibly keep an eye
on two hundred acres by themselves, and the safety of her
animals had to be her top priority.

Hawkeye Security came highly recommended to Samantha's father by his youngest brother, Hugh, an Oregon state
policeman. According to Hugh, the firm not only provided
more extensive training programs for their employees than
most, but also supplied them with state-of-the-art surveil-

lance equipment, including night-vision goggles and portable, battery-powered motion detectors and video cameras.

By six thirty that evening, armed strangers had descended upon the ranch and were rushing about, setting up camera surveillance and motion detectors. It fell to Samantha to help focus their efforts on key areas, all the places where her horses might be put out to graze and also on any outbuildings used for grain or hay storage. As a result, she was still outside at seven thirty, walking the property with Nona Redcliff, the security team's senior officer, a slender but well-muscled young woman of Native American ancestry.

When they reached the hay shed, Samantha asked, "How, exactly, will cameras protect this area? Pictures or videotapes reviewed after the fact won't stop someone from spraying my hay with poison."

Nona motioned to a white van parked near the stable. "There's an entire bank of monitors inside our van that picks up images via wireless transmission." She crouched by the equipment that Chuck, a blond underling, had just deposited on the ground. As she untangled cords, she explained, "These cameras are motion-activated. The moment the electronic eyes detect movement anywhere near this structure, the cameras will come on and send images to a monitor in the van. The person watching the monitors"—she thumbed her khaki uniform shirt—"namely me, will determine if there's a genuine threat. In short, Ms. Harrigan, if a mouse so much as twitches its tail near this hay, I'll know it." She swung her arm toward the farthest reaches of the ranch. "Same goes for the perimeters, except that the long-range motion detectors are marginally less sensitive and are also equipped with infrared heat detectors. A rabbit or small dog will be able to cross your fence lines, but any larger warm-blooded creature, animal or human, will trigger the detectors, alerting me in the van and transmitting real-time images onto my screens."

"Do the cameras work well in the dark?"

Nona pushed erect. "After dark, they automatically switch into night mode. The images are weird-looking, sort of gray-green, but they're clear enough."

Samantha could only wonder how much all this electronic surveillance might cost. Luckily her father had offered to pick up the tab, and he had deep pockets. "Well, it certainly sounds as if you have everything under control."

"Guaranteed," Nona assured her. "Well, maybe I should rephrase that. There'll be no more incidents on your ranch unless your perp is someone allowed to come and go—a friend, family member, or employee. That's why we asked you to supply us with a list of all individuals you want allowed on the property. If you've forgotten anyone, just let me know and I'll add the name." At Samantha's horrified look, Nona quickly added, "I'm not suggesting it's someone you know and trust, only that there's always that possibility. All the high-tech surveillance equipment in the world can't protect your animals from an inside job."

"I understand." Samantha mentally went back over the list of names. "Did I mention Dee Dee, our cleaning lady? Her daughter just gave birth to her first grandchild, and she's been out of town for about a month. I'm not sure when she'll be coming home, but when she does, I don't want her to be hassled. She's like a mother to me."

"I'm pretty sure she's on the list, but I'll double-check," Nona promised.

"Where do you want this?" Chuck asked, holding up a black box with dangling cords.

Nona started to excuse herself but stopped midsentence and narrowed her gaze on a green Dodge truck that had just parked beside the surveillance van. "Who's that?"

Samantha smiled. "My vet, Tucker Coulter. He's definitely on your list—right at the top, if I remember right."

Nona drew her two-way from her belt, keyed the mike, and spoke briefly with another guard who stood sentry at the arena personnel door, telling him that the vet should be allowed inside. Samantha considered walking over to the stable to say hello to Tucker, but her stomach rumbled with hunger and she had the weak shakes. She hadn't eaten in almost twenty-four hours. Talking with Tucker would have to wait.

After wolfing down a sandwich and an apple, Samantha was too exhausted to go back over to the stable. Her bones ached, her head felt muzzy, and she could barely lift her feet. The last time she'd slept had been on a cot at the equine center. She wasn't sure how many hours—or days—ago that had been, only that she'd reached a point beyond exhaustion and absolutely had to get some rest, preferably in her own bed for a change.

Fortunately, she actually felt safe in allowing herself that luxury with Nona Redcliff overseeing the surveillance of her ranch that night. Nona struck her as a person who took great pride in her performance.

After setting the house alarm system and calling her father to assure him she'd remembered to do so, Samantha knotted her hair atop her head, poured herself a glass of chilled white zinfandel, and wearily climbed the stairs. Once in the master suite, which she'd completely redone after the divorce to please her own simple tastes in decor, she began filling the jetted tub in the adjoining bathroom with piping-hot water, then stripped off her clothes and flung them over the juniper saddle tree in one corner of the bedroom. A neck-deep bubble bath, white wine, and the soothing fragrance of lighted lavender candles were sure to help her relax.

She sighed and closed her eyes as the hot water reached her chin. An image of Cilantro flashed in her mind, and she felt a brief stab of sadness, but it was just as quickly gone, replaced by a vision of Tucker's face. She thought of how his eyes darkened to the color of blue steel when he was concerned about a patient, and then she thought of his devastating grin, which always filled her with warmth. Then she remembered that afternoon at the river when he'd almost kissed her.

How would it feel to have Tucker's mouth on hers? She instinctively knew he'd start out gently, soothing away all her nervousness before he deepened the kiss. She imagined putting her hands on his shoulders, how all that warm strength and vibrant muscle would bunch under her fingertips. And then she fantasized about having his hands caressing her skin.

Her eyes blinked open. Imagining kissing him was all well and fine, but anything more than that was pretty much uncharted territory for her. Steve hadn't been a touchy-feely person. He'd made love to her as if it were a chore that he wanted to finish as quickly as possible. On her wedding night it had hurt terribly, because she'd been a virgin and wasn't aroused. After that, she'd followed Dee Dee's advice and never gone to bed without first using a personal lubricant. That had suited Steve's purposes just fine. When and if he wanted sex, which hadn't been often, he'd never wanted to engage in foreplay first.

Shame rose in her throat, thick and suffocating, as she recalled their couplings. It was humiliating for a woman to be intimate with a man who didn't find her desirable. Thinking back, she couldn't remember a single thing about her body that Steve had liked: small boobs, knobby knees, and protruding hip bones, which he'd always claimed poked him. And then there'd been his drinking to make matters worse. More than once he'd passed out on top of her immediately after ejaculating.

Maybe it wouldn't be that way with Tucker. He'd almost kissed her that afternoon at the river. She felt certain of that. Didn't it follow that he must be attracted to her? But what if he only *thought* he was and changed his mind after he saw her naked? The possibility made her cringe.

Why was she worrying about it, anyway? *Dumb, dumb, dumb.* It wasn't as if he'd given her any recent indication that he was thinking along those lines. So she shouldn't be either. It'd be awful if he wasn't interested and he realized she *was*. Or might be, she revised. She wasn't sure yet. Entering into another relationship would be a huge step for her, and then there was her faith to complicate matters. Engaging in sex before marriage was a mortal sin, not something she took lightly.

Sigh. Better to just not think about it. Tucker probably didn't even think of her in that way. She might have read more into his expression than had been there that day at the river. Maybe he hadn't been staring at her mouth at all. She could have had mud on her nose—or a string of algae on her upper lip. Just because a man appeared to be staring at a woman's mouth didn't necessarily mean he was about to kiss her, right? *Right.*

After soaking for over an hour and finishing the glass of wine, Samantha expected to feel drowsy, but she didn't. She was so exhausted she felt wired, too weary to accomplish anything useful, but too innervated to fall asleep. More wine, she decided. If another glass didn't help, maybe the whole bottle would do the trick.

She left the tub, toweled off, and drew on a white terry robe before going downstairs. Once in the kitchen, she went directly to the refrigerator, plucked the white zinfandel from the shelf, and moved to the table, bottle and goblet clasped in her hands. After refilling her glass, she sank down on a chair to leaf through an equine supply catalog that had come that day in the mail. She was staring sadly at a horse blanket eerily similar to Cilantro's when a loud knock at the door made her leap to her feet.

A glance at the windows told her it was fully dark outside. She checked her watch, saw that it was twenty after nine, and frowned. Jerome knew how exhausted she was and wouldn't dream of disturbing her unless it was an emergency. A chill of dread crawled up her spine as she went to the door.

"Who is it?"

"Tucker. You got a minute to talk?"

Samantha's gaze dropped to her robe. "I, um . . . I'm not really dressed for company."

"You don't need to make a fashion statement, honey. I just want to talk."

She tugged the collar of the robe close around her throat. "All I'm wearing is a robe, Tucker, and I'm naked underneath."

Long silence. "Totally naked?"

Of course, *totally.*

When she didn't answer his question, he said, "I'm sorry for coming so late. I had to take Tabasco's blood sample back to town." She heard his boots shuffle on the porch and imagined him shifting his weight to one leg, a habit of his when he grew frustrated. "Are you using the robe as an excuse not to let me in?"

"Why would I do that?"

"Because you're pissed at me about that report."

If that wasn't the silliest thing she'd ever heard. She started to tell him as much, but he cut her off.

"Filing that damned thing was the hardest thing I've ever done in my life. You have to believe that. Practically every word implicated you." Another long silence. When he spoke again, his voice was thick with emotion. "I'm in love with you, Sam. I think you already know that, but just in case you don't, there you have it. I'm in love with you."

She disengaged the dead bolt and jerked open the portal. He seemed to fill the entire doorway. He wore no jacket to protect him against the cool night air, only a blue shirt, jeans, and dusty boots. In the glow of the porch lights he was the epitome of tall, dark, and treacherously handsome, his shoulders thick and broad, his tanned forearms, extending below his rolled-back shirtsleeves, roped with powerful tendons.

"You're *what*?"

His gaze plummeted from her face to the vee of her collar. "You really *are* wearing a robe."

"Well, of *course* I'm wearing a robe. Why would I lie

about something like that? And don't change the subject. What did you just say?"

"When?"

"Just before I opened . . ." She saw the glint of mischief in his eyes. "You know precisely when. Did I or did I not hear you say—"

"That I love you?" he interrupted. "Absolutely not. You were imagining things. I am far too suave and sophisticated to *ever* tell a woman something like that through a closed door." He stepped onto the threshold and rested one muscular arm against the doorframe. Even as his beautiful mouth tipped into a grin, his eyes went dark and serious, just as they always did when he was deeply worried. "Please don't hate me for filing that report. I had no choice, honestly I didn't, and I'm sorrier than you can know that the police are breathing down your neck because of it."

"How do you know the police are—?"

"Your dad. He called to give me hell. Well, not really. He was actually pretty understanding after I explained that I was obligated by law to report the poisonings. But he was pretty pissed when we first started talking."

"Daddy always gets pissed when anything threatens me. I hope you didn't take him too seriously."

She thought about grabbing him by the front of his shirt, dragging him farther into the house, and kissing him. It was madness. For starters, she wasn't wearing a stitch of clothes under the robe, and there were still all the dos and don'ts of her faith to worry about. But it wasn't every day a man said he loved her, either, and she was positive she hadn't imagined it.

His gaze moved slowly over her face. Then it dropped lower. When he met her gaze again, he said, "You are the most beautiful thing I've ever clapped eyes on. Have I ever mentioned that?"

And then, as if she'd willed him to do it, he stepped into her kitchen and shut the door. She could tell by his expression that he meant to kiss her. Her heart started to pound. Her knees started to shake. She was finally going to find out how it would feel to have his mouth touch hers.

He cupped her face between his big hands, moving his thumbs lightly over her cheekbones in a feathery caress. When she looked into his eyes, her breath caught in her throat. His face drew closer, and then closer yet, until his features blurred and she could feel his breath on her lips. He smelled of coffee and mints, horses and male muskiness, and fresh night air. With gentle fingers, he loosened her hair and gathered it into his hands.

Just as their lips touched—just as she curled her hands over his shoulders to enjoy the feel of him—an ear-shattering wail filled the room, the sound so loud and unexpected, they leaped apart.

"What the *hell*?"

She'd been so focused on the kiss that it took her a moment to realize what had happened. "The alarm," she cried. "I totally *forgot*!" There was only a gap of a minute and a half before the siren went off after an entry door had been opened. She ran across the room to the panel, but when she got there, she couldn't remember the new code. "The numbers, what are the numbers?"

She felt his chest graze her back, felt the heat of him radiating through the terry cloth. He reached over her shoulder, punched in the new code, and then hit number one to shut off the siren. "Blue Blazes's weight, remember? Thirteen hundred plus."

The sudden silence seemed almost as loud as the wailing. Samantha went limp with relief, leaning against him for a second. Then she turned and pressed her back to the wall. "I'm not very good at remembering numbers."

"I'm excellent at it," he said huskily, "so I guess we're a perfect match."

He braced his hands on each side of her, leaned closer, and asked, "Where were we?"

"I think you were about to kiss me."

"I think you're right," he whispered, and then covered her mouth with his to finish the job.

The phone rang. He jerked away again, his eyes stormy. "*Damn!* I can't believe this." He glanced toward the ceiling. "Give me a break, God!"

Samantha couldn't believe this was happening, either. "It's probably the alarm company. Or maybe my dad. It could be one of my brothers, too. They're all on my emergency list."

"Wonderful." He rested his forehead against hers, the blue of his eyes eclipsing her vision. She felt his chest jerk and heard the low rumble of his laughter. "According to my calculations, we only have five more calls to go."

Just then a loud pounding came at the door. "Samantha!" Jerome yelled. "Are you all right?"

Then they heard Nona say, "Step back, sir. We're going in."

Samantha wondered if she'd been born under an unlucky star. She was twenty-nine years old, and for the first time in her life her body had been throbbing with physical desire. Now it seemed as if half the population of Crystal Falls was either phoning or knocking on her door.

"Well, hell." Tucker quickly straightened. "Don't kick the door down! Everything's all right. We just forgot to disarm the system."

Straightening her robe, Samantha scurried over to the door and drew it open. Backed by three security guards, Jerome stood on her welcome mat, looking like a thundercloud that was about to let loose on all creation. "What the Sam Hill is going on over here?"

"*Nothing.*" The phone still rang persistently. Samantha started to answer it, but Tucker forestalled her by saying, "I'll get it."

He strode across the kitchen to lift the portable unit from its base. "Hello, Tucker here." A moment of silence. "No, she's all right, Frank. I just dropped by to talk with her, and she forgot to disarm the system after opening the door." Another silence. "I appreciate that. We'll handle everything else. Yeah. Good night."

Samantha turned a questioning gaze on him as he ended the call.

"Your father says he'll call all your brothers to tell them it's okay. But he's worried you won't remember your password. If you can't, he says to call him."

"Of course I remember my password. Does he think I'm an idiot?" Samantha turned back to assure Jerome and Nona that everything was fine. "I'm sorry, Jerome. I was about to go to bed, and Tucker stopped by to—" She broke off and licked her bottom lip. "He, um, had something to tell me. Anyway, I forgot about the alarm being set when I opened the door."

Nona smiled. "I hoped it was something like that."

"You scared the living hell out of me," Jerome informed her.

"I'm sorry." Samantha looked at Nona. "I'm *really* so sorry. I didn't mean to frighten everyone."

"Well, all right then." Jerome squinted to see past her. Then he glanced at her robe. His jaw tightened. "If you're sure you're okay, I'll go back to bed."

"I'm perfectly okay."

After closing the door, Samantha leaned weakly against it. Meeting Tucker's gaze, she confessed, "I *am* an idiot. I don't remember my password."

"You don't?"

"In the year we've had the system we've never tripped the alarm, so I've had no occasion to use it."

"Well, that's simple to fix." He grabbed the phone again and dialed her dad's number by memory, which she thought was pretty amazing. Seconds later he arched his eyebrows again and gave her a wondering look as he ended the call. "Your password is 'Just Ducky'?"

It came to her then. "Yes. That's it."

He returned the phone to its base. "That's a strange password. How did you come up with it?"

"When things are fine, don't you ever say everything is just ducky?"

"No."

"Hmm. It made sense to me at the time."

Before he could respond, the phone rang again. He didn't immediately answer. Instead he smiled slightly, rubbed beside his nose, and said, "I have this really weird feeling."

"What kind of feeling?"

"That it wasn't meant— Oh, never mind, it's a stupid thought."

He answered the phone, spoke with the woman manning the phones at the security company, and then gave her the password. After listening for a moment, he proffered the phone to Samantha. "She wants to talk to you. I think she's afraid I have a gun to your head."

"A gun to my head?"

"Yeah. You really need another password to let them know if something like that ever happens."

"I can't remember the password I already have." She took the phone and spent a full two minutes assuring the woman at the other end of the line that she wasn't in life-threatening peril.

When the alarm debacle was finally over, she sank down on a chair at the table, so exhausted that her bones felt as if they'd turned to water. Tucker sat across from her. There was a gentle, indulgent smile in his eyes even though his expression was serious.

"I love you," he said, his voice gone gravelly and thick. "Did I happen to mention that?"

"Why?" she couldn't resist asking.

The smile finally reached his mouth, a glamorous smile that dazzled her, making her forget how tired she was. "Because you make me laugh," he replied. "Because you're kind and gentle and caring." He sighed and pushed his fingers through his hair. "You don't really want to hear all this sappy stuff, do you?"

"Yes."

He chuckled and rocked back on the chair. "The first time I ever clapped eyes on you, I was a goner. You were—" He broke off to think about it, then grinned and said, "*Extraordinary*. No bigger than a minute, but going toe-to-toe with a mean drunk twice your size. In addition to being brave, you're beautiful, smart, and loyal. I love everything about you."

"I wasn't mad at you about the report."

"I'm getting that."

"All you did was tell the truth. How could I be upset about that?"

He sat forward, the front legs of the chair thumping the floor. "Sometimes the truth is damning. I thought you might feel that I betrayed you."

Just the opposite was true. If he'd falsified any of the information on the report, she never would have been able to trust him again. "I admire your honesty, Tucker. I always have. I guess it's a phobia of mine, but I can't abide lying, not in any form or for any reason. I've been lied to way too many times."

He held her gaze. "I'll never do that to you, and that's a promise."

She believed him, and the realization almost brought tears to her eyes.

He rubbed a hand over his face and blinked, then rested his folded arms on the table. "I'm sorry I had such miserable timing tonight. I wasn't expecting all hell to break loose like it did."

"It wasn't your fault." Her heart fluttered into her throat. "Would you like to try again?"

"I'd like nothing better, but I've got this feeling we were interrupted for a reason. I think the Big Guy in the sky is telling me in a very *loud* way that there are more important matters that require our attention."

At that precise moment, she could think of few things more important than finishing that kiss. "Like what?"

"Like discussing the mess you're in."

Samantha didn't want to think about that. "I'm sure it's all going to come right in the end. In time, the police will dig deeper and realize I had nothing to do with the deaths of my horses."

"No," he said softly, "I'm afraid they won't, not if Steve Fisher has his way."

"What do you mean?"

"The bastard isn't just bent on harming your horses, sweetheart. He's going after you as well."

Samantha couldn't see why he believed Steve was coming after her. "I'm sorry; I'm not following."

"That day on the courthouse steps, when he promised to make you sorry for cheating him out of what he felt was rightfully his, he didn't intend to merely take the horses away from you. He meant to make you pay in far worse ways, with years and *years* of your life."

"In prison?" she asked thinly, even though she already knew the answer.

"Exactly."

An awful coldness moved through Samantha. Until that moment she hadn't analyzed Steve's motives. She'd believed he meant only to break her heart by harming the creatures she loved so much. "Oh, my God."

"Sweetheart, you've got to trust me." His blue eyes locked on hers, their expression imploring. "After all that Steve has done, I know trusting me or anyone else outside your family isn't easy for you. But, damn it, you have to try. Will you do that for me—just for a while? I may be your only ace in the hole."

Samantha already trusted him. It had happened bit by bit as she'd come to know him, but it was a done deal now. She trusted in his word. She admired his ethics. She respected his heartfelt concern for the animals he treated and his sterling professional standards. In short, she'd come to believe in him in a way she'd never thought might be possible.

"Oh, Tucker, I do trust you, honestly I do, but how on earth do you think you can help me?"

"How long does it take for an oral dose of morphine to affect a horse?"

"I . . ." Samantha searched her store of knowledge. "I don't know."

"I *do*. After a horse ingests a large amount of arsenic, how long does it take for the poison to take effect?"

Her response was the same. "I don't know."

"Neither do the cops, but I do. In fact, I know *exactly* what the window of time is. Was Steve in town shortly before or during that window of time? And where was he the day Blue Blazes went nuts from an opiate overdose?"

"I don't know," she whispered.

"Neither do I. But, damn it, we're going to find out. The son of a bitch is doing his damnedest to frame you. Everything I put into that report today implicates *you*. Who stands to gain financially by the deaths of those horses? *You*. Who had the most opportunities to poison them? *You*. Who has been around horses all her life and knew what morphine would do to Blue? *You*. Who had motive? *You*. He's trying to crucify you. If he has his way, you'll be put behind bars for a very long time. Do you know the penalty for cruelty to animals in this state?"

"I've never been cruel to my animals," she protested.

"I know you haven't, honey, but name me one thing crueler than feeding horses arsenic. If Steve has his way, the cops will arrest you on charges of cruelty to animals, and trust me, the penalty for animal abuse is pretty damned stiff in this state. Top that off with a conviction of attempted insurance fraud, and you could be an old woman by the time you're released from prison. It isn't the horses Steve's after. They're only a means to an end. He's out to get *you*."

What he was saying made a terrible kind of sense. She made a fist in her hair and stared at him in appalled horror. "Oh, Tucker, what on earth am I going to do?"

"You're going to trust me," he said evenly. "Right now the cops have their heads up their asses, because everything they've come up with so far points to you. We can't just sit back and let them reach the obvious conclusions. We have to blow all their theories sky-high." His eyes filled with that glint of determination she'd seen so many times when he fought to save an animal. Only this time it was her life on the line. "You don't honestly think I'm going to stand aside and let that son of a bitch do this to you."

Tugging his notepad from his shirt pocket, he said, "Down to brass tacks." He slapped the pad onto the table, leafed back several pages from the front, and began reading his notations aloud, reminding her with every word of the night Blue Blazes had gone loco and how long it had taken for the drug to leave his system. "According to Jerome, the cob was fed to the stallion sometime between ten and eleven, probably closer to eleven. Blue went nuts about twenty minutes after Jerome went upstairs. You told me yourself that Jerome would have given the cob to Blue Blazes toward the last, because his stall is at the back of the arena."

"Yes, that's right."

"Which makes the timing perfect. It takes from twenty to thirty minutes for an oral dose of opiate to affect a horse."

"We never had the cob analyzed, though."

"You and your father didn't think to have it analyzed, but I did, and the report corroborates our suspicion that the white powder was morphine, as do the blood panel results I had run on Blue Blazes that night. The lab tech told me she thought he was fed morphine tablets crushed into a powder that stuck to the molasses coating the cob particles."

Samantha stared at him blankly. "But we already knew it was morphine. How does any of this help me?"

"The cops are undoubtedly assuming that the cob was laced with morphine at feeding time, which implicates you or Jerome, because everyone else had left. Only I quizzed Jerome, if you'll remember, and the nighttime treats are dished up and put on a shelf at the end of day shift to save him time late at night. All he had to do was grab the bowls and take them to the designated stalls, not measure out all the cob."

Samantha still couldn't see why that seemed so significant to him. "I'm sorry. I'm still not following."

"Think." His blue eyes locked on hers. "Around four o'clock, maybe later, depending on when the day shift crew left that day, Blue Blazes's dish was filled with the appropriate amount of cob by either Kyle, Nan, or Carrie and put on the shelf in its designated spot, which is clearly marked by Blue's stall number. Between ten and eleven, Jerome removed the bowl from the shelf and took it to Blue's stall. What went on between four or five o'clock and ten or eleven? No one watched those dishes. It was afternoon when the bowl was put there and late evening when it was removed. The paddock doors were all open. Anybody could have sneaked onto the property during those hours and laced Blue's cob with morphine."

"Steve," she whispered.

"Exactly. If he was in town between four and ten, it's a nail in his coffin. It won't be enough, not standing alone. But what if we can prove he was also in town during the window of time for the arsenic to have been fed to Cilantro and Hickory? The horses were given their evening hay around six, but horses don't always eat all their hay immediately. They munch, walk away, nibble at their grain or grass in the paddock, and then come back. It can take two hours, sometimes three before they finish up. Arsenic's time of action is between a few to several hours. Was Steve in the area between six and nine that night? If so, he could have driven out

here to contaminate the hay after Jerome forked it into their stalls, and he would have been long gone before the horses started getting sick."

"The time frame works, I suppose."

"Damn straight it works. They were fed the hay at six, and they died around eleven. If Steve slipped into the stall sometime between six and seven to poison the hay, that leaves a four-hour lapse, plenty of time for the arsenic to do its work."

"But in your report, you suggested that outdated swine or poultry feed was the most likely arsenic source. How could feed be successfully mixed with hay?"

"Steve could have just dumped the feed on top."

"But wouldn't it have fallen down through the hay as the horses ate? They nudge the hay around a lot as they're eating."

"I'm guessing that the horses probably ate the feed first. It's tastier than hay as a general rule. But outdated feed isn't the only possible arsenic source. If you search through any old storage shed, you're likely to find outdated stuff on the shelves that may contain high concentrates of arsenic. It's also possible to order crap like that over the Internet and get it into the country undetected."

Samantha shivered as she recalled entering that stall to find the horses down. "Maybe we should check the floor of their stall for trace evidence."

"The cops have probably already done that, and in my opinion, the results of an analysis can only prove what we already know—that the horses died of arsenic poisoning. What we don't know is if Steve Fisher was within driving distance of this ranch during the crucial times. If we can prove he was, that will be two counts against the bastard, which will certainly be enough to make the cops take a serious look at him and serve him with a search warrant. I'd bet my last dollar they'll find trace evidence of arsenic somewhere on his property or inside his house."

"You've really thought this through."

"Of course I've thought it through—" He broke off and searched her gaze. "You're very important to me—the most important person in my life, as a matter of fact."

"We've only known each other about a month, Tucker."

"Yes, but it hasn't been an ordinary month," he replied. "We've been with each other in trying situations that most couples don't experience in a lifetime. You're one of the most wonderful people I've ever known." His Adam's apple bobbed as he swallowed hard. "I meant what I said earlier. I love you, Sammy."

She was standing on the edge of that high cliff again, and the earth was crumbling beneath her feet. Only this time she was ready to take the plunge. "I'm falling in love with you, too," she said tremulously. "It scares the hell out of me to say those words, Tucker, and it's even scarier to feel the way I do. I realize now that I never loved Steve, not really. I only thought I did. That said, he still had the power to break my heart, and a huge part of me is terrified to make myself vulnerable like that again."

"I know," was his only response, but somehow that was all she needed to hear.

Abandoning his notepad, he pushed to his feet, came around the table, and sat on a chair beside her. Before she guessed what he meant to do, he grabbed her wrist, tugged her toward him, and scooped her up onto his lap.

"Let's give that kiss another try, shall we?" he whispered.

He moved one hand up her spine to the nape of her neck, then pushed his fingers into her hair, tightening them into a fist over her curls. Before she could react or even breathe again, his mouth came down over hers, hot and demanding one moment, then sweetly hesitant the next. Every tender brush of his lips robbed her of the ability to think clearly and filled her with a painful yearning simply to be with him.

"Oh, Tucker," she murmured into his mouth.

He went from gentle to passionate in a heartbeat, his kiss

deepening, his tongue pushing past her lips to taste the inner recesses of her mouth. Samantha's head spun dizzily. She clutched his shoulders, half-afraid she might fall, because the whole room seemed to spin out of control. *This* was how desire felt. She'd yearned to experience it with Steve and never had. She'd believed at the time that she was too nervous, too self-conscious, or too inexperienced to feel real physical longing. Now, in Tucker's arms, she realized how wrong she'd been. With the right man, the needs sprang up from nowhere, and they made her forget everything, even the tenets of her faith.

Somehow they made their way to her living room. Somehow she ended up beneath him on the sofa. Somehow her robe disappeared, and he was learning her body with his mouth and hands, making her ache with need in places she hadn't even realized existed until now. When his mouth found her breast, she felt as if all the fireworks for a Fourth of July display went off inside her at once. She gasped, made fists in his hair, and arched her spine to accommodate him. When his denim-clad knee pushed between her thighs, she made no move to stop him.

She *wanted* this more than she'd ever wanted anything. It wasn't about choices. Her body was issuing primal demands as old as womankind, and every fiber of her being thrummed with urgency.

But Tucker suddenly jerked away. She blinked stupidly, her nerve endings screaming for him, her mind not able to grasp where he'd gone.

"Tucker?"

"I'm sorry," he rasped. "I just . . . No way, not like this."

Her searching gaze finally found him in the shadows. He'd slid off the sofa onto the floor. She pushed dizzily up on one elbow to look down at him. Light from the kitchen barely illuminated one side of his face. His eyes gleamed like chips of muted silver as he raked a hand through his hair. A muscle ticked in his cheek.

Samantha couldn't understand why he had stopped. His every gesture and even the rigid brace of his shoulders told her it hadn't been easy for him. So why had he drawn away? As she stared at him, her vision sharpened until she could see his expression, stony with resolve.

He released a shaky breath, leaned his head back to stare at the pitch blackness above them, and finally asked, "Have you ever known a couple who seems to have found absolute magic?"

Suddenly embarrassed to be lying there nude, Samantha wished for her robe and settled for a sofa pillow instead. As she drew it over her breasts, she said, "Not really, no. My parents, I guess. To this day my dad's never looked at another woman, so far as I know. But my mom died when I was born, and I never saw them together."

He shifted to brace his back against the coffee table so they were facing each other. "I'm surrounded by couples like that," he informed her in a gravelly voice. "People who truly love each other. For them, it goes way deeper than sex." He curled his fingers over open air and made a tight fist. "You can't see it, but it's real. Something wonderful and precious and rare." He paused for emphasis. "And now I think I've finally found it myself—with you."

Tears sprang to her eyes. "Oh, Tucker."

"Please don't think this is a line. I know it sounds corny."

Samantha hadn't been thinking anything of the kind, but the moment he spoke, she realized she should have been. Guys weren't romantic. She had four brothers and knew that for a fact. To them, the perfect date included sex, followed by pizza and beer, preferably sans females so they could belch and channel-surf in peace. They definitely avoided waking up in the morning with a head on the pillow next to theirs.

"So if it's not a line, what is it?"

He propped an elbow on his knee and pinched the bridge of his nose. "Hell, I don't know." Silence. Then, "An epiphany, I guess." He dropped his hand to gesture at the sofa. "This is how it always happens. I can't let it be that way with you. This is special. *You're* special. It can't be like all the other times when it meant nothing. I'm afraid it'll jinx us— that I'll blow it . . . that I'll end up wanting to kick myself for not treating you the way you deserve to be treated."

"I see."

"If you knew my family, maybe you'd understand. For starters, there's my parents. They've been married for . . . what? . . . forty years or more? And after all that time they still love each other. Then there are all my brothers, making happy with the loves of their lives and starting families. I'm the only one who's never found that with anyone. Until I met you, I'd started to believe I never would. Now, here we are. I'm crazy about you, and damned if I know what should come next."

Samantha brushed at her cheeks. "Do you know where my robe went?"

He gave her an odd look. Then he flipped over onto his knees to search for it. He returned with the white terry bunched in his fist and handed it to her. While Samantha drew the soft material over herself, he said, "It can't be about sex. Not only about that, anyway. Not when it's the real thing. There are steps to take, rules to follow. You don't just jump into it."

Samantha had been following the rules all her life. For once, she'd been ready to toss them all to the wind. She stuffed an arm down a sleeve and sat up, careful to keep herself covered while she finished donning the robe. "Is this some kind of role reversal?"

He chuckled humorlessly. "I guess maybe so. I can't do it like this, not with you."

She narrowed her eyes at him. "Only with other women?"

"Exactly," he said, then noted her expression and quickly added, "Not anymore, of course."

"Of course."

She pushed to her feet, stepped around the coffee table, and started toward the kitchen.

"Where are you going?"

"I have an appointment with a bottle of wine."

Moments later as she topped off her goblet with white zinfandel, he joined her in the kitchen. Over the rim of the goblet, she met his gaze. "Cheers."

He sank onto a chair. Samantha knew she'd never seen a handsomer man. After watching her gulp wine for a moment, he said, "I'm not very good with words sometimes."

"Really?" She curled her hand around the neck of the wine bottle. As she sloshed more into her glass, she said, "I never would've guessed."

"I've offended you."

Samantha thought about that for a moment. Aside from the fact that she suddenly felt about as desirable as a railroad tie compared to all the other women he'd slept with, she thought she'd handled the rejection fairly well. "My ego has been bruised a bit." She tried to smile. "With other women you forget all the rules and just go for it, but with me, your thought processes are still in fine working order." She lifted her glass to him. "That puts me pretty low on the desirability chart, the way I see it."

"That isn't how I meant it at all!"

She took another large swallow of wine. "It doesn't matter. You've actually done me a big favor. I'm a practicing Catholic, remember."

His dark brows snapped together. "What does your religion have to do with it?"

"Everything." She shrugged as she took another sip of wine. "We who practice can't screw around without paying a price." Sinking onto a chair across from him, she added, "You've spared me the ordeal of having to tell Father Mike all about it in confession tomorrow. I always go on Saturdays unless something comes up and I can't make it."

His bewildered expression gave way to stunned disbelief. "You *confess* having sex?"

Samantha shrugged. "I haven't yet. I only ever indulged within the bonds of holy matrimony. But I *would* have to confess it if I . . . we . . . well, you know."

"Damn." He rubbed a hand over his face and blinked. "I'll keep that in mind."

She imagined all the women he'd slept with and wondered if any of them had ever felt twinges of guilt afterward. Probably not. Raised as she'd been, she was archaic in her attitudes, completely out of sync with modern-day morality or the dating practices of her contemporaries. She should have been born a hundred years ago.

She stared at the kitchen window, which looked out on the front porch. Beyond the glass it was ink-black. It occurred to her that she hadn't reset the alarm. Now she'd have to go through the entire house when Tucker left to make sure all the windows were still locked. Just the thought of walking from room to room made her feel exhausted.

"It's late, Tucker. I'm so tired I can barely think. It's about time for you to go."

He didn't move, just sat there, studying her as if he'd finally finished assembling a puzzle, and she was an extra piece that didn't fit anywhere. "I've done it anyway, haven't I?"

She emptied her wineglass and set it on the table with a click. "Done what?"

"Blown it."

She couldn't think how to respond. "Tomorrow is another day," she said, once again trying to smile.

"Shit."

"It really is time to call it a night. I have to get some sleep."

"I can't leave, not on this note." He sat forward on his chair, braced his arms on his knees, and looked earnestly at her. "What did I do that was so wrong? When did showing a woman respect become a capital offense?"

She didn't want his respect. She'd needed him to desire her as much as she did him, and he hadn't. Not enough to forget everything, as she had, anyway, and anything less than that wasn't enough. She'd settled for half a loaf once. She never would again.

She pushed to her feet and went to the door. After drawing it open, she stood there, holding it ajar. "Good night, Tucker."

"Can't you just talk to me?"

"What would you like me to say?"

"'Go to hell' would work. I'm sorry, all right? If you want to have sex, I'm game. More than game. I'd like nothing better. I just thought—" He broke off and came to his feet. Collecting his tablet, he stuffed it in his shirt pocket. "Damn it, I don't know what I thought. I just wanted to get it right for once in my life. Can't you understand that?"

"Yes, only you didn't."

"Then give me some pointers. Don't just show me the door."

He looked so genuinely upset that Samantha softened. "Tomorrow," she told him. "We'll talk about it then."

"Swear it?"

"I never swear. It's against my religion."

Moments later Tucker was standing outside in the dark, watching the lights blink out inside Samantha's house. A part of him was sorely tempted to march back up the steps and pound on her door until she answered. Only then what? When he thought back over his dating experiences, beginning at sixteen, all he could remember was a blur of faces and a confusing jumble of female names. He'd long since lost count of how many times he'd scored—or at what point in his life he'd come to realize there had to be something more. He only knew that he'd eventually tired of the dance and started to yearn for what his brothers had found, one special woman and a relationship that really meant something.

Samantha was his special someone. He was convinced of that. Last spring, after reading an old family diary with his mother, he'd come to realize that magic between two people actually could exist—and that true love wasn't a fantasy. His parents had it. His brothers had found it as well. He'd also come to believe it was something very rare and not to be taken lightly.

He'd stopped himself from making love to Samantha tonight because of that. She was a rare treasure. It was kind of like stumbling across a vintage bottle of wine worth hundreds, maybe thousands of dollars. You didn't pull the cork and drink it from a paper cup while you wolfed down a hamburger. You saved it for a really momentous occasion, and even then you took small sips, savoring its taste and appreciating every swallow, wanting it to last.

He wanted what was growing between him and Samantha to last, and when he made love to her, he wanted it to be perfect, not a hurried joining on the sofa, with her feeling embarrassed and possibly used afterward.

"Is everything okay, Dr. Coulter?"

Tucker nearly jumped out of his skin. He turned to peer through the darkness. A man in a khaki uniform emerged from the shadows. As he drew closer, Tucker recognized the dark-haired guard he'd met earlier outside the arena.

"I was just leaving," he replied stupidly.

The fellow nodded. Glancing toward the now dark house, he said, "No need to worry about her. We've got this place buttoned up pretty tight."

Tucker believed it. They even had cameras at the main gate. He bade the man good-night and headed for his truck. Halfway there, he turned to walk backward, wondering which of the upstairs windows opened into Samantha's bedroom. One day soon, he vowed, he would be up there with her. Things hadn't gone well tonight, but he was no quitter, and as she had said, tomorrow was another day.

Chapter Fifteen

Samantha cracked open one eye, peered incredulously at the digital display on her bedside radio, and slowly assimilated that it was half past eight in the morning. Normally shock would have jerked her upright. She *never* slept this late. But her head felt as if an entire platoon of soldiers with two left feet were marching through her gray matter.

Pushing up on an elbow, she groaned and clenched her teeth. *The wine.* She sat up very slowly, then carefully straightened her spine. *Oh, God.* As she made her way to the bathroom, she remembered the good old days, prior to Tabasco's poisoning, when she had arisen sharply at four every morning, gone for a three-mile run, and been at the stables by five to make her rounds. Now nothing in her life was predictable or the same.

A few minutes later as she walked gingerly to the stable, she saw Carrie standing over Cilantro and Hickory's grave. Changing directions, she went to join her newest employee in sad contemplation of the freshly turned earth. Atop the grave rested some wildflowers bound together by a rubber band. The sight of them made Samantha's heart catch.

"Oh, Carrie, how thoughtful."

The young woman brushed her wet cheeks. "She was my favorite. I always sneaked her a treat when I came to work."

Her heavily lined eyes filled with fresh tears, black mascara bleeding from the corners. "She was always waiting when I went inside, and she'd call to me." Her lips quivered. "It was a cute whickering sound, and after she made it, she'd grunt and blow air through her nose."

Samantha knew the sound, had heard it hundreds of times, and now contemplated the heartbreaking fact that she would never hear it again. "Thank you for bringing her the flowers. She's here with us, I'm sure, and knows you thought of her."

"They're mostly just weeds." Carrie gestured at the pasture. "I walked along the fence to pick them."

Upon closer inspection, Samantha saw that the limp bouquet held dandelions, wild daisies, and short, anemic stubs of summer's last clover, the blossoms of which had faded from pink to almost white and were frosted with rust.

"It doesn't matter," she said, touching Carrie's arm. "They're the only kind of flowers Cilantro ever saw, so they're far more appropriate than an expensive bouquet would be."

Carrie turned an anguished gaze on Samantha. "She died really fast, right?"

Samantha considered the question. "In a matter of hours. All things considered, I suppose it was fast. I only wish she hadn't suffered so much."

"So she suffered a lot?"

Samantha nodded. She heard Carrie's breath catch.

"I hoped maybe it was quick, that she didn't feel much of anything," the other woman said.

"Oh, how I wish. But, no. It was a terrible way for her to die."

Carrie wheeled away. Samantha remained by the grave for a moment, thinking of her horse, and then she turned to follow her employee to the arena. En route she waved to Nona, who appeared to be leaving. Samantha supposed it was time for the morning shift change.

Once inside the building, she couldn't find Jerome. Spying Nan out in Blue's paddock, she swung up on the stall gate and hollered, "Have you seen Jerome anywhere?"

"He's in the office." Nan wore a plaid flannel shirt over her tank top this morning, a sure sign that autumn was on its way. "Don't ask me what's going on in there. It looked like a cowboy summit meeting."

Frowning sadly, Nan entered the stall area. "I am so sorry about Cilantro and Hickory, Samantha. It must have about killed you to find them."

Samantha hooked her arms over the top rail. Though Nan wasn't as effusive in her sorrow as Carrie had been, her blue eyes reflected heartfelt regret.

"I'm better today," Samantha assured her, then shrugged and tapped her temple. "I drowned my sorrows in a bottle of wine last night, and now I've got a doozy of a headache to keep my mind off it."

"Good for you. Whoever said alcohol can't cure our woes? Always works for me." Blond ponytail swinging through the rear opening of her ball cap, Nan came to stand at the gate. "I know it's not much consolation, but at least you can rest easy it won't happen again." She hooked a thumb toward the paddock. "Security guards are everywhere." She grinned. "That Latino guy is pretty hot."

"Hmm," Samantha said, dimly recalling the dark, slender man on her doorstep last night. "That should make your workday more interesting."

Nan sighed. "My luck, he's married. The really cute ones always are."

Samantha swung down from the rail. "Well, I'd better see what the summit meeting's about. Keep your fingers crossed. I'm in no mood for more bad news."

When Samantha entered the stable office where she did most of her paperwork, she was startled to find it nearly overflowing with men. Her father sat at the desk, facing a stranger in a blue suit. Tucker, her brothers, and Jerome stood wherever there was leaning room, Clint with an arm propped on the filing cabinet, Tucker next to a bookshelf, and the others lined up along the cedar-paneled walls.

Samantha felt Tucker's gaze on her, and pictures of last night flashed in her mind—how he'd kissed her, where he'd touched her, and how she'd moaned and arched up to him for more. In the bright light of morning the memories were embarrassing, and her cheeks went hot.

"What's going on?" she asked.

"Hi, sweetheart," her father said. "Come on in and shut the door."

When Samantha had done so, Frank pushed to his feet. "Let me introduce Ray Ballantine. He's a private detective."

The man in the suit stood up and turned to shake Samantha's hand. He was rotund and short, not much taller than she was, with dishwater blond hair, light blue eyes, a pronounced overbite, and pudgy features, not at all the stereotypical pulp-fiction private eye.

"'Ballantine will make it fine,'" he quipped. "If I can't make it fine, I'll at least make it better."

Samantha felt as if she were shaking hands with a used-car salesman featured in really awful television spots. "Hello, pleased to meet you," she said.

Frank resumed his seat, gesturing for Ballantine to do likewise. To Samantha, he said, "Tucker called me last night. We had a long talk, and we've decided that we can't sit on our laurels while the cops are investigating this mess and leaping to all the wrong conclusions. We need a professional investigator working on *your* behalf, someone who'll cut right to the chase and turn the magnifying glass away from you and directly onto Fisher."

Samantha crossed the room and perched on the low-hung windowsill. Avoiding Tucker's gaze, which made her skin burn, she focused her attention solely on her dad and Ballantine. Some clear plastic freezer bags filled with hay and what looked like dirt lay on the blotter between them.

"What's that?" she asked.

"Samples from the floor of Cilantro's stall," her father informed her. "More on that later." Gesturing to Ballantine, he asked, "Are you okay with this, honey?"

It would have been nice to be consulted before a third party had been brought into the mix, but after nearly thirty years of being her father's daughter, she had grown accustomed to decisions being made without her knowledge. "Isn't hiring our own investigator a little premature? I don't think the police are going to appreciate any interference."

Ballantine spoke up. "I never interfere with an investigation. I assist behind the scenes, exploring alternative theories." He smiled with dry humor, his two front teeth peeking out between his plump lips. "If I solve a case—and I often do—I volunteer my findings to the police, they follow up on the information, take credit for the bust, and everyone is happy. It isn't uncommon in situations like this for people to hire a private investigator if they can afford it."

Frank settled a worried gaze on his daughter. "They aren't even looking at Steve, honey. At this point they believe you're the culprit and see no reason to search further."

Goose bumps rose on Samantha's nape. "I'm their only suspect, in other words?"

"And you're likely to remain their only suspect if I can't turn up some dirt on somebody else," Ballantine declared. With each pronunciation, his lips tucked in at the corners, drawing tight to reveal his two buckteeth. He put Samantha in mind of a roly-poly squirrel with overflowing cheek pockets. "It's my practice to notify the police as soon as I'm brought in on an investigation," he went on. "Shortly after your father phoned me last night, I spoke with Detective Galloway. He was quick to inform me that this case would be a waste of my time. Some pellet samples that he removed from the floor of your feed room yesterday tested positive for arsenic."

Samantha's heart jerked in her chest. *"What?"*

"It's true, honey," her father assured her. "Ray got it

straight from Galloway. Someone scattered some kind of pellets on the floor of the feed room. I watched James sweep them into a plastic evidence bag yesterday. Apparently they hotfooted it back to the station and had their forensics tech work overtime to get an analysis back to them right away. It was outdated swine feed, just as Tucker suspected and noted in his report."

Samantha stiffened her body and clenched her teeth. It was the only way she could stop herself from screaming. After a moment of deafening silence, she gathered the composure to ask, "Why haven't they arrested me, then?"

Frank glanced at Ballantine, who cleared his throat and shifted on the castered chair like a child whose toes didn't quite reach the floor. "I'm sure they're working their way up to that, but for the moment the swine feed alone isn't enough evidence to make any charges stick."

"What more do they need?" she asked tremulously.

"It's not necessarily a case of what more they need. They just have to rule out all other possibilities before moving in." Ballantine rubbed his jaw. "The stable security at the time of the poisonings wasn't impenetrable, and it was particularly lax during the day. An outsider, namely your ex-husband, could have sneaked in, poisoned the horses, and left evidence in the feed room to frame you—or it could have been an employee who feels he's been wronged, or even a friend. They have to tie up every loose end and convince the district attorney they've got an airtight case against you before they make an arrest. Failing that, they'll have to take it before a grand jury for an indictment."

"We need to know if my ex-husband was in Crystal Falls during certain periods of time," Samantha said.

"Yes," Ballantine agreed. "Mr. Coulter has already supplied me with the dates and times in question. I'll do some computer searches when I return to my office and hopefully have some answers for you by early afternoon."

Samantha sought Tucker's gaze, then struggled to break

eye contact, her skin tingling as if he were physically touching her. He looked tired this morning, she realized, with faint smudges beneath his eyes. A green checked shirt fit snugly over his shoulders, the open collar revealing the burnished column of his throat and a tuft of dark chest hair. Seeing it reminded her that she'd never gotten his shirt off him last night to actually see his torso. *Oh, no.* He reserved that privilege for *other* women.

Anger and hurt tangled together within her and combusted into a fiery heat. Realizing that her father and Ballantine were still talking, she tuned back to the conversation. "Have the police checked on Steve's whereabouts on the dates in question yet?" she asked.

Ballantine shook his head. "As of last night when I spoke to Galloway, no. Your horses died only thirty-three hours ago. I know it seems like an eternity to you, but in work-shift time, only one business day has passed, and now it's Saturday. They probably won't get around to checking out Fisher until Monday."

Samantha could scarcely believe her ears. "My whole life is turned inside out, my horses are dead, and they aren't going to work over the weekend to get to the bottom of it? You're joking."

"They *may* put in a few case hours over the weekend," Ballantine replied. "Galloway sounded pretty hot about how horribly the horses died, so this may rank high on his list of cases he'd like to solve. On the other hand, we're talking about the Crystal Falls Police Department. It's not exactly the NYPD, if you get my gist, and it's *nothing* like in the television series."

"So I may be put on hold until next week, not knowing what's going to happen?"

Ballantine nodded, then shrugged. "Possibly, possibly not. It all depends on how this case falls into the lineup. The chief of police calls the shots. If he feels this case demands immediate attention, Galloway may put in some overtime to compile evidence against you over the weekend. If not, he may sleep in, go to the park with his grandkids, and have a barbecue tomorrow afternoon."

Samantha didn't like either of those options.

"On a bright note," Ballantine added, "you may get a lot of information from *me* over the weekend. All I need to find is one piece of evidence to prove Steve Fisher was in this area on one of the dates in question to cast some suspicion on him. It will be particularly effective if Fisher denies being in the area, and we can prove he's lying."

"How can you learn Steve's whereabouts on those dates by doing only computer searches?" she asked. "Don't you need to interview people and ask questions?"

"I will certainly do that if it proves necessary, but good detective work begins on the Internet, and personal interviews are only follow-up work, which often isn't necessary. The information I can find, via the computer, is not only compelling, but to a great extent inarguable." He smiled benignly. "My work is nothing at all like it's portrayed in popular fiction."

He opened a leather-bound notebook on the desk. "The secret to my successful investigative work is specialized software. For me to do any searches on Fisher will take time, of course, so I can't impress you with anything on him yet. I'll have to dig up all of his personal statistics first. Fortunately your father was kind enough to supply me with his"—he glanced up at Samantha and then at her brothers—"and yours as well, enabling me to provide you with some examples of what I can do when I have the necessary information."

He perused his notes. "Forgive me if the data I've gathered startles or embarrasses you. I've learned that this is often the only way I can convince people I'm worth my wages." He looked up at her father. "A little over a month ago on Wednesday night, August second, you dined at Michael Angelo's with Dee Dee Kirkpatrick, a lady whose name I learned only because she picked up a small portion of the tab. For appetizers, you selected tempura calamari. The wine you chose was a choice California merlot that I'm partial to myself. You tipped the waiter or waitress a generous seventy-five dollars. You also paid an extra fee for violin music during your meal. You settled your tab at seven forty-five. I estimate that you left the establishment at about eight. Later, you stopped for diesel at Farmers' Co-op Fuel and Oil. Need I go on?"

Frank Coulter's face had frozen into a dark, unreadable mask. For a long moment he said nothing. Then he ground out, "You can find out what I eat at a restaurant?"

"And *when* you eat it. Amazing, isn't it?" Ballantine smiled, clearly enjoying himself. "On an even more personal note, Mr. Harrigan, you apparently have a partial denture plate. The next evening at Safeway at precisely six forty-three, you bought a new toothbrush, a tube of Crest toothpaste, and a box of Efferdent. Who needs all three, *unless* he has a partial plate?" He glanced up. "If I were seriously investigating you, I would discover which of your teeth are missing and exactly what kind of bridgework you have, but that hardly seems necessary merely to prove a point. You also love *Benji* films. You rented three the following Monday night at the Video Den and bought two giant popcorns. Unless you have a gargantuan appetite for popcorn, I can only assume you had company while you munched your way through the trio of films." With a lift of one pale eyebrow, he added, "All of this transpired in Crystal Falls, of course, and I have the exact times of every transaction if you'd like to hear them."

In that moment Samantha stopped seeing Ballantine as an enterprising squirrel and decided he was a genius.

Samantha's father clearly wasn't as impressed, or perhaps he merely resented the invasion of privacy. "The exact times won't be necessary." He scanned the room, meeting the startled gazes of his children. "Before Dee Dee left to go visit her daughter, I took her out to dinner, and we watched *Benji* movies at her place a few nights later. Big deal. You can stop looking at me as if I committed adultery."

Dee Dee, the family housekeeper, was a plump, attractive redhead in her late fifties who'd been Samantha's only mother figure growing up. Nowadays, she divided her time between the six Harrigan households, focusing primarily on Frank's residence, but also mucking out his children's homes once a week. She'd gone to California over a month ago to attend the birth of her first grandchild and had stayed to enjoy the baby for a few weeks. Everyone missed her, but now Samantha had cause to wonder if her father hadn't been missing her most of all.

"You're dating Dee Dee?" Clint inquired, his expression scandalized. "How long has *that* been going on?"

"How long has *what* been going on?" Frank sent Ballantine a searing glare that would have dropped less stalwart men in their tracks. "We're friends, for God's sake. Don't try to make something sordid out of *Benji* and two cartons of popcorn."

Ray Ballantine shifted on his seat and turned the page. "I don't intend to unveil dark secrets, Mr. Harrigan, only to prove there is no such thing as privacy anymore. A certain individual in this room bought a case of Trojan condoms a little over a week ago. On last Tuesday evening, to be precise, at a little after eight o'clock, at Pay Right Pharmacy."

A flush of scarlet crept up Quincy's neck. He quickly dipped his head, but not before Samantha caught the mortified expression on his face. A whole *case* of condoms? She could scarcely believe her ears.

Ballantine closed the notebook and sat back on his chair. "If you do it, I can track it. Well, in most cases, anyway. I can't see through the walls of your home—unless you rent videos through your satellite provider. Watch porn on dish, and I can tell you exactly what film you watched, and when you watched it." He shrugged and grinned. "I ran a check on all of you last night in preparation for this meeting." He glanced up at no one in particular and beamed a knowing smile. "The Internet never sleeps."

Leaving his truck parked on the street, Tucker ambled across his parents' front lawn, snapping his fingers to make sure Max stayed at his heels. A cute female poodle lived next door, and ever since first rubbing noses with her through the bushes along the drive, the rottweiler had been hot to take her for a romantic stroll. Tucker didn't know if Cheri was spayed. With his luck she wasn't, and his pedigreed, intact brute of a dog would knock her up. The results were too awful to contemplate, half-size rottweilers with topknots and pom-pom tails. Max was already the proud papa of six mixed rotties with long cocker ears. Thank God Lady's owner had taken it all in good humor and assumed half the blame.

"*No,*" Tucker growled when Max tried to wander away. "Get it through your thick skull; she isn't for you."

Sounds from the backyard told Tucker his parents were spending their Saturday afternoon out in the garden. He circled around to the left of the garage and unlatched the side gate, ushering Max through the opening ahead of him. As always when he visited, Tucker thought how sad it was that his father had been reduced to owning a small city lot when he'd once had hundreds of acres of prime ranchland.

As Tucker rounded the back corner of the garage, Harv Coulter's dark head appeared above a row of robust tomato plants laden with deep red fruit. "Well, now, just look what the cat dragged in."

Tucker's mother, who was much shorter than her husband, parted the vines to peer through at her son, her plump, pretty features lighting up with pleasure. "Hello, dear heart! And just look, you've brought our sweet Max, and I have no biscuits in my apron pockets."

Snub tail wagging wildly, Max made a beeline for Mary Coulter, tromping over her world-class cabbages as he went.

Tucker's mother, now in grandmother mode, pushed through the tomatoes to crouch down and welcome the dog with a fierce hug.

"Oh, you're such a love," Mary said. "Yes, you're Grandma's precious boy." She laughed and almost toppled backward when Max pushed at her apron pockets with his broad nose. "There's nothing for you, I'm afraid. Come with me to the kitchen, and Grandma will find you something." To Tucker, she said, "We have iced tea in the fridge. Would you like a glass, sweetheart?"

More careful of the vegetables than his dog had been, Tucker sauntered toward the tomato patch. "No, thanks, Mom. I just dropped by to chat with Dad for a few minutes."

"Oh. Well." Mary went up on her tiptoes to give him a quick hug, ruffling his hair and tweaking his cheek. "I'll leave you alone then. Max and I are on a mission."

Harv resumed picking tomatoes as his wife headed for the house. "Zeke was the last one of you boys who cornered me in my tomato patch."

Tucker's curiosity was piqued. Of all his brothers, Jake and Zeke were the most squared-away. Tucker couldn't imagine either of them ever needing advice. "What did Zeke need to talk to you about?"

"That'll stay between me, Zeke, and the canned tomatoes in your mama's pantry," Harv replied. Then he frowned. "I think it was when I harvested last year's tomatoes, anyhow. Could be it was the year before that. Gettin' hard to keep track anymore, with everyone gettin' married, pregnant, or christenin' a baby. Isn't a week goes by that your mother's not baking a birthday cake."

That was a slight exaggeration, but not by much, and Tucker understood what his father meant. In the Coulter family, the calendar always seemed to be filled with special events. "Need some help picking?"

"Nope. Zeke offered to help pick, too, as I recall. Didn't have his mind on my tomatoes and bruised half of 'em."

Harv gently placed a large piece of fruit in his garden basket. "What's the problem, son?"

"What makes you think I've got a problem?"

"Your hair's not combed, your shirt's wrinkled, and you look like you've been on a three-day drunk."

Tucker tugged on his earlobe. "It's been a rough month."

"I can see that."

"Actually, Dad, I just wanted to pick your brain, if you don't mind."

"Fine by me. Start pickin'."

Tucker thought for a moment. "I'm not really sure where to start."

"Well, now, that's a pickle." Harv left off picking tomatoes and removed his garden gloves. "It about a woman?"

"What makes you think that?"

Harv grinned. "You attended university for how many years? After all that schoolin', you know most everything. I can't think of much else you'd want to pick my brain about."

Tucker sighed. "It is about a woman, actually. I've finally met someone really special."

"Hmm." Harv tucked his gloves over his belt, motioned for Tucker to follow him, and made his way toward the compost pile at the far back corner of the yard. He sat on the rim of the raised enclosure and motioned for Tucker to join him. "More private back here, just in case your mother comes back outside."

Tucker took a seat, crossed his ankles, and folded his arms. "About this lady I've met. Last night, when we were alone, I kissed her. One thing led to another, and before I knew it, we were on her sofa and almost . . . well, you know."

Harv grunted to let Tucker know he was following so far.

"Anyway, as much as I wanted her, it felt all wrong somehow. I've been in a lot of relationships."

"You don't say?"

Tucker decided to ignore that. His parents had never made a secret of the fact that they disapproved of his dating habits and apparent inability to stick with one woman for any length of time. "In the past, that's how it's always gone, straight into bed and nothing special to mark the moment. With this lady, that just doesn't feel appropriate."

Harv stared thoughtfully at the ground. "When you meet the *right* lady, son, hopping into bed with her immediately usually doesn't feel appropriate. When you really care, it's not just about the sex anymore. Everything you say and do suddenly becomes very important. An investment in the future, I reckon you might say."

"Exactly." Tucker was relieved to hear his father put his feelings into words. "I've been hung up on her since I first met her, and it's not just a physical attraction, though that's a big part of it." He pressed his fist to his diaphragm. "I feel it in my gut. You know? That she's the one, I mean."

"Congratulations. I was startin' to worry it might never happen for you."

"Me, too," Tucker confessed. "And now that it has, I don't want to screw it up."

"Can't say I blame you there. It's not every day you find a really special lady you think you can spend the rest of your life with. Only happened once for me, and I think it's fair to say that's how it is for most folks."

"Only I did screw it up," Tucker inserted. "Big-time, I'm afraid."

"How in hell did you do that?"

"By calling a halt to everything last night." Tucker gestured with one hand. "We were . . . well, you know . . . at the point of no return. Almost, anyway. And bang, like a fist between my eyes, I realized it wasn't right, that I couldn't let it go any farther. Not until I could make it more special somehow. Only that isn't how she took it, and nothing I said changed her mind. I think she felt . . . I don't know . . . like maybe I didn't really want her or something. And that wasn't it at *all.*"

"What makes you think she thought that?"

"She made a comment about my never stopping with other women, only with her. Since it was pretty much true, I couldn't deny it. But she interpreted it all wrong. I stopped because I wanted her so much *more* than I'd ever wanted anyone else, not because I wanted her *less*."

"Oh, boy."

"I don't know what to do, Dad. She's still upset with me today. Every time I so much as look at her, she turns as red as one of your tomatoes, and she won't talk to me unless she absolutely has to." Tucker lifted his hands in helpless bewilderment. "I don't know what the frigging hell to do."

"Oh, boy."

Tucker angled his father a sharp look. "Is that all you've got to say? 'Oh, boy'? I need help here."

"I can see you do." Harv rested his hands on his spread knees. "But female feelings ain't exactly my specialty."

"They *aren't*? After all these years with Mom, it seems to me you should be something of an expert."

Harv snorted. "I love that woman so much it hurts, and I'd move heaven and earth to make her happy. The problem is, I'm never quite sure what it is she actually wants unless she decides to tell me, which most times she won't."

"Why not? Does she think you're a mind reader?"

"That pretty much nails it on the head. She wants me to be, anyhow, and most of our troubles arise because I'm lousy at it."

"That makes no sense at all."

"Does to her. Women don't think like we do, son. I'm supposed to understand how she feels without her drawin' me a picture. Sooner you learn that, the better off you'll be."

"You've been a lot of help."

Harv chuckled, pushed to his feet, and laid a big hand over Tucker's shoulder. "I'm sorry. You dug your way into this hole. It's for you to dig your way out."

Tucker watched his father walk away. Then he released a taut breath and spent several thoughtful seconds observing an industrious ant that was trying to carry a mulch particle twice its size over uneven ground. Two steps forward, several back. Tucker felt as if he and the insect had a lot in common.

The sound of approaching footsteps brought him back to the present. He glanced up and saw his mother walking toward him, Max trudging adoringly at her heels.

"Your father says you need to talk to me?"

Well, now, isn't this just fine. He'd have his father's head for this piece of work. "Not really," he said. "What made him think that?"

Mary perched beside him on the edge of the compost enclosure. "He says you've met someone special and hurt her feelings. He thought I might be able to give you some advice."

Tucker considered the possibility and mentally shuddered. *No way.* He went to his mom for hot pie à la mode on a winter afternoon, but never for advice about his love life.

"How did you hurt her feelings?" Mary asked, her blue eyes aching with motherly concern.

"It's personal, Mom."

"Ah," she said. "Shall we play ten guesses? You said something incredibly stupid." She thought for a moment. "She asked if her dress made her look fat, and you said another one looked better on her, unspoken message being that she *did* look fat, which isn't what you meant but how she took it."

Tucker gave his mother a horrified look. "Are you women *really* that sensitive?"

Mary laughed. "We call it being perceptive."

"And put words in our mouths that we'd never think of saying?"

"Sometimes. Am I warm with my guess?"

"Totally off the mark," he assured her, only in a crazy sort of way, she'd come awfully close. "It was a misunderstanding, though, and I'm pretty sure I hurt her feelings without meaning to, and nothing I say makes it better."

Mary made another guess, Tucker shook his head, and the guessing game continued until Tucker tired of the nonsense and blurted out the details.

"Oh, my," Mary whispered when she'd heard the tale.

"What's that mean?" Tucker asked worriedly, not liking her tone.

"Just that it's a very ticklish problem," Mary replied. "You didn't just hurt her feelings, sweetheart; you struck a terrible blow to her feminine pride." At her son's blank look, Mary sighed. "Dear heavens, you're as inept at this sort of thing as your father is."

Tucker didn't like the sound of that, either. "I'm not inept. Confused, more like. And I'm not sure how to mend my fences with her."

"I would advise you not to stop the next time around," Mary said, "but that goes against everything I believe. Unless, of course, you marry her first."

"People don't get married first anymore."

"They don't?"

Tucker renewed his vow to have his father's head for putting him in this position. "Most people don't," he revised. "It's really old-fashioned."

"There's something to be said for old-fashioned," Mary replied. "You wouldn't be in this mess if you'd ever once listened to your mother and refrained from engaging in physical intimacy outside marriage. You would have kissed the girl, told her how beautiful she is, and left before you shoved that size-twelve boot in your mouth."

Tucker couldn't argue that point, so he settled for saying, "Size thirteen."

"That's even worse," she said with a warm laugh.

"What am I going to do, Mom? I really care about her."

Mary shook her head. "I don't know. You might try talking to her and telling her how you feel. That's what your father always does."

"Dad doesn't stick his foot in his mouth that often anymore, does he?"

She gave him an incredulous look. "Of *course*. Sometimes I think the man was born with it there. Just last week I was studying myself in the mirror, moaning and groaning about how old I'm starting to look. I wanted him to tell me he still thinks I'm beautiful. But you know what he said?"

"No, what?"

"That he looks older than dirt, too, so we make a fine pair."

Tucker choked back a startled laugh. "Seriously? Dad said that?"

"He did, and it hurt my feelings. He went around half the day, scratching his head, without a clue why I was mad at him. When he finally figured it out, he went to town and bought me a dozen roses. On the card, he wrote, 'To my Mary girl, who'll always be the prettiest rose of all.'" Mary beamed a happy smile. "I didn't believe a word of it, of course. I'm not *blind*, after all. But I forgave him all the same. By going clear to town and to all that bother, he told me how much he loves me, and that was all I really needed to know."

Tucker thought about that. Then he narrowed an eye at his mother. "So women never outgrow it?"

"Outgrow what?"

"Being"—he almost said "absurdly sensitive," but caught himself just in time—"perceptive."

Mary laughed and hugged his arm. "No, dear heart, I'm afraid not. We remain *perceptive* until the end."

They sat quietly for a while, listening to the leaves of the oak tree rustling in the breeze and a bird singing in the yard next door. Max, who'd curled up near Tucker's feet, finally began to snore.

"So," Mary said softly, "when will we get to meet this *special* young lady?"

Tucker rested his cheek atop her head. "Sometime shortly after she starts talking to me again, I guess. Would two dozen roses work, do you think?"

Mary tipped her head back to grin at him. "Possibly, if you send them every day for a week."

Thirty minutes later, Tucker hunched over the far end of the floral shop counter, trying to compose a romantic note to Samantha. So far he'd ruined five cards, and he still wasn't happy with the results. *I think you're beautiful.* How original was that? *I'm sorry about last night.* Definitely not a keeper. It didn't seem right to steal his father's words, but Tucker was sorely tempted. The old man might be a lousy mind reader, but he had a few tried-and-true lines memorized. Comparing his mom to a rose and saying she would always be the prettiest one of all had been absolutely *brilliant.*

In the end, Tucker asked for a sixth card, committed plagiarism, and arranged for the dozen roses to be delivered before closing time that day. The older woman who rang up the purchase smiled knowingly as she read the card.

"Oh, how nice. You're very good with words, Mr. Coulter. She'll *love* it."

Samantha answered the stable phone just as a security guard entered the arena via the personnel door and loped across the exercise area toward her. "Hello, Sage Creek Quarter Horse Ranch. How may I help you?"

"Hi, sis." Quincy's voice fairly boomed over the airway, and a squeaking sound blasted in her ear. He had a new, hands-free cell phone with a clip-on earpiece that picked up ambient noise and shrieked occasionally. "Has the gerbil been in touch yet?"

"The who?" she repeated blankly.

"Ballantine. He has to have come up with something on Fisher by now."

Samantha said, "Hold on just a second," and cupped her

hand over the mouthpiece to see what the security guard wanted. Judging by his looks, she guessed him to be Nan's sexy Latino. "What's up?"

All shiny black hair, copper skin, brown eyes, and inflated muscles, the guy had dark spots of sweat on his uniform shirt. "There's a delivery. I need your permission to sign for it."

Most of the deliveries were to the ranch, not to her personally, and it was her policy never to let anyone else but Jerome sign for them. She didn't want another bad load of hay. "Where's my foreman?"

The man shrugged. "Dunno. I haven't seen him for a bit."

"Is it a feed or hay delivery?"

"No, ma'am, I don't think so. It's a lady in a green uniform, driving a little red economy car. A magnetic sign on the door says, 'Floral Fantasies.'"

"Oh." Samantha was intrigued, for she never received flowers. Maybe they were from her dad or one of her brothers, a little something to brighten her day because so many things had been going wrong lately. "It's fine for you to sign for me then," she told the guard. "Just put the delivery on my front porch." As he turned to jog away, she called, "Is Nona back on duty tonight?"

"Yes, ma'am," he answered, running backward. "She'll be here at nine."

Samantha was relieved to hear it. All of the security people seemed competent enough, but Nona Redcliff had impressed Samantha with her knowledge and professional manner.

"I'm back," she said into the phone. "Sorry about the interruption, Quincy. With so many people milling around, there's not a moment's peace."

"No problem. I just called for an update. What has the gerbil come up with?"

"That isn't nice."

"I guess we can call him the condom sleuth."

Samantha grinned in spite of herself. She still couldn't believe her brother had bought an entire case of prophylactics. Maybe it was a whole year's supply. "Why don't we just call him the genius? I know he's a strange-looking fellow, but I was impressed with his demonstration."

"So has he come up with anything on Fisher yet?"

"Not that I've heard. I imagine he'll probably check in with Dad, not me. He'll be paying the bill, after all."

Quincy sighed. "Well, I hope we hear something soon."

Samantha seconded that. If Ballantine couldn't find anything to hang Steve with, it would be her neck in the noose.

Chapter Sixteen

*R*oses. Samantha's hands trembled as she lifted them from the long white box and drew back the green paper. She knew the instant she saw the bloodred blossoms that they hadn't been sent by her father or one of her brothers. They were from Tucker. Had to be.

Like a child saving the best part for last, she left the card in the box while she found a vase, snipped the rose stems, added flower food to the water, and then arranged the blossoms and delicate ferns in fans of scarlet against backdrops of green. She set the roses at the center of the table, then stood back to admire them. Definitely from Tucker. Her father or brothers would have sent wildflowers, thinking she'd like them better because she was so often outdoors and simple in her tastes. *Not.* She did love wildflowers, of course, but deep in her feminine heart of hearts, roses were far more special.

When she finally opened the card and read the message, she couldn't help but smile and press the card over her heart. *How sweet.* She'd seen Tucker's longhand on more than one occasion and instantly recognized his bold scrawl. It touched her that he'd gone to all the trouble to drop by the florist's to choose the flowers personally instead of simply ordering them over the phone, and that he'd written the note himself.

Not that she believed a word of it. But it was still lovely to pretend, just for a moment, that she was beautiful and desirable.

Stepping into the downstairs bathroom, she took a long, hard look at herself in the mirror. The slender young woman who stared back at her was far from gorgeous, but for the first time in a very long while, Samantha was able to focus on her good points instead of the bad. The oval shape of her face would never give anyone nightmares, her lips were nicely defined, and her nose, though a little too much like her father's to be feminine, wasn't really that big. Leaning close to the glass, she decided her eyes were her best feature, large, dark, and naturally lined with thick, black lashes.

Sudden, poignant memories of herself standing before a mirror as a teenager flashed through Samantha's mind. Trying to fix her hair, learning to apply makeup. In those days she'd never felt plain or downright homely because her father had frequently told her just the opposite: that she was the prettiest girl in town. As an adult, dispassionately taking inventory of her reflection, Samantha decided that the truth fell somewhere in the middle. She wasn't as unattractive as Steve had so often claimed, and she wasn't the most beautiful woman in Crystal Falls, either. But she *was* pretty, in her own way, and maybe, just maybe, in the eyes of one special man, she truly was the loveliest rose of all.

Curling her hands over the edge of the sink, Samantha took a deep, cleansing breath, and then slowly released it, turning loose of all the old hurts. With her life in such turmoil because of Steve Fisher, it was probably crazy, but she finally felt free of him—totally, absolutely, and permanently *free*.

As Tucker parked his Dodge outside the equine clinic, he caught movement in his side mirror and realized a man carrying a camera was hurrying toward the truck. *What now?* He pushed open the door, about to ask what the guy wanted, when a flash went off in his eyes.

"You're Tucker Coulter, right, Samantha Harrigan's vet?" the man asked. He jerked a plastic ID card from his shirt pocket. "Royce Mulligan, *Crystal Falls Daily*. How did you feel when you realized Ms. Harrigan poisoned her own horses for the insurance money?"

"I never realized any such thing." Tucker slammed the truck door hard behind him.

"The reports you filed are now public record, Dr. Coulter. All the facts implicate Ms. Harrigan. She's knowledgeable about horses, she alone stands to gain financially, and, according to the police, though they're working on some other leads, they have no other suspects at this time."

Tucker wanted so badly to mention Fisher's name. But he instinctively knew not to tip their hand. Let the bastard think he'd gotten away with it and that no one suspected him. "No comment," he said, shoving past the reporter, who refused to get out of the way. "And be careful what you print, buster. Frank Harrigan will haul your ass into court for slander so fast it will make your head spin."

As the camera flashed again, Tucker entered his clinic and slammed the door closed in the reporter's face. He was shaking, he realized. Talk about getting blindsided. He hadn't considered the possibility that local newshounds might pick up this story. *Stupid, so stupid.* Samantha was Frank Harrigan's daughter. The man was a baron in the horse-breeding industry and famous in his way, a self-made millionaire. Juicy scandals about wealthy, important people sold newsprint.

Tucker jerked his cell phone from his belt and dialed the number of the Sage Creek Ranch. If the reporters were breathing down his neck, they were going to try to catch Samantha off guard, too. At least she had security out at her place now. But he still needed to warn her.

Samantha heard a ruckus outside and hurried out onto the front porch to see what was happening. The Latino security guard stood nose-to-nose with a redheaded woman, behind whom was parked a white van splashed with a local television station's logo. The two were arguing furiously, the guard's posture threatening, the female reporter's determined.

"I merely want to interview Ms. Harrigan. You can watch my every move if you like, but I'm not leaving without speaking to her first."

"This ranch is under tight security. You aren't authorized to be here!" the guard insisted.

A man inside the van saw Samantha on the porch and hurriedly exited the vehicle. To her horror, he drew a video camera from the back, rested it on his shoulder, and was already filming as he came around the front bumper.

"There she is!" he shouted to his female associate. "Ms. Harrigan, can you answer some questions?"

Samantha couldn't make her feet move. She stood frozen, watching the man pan the front of her home with his camera and then zero in on her.

The story was on the six-o'clock news. Tucker got word of it via cell phone at twenty after the hour as he was driving out to Samantha's ranch.

"Are you watching the news?" Isaiah asked.

"No." Tucker flipped on the turn signal and adjusted his visor to block the sun from his eyes. "Should I be?"

"Ah, damn, Tucker, they're crucifying her."

"Samantha?"

"Who else? Of course, Samantha. Whatever happened to being innocent until proven guilty? This is bad, Tucker, really bad. The female reporter isn't flat-out accusing her of anything, but the way she's asking the questions implies one hell of a lot." A brief silence. "I'm recording it. You need to see this."

Tucker shoved harder on the accelerator, sending Max into a sprawl against the back of the bench seat. "I'm on my way out to her place as we speak."

"Too late now," Isaiah replied. "The damage is already done."

Tucker half expected to find his lady fair hiding inside her house. Instead she was in the stable, working like a dervish at cleaning stalls. When she saw him, she didn't stop shoveling, just gave him her back and increased her pace. Her blue chambray work shirt sported a dark blue line of sweat down her spine. Her beautiful black hair sprang out the back of her ball cap like a garden bush badly in need of sculpturing. The seat of her jeans was also dirty. But in Tucker's opinion, she was still incredibly beautiful, and effortlessly so.

He folded his arms over the top of the stall gate, willing to wait her out. Nutmeg, a pretty bay mare and the occupant of the enclosure, was out in her paddock, dining on her evening ration of hay. The floor of the stall looked as if it had been cleaned only recently, a telltale sign to Tucker that Samantha was working just to be working, not because the chore really needed to be done. He completely understood the tactic; when he was upset, he often threw himself into a task to hold his thoughts at bay.

When the wheelbarrow was brimming with what appeared to be mostly clean straw, Samantha went outside to dump it, not returning for a couple of minutes. In the interim, Nan approached from Tucker's left, startling him with her presence.

"I thought all of you had left," he said.

She joined him at the gate. "Nah, not yet. Sometimes we get out of here shortly after six, but other times it's almost seven. It depends on whether or not Jerome needs us to help with the evening hay. Today was hectic, so we all stayed late to help him catch up."

"How many of you work full-time?" Tucker asked, partly to keep the conversation going, but also to avoid hearing why the day had been so hectic. He'd met Nan in passing

and didn't feel comfortable discussing the TV crew's visit
with her. "Three, four?"

"Me, Kyle, and Mac are the full-time underlings," she
replied.

"Mac?"

"You haven't met him. He's been off on vacation. Next
to Jerome, and excluding all the Harrigans, of course, he's
one of the best trainers around. Carrie, the stocky gal, and
Ronnie Post, the little redhead with dimples, are part-timers
for now. When she can afford it, Samantha plans to increase
their hours."

"I don't recall ever seeing Ronnie."

Nan's pretty face broke into an affectionate grin. "Yeah,
well, if she was working in a stall when you walked by, you
wouldn't have seen her. If she's five feet tall, I'll eat my hat.
Vertically challenged, that's our Ronnie. Great with horses,
though."

Nan gazed thoughtfully into the paddock, her fair brows
drawn together in a frown. Finally she said, "Am I wrong
to suspect that you and Samantha have become an item, Dr.
Coulter?"

Tucker was taken off guard by the question. "What makes
you think that?"

"Call it female intuition." Nan held up a hand. "You don't
have to answer. It's none of my business, really. It's just that
I care about Samantha, and to be straight out with it, I hope
you won't hurt her. I hired on right after she got divorced,
so I never met Steve Fisher, but judging from what I've seen
and heard, he's a world-class asshole. The next time around,
Sam deserves happiness, not heartache."

Tucker totally agreed and decided he liked Nan Branson. Her loyalty to her boss told him a lot. "I'll keep that in
mind," he settled for saying.

A twinkle warmed the stable hand's clear blue eyes. "See
that you do."

Tucker was almost smiling as she walked away, *almost*

being the key word. The day had brought too many worries and concerns for him to relax enough to be amused about much of anything.

Samantha returned to the stall just then, this time without the wheelbarrow. Shoulders straight, small chin lifted, she strode directly toward him, her gaze unwavering on his. "Tucker, we need to talk."

He'd been about to say the same thing and had expected her to argue. "I agree. Will the stable office do?"

She shook her head. "Not enough privacy. How about walking over to the house with me?"

Bracing one hand on the gate rail, Tucker vaulted over into the enclosure and fell into step beside her to exit the building via the paddock. When they'd cleared the fence and picked up the pace, he expected her to say something more, but she remained stubbornly silent. He felt eyes on them as they crossed the parking area to her small front yard, which sported only a few patches of hardy grass surrounded by packed dirt. He thought of his English garden, with its stepping-stones, trellises, and ornate benches, and wondered how Samantha would feel about having at least a few flowers here and there and maybe some ornamental shrubs.

That was a conversation better left for later. "The security guards are watching us," he said. "I can feel eyes boring into my back."

"I hate it," she blurted out. "The solitude is one of my favorite things about ranching, and now he's destroyed that, too."

Tucker didn't need to ask who "he" was. "It's only temporary," he assured her. "With Ray Ballantine working behind the scenes, this will all be resolved before you know it."

"Oh, I hope so," she said softly as she led the way up her porch steps.

"I know so. Ballantine came highly recommended to me by Rafe Kendrick."

She hesitated midstep to flash him a startled look. "You know Rafe Kendrick?"

Like the Harrigans, the Kendricks were a well-known ranching family in the area, the only difference being that they'd started up their business with thousands of acres, not merely twelve hundred, and they were now wealthy beyond most people's comprehension.

"I know him quite well," Tucker replied. "My little sister, Bethany, is married to his brother, Ryan. The night Blue Blazes was doped, it was Ann Kendrick who called Saint Matthews and pulled strings to get the blood panels run at the hospital lab."

"Seriously?" She looked amazed. "My goodness, Dr. Coulter, you have friends in high places."

Tucker remembered that year's Fourth of July family celebration, on private Crystal Falls lakefront, all owned by the Kendrick family. Keefe Kendrick, the family patriarch, reminded Tucker strongly of his own father, a tall, aging cowboy who said *ain't* more often than not, sneaked occasional cigarettes behind his wife's back, and loved to hear a good joke.

"The Kendricks would find that assessment very amusing," he told her. "They're ranchers, just like you, very down-to-earth and unassuming, despite their wealth. You'd like them."

"I've heard that about them," she said as she pushed open the door and led the way into her kitchen. Tucker immediately noticed the roses on the table. He drew out a chair and straddled it, hoping the flowers had served their purpose and at least partially assuaged her hurt feelings.

She went to stand across the room with her hips braced against the counter. "I'm not sure how to say this, Tucker, except straight out. I'm sacking you."

The words exploded like a small bomb in the otherwise quiet room. She met his incredulous gaze with big brown eyes that glittered with stubborn resolve.

"Pardon me?"

"You heard me. On Monday, please figure up my bill and get it in the mail. I'll settle up with you by the end of the week."

Dimly, Tucker was aware of the wall clock ticking somewhere behind him, and of the refrigerator humming. "But Tabasco is still—"

"Tabasco is far enough along in his recovery to survive a change of vets. I am no longer in need of your services."

Stunned, Tucker couldn't immediately think of anything to say. Finally he asked, "Do you blame me because Cilantro and Hickory died? Is that it?"

"Of course not. You're a fabulous vet. No one could have saved them. They were beyond help before I even found them. We both know that."

"Then *why*? Because of last night?"

He saw her jaw muscles tighten. "I don't want to get into all my reasons. Suffice it to say it's nothing personal and is completely unrelated to your performance as a vet. I just don't want you as *my* vet anymore."

Tucker pushed to his feet. "Just like that. I worked around the clock for days, trying to save Tabasco. Now"—he snapped his fingers—"with no explanation, you're giving me the boot?"

"You'll be well compensated for your time. Pad my bill as much as you deem suitable, and I'll cut you a check." She shoved away from the counter and walked to the door. After opening it, she said, "Thank you for all you've done. I'll always be grateful. But now I want you out of it."

Tucker was already out on the porch, and she'd closed the door firmly behind him when his stunned mind finally grasped what she'd said at the very last. *I want you out of it.* Not *I want you gone.* Not *It's been nice knowing you.*" Not *We're finished.* She just wanted him out of it. And suddenly he knew why.

He promptly turned around and went back inside. She was

sitting at the table with her head cradled on her folded arms. When she realized he'd reentered the room, she snapped erect, her eyes glistening with tears he hadn't given her time to shed. Tucker closed the door behind him and leaned his back against it.

"Why do you want me out of it?" he asked, already knowing the answer to his question and loving her all the more because he did.

"I don't owe you any explanation," she retorted tremulously. "Just go, Tucker. It's a business decision, and I have every right to make it. Just go."

He leaned more of his weight against the door, folded his arms over his chest, and hooked the heel of one boot over the ankle of the other. "I'm not going anywhere. The last time I allowed a woman to protect me, I was a snot-nosed brat who couldn't cross the street without holding someone's hand. I'm a big boy now. I don't need you or anyone else to watch out for me."

"You *have* to dissociate yourself from me," she cried, standing up so fast her chair almost toppled. "Do you have any idea what they're *implying*? It's bad enough that my good name is being ripped to shreds. I won't allow yours to be destroyed, too!"

"It's not your choice to make."

"It most certainly *is*!" she cried shrilly. "You're a *vet*, Tucker, a rising star in specialized equine care. If people get it into their heads that you're personally involved with a woman who poisoned her own horses for financial gain—or worse, that you turned a blind eye and allowed it to happen—your career will be ruined. Even if it all comes right in the end, the accusations will remain in people's memories. Do you honestly believe they'll call you when one of their horses gets sick?"

She had a point, and Tucker knew it. If he stood by her through this, he might be flushing his career and all his dreams straight down the toilet. Only in the end, what was it all about if he had no one to share his life with?

"I love you," he said thickly. "If it comes to a choice between you or my career, the career will come in second every time."

She locked her arms around her waist. "You don't love me. You barely know me."

"That's not true. If you only look at the actual time I've known you, I suppose it's fair to say it's happened really fast. But we haven't been together under ordinary circumstances. I've watched you go through one catastrophe after another ever since we met. No romantic candlelight dinners, no walks in the moonlight, no meaningless small talk, trying to get to know you. I've *seen* who you are, sweetheart. It's apparent in the way you care for your horses, in the way you keep putting one foot in front of the other when most people would have already dropped in their tracks from sheer exhaustion. You're a loving, loyal, and caring person. Your employees adore you, your horses adore you, your father and brothers adore you, and now so do I."

Her chin started to quiver. "I love you, too. That's why I have to get you out of this. Do you think they'll care if they wrongly destroy your reputation? Think again. All they care about is the story and how well it sells papers or draws viewers. What of Isaiah? What of your practice? This could bleed over onto your brother and hurt his career as well."

"Isaiah is a damned good vet, and his practice isn't going to go under because of a little mudslinging in the local news. Things may get rough for a while, but he'll survive, and gladly. We Coulters stick together. If someone takes a shot at one of us, he takes a shot at all of us. That's just how it is."

"I'm not a Coulter."

"No," he said softly, "but you're soon going to be, if I have anything to say about it." When her chin came up in stubborn defiance, he added, "I don't expect you to take my name. You've built your business as Samantha Harrigan, and it probably wouldn't be wise to change that now. But you will have to marry me."

She swung away. "Don't be ridiculous. I'm not marrying you or anyone else. I'd rather have a tooth pulled without Novocain."

"Poor Father Mike."

Pacing back and forth, she threw up her hands. "What does Father Mike have to do with it?"

"Because until you change your mind, he'll be blushing clear to the roots of his hair every Saturday when we go to confession."

She whirled to face him and gave a startled little gasp when she found him almost on top of her. *"We?"*

"Of course, *we*. Do you think I'd let you go alone when I'm as guilty as you are?"

"Don't be absurd. You can't go to confession." She retreated a step to put distance between them. "You're not Catholic."

"I am so. I was baptized in the Church, at any rate, and I know how to say the first and last parts of a Hail Mary."

"That doesn't make you a Catholic."

"Then I'll do whatever's necessary to become one. Your faith is a huge part of who you are. If we're going to get married and raise a family, I want to share that with you."

She shook her head as if to clear her thoughts, an odd little gesture that suggested mainframe overload. Pressing her fingertips to her temples, she said, "You're out of your mind."

"Guilty as charged. I'm crazy in love with you, at any rate."

She lifted a bruised, aching gaze to his, her expression almost pleading. "I'll make a bargain with you, then."

"What kind of bargain?"

"You leave right now. You dissociate yourself from me." She held up a hand. "Not forever. Just until this is over. When my name has been cleared, we'll start back up where we left off."

Tucker grasped her by the shoulders. "No way, sweetheart. Truly loving someone means sticking tight through thick and thin, good times and bad. I love you, and I'm here to stay."

Before she could argue, Tucker dipped his head and settled his mouth over hers. For just an instant she tried to arch away from him. But then, with a soft sob of surrender, she made fists on his shirt and kissed him back.

When he allowed her to come up for air, she gulped and said, "There are conditions."

"What kind of conditions?" he asked as he nibbled on her ear.

"That you'll respect me as an equal, always, no exceptions," she said with a shiver of sensual delight.

"No problem."

"And you have to let me make my own decisions."

"Absolutely." He touched the tip of his tongue to the sensitive spot just under her earlobe. "I wouldn't want it any other way."

She moaned softly. "And you have to let me take risks. I've been sheltered and protected all my life. I'm sick of it."

Tucker didn't like the idea of her taking risks. On the other hand, he'd seen her family in action and understood her need to feel independent and in charge of her life. "Will you consult with me first and at least listen to what I think before you put yourself at risk?"

She shivered again and pressed closer. "Just so long as you don't try to call all the shots."

"I won't," he promised. "Anything else?"

"Yes." Her hot, moist breath wafted over the exposed skin at the collar of his shirt. "You have to be faithful, no ifs, ands, or buts."

"I'll go you one better and swear I'll never even so much as *look* at another woman that way."

She tipped her head back to gaze up at him with passion-glazed eyes, her soft lips parted in invitation. "Then you can stay," she whispered.

*   *   *

Samantha felt like a bit of flotsam drifting aimlessly in a current of warm water as Tucker carried her upstairs. He didn't allow her time to think about what they were doing—or about the consequences. Nor did he pause before depositing her on the bed to remove her clothing. If he'd stopped kissing her long enough to let her draw more than one breath—or if he'd hesitated for just a second to unbutton her shirt—she might have been able to collect her thoughts and call a halt before anything more happened.

He did neither of those things. Instead he gently laid her on the mattress and followed her down, never so much as removing his mouth from hers. And his hands seemed to be everywhere—big, hard, warm, and gentle hands that knew just how and where to touch to make her lose what was left of her sanity.

"Oh, Tucker," she whispered as he peeled her shirt away and bent to trail hot kisses along her throat as he unfastened her bra. "I love you."

He was willing to sacrifice his career for her? Dizzily she marveled at that. During her marriage it had always been about Steve. Steve's needs, Steve's expectations, Steve's desires. He'd never cared a whit about her feelings or her happiness, and he'd definitely never stood by her through anything. The knowledge that Tucker not only wanted to stand by her, but insisted on it, regardless of the cost to himself, went a long way toward convincing her that maybe, just maybe, there actually was such a thing as true love.

The loveliest rose of all.

As her bra fell away and cold air touched her nipples, his hot mouth and hand were there to cover her sensitive flesh. She gasped and arched her spine as jolt after jolt of delicious sensation streaked through her. Making fists in his hair, she clung to him, her mind spinning as liquid heat swirled deep into her belly and became molten fire. She could no longer form a complete thought and didn't try. *Tucker.* He made her feel as if she were flying.

After attending to her breasts, he moved his mouth in a burning trail downward, tracing each of her ribs with his tongue, then moving lower, tugging her jeans down over her hips as he went. Dimly Samantha realized where he was headed and tried to clamp her knees together. But he was having none of that, and again, he allowed her no time to think. Before she could even formulate the word *no,* the heat of his mouth had covered her, and with the first flick of his tongue, every rational thought in her head drained out through her ears.

It was . . . *incredible.* She arched her hips, felt his broad shoulders move between her legs, and then she was soaring.

"Tucker!"

In some distant part of her mind, she heard herself making sounds. Little moans, guttural whimpers, and even shrill shrieks, but she couldn't make herself stop. Higher and higher he took her, until the pressure within her was almost painful. Just when she thought she could bear it no more, he sent her over the edge into a dark, spiraling fall shot through with sparkling lights, and the most delicious sense of satisfaction she'd ever experienced moved through her, as thick and sweet as warm honey.

Her body was still in spasms when he rose over her, all dark, wavy hair, intense blue eyes, and bronzed skin. Muscles rippled and bunched in his shoulders as he braced himself above her. Vaguely, she registered that he'd removed his shirt. The next second she realized he'd also unfastened his pants, because the long, hard heat of him thrust into her.

She'd thought never to experience anything to equal what he'd just done to her, but, oh, how wrong she was. Her body quickened around him as he established a fast, relentless rhythm, and each time he plunged deep, sensation exploded within her. The feelings were so intense they almost frightened her.

"Tucker?"

"Just hug my neck," he whispered gruffly.

And she did, clinging to him as he carried her farther and higher toward that point of almost painful need yet again. Only this time, she knew how it would end, and she wanted to experience those feelings with him more than she'd ever wanted anything.

Suddenly she felt every muscle in his body snap tight, and his pace slowed to hard, evenly spaced thrusts that brought her teeth together and made everything feminine within her pulse with pleasure until she exploded on a rush of sensual climax that robbed her of breath.

Afterward he collapsed, shifting his body slightly to one side to avoid crushing her, yet still partly on top of her, his right arm hooked around her waist. Limp with exhaustion, she was happy to simply lie there, feeling the furious thrum of his heartbeats move through her. Neither of them spoke. They were too busy trying to catch their breath.

When at last their heart rates settled down to normal, he stirred, pushing up on one elbow to gaze solemnly down at her. What they'd done was just beginning to dawn on her, and she expected him to say something foolishly romantic to make her feel better.

Instead he said, "I can't believe it. I've fallen head over heels in love with a screamer."

The outrageous observation tugged a startled laugh from her, and he treated her to one of those stunning, trademark grins that made him look both boyishly mischievous and dangerously masculine at once. Her heart filled with absolute wonder. How could anyone so handsome and accomplished, who could surely have any woman he wanted, possibly be in love with *her*? But he was. *Knowing* that, feeling absolutely *certain* of that, was one of the sweetest gifts anyone had ever given her.

"I love you," he said softly, and dipped his head to trail his lips over her brows.

"I love you, too," she murmured. "I love you so very much."

He drew back to meet her gaze, all trace of a smile gone from his face. "I know you do," he whispered. "And I'm right there with you, sweetheart, loving you with my whole heart and soul."

"Samantha Jane?" a male voice yelled from somewhere downstairs. "You in here, darlin'?"

"Oh, my *God*, it's *Daddy!*" she whispered.

Tucker looked as horrified as she felt. He sprang off the bed as if it had suddenly turned into hot coals, grabbed his shirt and jerked it on, and then left off dressing himself to collect her clothing. Before she quite realized what he was about, he'd shoved her bra straps up her arms, fastened the hooks, and already had one of her arms pushed into a shirt-sleeve. Samantha gulped back a demented giggle because the bra was inside out, and she couldn't imagine how he'd managed to fasten it.

"What are we *doing*?" he suddenly asked.

She clamped a hand over his mouth. "Shh, he'll hear."

He turned his head aside and whispered, "We're both consenting adults. Why are we acting like a couple of guilty kids?"

"Because," she whispered back, "he's my *father*."

"Right," he replied, as if that made total sense. "Your father. *Damn*."

He tucked in the tails of his shirt with hard thrusts and fastened his jeans. As he buckled his belt, he said, "Where do you want me to hide?"

It meant the world to her that he understood how she felt. "In the bathroom. I'll holler up when he's gone."

In a flurry of movement Samantha jerked on her jeans, finished donning her shirt, pulled on one boot, and then couldn't find the other one. "Damn, damn, *damn*." She toed the boot back off, only then registering that she had just made love to the handsomest man she'd ever met with her socks still on. "Just a minute, Dad!" she called. "I'll be right down. You woke me from a nap."

Tucker rolled his eyes, clearly unimpressed with her ability to lie convincingly. Samantha didn't care. She was not, absolutely *not*, going to let her father know that she'd been having sex with her veterinarian.

She hurried out onto the landing, raced down the stairs, stopped just outside the kitchen to frantically finger-comb her hair, and then calmly entered the kitchen. "Hi!" she said brightly.

Her father treated her to a long study, much as he had long ago when she'd gotten into mischief as a child and tried to pull the wool over his eyes. "Kind of late in the day for a nap, isn't it?" he observed.

"Yes, well." She pushed at her hair again. And then, to her horror, she saw her ball cap lying in the middle of the kitchen floor. "I was just so exhausted, I couldn't keep my eyes open." Acting casual, she made a beeline for the hat. "I guess the last few weeks have taken a toll." Yawning for effect and hoping to keep his attention on her face, she kicked the hat under the table. "I can't seem to get enough sleep."

"Tucker exhausted, too?" he asked, his expression deadpan but for the questioning lift of his eyebrows.

"Tucker?" she echoed stupidly.

"Jerome saw the two of you walkin' this way, and Tucker's nowhere to be found in the stables. Given that his truck and dog are still outside, it follows he must be here." He waited a beat. "Maybe you should go back upstairs and check to see if he's under the bed."

Samantha felt fiery heat surge into her cheeks. She jumped with a guilty start when Tucker spoke up from behind her. "No need to go searching. I'm right here." His boot heels tapped the floor as he came to stand at her side. "Before you blow your stack, Frank, it's not how it looks."

Frank thumbed up the brim of his hat to give Tucker an expectant look. "How is it then?"

"I plan to marry her as soon as I can convince her to have me."

Frank settled a questioning gaze on his daughter. After a long silence he said, "If you need convincin', Samantha Jane, you're not as smart as I thought you were."

Samantha still hadn't managed an intelligent response when her father swept off his hat, hooked it over the back of one of the chairs, and sat down.

"We need to talk, ladies and gents. I just got a call from Ray Ballantine, and the news about Fisher isn't good."

Chapter Seventeen

Samantha sat at the table beside Tucker, facing her father. Her heart was still slamming, and her face felt hot. It was more than a little unsettling to meet her dad's gaze when her body still thrummed in the afterglow of having had glorious sex. It didn't help that the experience had been a new one for her. She still wanted to be upstairs in Tucker's arms. She needed some private, quiet time to go back over all of it in her mind, and then hold it close to her heart and marvel that something so beautiful had happened to *her*. Instead she was involved in a discussion she couldn't concentrate on, her skin felt sticky, and the rough lace of her inside-out bra chafed her nipples every time she moved.

"Samantha Jane?"

With a guilty start, she forced her attention back on her father. "I'm sorry. What did you say?"

He studied her solemnly. "This may be one of the most important conversations we've ever had or will ever have. You need to listen." At her nod, he repeated himself. "Steve Fisher was in Boise, Idaho, at a bull-ridin' event on the weekend Tabasco first got sick. He was in Denver at another rodeo the night Blue Blazes was doped. On Thursday, there's no way he could have been here to poison Cilantro and Hickory. He was clear down in Sacramento."

As she absorbed that information, Samantha felt an awful coldness move through her. "So it wasn't Steve after all?"

Her dad shoved his thick, calloused fingers through his hair. "Apparently not. Ballantine checked with every possible airline to make sure Fisher didn't hop on a puddle jumper to get back here, do the deed, and then leave again. The man wasn't on any of the flights, and in this day and age, with heightened security even at smaller airports, his flyin' under another name is highly unlikely. Ray also assured me that on two occasions, there were no flights available into Redmond for Steve to have taken."

"Maybe he flew back to Portland and drove down here," Samantha suggested. "If you break the speed limit, you can make it in three hours."

Frank shook his head. "Ballantine thought of that. After goin' over all the information Tucker gave him, he determined that Steve couldn't possibly have pulled it off. The times of the flight arrivals in Portland, along with the drivin' time, just don't add up and coincide with the times Tucker estimated the dope and poison had to have been ingested."

"Is Ballantine *positive* Fisher was actually that far away all three times?" Tucker asked angrily. "If he's tracking the bastard by purchases that were made, maybe it wasn't Steve using his credit card. I've used my brothers' cards occasionally, and they've used mine. We just forge each other's names. Most times they don't ask for picture ID when it's a small purchase. Credit card activity in those locations doesn't absolutely prove Steve was there."

Frank shook his head again. "That was my first thought, too, but there's other evidence. Steve actually competed in bull-ridin' events at all three locations. In each instance hundreds of people saw him perform. Even worse, he took first place in the Sacramento competition, attended the winner's banquet afterward, and gave a speech. He was there, all right."

The room fell ominously silent while Samantha and

Tucker struggled to assimilate that. "I was so *sure*," she said tautly. "Who else but Steve would do something so vile?"

"I don't know," her father replied. "I only know we have to find out, honey. If we don't, you're in big trouble."

Tucker's big, warm hand encircled hers beneath the table. It helped soothe her to feel the heat of his wide wrist resting on her thigh.

"Ballantine has concluded that it has to have been some-one else," her father went on. Looking directly at his daugh-ter, he added, "Someone on the inside."

"The inside?" she repeated stupidly.

Frank nodded. "I know it's not a nice thing to think about, but with Steve completely out of the picture, we've got to fo-cus on anyone else who has access to your horses. Ballantine wants permission to investigate all of your employees first. If that turns up nothin', he'll turn the magnifyin' glass on everyone else—delivery people, friends, even family."

"No." Samantha shook her head. "Family, Dad? That's *crazy*."

"I know it," Frank agreed. "And I don't believe for a min-ute that he'll turn up anything on any of us. Unfortunately, honey, I can't be so sure about your employees. People can seem one way and be another, especially when you don't know 'em well. I'd like your authorization to put every damned one of 'em under Ballantine's magnifyin' glass."

Samantha clung to Tucker's hand now. "Nan? Ronnie?" She remembered the pathetic bouquet of weeds that Car-rie had picked for Cilantro's grave, and the anguish on the young woman's face. "They're not just employees, Daddy. They're my *friends*. I trust them."

"I know it, but maybe you shouldn't."

"Not even Nan?" Samantha couldn't count the times that she and Nan had laughed until they were weak over some bit of girlish nonsense. She couldn't in her heart believe that Nan had a mean bone in her entire body. Or Carrie, either, for that matter. "If Nan ever finds out I had her investigated, just

think how she'll feel. It would be a terrible slap in the face."
She thought of Kyle and shook her head again. Though the
stable hand made a constant pest of himself by coming on to
her and every other woman in her employ, Samantha didn't,
couldn't, believe that he would do something so vicious.
"No," she said. "I want to find out who did this, but we have
to set limits on how far we'll go. Those special programs of
Ballantine's invade people's privacy."

"I'll go first," Tucker said softly. Angling a determined
look at Samantha, he said, "If I don't have a problem with
being investigated, no one else should take it personally, either. A crime has been committed—a *terrible* crime. It may
be an invasion of Nan's privacy if Ballantine documents
when and where she last bought tampons or discovers that
she reads soft porn, but keep it in perspective. Compared to
what Cilantro and Hickory were subjected to, it's nothing."

"You, investigated?" she echoed. "Why would I even
consider—"

"Several reasons," he interjected, "starting with the fact
that I'm in love with you. Maybe I'm insanely jealous and
got pissed, thinking you smiled wrong at Jerome or Kyle."

"That's *absurd.*"

"Absurd, yes, but also possible. Like your dad says, people can seem one way and be another. What do you really
know about me?"

"I know everything I need to know," she said softly, hearing the echo of his words to her only a short time ago. "You'd
never poison one of my horses. I *know* it. I don't need a report from Ray Ballantine to tell me that."

Tucker's blue eyes went cloudy with tenderness. He
gave her hand an affectionate squeeze. "Thank you for that,
Sammy. It means more to me than I can say. But it still makes
sense for me to go first. I have access to morphine. I met you
only a short while before all of this came down. I frequently
visit farms and ranches, giving me an opportunity to get my
hands on outdated swine feed or sprays that contain arseni-

cals. I also have the knowledge to pull it off. Lastly, if any of your employees find out they've been investigated and are offended, you can mollify them with the response that *everyone* was investigated, even your vet."

"I don't like it," she protested.

"You'll like goin' to jail even less," her father retorted. He gave Tucker an admiring look. "I'll go next." His hard mouth tipped into a grin. "Why not?" He returned his gaze to his daughter. "You can tell your employees that you had your own father checked out." He lifted his hands. "Aside from popcorn and *Benji* films at Dee Dee's place, I've got nothin' to hide. Anyone who gets totally pissed is someone worth lookin' closer at, if you ask me."

"Even Jerome?" Samantha said shakily.

"Jerome won't give a shit," her father replied. "If he was here, he'd be linin' up behind me and Tucker to go on Ballantine's list. He loves you, honey. And he loved Cilantro, too. He wants to catch the person who killed her every bit as much as we do."

"I have to talk to him first," Samantha insisted. "I can live without the rest of them, but not Jerome. He's like part of our family."

"I'll talk to him," her father assured her. "If he objects to being scrutinized, we'll honor his wishes. But I'll be mightily surprised if he does. Jerome has no secrets that are worth keepin'. If he's ashamed to do somethin', he doesn't do it, plain and simple."

"All right," Samantha pushed out, but the words came hard. By giving her permission, she was acknowledging the possibility that someone on her payroll, someone she cared about and genuinely liked, was as heartless and evil as Steve Fisher. What did that say for the world she lived in?

Her father pushed up from his seat to cross the kitchen and make some coffee. As he rinsed the basket and reusable filter, he asked, "Is there anyone, anyone at all who works for you, who may have reason to hate you, honey?"

Samantha drew her hand from Tucker's and wrapped her arms around her waist. "I don't think so. I try to be a good boss. Maybe I fail in that sometimes, but mostly I think I'm fair."

As he measured out coffee, Frank said, "I don't necessarily mean that you did somethin' to deserve the hatred. And maybe *hatred* is the wrong word. Take Kyle, for instance, always struttin' his stuff and makin' eyes at you. A second ago, Tucker talked about the possibility that he could be insanely jealous. Could the same hold true for Kyle?" He slapped the basket drawer closed on the coffeemaker and pushed the brewing button. "You're a beautiful woman. The man works with you day in and day out. It's entirely possible that what you laugh off and make light of is very serious to him."

"It's not like that, Dad." Samantha started to say that Frank thought she was beautiful only because he was her father, but knowing and loving Tucker had wrought a change within her, and she no longer felt second-rate. "To Kyle I'm just another mark. He comes on to everyone. That's just *him*. He may be serious, in a joking sort of way, but he doesn't get mad when he's turned down. He just regroups and tries again."

Her father drew three mugs from the cupboard. "You got your tablet in your pocket, Tucker?"

"I *always* have my tablet."

"Start taking notes then," Frank advised. "We need to make a list."

"A list of what?" Samantha asked.

"Suspects," her father replied. "People who may have a reason to want to hurt you, or kill your horses, or damage your reputation, even if it seems far-fetched." To Tucker, he added, "This may take a while. If you'd like to bring your dog in, I'm sure Samantha wouldn't mind."

Three pieces of jerky and two bowls of water later, Max lay asleep with his head on Samantha's stocking feet as the discussion continued. In less than an hour, everyone in Samantha's employ had been scrutinized except Jerome, and it had been determined that each person might, for one reason or another, have it in for Samantha.

"I still find it hard to swallow that it could be Nan," Samantha said for at least the third time. "We're *friends*."

"She's also working her ass off for a piddlin' wage."

"I pay her decent money," Samantha argued.

"For a rancher still strugglin' to make it, you pay her decent," Frank retorted. "But she may not see it that way. She's got an apartment; you've got a nice home. She drives a rattletrap economy car; you drive a new four-wheel-drive Ford. Trust me, honey, I've been there, with hired hands who hated my guts just for bein' their boss. It didn't matter that I worked harder than they did and went without, tryin' to make ends meet. In their eyes, I was a little rich boy who'd inherited this land and had every damned thing handed to me on a silver platter."

"All right, all right," Samantha said in defeat. "It's a long shot, but we can put down her name, I guess."

She glanced over Tucker's arm to peruse the list again. Even the quiet, unassuming Carrie had come under fire, the contention of Frank and Tucker being that the woman was homely, friendless, and might secretly resent Samantha for making her feel inferior. In Samantha's opinion, their arguments held no water. She'd seen the anguish in Carrie's eyes when she'd stood over Cilantro's grave. The woman's tears had not been faked.

"I'm exhausted," Samantha said, sinking back in her chair. "Put everybody on the list. I don't care."

Frank held out his hand for the sheet of paper Tucker had just torn from the tablet. "I'll be leavin' then so you can get some rest while I call Ballantine."

Samantha held up her arms to give her father a farewell hug. He returned the embrace, pressing a kiss to her forehead. "Stop your frettin'," he commanded. "Ray Ballantine's a good man. He'll do his best not to offend your friends if he feels it's necessary to question them. And if he finds nothing on 'em, they'll probably never even know he investigated them."

After her father left, Samantha found it difficult to look at Tucker. In the cold aftermath of their lovemaking, she felt a little embarrassed over some of the intimacies she had so wholeheartedly engaged in. Okay, a *lot* embarrassed. And to top it all off, she'd been so into it that she'd actually screamed.

"Hey," he said softly. "What's wrong?"

"Nothing."

He caught her chin and forced her to look at him. After studying her for a long moment, he said, "You're blushing."

"No, I'm not."

"That's two in less than a minute."

"Two what?"

"Fibs. Fib number one, if it's bothering you, it isn't nothing. Fib number two, you *are* blushing, which tells me you're either upset about something or embarrassed." He narrowed his blue eyes slightly. "Let me guess. You're remembering what we did, and you're feeling uncomfortable."

"Do we *have* to go there?"

Keeping a firm grip on her chin, he leaned close, eclipsing her vision with a blur of masculine features as he traced the line of her cheekbone with warm, silken lips. His breath smelled faintly of coffee and moved over her skin like a caress. And to her dismay, just that fast, she wanted him again.

"I can't," she murmured. "I need time to think."

"I'm afraid to let you think," he whispered. "Just *feel.* This is right. You know it, and I know it. I've never felt this way with anyone. Just one touch, and my heart's already pounding."

"It *isn't* right," she protested. "At least, not for me."

She thought of how she'd felt facing her father afterward, knowing that he knew. It had *not* been a good feeling. Perhaps it was hopelessly old-fashioned—and maybe the whole rest of the world had long since changed—but she hadn't, not until today, and now she felt all mixed-up, happy and sad, both at once, as if she'd found something absolutely priceless but had lost something precious as well.

Tucker sighed and pressed his forehead to hers. "Is this about the confession thing again?"

Samantha squeezed her eyes closed, embarrassed about who she was and what she believed. "I know my feelings are antiquated. I'm probably the first woman you've ever taken to bed who thinks it's wrong. But that's who I am, Tucker. It's how I believe. I not only *can't* change it, but I don't *want* to change it."

"God, you sound like my mother." When she tried to jerk away, he curled a strong hand over her nape and held her fast. "I don't mean it as an insult. My mom's the sweetest person I've ever known—until I met you."

Samantha squeezed her eyes closed.

"And here's another news flash for you," he went on. "*I* don't want you to change. Get that through your head: I love you just as you are. Correction. Your being who you are is *why* I love you. Does that make sense?"

She nodded but still felt mixed-up, because being with him that way had been the most incredible experience of her entire life. And she already wanted to experience it again. "Oh, Tucker."

"What?" he whispered.

She turned her face slightly, hoping his lips might meet hers in a kiss that would rob her of thought and give her the excuse she needed to make love with him again. Just *once*. Or maybe dozens of times. She could be like a dieter on an eating binge, gobbling him up over the entire next week, and then swearing off on Saturday, promising herself and God that she'd never indulge again.

The thought was so crazy yet appealing that it made her smile.

"What?" he asked again.

"I'm just wishing I weren't such a fuddy-duddy. I *am* a

little embarrassed about what we did," she confessed, "but mostly I just wish we could do it again."

He chuckled and pressed his face against her hair. "Me, too." He fell quiet for a moment, and then he added, "I can't believe I'm about to say this, but maybe we should abstain from this point forward. I don't want you feeling guilty. It's supposed to be a beautiful thing, something really precious and wonderful."

And it had been, Samantha thought. It wasn't his fault that she was impossibly old-fashioned, with an overactive conscience and an overdose of Catholic guilt.

Grasping her by the shoulders, he set her slightly away from him so they could look into each other's eyes. "So here's what we're going to do. No more sex. We'll go together next Saturday to talk with Father Mike."

"That isn't how it works, Tucker. You go to confession alone. It's only between you, the priest, and God, no fourth party allowed."

"How does that make sense? If we did it together, why can't we fess up together?"

"I suppose we could talk with him together. But it wouldn't count as a confession, and I wouldn't receive absolution."

"You wouldn't receive *what*?"

Samantha searched his face and then burst out laughing. If Tucker Coulter became a Catholic, the Church might never be the same.

"What's so funny?"

"Nothing." In that moment, Samantha accepted, deep within her, that she'd been in love with him for a very long time—a few weeks that felt like a lifetime. She loved the way his eyes twinkled with mischief, the way his firm mouth tipped slowly into a grin, the way he rubbed beside his nose when he was discomfited, and most especially she loved the way he could make her laugh when she least expected it. How many men would consider going with her to confession? Not many, she felt sure. "I really don't need you to go with me to see Father Mike. We're friends. He'll talk with me and try to advise me. He won't yell or anything."

"I'm going," he said firmly. "It's partly my fault you did it. And besides, that's not all I want to talk to him about."

"What else?"

"About the hoops I have to jump through to become a practicing Catholic and marry you."

"Don't put it quite that way to Father Mike. You need to feel a burning desire before he'll even *discuss* your becoming a practicing Catholic."

He dipped his head to kiss the end of her nose. "Trust me, I feel a burning desire."

"Not *that* kind of desire. And it isn't absolutely necessary for you to share my beliefs, anyway," she informed him. "The Church is far more lenient about that nowadays. Optimally, it's best if both people are Catholic, but it's not—"

"I'm becoming a practicing Catholic," he interrupted. "It's what I want for several reasons, not the least of which is that it will make my mother extremely happy. She'll be beside herself with joy and weep rivers of tears if one of her sons is married in the Church. My father will have to bypass handkerchiefs and go equipped with a bath towel to mop up after her."

"I haven't officially said yes yet, you know."

"A small wrinkle," he said with a grin. "You are free to marry me, right? In the eyes of the Church, I mean."

"Yes—after my divorce, Father Mike helped me get a papal dispensation in record time. He even testified on my behalf about Steve's complete disregard for the sacrament of marriage and his repeated infidelities, which started the first week after the wedding."

"Back up. After your divorce, you got a *what*?"

Shortly after midnight Samantha's phone rang, and the sound sent her heart clear into her throat. Coming upright from a sound sleep, she grabbed the portable.

"Yes? What's wrong?"

"Nothing, it's just me," the deep voice that had been whispering in her dreams said softly. "I'm sorry for waking you up, but I just got off call, and I had to hear your voice."

Samantha smiled before her eyes came fully open. "Tucker?"

"Does some other man call at this hour just to hear your voice? If so, give me his name, and I'll kill him."

Her smile became a full-blown grin. "No, no one else," she murmured. "Only you."

"Damned good thing. I could get crazy." Silence. "Say you love me."

Her heart twisted, not because it would be a lie, but because saying the words, verbalizing the commitment, still came hard for her. "Oh, Tucker. I just—"

"It's *so* easy. Just repeat after me. *I.*"

Her smile went all soft. "I," she repeated softly.

"Love," he prompted.

"Love," she repeated.

"You," he whispered in a gravelly voice.

"You," she said.

"Thank you. I'll be able to sleep now."

She settled back against the pillow, which still smelled faintly of him, and she wished with all her heart that his big, strong arms were wrapped around her. "Where are you, in bed?"

"Don't I wish. I just left the clinic and I'm heading home. For the first time in my career I flaked out on Isaiah and went in late, not answering my pager. That's what you've done to me, lady. Nothing else matters to me but you. Isaiah was royally pissed. It's my weekend to work. I think he had a hot Saturday night with Laura planned, and the emergency calls ruined it."

She snuggled deeper into the blankets. "What's she like?"

"Laura? She's a total doll. You'll take one look and be instant friends. It's a rule in our family. All the ladies have to be angels."

"Uh-oh, my halo is a bit tarnished at the moment."

"I'll spit-shine it up for you. Confession on Saturday, a trip to the altar as fast as I can manage it. No more angst."

Samantha was losing touch with her angst. Deep in her heart she found it difficult to believe that anything that happened between them could be wrong, because she loved him so much it hurt. "Have you ever been on a strict diet?"

"In high school for wrestling. I used to starve and run the stairs to get one pound under heavyweight so I could kick ass. Why?"

Samantha could remember Parker and Quincy doing that, only they'd been starving to make lightweight. "After making weight, did you ever binge?"

"I once devoured three giant pizzas in one sitting. Why?"

Samantha closed her eyes, remembering when he'd been there with her several hours ago, and she *wanted*. It was a yearning that went clear to the marrow of her bones. "I was just thinking."

"About what?"

"Earlier, and how fabulous it was. And that I have a whole week before I have to go to confession. I don't think my penance would be any worse for three or maybe even a dozen pizzas than it would be for one."

"Penance?"

She almost giggled. "Tucker, you have a lot to learn before you can receive your First Communion. You'll have to study for a year."

"Bullshit. I'll have it down in a week. I have a photographic memory."

She laughed again. "Father Mike will *not* allow you to receive the eucharist in a week."

"Why not? Technically I'm already a Catholic. But forget that. Let's go back to talking about bingeing on pizza."

Samantha sighed regretfully. "Forget I said it. There's a huge part of me that wishes I could be less uptight and just go for it. But another part of me still feels seven years old, when there was never a gray area between right and wrong."

"The very fact that you see what we did as a gray area tells me we can't go there. I don't want you to feel that way. No sex. I'm sticking by the decision. How hard can it be to abstain? Priests are celibate. If they can do it, I sure as hell can."

Chapter Eighteen

Tucker felt confident in his ability to simply say no, the only fly in the ointment his memory of Samantha saying she was tempted to binge on sex the entire next week. He might be with her now instead of going home to a cold, empty bed. Only then what? Raised as she'd been, she'd agonize about it whenever they were apart, and he didn't want that. It wasn't about right or wrong or the gray areas in between, but about how she felt.

Sometimes a guy just had to be strong.

Once in the house, Tucker fed Max, freshened the dog's water, and then belted down two whiskeys, chased with a cold shower. *Hell, yes.* He could do this. All it would take was keeping his gonads shriveled to the size of raisins. As he toweled off, he briefly considered jumping in his truck, driving like a maniac to Samantha's ranch, and making love to her until dawn. Resisting the urge was one of the hardest things he'd ever done in his life, for he knew that she was probably awake, too, and would undoubtedly welcome him.

Later Tucker wondered just how long it would take him to become a practicing Catholic. Weeks, months? He refused to contemplate the possibility of a year. How would he keep his hands off of her for so long? He toyed with the idea of writing himself a script for an anaphrodisiac. Not that he'd ever researched that particular family of drugs. What red-blooded American male wanted to take medication that caused erectile dysfunction?

Sleep came hard, and he soon awakened, his brain electrically charged with a new angle on the poisonings of Samantha's horses. Maybe Steve Fisher hadn't been anywhere near Crystal Falls when the crimes were committed, but that didn't mean he couldn't have hired it done. That was *it*, Tucker thought. Had to be it. Fisher could still be behind the poisonings.

It was the only theory that made sense. Nan Branson hadn't killed those horses. Tucker felt certain of that. And judging by the little he'd seen of Carrie Dobson, the poor woman didn't have enough self-confidence to make a decision by herself, let alone plan and commit a horrible crime. That left only the little redhead, Ronnie, who worked so few hours per week that Tucker had never seen her, or Kyle, the muscular boy toy who couldn't convince any of the ladies to play with him. Tucker couldn't say he *liked* Kyle, but his instincts told him the dude was oversexed, not vicious.

Tossing and turning, Tucker waited for dawn to brighten the sky. Then he went downstairs to make a strong pot of coffee, collected the Sunday paper from the porch, and settled at the dining room table to while away another hour before calling Ray Ballantine. The instant he unrolled the paper, his stomach took a hard downward plunge. His own face stared back at him from the front page. Next to the photo of Tucker was a grainy, dated picture of Samantha, a graduation bust shot of her in cap and gown. She looked very young and incredibly innocent. Tucker couldn't tell if the photo had been taken when she graduated from high school or college. He knew only that he loved every line of her sweet face and would have moved mountains to keep her from seeing the headline, which read, TWO HORSES DIE OF ARSENIC POISONING. The story that followed didn't flat-out accuse Samantha of poisoning the animals, but the reporter who'd written the piece had done a very slick job of implying that she had. It would be Tucker's luck that she'd try to give him the boot again. Knowing she might do just that in an attempt to protect him, he loved her all the more.

It was still too early to call Ballantine, but Tucker had no such compunction about waking his brother. Isaiah answered on the third ring, his voice gruff with sleep.

"Have you seen the Sunday paper?" Tucker asked.

"Hell, no. It's barely daylight, and it's my day off."

"I need you to go on call for me, Isaiah. I know it's my turn, and I promise to make it up to you, but I need the day off. When Samantha sees this story, I have to be with her. She's going to freak."

"That bad, huh?"

"Worse than bad. I'm tempted to hire a lawyer to sue the pants off the newspaper, but Frank will probably beat me to it."

Sounding more awake, Isaiah said, "I hate when people say it, but I told you so. Next they may turn the spotlight on you."

After breaking the connection with his brother, Tucker went upstairs to shave and get dressed. When he returned to the kitchen half an hour later, it was nearly six thirty, late enough, in his opinion, to roust Ballantine out of bed and tell him to meet him at the Sage Creek Ranch.

Ray Ballantine held court at Samantha's kitchen table. Four of the formal dining room chairs had to be commandeered for seating. Everyone in Samantha's family had shown up for the meeting, and so had Jerome, who'd called in Kyle and Carrie to cover for him at the stable.

Tucker endeavored to keep the focus on Ballantine's investigation, not the newspaper story, but that proved to be no easy task. Clint Harrigan was so furious that his tanned face looked gray, and he sat with his arms across his chest, both fists clenched. Quincy busily honed the blade of his pocketknife, his sweeps with the whetstone slow and precise, his expression murderous. Samantha kept whispering, "I can't *believe* this. I just can't. If you don't dissociate yourself from me, Tucker, your practice will be *ruined*."

"I'm not particularly worried about my practice right now," Tucker finally told her. "I'm far more worried that the cops will take this story as a vote of public opinion and show up on your doorstep with a warrant for your arrest."

"Why can't Sammy just forgo the insurance money?" Zach suggested. "If she doesn't file the claims, how can they make a charge of fraud stick?"

"Intent to defraud is almost as serious a crime as actually committing fraud," Ballantine explained. "In order to protect your sister, we have to find out who actually poisoned the horses." As he opened a manila file folder on top of a stack, he angled a glance at Tucker. "It had already occurred to me that Fisher might have hired someone to do the dirty work, so I've checked that out. So far I've found no evidence that he paid anyone a large sum of money by check, and no significant sums have been withdrawn from his account." The detective's lip curled. "Not that he could afford to make a payoff. The man is in debt to his eyebrows and almost broke. He has only a little over three thousand in his checking, and his savings account has been closed."

Frank swore under his breath. "How can that be? Just over a year ago, he was issued a draft from my savings account for over a million dollars."

"Fisher managed," Ballantine assured them. "He purchased a new truck, a horse trailer with living quarters that set him back almost three hundred grand, and a roping horse that cost the earth. There was about four hundred thousand left, but that went quickly on—if you'll pardon the cliché—wine, women, and song. And I do mean that literally. Seven months ago he ordered five cases of Dom Pérignon, vintage 1964, at over five hundred dollars a bottle."

"Holy *shit*," Parker whispered. "What'd he do, take a bath in the stuff?"

Quincy looked up from his knife. "What the hell is Dom Pérignon?"

"Expensive champagne," Clint supplied. "On an *extremely* special occasion, I might spring for one nonvintage bottle, but it'd *still* make my teeth ache to sign the tab."

"Steve likes to impress the ladies," Samantha said softly. "He used to spend a lot on microbrewery beers and expensive blends of whiskey."

Frank rubbed a hand over his face, clearly finding it difficult to believe that his daughter's ex-husband had blown over a million dollars of his hard-earned money. "Well, I hope he enjoyed himself. There'll be no more where that came from, not one damned cent."

Tucker didn't care what Fisher had spent the million on, unless the information might clear Samantha of suspicion. "So essentially what you're saying, Ray, is that Steve couldn't have hired someone to perpetrate the crime."

"Pretty much," the detective conceded, "unless I've missed something. I tend to think not, but I'm still digging."

"Which leaves us where?" Jerome asked. "Have you found any dirt on any of the employees?"

The detective sighed. His plump countenance showed evidence of sleep deprivation, which told Tucker the man had been burning the midnight oil, trying to find something, anything that seemed out of the ordinary.

"So far nothing leaps out at me," he said. "I have learned that Nan Branson's mother is a nurse practitioner who can write prescriptions, so it's possible, if not probable, that the young lady could have forged a script to get her hands on some morphine tablets. Ronnie Post is coming out clean as a whistle, except that her grandmother had a hip replacement a couple of months ago and might have been given a morphine derivative for pain."

"You can't find out for sure?" Zach asked.

Ballantine shook his head. "With the Privacy Act, it's extremely difficult for me to dig up any medical information without hacking my way into the medical community's system. I'd be breaking the law, which I prefer never to do, and I suspect any evidential material I found would be unusable in a court of law.

"That said, it's still possible that Post's grandmother may have taken morphine for pain during her recovery. So it's not too far-fetched to think that the granddaughter could have stolen a few of the tablets." He leafed through his notes. "Both Post and Branson have been equine enthusiasts most of their lives, but neither of them ever lived on a farm nor has relatives who do, making it highly unlikely that they might have access to agricultural sprays or outdated swine feed. I'll continue to do searches on them, but my gut's telling me they're clean."

"Carrie Dobson used to work as an aide for a nursing agency," Jerome inserted. "She still occasionally works a shift for them. In-home elderly care, I think."

"I was just getting to that," Ballantine said with a weary smile that displayed his protruding front teeth. "Miss Dobson *does* care for the elderly, who are sometimes terminal and given strong doses of opiates to ease their suffering. I've spoken to the agency administrator where Dobson still works occasionally, and she swears on her life that they employ a check-and-balance inventory system at every shift change, making it impossible for one of their employees to make off with even one narcotic tablet, let alone several.

"But, as strict and careful as all nursing agencies are, in-home caregivers *have* managed to steal drugs. There are countless documented instances of it, in fact. Sometimes a nurse steals a drug and black-markets it on the street. Other times a caregiver will steal drugs to support his or her own habit."

"How do they manage that?" Tucker asked. "We have controlled substances under lock and key at our clinic, and we, too, keep careful track of the inventory. Every dispensation is recorded and logged in to a computer. If a shortage occurs, we're instantly aware of it. I thought similar procedures were required by law everywhere."

Ballantine nodded. "They are. But someone can still steal the drugs a little at a time, simply by failing to administer the recorded doses to patients. In-home elderly care offers more opportunity for sleight of hand because there is no on-site supervision, and many of the patients are either too old, weak, or mentally impaired to complain if they don't get their pain medication. The nurse enters the dose into the logbook, pockets the pills, and gives the patient a sugar tablet or nothing at all."

"That's awful," Zach said. "So the old person just suffers?"

"Pretty much, yes, until the next nurse comes on shift."

Samantha spoke up. "I can't *believe* that of Carrie. I'm sorry, but she's got a tender heart, and she'd just never do such a thing. I'm certain of it."

Tucker pretty much shared the sentiment, but he was also jaded enough about human nature to realize that even the kindest people sometimes did horribly cruel things. He saw evidence of that far too often in his line of work.

"What we have to focus on is *why* she might do it," he interjected. "With enough motive, people will do almost anything." He leveled a hard look at Ballantine. "Put the magnifying glass on Dobson," he said, "and on Branson and Post as well. All three of them could have gotten the morphine. Maybe if you take as hard a look at them as you have Fisher, something suspicious will leap out at you."

A knock came at the door just then. Tucker got up to answer the summons, thinking it was probably a security guard with a question. His heart felt as if it dived clear to his knees when he found two gentlemen in suits standing on the porch. Tucker knew they were cops before the elder one flashed his badge.

"Is Samantha Harrigan in?" the gray-haired fellow asked.

When Samantha came to stand beside Tucker in the doorway, the man said, "Samantha Harrigan, we have a warrant to search your residence."

"For what?" Frank demanded, his boots slapping the slate as he came to stand behind his daughter.

"Morphine, outdated swine feed, or any other substance containing arsenicals." The man thrust the warrant into Samantha's hands, then pushed past her and Tucker, the younger blond detective right at his heels. "You take the kitchen," the older policeman ordered over his shoulder. "I'll take the living room, and we'll fan out from there."

When the blond plugged the sink with a stopper and started dumping the contents of cereal boxes into it, Tucker turned to Frank. "Call a lawyer. *Now.* She's going to need representation."

It was all Tucker could think to do. When he spun back around, the younger detective was cutting open a cardboard drum of iodized salt and spilling granules everywhere.

"Do you have to make such a mess, asshole?" Clint demanded. "How would you like to have everything in your kitchen dumped in the sink?"

Tucker went to curl a hand over Clint's shoulder. "Keep your temper. If he dumped all of it on the counter, it'd be a whole lot worse."

All the starch went out of Clint's spine. Jerking away from Tucker, he turned on his father. "For God's sake, do something, Dad. It sounds like the other guy's tearing the living room apart!"

Visibly shaken, Frank cast a last worried look at his daughter, then drew his cell phone from his belt and stared at it as if he'd forgotten between one heartbeat and the next what he needed to do.

"An attorney," Tucker reminded him.

And then Tucker was off for the living room. The sight that greeted his eyes made his blood boil. The leather cushions of the sofa and chairs had been unzipped, the foam tossed willy-nilly onto the floor. Drawers had been upended, the contents spilled out and then walked on. He'd never seen such destruction or imagined it could occur so quickly.

When he returned to the kitchen, Samantha looked as if she were in shock. The younger detective was even going through her refrigerator. Evidence bags, filled with unidentifiable substances, already lined the kitchen counter. She hid her face against Tucker's shirt when he looped an arm around her shoulders.

"I can't believe this is happening," she said.

Tucker shared the sentiment, but it *was* happening, and he couldn't think of one damned thing he could do to stop it. When Tucker saw the older detective heading for the stairs, he handed Samantha off to her father and followed the man. The detective went directly to the first bedroom along the hall, jerked all the blankets and sheets from the bed, and slit open the mattress with a box cutter.

"What the *hell*?" Tucker was across the room in two strides. "That thing probably cost a thousand dollars, you son of a bitch." Before Tucker could say more, Clint's hard hand clamped around his arm and he was pulled back a step.

"Let it go," Clint told him. "It's not worth your getting arrested."

Tucker swung away, unable to watch any more without losing his temper and doing something he'd regret. Samantha's entire house was being turned inside out. It would take hours to set it right and possibly thousands of dollars to replace the damaged items. He couldn't frigging believe the law allowed this kind of thing to happen.

Frank Harrigan's attorney specialized in equine contractual agreements. Whenever a Harrigan bought or sold a horse, John McKay drew up the legal documents. As good as McKay was at his job, he wasn't the kind of attorney Samantha needed.

Tucker called Rafe Kendrick. Within five minutes he had the name of Sterling Johnson, the best criminal defense attorney in Crystal Falls. Affiliated with an interstate firm renowned for winning court cases, he had once been retained to defend Zeke's wife, Natalie, when her ex-husband had been murdered. Though it was a Sunday, Johnson took Tucker's call and agreed to see Samantha in his office the following day at one o'clock.

In the meantime, all Tucker could do was join Samantha's father and brothers in putting the house back in order after the detectives left. While they worked, Samantha wandered from room to room, her face pale and drawn, trying to rescue mementos and other items that were precious to her.

When as much of the damage had been repaired as possible, Tucker went in search of the woman he loved. He found her in the downstairs office, straightening the inside of the safe. She glanced up as he entered the room.

"They took samples of my *cereal*," she said. Wide with fright, her eyes clung to his. "What if someone planted morphine or arsenic somewhere in the house?"

The same thought had already occurred to Tucker, and he could think of little to say that might comfort her. Instead he drew her to her feet and locked both arms around her.

"It'll be okay," he whispered fiercely. As he made that vow, Tucker made another promise to himself: that he would confess to poisoning the horses himself before he allowed her to be arrested. The very thought of Samantha behind bars made him heartsick. "It'll be all right, I swear."

Work had always been Samantha's panacea for all ills. If she had a headache, she worked through it. If she had a problem to solve, she always worked until an answer came to her. During her marriage, she'd worked her way through one heartbreak and betrayal after another. Aside from praying, which she could do anywhere, straining her muscles, building up a sweat, and flirting with exhaustion were the only ways she knew to cope when life's problems seemed overwhelming.

That afternoon and evening were no exception. She dispatched all the males who wanted to hover over her, insisting that her father and brothers go home and that Tucker go to his clinic. When she'd gotten all of them out of her hair, she went to the stables, where there was always something to be done. Because it never failed to soothe her, she chose to bathe and groom the horses, a wet, strenuous, but fulfilling job that afforded her quiet time with the animals she so dearly loved.

Carrie lent her assistance. Samantha appreciated the other woman's silence far more than she did the help. Carrie seemed to sense that any attempt at small talk wouldn't be appreciated.

Shortly after four that afternoon, Samantha glimpsed movement at the front entrance of the arena and glanced up to see Jerome, Ballantine, her dad, all her brothers, and Tucker enter the building. Their grim expressions told her they weren't bringing good news. Stepping to the stall gate, Samantha waited for them to reach her. To her surprise, her father didn't even bother to say hello. Instead he leveled a cold glare on Carrie, who was brushing Nutmeg's mane.

"Miss Dobson, may we have a word with you?"

Carrie paled slightly. Dropping the brush to the ground, she dusted her palms clean on her jeans. "Sure," she said, walking over to join Samantha at the gate. "What about?"

"It's a conversation that should take place in the office, I think." Frank gestured for Carrie to exit the stall and turned to lead the way. "It shouldn't take long. Samantha, can you join us?"

Curious, Samantha trailed after Carrie to join the men. After she entered the office, Tucker closed the door behind her and ran the dead bolt home with an ominous click. Samantha sent him a wondering look but could read nothing in his expression. Her father sat behind the desk and motioned for Carrie to take the other chair. Like a scared rabbit searching for a bolt-hole, the stocky woman looked nervously over her shoulder. Samantha's heart squeezed, for in that moment she knew Carrie was somehow involved in the poisonings.

Frank Harrigan's voice cut through the sudden silence as viciously as a razor. "How long have you been intimately involved with Steve Fisher?"

The question ran through Samantha like an electrical jolt, and suddenly the changes in Carrie's appearance all made sense. Steve had a strong preference for slender, busty blondes who wore lots of makeup.

Carrie grew very still and squeaked, "Who?"

"Don't," Frank snapped. He quickly introduced Ray Ballantine and explained how the private eye went about investigating people. "We know about your relationship with Fisher. I will give you this one chance, and only this one chance, to come clean of your own accord. The police are bound to go a lot easier on you if you cooperate and don't waste anyone's time tryin' to lie your way out of it."

"I don't know what you're talking about."

Frank drew a piece of paper from his shirt pocket. After unfolding it, he said, "You attended a rodeo in Montana a little over a week ago to watch Fisher compete in a bull ridin' event."

"So? That proves nothing. Lots of people go to rodeos."

"Lots of people don't spend the night at the Whispering Pines Motel with Steve Fisher."

"You can't prove I was with Steve."

"Can't we? Do you think motel clerks wear blinders? We have two witnesses who are willing to testify in court that you *were* there with Fisher." Frank jerked his cell phone from his belt, flipped it open, and gave Carrie a smoldering look. "The game is up. You either start talkin', or I'm handin' you over to the police. Trust me when I say you'll talk when they have you in custody. It isn't only the one night you spent with Fisher that's been documented, Miss Dobson, but *several* nights. You can lie until you're blue in the face that you don't know the man, but the evidence proves otherwise.

We know how you got the morphine. We also know where Steve Fisher got the swine feed and that he convinced you to use it to kill the horses. What's the punishment for stealin' a controlled substance, Ray?"

"It's a federal offense, if I recall correctly, with a minimum and maximum penalty. If Ms. Dobson cooperates, the judge will probably go easy on her because it's a first offense. But if she doesn't cooperate . . . well, it's hard to say."

"And for feeding the horses swine feed that contained arsenic?"

"For that crime, a judge may put her behind bars until she's an old woman. Unless, of course, she can convince the police that Fisher was the mastermind and she only did what he told her. In that event, I don't think her sentence will be quite so harsh."

Frank waited. When Carrie remained stubbornly silent, he said softly, "It's your funeral," and started dialing the phone.

"Wait!" Carrie cried. "Wait."

Frank immediately stopped punching buttons.

"I never wanted to hurt the horses!" she cried. "You have to believe me. I *loved* Cilantro. I didn't want to kill her." And then she burst into hysterical tears. Swinging her arm toward Samantha, she wailed, "It's *her* fault. Why does she have to be such a *bitch*?"

The ensuing accusations leveled against Samantha were outrageous—a long story, which obviously originated with Steve.

"You're a cruel, heartless viper who sank her fangs into him, broke his heart, destroyed his self-esteem, humiliated him every chance you got, and then used your father's money to annihilate him in divorce court and wrongfully rob him of what was rightfully his," Carrie ranted. "You got *everything.* After all his hard work—five *years* of sweating blood to build this ranch into what it is today—he didn't get one red cent!"

Instead of denying the charge, Frank said, "The bastard didn't have a red cent coming to him."

Carrie shot up from her chair and pointed accusingly at Frank, her face contorted, mascara streaming from her eyes. "*That's* why I helped him. People like *you*, who walk all over people like him and me." Her voice quavered with absolute contempt. "He can barely pay his bills, while *she* lives in a fancy house and struts around here, acting like the big boss and issuing orders. When Steve found a way to get what he had coming to him, of *course* I agreed to help him!"

"So you poisoned the horses for him." Frank rocked back on his chair.

"Yes." Carrie covered her face with trembling hands. "I *hated* doing it, but I *had* to help him. I love him. Nobody's ever loved him until me. I didn't want to kill the horses, but it was the only way he could get any money."

Frank's eyes narrowed. "Insurance," he said softly. He shot abruptly to his feet, his gaze shifting to Samantha. "Of *course*. I'll bet he got insurance on the horses when you were still married and never canceled the policies." He looked at Ballantine. "Get on it. He probably paid the initial premiums with a check from the ranch account. I don't know how he paid this year's premiums, but there has to be a record somewhere."

Ballantine nodded. "I probably saw it and thought nothing of it. Everyone has to pay for insurance of one kind or another."

"This will be to a company that offers equine mortality insurance."

Carrie had collapsed on the chair and bent forward to hug her knees. "He said we'd get married," she wailed. "That we'd go away together, and he'd make it all up to me. I didn't *want* to hurt the horses. It was the only way he could get enough money for us to be together."

Watching Carrie sob, Samantha felt nothing but contempt for the woman. There was no excuse for what she had done.

"Did you get all that?" Frank asked Clint.

Clint held up a recorder no larger than his palm. "Every word."

Frank stopped to gaze down at Carrie's jerking shoulders. Instead of reflecting anger, his expression was sad. "I'm sorry for you, honey. You're not the first young woman whose life has been destroyed by that lyin', conscienceless bastard, but I swear on all that's holy that you're gonna be the last."

Samantha swung away toward the door. The very air in the office felt tainted, and she could barely breathe. Already with his cell phone to his ear, Tucker disengaged the dead bolt. As she escaped the room, she heard him say, "This is Tucker Coulter. I need to speak with Detective Galloway."

Darkness had long since blanketed the ranch when Samantha let herself into Blue Blazes's stall to give the stallion his nightly ration of cob. Across the arena she could hear the low inflections of Jerome's voice as he performed the same task for another horse. *Normalcy*. Only that morning, she had despaired that anything in her life would ever be right again, but now it was almost over. Carrie was in jail, and there was a warrant out for Steve's arrest. He would soon join his treacherous accomplice behind bars.

Samantha still could find no sympathy in her heart for Carrie. Yes, Steve Fisher was a charming, attractive, and dangerously manipulative man, but there were lines a woman should never cross, no matter how desperately she yearned to be loved. Carrie Dobson was a pathetic excuse for a human being, so far as Samantha was concerned. If she lived to be a hundred, she would never forget the awful way Cilantro and her baby had died. There were many things she might be able to forgive, but that heartless act wasn't one of them. She hoped Steve and Carrie paid dearly for what they'd done.

"Ah, Blue," she whispered, resting her cheek against the

stallion's withers while he enjoyed his bedtime treat. "It's so good not to feel afraid for you anymore. So very *good*."

Samantha heard a slight sound behind her and smiled in expectation. Tucker was due to show up at any moment. He'd called from his cell phone only a few minutes earlier to tell her he was just leaving the equine clinic and was on his way to the ranch. An emergency call about a sick horse had taken him away from her side at around seven. The mare was stabilized now, and Tucker felt safe about leaving her in the competent hands of his night tech.

"I thought you'd never get here," she said as she turned to give him a welcoming smile.

Her heart went still in her chest when she found Steve Fisher standing behind her. He smiled coldly. "Been counting the minutes, Samantha Jane?"

As her heart slogged back into an uneven rhythm, Samantha looked past him to the opposite side of the arena.

"Forget it. Jerome is out cold. He won't come to your rescue." He glanced around the stall. "And, uh-oh, I don't see a single chair that you can club me with."

Samantha didn't ask how he'd gotten into the building. She and Jerome hadn't set the alarm. With Carrie behind bars, Steve running from the police, and the ranch still under tight security, they hadn't believed such measures were still necessary until Jerome locked up for the night. "How did you get past the guards?"

Steve tipped his black Stetson and smiled derisively. "Meet Mac, your trainer, back off vacation. They've never seen the man. I just said howdy, flashed a fake picture ID, and walked right in. Bless Carrie's heart for keeping me informed of everything happening here, including the fact that you put Mac's name on the list of trusted personnel."

Samantha glanced across the arena again, wondering what he'd done to Jerome. "Why are you here, Steve? You're only going to dig yourself a deeper hole if you cause any more trouble. Why not turn yourself in and make it easier on yourself?"

"And let you go happily on with your life while I serve time in prison?" The smell of whiskey wafted to her nostrils, and she knew he was crazy drunk. "No way, sweet cheeks. I'll be locked up for years either way. Before they slap the cuffs on me, I intend to settle the score between us once and for all."

He was on her then, his taller and heavier body slamming into hers and knocking her backward. When she hit the ground he landed on top of her, crushing all the breath from her. Before she could breathe again, his hands were at her throat, his thumbs digging into her larynx. Her lungs hitched, grabbing frantically for oxygen. He only smiled and tightened his grip.

"How's it feel, bitch? You're gonna die, and the last thing you'll see is my face. Forever, remember? Until death do we part. I said I'd make you regret leaving me. I keep my promises."

Black spots danced in front of Samantha's eyes. Her body pulsated with an overwhelming urgency to breathe, only she couldn't. She dug in hard with her nails at his wrists in a last, desperate attempt to break his hold on her throat, but his grip was like a vise, and his eyes gleamed dementedly into hers. *Suffocating, I'm suffocating.* She'd felt this way once before, and suddenly she remembered how she'd escaped him the last time. *Clint.* He'd taught her to jab at the inside corners of an assailant's eyes with her thumbs. *Go for his gray matter,* Clint had drilled her. *He'll turn loose, and when he does, run like hell.*

"Nobody screws me over and gets away with it," he snarled in her face. "Payback time, baby." He assumed a singsong tone. "Say bye-bye to Daddy."

Praying Steve was too drunk to be expecting it, Samantha let go of his wrists, stiffened her thumbs, and jabbed at his eyes. Bellowing, he jerked back, released his hold on her throat, and cupped his hands over his face. All she could see between the inverted V of his hands was his nose, so she went for that next, striking out with the heel of her hand with all her strength. He squealed and rolled away from her.

Black spots still dancing in her vision, she clambered to her feet, almost went back down, and grabbed the wall for support. Blue Blazes was shrieking and rearing. Knowing the stallion would never harm her, Samantha kept her gaze fixed on Steve. As her senses slowly righted themselves, she was able to stand without clinging to the boards, and in that moment she *knew* he would kill her if she let him get back on his feet. Terror pounded through her veins, blurring her reason. She retreated a step and tensed to kick him with all her might—in the face, in the groin. It didn't matter where, as long as he stayed down.

Just as Samantha moved to follow through on her panicky thoughts, she remembered the last time Steve Fisher had almost killed her. She'd lost it that night, reacting with mindless fear, and what she'd done had haunted her ever since. Now he was back, and just like before, he was dragging her down to his level. *No.* She wouldn't go there this time. *Couldn't* go there. It wasn't necessary.

Wheeling around, she threw herself at the paddock doors, which she'd barred shut after bringing Nutmeg into her stall. Struggling to lift the plank, she shrieked when Steve's hand locked around her calf. "No!" she cried, turning to fight him off. "Let *go* of me."

Using her jeans, Steve dragged himself into a crouch. Samantha knifed her knee up, catching him on the chin. When he fell away from her, she finally got the doors open. Throwing her weight against the wooden panels, she lost her balance and rolled out into the paddock.

"Help!" she screamed. "Somebody help me!"

Tucker had climbed out of his truck and was reaching for a lightweight jacket to ward off the evening chill when he heard Samantha's screams. He cocked his head, determined that she was somewhere outside to the left of the arena, and broke into a run to circle the building. He reached the paddock just as three male security guards were vaulting over the fence. By the time Tucker could enter the enclosure, Nona Redcliff was also on the scene, shouting orders to her guards, helping them wrestle a man to the ground, and then backing off to use her cell phone to contact the police.

Tucker knew without asking that the guy they'd just overpowered was Steve Fisher. He hurried over to Samantha, still lying prone on the scattered hay. "Are you okay? Talk to me. Did the bastard hurt you?" He ran his hands over her legs and arms. "Are you all right?"

Speaking incoherently between sobs, she sat up and locked her slender arms around his neck. "I'm fine," she finally managed to croak. "I'm okay. Oh, God, Tucker, he tried to strangle me."

Tucker sat so he could pull her trembling form onto his lap. "It's over. It's all right now. The cops will be here soon."

She pressed her face against his neck. "Jerome . . . he did something to Jerome. He was working at the other side of the arena."

Tucker couldn't bring himself to leave her just yet. "Nona!" he yelled. "Find the foreman. He's somewhere inside the building and may be hurt."

Nona gave him a thumbs-up and hurried inside. Tucker returned his attention to Samantha. He'd almost lost her, he realized. Thank God she'd escaped Fisher's hold and run outside to yell for help.

Within seconds the paddock and stables were crawling with more security guards, who were shouting, performing emergency first aid on Jerome, and summoning an ambulance. All that was left for Tucker to do was cradle the woman he loved in his arms.

Much later, when Jerome had been transported to the hospital by ambulance for a concussion and Steve Fisher had been transported by squad car to a jail cell, Tucker and Samantha still sat huddled together on the floor of Blue Blazes's stall.

"Do you think Jerome will be okay?" she asked.

"I'm sure of it," he replied. "It's only a concussion. The paramedics told me he'll probably come home tomorrow." He rested his chin atop her head. "Take a deep breath and slowly release it. Everything is finally looking up, lady."

"I'm glad my dad and brothers didn't show up until *after* the hullabaloo was over."

He chuckled. "Amen. Your father and Clint had murder in their eyes."

Samantha rubbed her cheek against his shirtsleeve and hugged his arm. "So did I at one point. When he rolled off me, I wanted to start kicking him and never stop."

"But you didn't."

She sighed. "No. He was down. I knew there was help right outside. It wasn't like last time, when it was him or me."

"I'm proud of you."

"For stopping?"

She felt him grin against her hair. "No, for taking him down. You're quite a woman, Samantha Harrigan."

Samantha wasn't so sure about that, but she did know she felt at peace with the way she had handled the situation this time. "Now all that's left is to restore your reputation. I don't know if your practice will ever recover. People have long memories."

"No worries. The front page of tomorrow's paper will have Steve's and Carrie's pictures plastered all over it, and the *Crystal Falls Daily* will also make a full front-page retraction and a public apology to you for implying you had anything to do with the deaths of your horses."

She stirred to look up at his face. "Really? How do you know?"

"Because I'm calling in the morning to threaten them with a lawsuit if they don't, and I imagine your dad will, too."

Samantha laughed. "That should work."

They fell silent for a bit. Then she whispered, "How is it possible to feel so many emotions in one day? Anger, hopelessness, terror, and now I'm so happy I could bust. I'm ready for life to settle down a little bit."

"As long as I'm part of it, I'll second that."

Samantha hugged his arm more tightly, trying to imagine life without him. "Oh, you'll be part of it. You can count on it."

"Is that finally an official yes?" he asked.

"To what?" she countered, unable to resist teasing him.

"To my proposal of marriage."

"Nope."

"It's not?" He sounded just a little worried.

"I want an old-fashioned proposal. You have to bring me flowers, and you have to get on your knees, and I won't say yes until you show me a ring."

She felt him grin again. "I can handle the flowers and the ring."

"On one knee, then?"

He laughed. "You drive a hard bargain, lady. Okay, I'll get down on one knee. But only if you promise to say yes once I'm down there."

"Deal."

Epilogue

Samantha stood in the vestibule of the church, clinging to her father's arm, so nervous she felt sure her legs might buckle. Instead of bridal white, she wore a brown, calf-length, suede riding skirt, a Lady Wrangler dress blouse, brand-new riding boots, and a Stetson with elasticized ecru netting around the crown to create a veil. In her right hand she held a simple bouquet of wildflowers.

"Are you *sure* I look all right?" she asked Dee Dee, who kept tugging at the veil and smoothing Samantha's blouse. "Maybe I should've worn a gown."

"Nonsense!" the plump redhead scolded. "You look absolutely *perfect*."

Samantha glanced up at her father for confirmation and saw tears in his eyes. "You're the second-most beautiful bride I've ever seen, and that's pure partiality on my part, lovin' your mama like I did." He placed his hand over hers where it rested on his arm. "I feel good about this. That boy will take fine care of you. I'm finally *done*."

"Done?"

"Raisin' kids. Now it's my turn. I'll never find another love like I had with your mother. But I'm thinkin' there's such a thing as bein' close friends, havin' fun, and havin' someone I care about to grow old with. How would you feel about that?"

Samantha's nerves were jangling, and she could barely make sense of what her father was saying. "How would I feel about what?"

"Me and Dee Dee. I care about her, she cares about me, and neither of us is expectin' rockets to go off. Would it bother you if we moved past *Benji* movies and popcorn, and got married?"

Samantha was so taken aback that she momentarily forgot she was about to walk down the aisle. "Oh, *Daddy*!" Holding her bouquet out to one side to protect the flowers, she hugged her father's neck. "I love Dee Dee. You know that." Then she turned to hug the plump redhead who'd been the only mother she'd ever known. "What a *wonderful* wedding gift. I'm so happy for you both!"

Dee Dee returned Samantha's embrace, then drew away to straighten the bridal veil again. "I knew you would be."

Organ music suddenly thrummed through the building, and Samantha's father stiffened. "I think the curtains just went up, and we haven't made our entrance yet. Shake a leg, honey."

Seconds later they entered at the back of the church and progressed up the aisle, with Tucker's nephew Sly, the ring bearer, and Rafe Kendrick's daughter Amelia, the flower girl, leading the way. Dressed in Western-style slacks and shirt, Tucker stood off to the right before the altar with two of his brothers and two of hers beside him. Jake had accepted the honor of being Tucker's best man.

Both the bride's and groom's sides of the church were packed. Samantha felt certain she'd never had so many eyes trained on her at once, and her attack of jitters grew worse with every step she took. She and Tucker had wanted to have a small, personal wedding, but in the end, three hundred people had been invited to attend the nuptial Mass, making the country theme seem a little *too* simple to be appropriate. Now she wished she'd worn a conventional wedding gown. How stupid to be wearing a riding skirt when so many of the guests had shown up in fancy dresses and suits.

Samantha felt an almost overwhelming urge to giggle hysterically. But then her gaze met Tucker's, he smiled at her, and the world fell away. Scarcely aware of her dad beside her, she moved toward the man who'd become her everything. *It's fine,* his smile told her. *This is our wedding. If they don't like it, they can make tracks.*

A second later he took her hand, and from that moment forward, everything happened in a blur for Samantha. She and Tucker said their vows to each other, and then they knelt in front of the altar to receive communion together for the first time as man and wife.

For Samantha, it was the most beautiful moment of her life. As if God were smiling down upon them, winter sunlight suddenly peeked out from behind the snow clouds to shine through the stained-glass windows, bathing both her and Tucker in a warm, muted rainbow of brilliance. It was a sign. She felt *sure* it was a sign, and Tucker evidently felt it too, for he gave her hand a hard squeeze, then lifted his gaze toward the angels painted on the cathedral dome above them.

Once at the church hall where the reception was to be held, Tucker kept one arm locked firmly around his wife's waist. Though he knew the party after a wedding was nearly as important as the nuptials, he wanted only to spirit her away to begin their honeymoon, two blissful weeks in Jamaica away from both their families. He meant to make the most of Jamaica, making love to his beautiful bride every single chance he got. If she insisted on sunbathing on the beach, he would oblige her, but he mainly hoped to keep her in bed. After waiting for almost five months, a guy had his priorities.

"What are you thinking?" she asked.

"About bingeing after a long starvation diet."

She giggled. Then she sobered. "I'm eager, too. Three giant pizzas at one sitting sound really good."

Tucker was about to suggest they duck out on their own reception when he noticed his sister, her husband, all of his brothers and their wives gathered around Father Mike. "What do you suppose they're bending Father's ear about?"

Samantha smiled. "Molly's a cradle Catholic. She mentioned to me just last week that she's gotten her first marriage annulled and would like to have her marriage to Jake blessed by the Church so she can start receiving communion again. She also wants to raise her kids Catholic."

Tucker wondered how Jake was handling that news. Catholicism wasn't for everybody. Drawing Samantha into a walk beside him, he worked his way through the throngs of people to reach Father Mike's side. As he and Samantha drew close, Tucker heard Jake say, "I'd like to begin instruction."

"Not a problem," Father Mike said with a happy grin. A plump, balding man with the surname O'Flannery, he was everyone's picture of an Irish priest, with graying dark hair, merry blue eyes, and just a bit of a brogue. "I teach every Wednesday night and Thursday morning. We'll make it a family affair."

Tucker noticed his mother just then. She stood at Molly's side, weeping copiously. The handkerchief in her hand was so wet it was almost dripping. When she saw Tucker and Samantha, she let loose with a new flood and flapped the soaked cloth in front of her contorted face, making Tucker want to duck.

"Mom's a little overcome with joy." Hank came to stand at Tucker's side, and as if by mutual but unspoken assent, they moved away to talk more privately. "All her kids, coming back to the Church."

"All?"

"Yes, and it's *your* fault." Hank arched his dark eyebrows. "Why didn't you marry a Baptist, or a Methodist, or an Episcopalian? Mom wouldn't have gone on a campaign." He cast an apologetic glance at Samantha. "No offense intended. You're the perfect woman for Tucker. I just wish . . . Oh, never mind."

"A campaign?" Tucker pressed. "Mom's on a campaign?"

"To get us all back in church. Ever since you started taking instruction, she's been a busy beaver, planting ideas in my wife's head about how families should worship together." Hank took off his hat and plucked a flask from inside the crown. After taking a drink, he offered it to Tucker. "Jim Beam. I'm not celebrating my brother's marriage with bubbly." He added hopefully, "Maybe I'll get excommunicated before I start."

Tucker was about to refuse when his wife plucked the flask from his brother's hand, drew off the cap, and said, "Here's mud in your eye." Then she took an impressively large gulp, whistled in air, and said, "Not bad stuff."

"You'd better watch out," Hank cautioned. "The priest will see you."

Samantha grinned. "You're right. Hide it, quick. He'll drink all the rest."

Hank looked amazed. "You're pulling my leg. Right?"

"Good grief, no. Haven't you ever heard of Irish whiskey?"

Hank nodded. "Another question. What, exactly, does that toast mean? I've heard it all my life, but it's never made a lick of sense."

"Mud in your eye?" Samantha grinned. "It originated among horse racing jockeys. At the end of a race, the winning jockey would say, 'Here's mud in your eye,' meaning that his horse's rear hooves had just flung mud in his opponent's eye. Not very gracious, but that's how it started."

"You're phenomenal." Eyes twinkling with mischief, Hank proffered the flask again. "Want another hit?"

"Don't you dare." Tucker pushed the flask away. "You will *not* get my wife drunk on my wedding day."

"Good point." Hank took another swig himself and then wandered off toward Father Mike, clearly bent on testing the waters of Catholicism with a little Jim Beam.

Tucker was still laughing when he and Samantha went to cut their wedding cake. After posing for pictures and hearing way too many toasts, they shared a piece of cake and were finally able to run toward Tucker's waiting Dodge under a deluge of birdseed.

Before jumping into the truck, which had been covered with white graffiti and streamers of toilet paper, and with tin cans attached to the back bumper, Samantha turned to throw her bouquet. Clint, who just happened to be standing toward the front, got nailed dead center in the chest and instinctively caught the flowers.

"No *way*," he said.

He was still saying, "No way," when Tucker started the truck and drove off. Samantha scooted across the seat to snuggle up next to him. When Tucker looked down at her, she fairly glowed with happiness.

"You threw it at Clint on purpose," he accused.

She giggled and shrugged. "Of course. I don't know if there's anything to the superstition. Believing in that kind of thing is against our religion. But who knows? It's time for him to find someone. Maybe it'll work." She glanced at her watch. "We have three hours before our flight. We only need to be at our little Redmond airport thirty minutes in advance. How do you feel about stopping off at my place for something I need?"

Tucker really just wanted to be on their way, but he had a mother and sister and understood what a catastrophe it would be if she'd forgotten something she thought was important. Underwear, maybe, or mascara, or, God forbid, her own special shade of lipstick. Only she didn't wear lipstick.

Sending her a wondering look he said, "Sure, sweetheart. What do you need?"

"You," she said softly. "Right now, as soon as possible. I absolutely need you. And I always will, for the rest of my life."

Tucker almost drove off into a ditch.

Beautiful Gifts

Chapter One

No Name, Colorado
July 1887

Hindsight is always better than foresight. Faith Randolph had heard that old adage since early childhood, but for the life of her, she couldn't see how it applied now. Though the decision she had made two months ago to flee Brooklyn had ended with her and her six-year-old daughter, Charity, sleeping behind the livery stable these last three nights and picking through trash bins for food, Faith wouldn't have gone back in time to do a single thing differently. Her daughter's survival had been at stake.

In retrospect, Faith did wish that she'd been less trusting of her fellow travelers. She'd never expected all her money to be stolen from her reticule while she napped at a way station. Now only a single penny stood between her child and starvation.

"Maman," Charity wailed, "I'm hungry."

Faith squeezed the child's grubby little hand as they trudged along the plank boardwalk for what seemed the hundredth time that morning. "I know, sweetness. Let's say a little prayer that Maman will find a position of employment soon."

Faith's feet hurt, and her throat burned with thirst. It was approaching noon, and the morning's coolness was fast giving way to sweltering afternoon heat. Soon she'd have to take Charity back to the livery stable so the child could have some water. Just the thought made Faith shudder. Back in Brooklyn, they would be lunching in the formal dining room, clad in fashionable day dresses. Here, they were reduced to wearing servant's clothing to disguise their identities, eating morsels of food others had tossed away, and drinking from a horse trough.

I will not cry, Faith assured herself as she stared across the unpaved street at the Golden Slipper, No Name's only saloon. Judging by the scantily clad women she'd glimpsed through the upper windows, she suspected the establishment also served as the town brothel. A sign posted outside the batwing doors read, DANCING GIRLS WANTED. It was the only job advertisement she had seen. Shoving a tendril of sable hair from her eyes, she thought, *Not that, please, God.* She'd do what was necessary to care for her daughter, but she sincerely hoped she could find something respectable.

"Maman, look!" Charity cried, her voice edged with more excitement than Faith had heard in two weeks. "That man is selling candy."

The peddler seemed to feel their eyes on him. After anchoring the doors of his wagon open, he waved them closer. "Come, madam. Have a look at my wares. I've a little of everything here, including a sweet for the child."

Faith would have ignored the hawker, but Charity started across the dusty thoroughfare, tugging her mother along behind her.

"And what would suit yer fancy, my fine little miss?" the peddler asked as Faith and Charity reached the wagon.

Taking in the display of candy, Faith could well imagine how Charity's mouth must be watering. "I'm sorry," she informed the man politely, "but I'm temporarily without coin."

"No worries. 'Tis a gift I'll be making of it." The peddler

waved his hand over the collection of sweets. "What do ye fancy, lass?"

"Peppermint!" Charity cried. "I *love* peppermint."

The eager hunger in Charity's large brown eyes forced Faith to swallow her pride and say, "Thank you, sir. You're very kind."

The hawker handed Charity a striped stick of candy. While her daughter popped the sweet into her mouth, Faith took inventory of the other wares. It seemed only polite to feign some interest, given the fact that the peddler had just given her child a treat.

Faith's gaze snagged on a lovely dress, hanging toward the back of the displays on a rod crowded with garments far less fine. A wedding gown? For reasons beyond her, Faith couldn't stop staring at the dress.

"Ah, so it's an eye for silk and lace that ye have," the peddler said with a chuckle. Using a wooden drop-down step, he pushed himself up to take the gown from the rod. "Not that I can be blaming ye. 'Tis a fine piece of frippery." He swatted at the garment and sent a layer of dust flying. "Sadly, I've been packing it around for nigh on a year. Not much of a demand for fancy wedding dresses in these parts. It's taking up space I could put to more profitable use."

He pushed the dress at Faith.

"No, no," she protested, even though she'd never seen anything quite so lovely. The gown had simple, elegant lines, which had always been her preference. The ivory silk underlay was sleeveless with a scalloped, fitted bodice, a fitted waist, and a full skirt that fell in graceful folds. The lace overlay was long-sleeved and high-necked with a delicate band collar, fastening down the front with countless lace-covered buttons. The effect was modest, yet alluring as well. "I've no use for a wedding gown, I'm afraid."

The peddler shoved the dress closer, and Faith couldn't resist touching it. Her fingertips tingled oddly the instant they grazed the lace, and inexplicable warmth coursed up her arm.

"Oh, my," she said breathlessly.

"It's perfect for ye," the peddler said. "Take it, please."

Faith laughed and shook her head.

"Come, lass, humor a silly old man. Ye're meant to have this dress. I feel it in me bones."

The peddler was so charmingly insistent that Faith would have felt rude had she refused. The strange tingle of warmth suffused her entire body when she took the dress into her arms.

"Words fail me. It's lovely. Thank you, sir."

"Off with ye," the peddler said with a pleased smile. "Mayhap the dress will bring good fortune yer way. It's needin' a husband, ye are, lass, someone to care fer ye and the little one."

Faith shook her head. She had endured marital bliss for seven long years, enough to last her a lifetime.

Charity had a skip in her step as they continued along the boardwalk. Faith attributed the child's increased energy to the ingestion of sugar. Candy wasn't very nourishing, but at least it was something.

As she had countless times over the last three days, Faith scanned the shop windows for job advertisements as they walked. When they reached the mercantile, she chanced to see a small sign taped to the door glass. In block letters, it read, HOUSEKEEPER NEEDED. In smaller letters, it said, "Experience required. Apply at the O'Shannessy place."

Faith's heart felt as if it might leap from her chest. Charity gave her an inquiring glance. "Is something wrong, Maman?"

"It's a job posting," she managed to squeeze out. "Someone needs a housekeeper."

Charity squinted up at the sign. "Do you suppose you can be a housekeeper, Maman?"

"Of *course*." How difficult could it be to keep a house?

Granted, Faith had grown up in a home fully staffed with servants, rarely turning her hand to do much of anything. But she had supervised the work of servants these last eight years, first in her father's household and later in her husband's. That qualified as experience, didn't it? "Anyone can be a housekeeper. There isn't much to it."

Charity flashed a sticky grin. "Wonderful, Maman. Now what do we do?"

Tucking the wedding dress under one arm, Faith bent to grasp her daughter's elbow and hurried into the store. "Excuse me, sir?" She pressed close to the counter, willing the burly, gray-haired shopkeeper to glance up from a list of figures that he was tallying. "I need a bit of assistance, if you please. Would you be so kind as to direct me to the O'Shannessy place?"

The shopkeeper finally looked up, his frown indicating that he resented the interruption.

Faith hastened to add, "I'm interested in the advertisement on your door window."

The man's gaze sharpened on hers. "That old posting? It's been hanging there for months. The position is probably filled."

"Months?" Faith repeated stupidly. "Oh, but, no, that can't be. I've been past your shop countless times over the last three days. I would have noticed the sign had it been there earlier."

"Trust me, lady, it was there. Patrick O'Shannessy put it up last August. He's probably not needing anyone now."

Faith's heart sank, but this was the only respectable job posting she'd seen. "I believe I shall check into it, anyway."

"It's your time you'll be wasting." He jabbed a beefy thumb in the direction she needed to go. "The O'Shannessy place is a handful of miles that way."

Tugging Charity along behind her, Faith exited the shop and turned in the direction that the shopkeeper had indicated. She and Charity had only just left the town proper when the child asked, "How far is it, Maman? When will we get there?"

"Soon," Faith replied, mustering as much cheerfulness as she could, given the fact that she was already footsore and weak with hunger.

Please, God, she prayed silently as she fixed her gaze on the dusty, forbidding horizon that danced in heat waves before them. *Don't let it be too far. And, please, please, let the position still be open. This is my last hope.*

Chapter Two

Faith was stumbling over the hem of her dress, so exhausted she could barely keep going. Charity had long since fallen silent. Faith was grateful the questions had ceased, for she feared that they were lost. They had walked at least five miles on the rutted road, one plodding step after another, their shoes sending up clouds of dust that stained the hem of Faith's dress and Charity's stockings. *Lost.* The word circled endlessly in Faith's mind.

Though she looked in all directions for a rooftop, she saw nothing. Finally she stumbled to a stop, convinced that the shopkeeper had pointed them in the wrong direction. Charity drew up beside her and pushed at her dark, sweat-dampened hair. "Why are we stopping, Maman?"

Because I'm afraid we're lost, and I don't know what to do, Faith thought dismally. There were undoubtedly large predators in this godforsaken land. She had no weapon with which to defend her child and wouldn't have known how to use one anyway. Never in her life had she felt so inept and useless.

"I just need to rest a moment," Faith lied.

Charity plopped down on a rock at the side of the road. "I'm tired, Maman, and I'm so very hungry. Do you suppose the O'Shannessys will feed us?"

"Perhaps. People who can afford to hire household servants are usually well off, and it has been my experience that the wealthy are inclined to be generous to those less fortunate."

"Are we the less fortunate now, Maman?"

Speaking around a lump in her throat, Faith said, "We are, I'm afraid."

Sinking onto a rock near her daughter, she considered her options. They had been walking for two or three hours, making it midafternoon. In another three hours, the summer sun would start to set over the Rockies. What if they kept going and never came upon the O'Shannessy place? She and her daughter could be stranded out here all night.

Faith had about decided to turn back when Charity abandoned her rock and skipped a ways up the road. At the crest, she cried, "I can see a house!"

As Faith scrambled to her feet, a wave of dizziness washed over her. The wedding gown that she'd been carrying under one arm slipped from her grasp and fell in the dirt.

"Oh, no!" Charity cried as she raced back to her mother. "Oh, Maman!" The child picked up the dress and brushed uselessly at the dirt stains. "Do you suppose you can wash it?"

It took a great deal of know-how to clean fine silk. "No, sweetness, I'm afraid it's ruined."

Faith almost tossed the dress away, but something stopped her. It was madness, she knew. The last thing she needed right now was a wedding dress. But crazy or not, she tucked the gown back under her arm.

As she followed Charity up the incline, her limbs felt oddly numb and leaden. Over the last three days, most of the morsels of food she'd found in the trash barrels had gone to her daughter. That was only as it should be, but now exhaustion and lack of nourishment seemed to be taking their toll. She had to force her feet to keep moving.

When they finally crested the rise, she stared stupidly

at a large, two-story house surrounded by outbuildings and fences.

"We're there, Maman," Charity cried. "This must be it."

Even from a distance, the house looked in sorry need of repairs and paint. It wasn't what Faith had pictured. "Perhaps it's the caretaker's residence," she mused aloud, "similar to our servant quarters at home."

"I just hope you get the job and they feed us."

A few minutes later, when they reached the house, Faith could only stare in hopeless dismay. There were no other dwellings in sight to indicate that this was a caretaker's quarters. The rickety picket fence surrounded a yard littered with all manner of equipment, everything from rusty old plow rakes to discarded washboards.

"Can I help you?"

Faith nearly parted company with her skin at the sound of the man's voice. She blinked against the slanting sun, brought him into focus, and then just gaped. The man rounding the corner of the house was tall and muscular, with dark auburn hair, countless freckles muted by a lifetime in the harsh sun, and startling blue eyes. He looked to be in his twenties, possibly twenty-three or twenty-four, her senior by only one or two years.

When he came to a halt about five feet from the fence, his stance was that of a dock ruffian, hands resting at his lean waist, one hip cocked, his opposite leg bent at the knee. He wore faded denim pants and a blue work shirt patched at the elbows. The wash-worn clothing hugged his body, displaying the powerful breadth of his shoulders and bulging upper arms. In a rough and very earthy way, he was extraordinarily handsome, the kind of man Faith might have admired at a distance in the recent past, but not someone to whom she ever would have spoken.

"I, um—" Angry with herself for losing her train of thought, she swallowed and started over. "I'm looking for Mr. O'Shannessy."

"You've found him." His brilliant blue eyes met hers, the directness of his gaze unsettling. "I'm Patrick O'Shannessy." He looked past her at the road. Then he cut a quick glance at Charity, who had pressed close to Faith's skirts. "How'd you get here?"

"We walked, sir."

"All the way from town?" Incredulity laced his voice. "Jesus H. Christ. Are you out of your mind, lady?"

Faith's spine snapped taut. Before caution could still her tongue, she said, "My good sir, with all due respect I will remind you that a child is present."

He gave her a bewildered look, prompting Faith to add, "Your language. Some phrases are inappropriate in the presence of a little girl." Or in the presence of a lady, for that matter.

"My apologies." His thick auburn brows arched high. Then he swiped a hand over his mouth. "Sounds to me like you hail from some place back east."

"Brooklyn." Faith immediately wanted to bite her tongue. The less this man knew about them, the better. There was no doubt a large and very attractive reward being offered by her father for information about her and Charity's whereabouts.

"Brooklyn, New York?" When she nodded, he said, "You're a long way from home. What exactly can I do for you?"

"I saw your advertisement at the mercantile."

"I'll be damned. I had about given up on that. Are you experienced?"

Faith felt confident that she could learn to do almost anything. "I am, most certainly." It was only half a lie. She had supervised housekeepers, after all.

"I was hoping to find someone older."

"What I lack in years I make up for in knowledge and skill, Mr. O'Shannessy."

"It isn't that." He hooked a thumb over his shoulder at the house. "I'm a bachelor. I'm not sure how it would work with you living here. I sure as hell don't plan to sleep in the barn in order to keep tongues from wagging."

Faith was encouraged to learn that he even recognized the impropriety of such an arrangement. His language was appalling. In Brooklyn, the gentlemen cursed only while in the company of other gentlemen.

Patrick took thoughtful measure of the woman and her kid. Ever since his sister, Caitlin, had married Ace Keegan two years ago and moved to the neighboring Paradise Ranch, he'd been in desperate need of a housekeeper. For several months after Caitlin's marriage, he'd convalesced from a bullet wound in his back, and then, after regaining his strength, he'd spent most of his waking hours trying to get his ranch back on its feet. In a nutshell, he was tired of working himself into an exhausted stupor only to come in at night to a dirty house and no food on the table.

He'd been advertising for help for almost a year, hoping that a stocky, no-nonsense widow might apply for the job. Never in his wildest dreams had he pictured a beautiful young woman like this. She had a wealth of curly dark hair, some of which had escaped from its pins to trail like dribbles of hot fudge over her slender shoulders. Even worse, she had large, pleading brown eyes that he found irresistibly appealing.

"I'm sorry," he said, trying to gentle the words with a smile, "but I don't think you're right for the job." She looked ready to drop in her tracks. He couldn't see her milking the cows of a morning or managing to carry the brimming five-gallon buckets back to the house. "I need someone with a little more bulk."

Her small chin came up. "I'm stronger than I look, Mr. O'Shannessy." A telltale quiver attacked one corner of her soft mouth. "You shan't regret hiring me."

Her fancy speech alone was enough to make him run in the opposite direction. *Shan't?* Nobody hereabouts talked like that.

"I'm sorry," he repeated, trying to avoid looking at the child. He felt terrible about turning them away. "I need an older woman."

She finally nodded. "Very well. I apologize for taking up your time."

Patrick was about to offer them a ride back to town when all the starch suddenly left the woman's spine. The next second, she crumpled like a rag doll, hitting the weed-pocked dirt in a limp sprawl.

Bracing a hand on the fence, Patrick vaulted over the pickets. "Lady?" He dropped to his knees beside her. The little girl started to cry, a shrill, broken wail that made his ears ring. "Jesus," he whispered as he felt the woman's wrist for a pulse. "It's okay," he told the child. "She's just fainted."

"Maman!" the child sobbed, tugging on her mother's sleeve. "Maman, wake up. Please, wake up!"

Maman? Mother and child were ducks out of water in a place like this. Patrick lightly tapped the woman's cheeks, hoping to revive her. Not even a flutter of lashes rewarded his efforts. "Get back," he ordered the child as he lifted the mother into his arms.

She weighed little more than a child herself, he thought. Her head lolled over his arm, exposing the delicate arch of her throat. He tried to shift his hold to support her neck, but it was like trying to juggle a limp rag, and no matter how hard he tried, his hands seemed to find feminine softness better left untouched.

Angling sideways to get through the gate, Patrick carried his burden toward the house, the child wailing at his heels. Once inside, he hurried up the hallway that bisected the first floor, his goal the kitchen at the rear.

Once there, he rested the woman's rump on the edge of the table and cleared the surface behind her with a sweep of one arm, sending his breakfast plate and coffee mug clattering to the bare planked floor.

"Quiet!" he barked at the child, his voice much harsher

than he intended. He tipped the mother over onto her back and winced when her head struck the wood with a loud *thunk*. "She's going to be fine, sweetheart. She just fainted, is all."

"Maman never faints."

"It's a long way from town in the heat of the afternoon," he mused aloud. He'd seen strong men pass out in the fields when they worked too long under the hot summer sun. "We'll get some water down her. That'll probably bring her around."

"She's hungry, too," the little girl revealed brokenly. "She's been giving all the garbage she finds to me."

Patrick's heart caught. He gave the child a horrified look, hoping to God he'd misunderstood her. "Garbage, did you say?"

The child nodded, her dark curls bobbing. "Someone stole all our money while we were sleeping at a stage station. All Maman has left is a penny they missed at the bottom of her reticule. She's been trying to find a position of gainful employment ever since we arrived in No Name, but there are no jobs."

The child used words twice as big as she was, her eastern twang sounding strange to Patrick's ears. "Where on earth have you been staying?"

The little girl blinked her huge brown eyes and swallowed convulsively. "We've been sneaking into the livery stable to sleep in the hay. Maman hid our satchels under an overturned trough out back."

Patrick almost let fly with another "Jesus H. Christ." He managed to hold his tongue and said instead, "You'll find some corn bread in the warmer and some milk in the icebox, honey. Get yourself something to eat while I tend to your ma."

The child cast an anxious glance at her mother.

"She's going to be fine," Patrick assured her with far more confidence than he felt. "Before you've finished eating, she'll be awake and right as rain, I'll wager."

"Are you quite certain?" the child asked in a quivering voice.

The woman's pallor concerned Patrick, and her pulse felt weak and irregular. "I'm pretty certain. Mind what I say, now. You need to get some food in your belly. I can only care for one fainting lady at a time."

The child licked her lips and glanced hungrily around the kitchen. "Where's the warmer?"

The question brought Patrick's head up. Had she never seen a kitchen? "The top shelf of the stove."

She turned to stare at the old cooking range.

"There's a stool in the corner," Patrick told her as he unfastened the woman's collar. "You can use it to climb up. And mind you, don't go spilling the milk. You'll find a clean glass there in the cupboard to the right of the sink."

The little girl made short work of dragging the stool across the floor. While she fetched the corn bread, Patrick unfastened the woman's threadbare gown to midchest, trying his best to ignore the swell of her breasts above the lacy chemise and the flawless ivory of her skin. No luck. It wasn't every day that he found himself partly disrobing an unconscious female, after all. Suddenly all thumbs, he placed a cool, damp cloth at the base of her slender throat and pumped a glass of water to moisten her parched lips.

Her cheeks bulging with bread, the child asked, "And where, pray tell, is your icebox, sir?"

A recent addition to the outdated kitchen, the icebox sat in plain sight at the end of the counter. Patrick gave the little girl another wondering look. The drab and worn condition of her clothing indicated to Patrick that she and her mother were poor, not members of the pampered upper class who supped at fine tables on food prepared by servants.

After directing the child to the icebox, Patrick returned his attention to his patient. Her pallor alarmed him, and he wished now that he'd thought to ask her name. If the worst happened, he would have to contact her relatives back east and arrange for someone to come fetch the child.

"What's your name, honey?" he asked the little girl.

Her rosebud mouth ringed with milk, she stared at him with wary eyes. "Charity," she finally revealed.

Patrick offered her a smile. "My name is Patrick, Paddy to my friends. My last name is O'Shannessy." He let that hang there for a moment. Then he asked, "What's yours?"

She pursed her lips. "I'm not allowed to say, sir."

"Not allowed to tell me your last name?" He gave a low laugh. "Why not?"

"Because we've run away."

"Run away?" The phrase filled his mind with memories that he had tried very hard to forget. "Who are you running away from?"

"My grandfathers. My papa passed away two years ago, and they are trying to make Maman get married again to a perfectly awful man. He has a nasty disposition, and he quite dislikes me. When Maman discovered that he had enrolled me in a boarding school far away from Brooklyn and planned to keep me there all year long, she decided we had to leave." The child shrugged and nibbled her lower lip, the glass of milk clutched to her narrow chest. "One night when everyone was asleep, she sneaked me out of the house, and we embarked on our journey here."

"In servants' clothing," he guessed aloud.

Charity nodded. "It's not as if she *stole* the clothing. She replaced everything she took with garments of ours, which were much finer. I'm sure the upstairs maid and her little girl were delighted when they awakened the next morning."

"I imagine they were."

The picture forming in Patrick's mind wasn't pretty. In Colorado, a young woman was still occasionally coerced into marrying a man not of her choosing, but for the most part, such archaic marital arrangements were a thing of the past.

Charity dimpled her cheek in a mischievous grin. "I doubt that Grandfather Maxwell, Maman's papa, was very pleased, though. Maman emptied all his household coffers before we left."

Patrick chuckled, then returned his attention to his patient. When he trickled some water into her mouth, she choked and moaned.

"How on earth did you end up here?" he asked.

"We hoped to reach a place called San Francisco, but when our money was stolen, we couldn't go on."

San Francisco was the devil's lair for impoverished young women, especially beautiful ones. In Patrick's estimation, it was probably a blessing in disguise that they had been robbed and ended up stranded in No Name.

"Now," the little girl added forlornly, "we are without resources and have nowhere to go."

Patrick didn't consider himself to be an overly charitable man, but he wasn't so coldhearted that he could turn away an impoverished young mother and child. Tomorrow he'd go into No Name to retrieve their satchels. While he was there, he would visit the community church. Surely there was a respectable family in town that needed a housekeeper.

Chapter Three

Faith drifted slowly awake to the morning sunlight. After blinking her surroundings into focus, she was startled to discover that she was abed in a strange room. There were feminine touches—lace curtains at the windows, an ornate hurricane lamp on the bedside table, and tatted lace doilies on the battered surfaces of the dresser. An old, scarred armoire loomed like a dark specter in one corner of the room.

Faith pushed slowly to a sitting position. Her head spun sickeningly, and she pressed a trembling hand to her throat. Where was she? More important, where was her daughter?

Memory of the previous day came rushing back to her. *Patrick O'Shannessy.* She recalled his saying that she wouldn't suit for the housekeeping position. After that, she had no memory at all.

She trailed a hand from her throat to her upper chest and gasped in dismay. She wore only her chemise. Her gown, pantalets, and corset had vanished. Appalled, she pulled the faded coverlet taut over her bare legs and cast a frantic look around the room in search of her clothing.

The faint sound of a child's laughter drifted to her ears. She swung out of bed, pushed to her feet, and promptly almost fell on her face. Putting a hand on the wall to keep her balance, she went to the armoire, where she found her missing garments hanging inside on the rod. The ruined wedding gown was nowhere in sight, but Faith had more pressing concerns at the moment, namely getting some clothes on.

Making her precarious way back to the bed, she grasped the bedpost for support while she dressed. Then she sat on the edge of the mattress to lace her kid boots, which proved to be more of a challenge. She was so light-headed that every time she leaned over she almost pitched to the floor.

"What in God's name are you doing?"

Faith glanced up. Patrick O'Shannessy loomed in the open doorway. This morning he wore a fresh pair of faded denim trousers topped by a green work shirt. The neck of the shirt hung open, revealing burnished chest hair and more muscle than a woman cared to see when at the mercy of a stranger.

"I am *en dishabille,* sir," she said with as much hauteur as she could manage. "A gentleman would refrain from entering my bedchamber uninvited."

"You're on dissa what?"

"En dishabille," she repeated. "In an improper state of dress."

"Ah." The corner of his firm mouth twitched. He ran an unsettling blue gaze over her as he rested a brawny shoulder against the doorjamb. "One thing I've never claimed to be is a gentleman."

Faith had determined that for herself the previous afternoon.

"And, beggin' your pardon, ma'am, but this bedchamber happens to be mine, not yours. If I want to enter uninvited, I reckon I can."

Faith had no ready comeback for that, either. The bedchamber did indeed belong to him. It was she who was the interloper. "That being the case, I shall collect my daughter and relieve you of our presence, Mr. O'Shannessy." She ran trembling fingers up the front of her bodice to be sure it was properly fastened, the thought not far from her mind that it had undoubtedly been his strong fingers that had last touched the buttons. "I appreciate your generous hospitality and apologize for the imposition." She pushed weakly to her feet. "I must have swooned from the heat."

"I'm glad to see that you found your things." He pointed to a trunk at the foot of the bed. "I stowed the wedding gown in there." His gaze moved slowly over her. "It's a real pretty dress. You plannin' on using it anytime soon?"

"Using it?"

"Yeah, you know, to get hitched."

Hitched? She could only surmise that he referred to the institution of marriage. "Most assuredly not." She recalled the dirt stains all over the skirt. "And even if I were, the dress is ruined."

He frowned slightly. "It looked fine to me."

Faith seriously doubted that the dress would ever look fine again, but she chose to let the comment pass and concentrate on more imminent concerns, namely getting out of there. Despite her announcement that she intended to leave, he remained in the doorway, much like a huge tree that had put down roots.

"Do you always talk like that?" he asked.

"Like what?"

"Like you've got a bad case of the highfalutins."

Faith swayed and grabbed the bedpost. O'Shannessy was across the room in a beat. Instead of grasping her elbow as a gentleman might, he cinched a strong arm around her waist, his big hand splayed familiarly over her side, his thumb resting in unacceptably close proximity to the underside of her breast.

"Please, Mr. O'Shannessy, unhand me."

"Damned if I will. You're so weak you can barely stand." If anything, he tightened his hold. "Let me help you downstairs. You'll feel better with some food in your belly."

"I must collect my daughter and go. It's no short distance back to town."

"You're not going anywhere," he informed her as he half carried her toward the door. "The way Charity tells it, you have no place to go and no money to get there. I'll check around in town today to see if I can come up with a more suitable arrangement. If not, there's no denying that I need a housekeeper, and you clearly need a job. We'll have to iron out the wrinkles somehow."

Wrinkles? His thumb had found a resting place in the hollow just under her breast, the touch seeming to burn through all three layers of her clothing.

"I fear that I cannot work for you after all, Mr. O'Shannessy. You've no wife. I'm a widow. Gossip about such an arrangement would abound."

At the top of the stairs, he pulled her closer to his side. "Watch your step, darlin'. It's a long way to the bottom."

Try as she might, Faith couldn't bring the treads into clear focus. Terrified of falling, she knotted her right fist on the front of his shirt.

"I've got you," he assured her huskily.

He had her, all right. A hysterical giggle bubbled at the back of Faith's throat. "I truly can't stay here," she told him again.

"If no one else in town needs a housekeeper, what're your options? There are very few jobs for decent young women in No Name."

"I shall manage, Mr. O'Shannessy."

"Right. You'll end up working on your back to keep food in your daughter's mouth. Somehow I don't think you're cut out for that particular profession."

"On my back?" They reached the bottom of the stairs, at which point Faith hoped he might release her. Only, of course, he didn't. "I'm sorry. To what sort of work are you referring?"

"You know damned well what I mean," he said huskily. "You didn't find that child under a cabbage plant."

Scalding heat rushed to Faith's cheeks. For a moment

she yearned to kick him, and then in the next she wanted to kick herself for asking such a stupid question. She was no innocent, fresh from the schoolroom. She was simply too addlepated at the moment to make sense of what he was saying.

His steely arm still locked around her, he stopped outside a door at the end of the hallway. After giving her a direct, searing look that completely unnerved her, he lowered his voice and said, "Gossip will definitely *abound* if you're reduced to that. Seems to me you'll be a lot better off staying here, the impropriety of it be damned."

She'd never had the misfortune to meet anyone so plainspoken and crass.

"You wouldn't last one night at the Golden Slipper," he went on relentlessly. "A fair half of the men who frequent the place are prospectors—rough, filthy fellows with little or no regard for the unfortunate females who service them. And what of Charity? Will you tuck her away in the armoire while you're entertaining? That's no way to raise a child."

Little black spots danced before Faith's eyes. Yesterday when she'd looked across the street at the saloon, she hadn't allowed herself to think beyond the foul-smelling men who swilled liquor inside the establishment. Now Patrick O'Shannessy's words had drawn a brutally clear picture of what would surely transpire if she returned to No Name and pushed through those swinging doors to seek employment.

"No," she said shakily. "No, never that."

"I hope to hell not. Charity's a sweet little thing. I'll check around to see if someone else needs a housekeeper. If not, you and the child can stay here."

He opened the door onto a roomy kitchen that apparently served as the dining area as well.

"Maman!" Charity bounced up from a scarred, handhewn table. "Oh, Maman!" The child raced across the room to clamp her thin arms around Faith's skirts. "I was ever so worried. Paddy promised that you'd come perfectly to rights, but you were so white and still last night when he put you to bed. I was beside myself with worry."

"Careful, sweetheart," Patrick warned when Charity hugged Faith's legs more tightly and swayed to and fro. "Your ma is pretty unsteady on her feet. Did you eat all the flapjacks? I think she'll feel better once she gets some grub in her belly."

Charity reared back to beam a smile. "I only ate three."

"Only three?" Patrick led Faith to a chair and gently lowered her to the seat. Before he released her, he leaned low to search her face. "You steady on, darlin'? I don't want you toppling off onto the floor."

Faith grasped the edge of the table to support herself. "I'm fine," she said, even though her head was still swimming and all her limbs quivered with weakness. Now that she was sitting down, at least her vision had cleared.

He left her to rattle about at the stove. It was an antiquated monstrosity that required wood for fuel. At home, gas ranges were all the rage. *Thank goodness it's not my worry,* she thought with some relief. A housekeeper's duties did not extend into the kitchen, a fortunate thing given the fact that she couldn't cook.

"How do you take your coffee?" he asked.

Faith generally preferred a nice cup of tea, but at the moment anything hot and wet sounded utterly divine. "With cream and sugar, thank you."

He came to the table, poured some cream from a small pitcher into a large blue mug, and then set himself to the task of chipping sugar from a block. Faith watched the process with some interest. At home, the sugar arrived at table in a dainty bowl.

"Here you go." He slid the mug toward her, handed her a spoon for stirring, and presented her with his broad back again as he returned to the stove. "How many eggs?"

Her stomach growled. "One, please."

He sent her a scolding look over his shoulder. "Ah, come

now. Charity tells me you haven't eaten in days. Two, at least. Don't worry about running me low. The chickens are laying over a dozen a day right now."

"Two, then."

"Flapjacks?" He sent her another inquiring look. "I made a heap. They may not compare to the fancy breakfast fare you're used to, but they're delicious drowned in butter and warm honey."

At home, the pancakes were the size of a silver dollar. And how did he know that she was accustomed to fancier fare? "Six, please."

His eyebrow shot up. "Six?"

"Yes, please, if you've plenty."

"Let's start with three," he suggested. "I know you're hungry, and I'm happy to feed you, but I don't want you busting a gut."

Busting a gut? The expression almost made her shudder. "Does everyone in this vicinity talk the way you do?"

"Mostly. Amazing, isn't it? We're from the same country, but we speak different languages." He retraced his steps to the table, carrying a plate fairly heaped with food. "Here you go. Honey and butter are right in front of you."

"Oh, *my*." Faith stared in startled amazement at the three pancakes, which were nearly the size of the plate and half an inch thick. "I shall never be able to eat all this. The cakes at home are quite small. I had no idea."

He flipped a chair around and straddled the seat. Folding his arms over the back, he flashed her a slow grin that reminded her of just how handsome he was. "No worries. If you can't get 'em down, they'll make great hog slop."

Hog slop? Back home, such a phrase never would have been uttered at the table. For the moment, however, Faith was far too hungry to mind. With her first bite of flapjack, she nearly moaned. The honey and butter melted over her tongue, warm and sweet. She closed her eyes and went, "Mmm."

Watching Faith eat made Patrick wish he could have her in his bed, making those low sounds of pleasure. He immediately banished the thought. If there were no other housekeeping positions in No Name, he would have to hire her himself. Being a bachelor, he had physical needs that were rarely satisfied, and Faith was a tempting little swatch of calico, fragilely made but sweetly rounded in all the right places. If he allowed himself to entertain improper thoughts about her, he might eventually find himself trying to charm her out of those fancy bloomers he'd glimpsed last night.

Chapter Four

Faith was too weak to work that first day. Even with the hearty breakfast to rebuild her strength, her head went a little dizzy every time she stood up. After she'd enjoyed her morning repast, Patrick O'Shannessy ushered her to an old horsehair settee in the sitting room and insisted that she stay there.

"I can't lie about all day, Mr. O'Shannessy," she protested. "I must make myself useful to repay you for your kindness."

"We'll worry about paybacks tomorrow."

In Faith's experience, a wise woman never allowed herself to be indebted to a stranger, especially not one so virile and masculine. There was a hungry look in Patrick O'Shannessy's eyes that made her uneasy whenever his gaze settled on her.

He stepped over to an old cherry bookshelf. While he rummaged through the dusty tomes, Faith took stock of the room. Before the door lay a colorful braided rug that looked handmade. Most of the wall hangings looked handmade as well, dried flowers under glass and pretty ovals of needlepoint. The only exceptions were some family portraits that hung above a table near the hallway door, one of a small, pretty woman and a brawny older man who bore a striking resemblance to her rough-mannered host.

"Your parents?" she ventured.

Patrick glanced over at the likenesses. "My mother, yes."

"She's lovely," Faith said. And then, "Who is the man?"

He took so long to reply that Faith wondered if he had heard her question. "That's Connor O'Shannessy, my biological sire."

The cold hatred in his voice sent a chill chasing up Faith's spine.

"If I had another portrait of my mother," he added, "I'd burn that one so I'd never have to look at his face again."

Patrick O'Shannessy would see his father's face for the rest of his life whenever he looked into a mirror, Faith thought sadly. She trailed her gaze lower, to a portrait of two children—a girl, who looked to be the older, and a little boy with an impish grin and freckles.

"Is the other portrait you and your sister?"

His expression softened. "Yes. I was seven, or thereabouts. Caitlin is two years my senior, so she was about nine, maybe ten."

The warmth in his voice told Faith that he loved his sister very much. He straightened from the bookshelf and returned to the settee with a thick tome. His stride, Faith noticed, was distinctly masculine, his lean hips and muscular legs working together in an easy, undulating harmony of power and grace.

"Caitlin used to read to me from this book." He winked at Charity. "Have you ever heard 'The Emperor's New Clothes' or 'The Ugly Duckling'?"

Charity sat primly on the edge of the settee, tugging at the hem of her borrowed dress to cover her knobby knees. "Yes, but I'd enjoy hearing both again."

"There you go," Patrick told Faith as he handed her the collection of fairy tales. "Your day's work is cut out for you."

Moments after Patrick left the sitting room, Faith heard him rattling around in the kitchen. She glanced at her daughter. "Was Mr. O'Shannessy kind to you last night?"

"Very kind, Maman. He fixed me fried chicken and spuds for supper, and for dessert he made chocolate gravy over biscuits."

"The proper term is 'potatoes,' dear heart."

"Paddy calls them 'spuds.' "

"Yes, well, Mr. O'Shannessy speaks like a dock ruffian. And one other thing, sweetie. Proper young ladies don't address gentlemen outside their family by their given names—or by their nicknames."

"But, Maman, he asked me to call him Paddy. He says my calling him Mr. O'Shannessy makes him feel older than Methuselah."

"Nevertheless, it's improper. Just because we've come to Colorado is no sign that we must abandon all semblance of propriety. Do you understand?"

Charity scrunched her nose. "I understand, Maman. It's just—"

Faith opened the storybook. "It's just what?"

The child sighed and rolled her eyes. "We're not in Brooklyn anymore, Maman. People are different here. If we're going to stay, we must try to be like everyone else. Otherwise, we'll never fit in."

Although Faith saw the wisdom in her daughter's observation, she was not yet prepared to abandon all the social mores drilled into her since childhood.

"Humor me," she said with a smile. "Perhaps after I've been here for a while, I'll no longer find terms like 'hog slop' and 'busting a gut' so offensive."

Charity giggled. It was a wonderful sound to Faith's ears, one that she hadn't heard in months. "That's just the way he talks, Maman. He doesn't mean to be offensive."

"I'm sure he doesn't," Faith conceded.

"I like him," Charity added. "He was ever so nice to me last night, and he took very good care of you."

Her cheeks going warm with embarrassment, Faith ran nervous fingertips down the line of buttons on her bodice.

"I'm glad that we came here," Charity said fervently. "Not to No Name, but *here,* to Mr. O'Shannessy's house."

"It sounds as if the two of you have become fast friends." Faith smoothed the yellowed pages of the book. "I do hope you remembered the need for discretion. We'll be in a fine pickle if your grandfathers somehow learn of our presence here and come to fetch us home."

Charity bobbed her dark head. "Oh, yes, Maman, I was very discreet. When he asked my last name, I told him I wasn't allowed to say. He was very understanding when I explained our situation."

The hair at the nape of Faith's neck prickled. When she searched her daughter's big, guileless brown eyes, her heart sank. Unless she missed her guess, Patrick O'Shannessy now knew far too much about them. Faith couldn't really blame Charity for that. She was an extremely bright child, but she was still only six years old. Children her age trusted a bit too easily and had a tendency to be loose-tongued with adults. And in all fairness, Faith hadn't been the soul of discretion herself. Yesterday when O'Shannessy had asked where they were from, she should have fabricated a clever lie instead of blurting out the truth.

Faith could only pray that the man could be trusted. Judging by the condition of his home, he was barely scraping out a living on this patch of land. A large monetary reward for information about two runaways might be very attractive to him.

A half hour later, Patrick O'Shannessy returned to the sitting room. His wavy auburn hair looked damp and had been slicked back from his face. He wore what Faith surmised was a dress shirt in these parts, white linen and open at the collar, the cuffed sleeves folded back over his thick, tanned forearms.

"I'll be taking off for town now," he informed them. "I put

on some stew for supper tonight. The fire is low, but it might be a good idea to keep an eye on it."

"Of course," Faith assured him.

He drew a gold watch from his pocket. "I'll be four hours or so. You feelin' all right?"

Faith nodded. "Just a bit weak, Mr. O'Shannessy."

When their host had left the house, Faith and Charity adjourned to the kitchen to stand at the stove. Faith stared nervously at the pot. "I've never watched over a stew before."

Charity lifted her thin shoulders in a bewildered shrug.

Using a dingy pad, Faith removed the lid from the pot and peered in at the slowly bubbling concoction. "Mm, it smells like Cook's Irish stew."

"I miss Cook's stew. Don't you?"

"I do." Faith missed many things from home. She resettled the lid on the pot. "It looks fine to me. Here in a bit, perhaps I'll give it a stir or two."

"Just so, Maman. I can remember Cook stirring the stew now and again."

Three and a half hours later, Patrick was headed for home. He had managed to find Faith and Charity's satchels, which now rode saddlebag fashion behind him over the rump of his horse, but his trip to town had been fruitless otherwise. He'd spoken to the pastor at the community church, and so far as the man knew, no one in No Name was in need of a housekeeper. There were no other respectable positions of employment available for a young woman, either.

It seemed that Patrick had himself a new housekeeper. And wasn't that a fine kettle of fish? Every time he looked at the woman, his mouth went to watering. She was a beautiful female, make no mistake—one of the prettiest that he'd ever seen. How in the hell was he going to rub elbows with her, day in and day out, and manage to keep his hands to himself?

In his thoughtless and drunken younger years, Patrick would have solved his dilemma with a Saturday-night visit to the upstairs rooms of the saloon, but now that he was older, his conscience bothered him if he even thought about it. That left him only one option: taking lots of midnight swims in the ice-cold creek near his house. Somehow that solution didn't strike him as being very appealing.

"I hope you fine ladies like stew," Patrick O'Shannessy said that evening as he ladled up servings from the cast-iron pot that Faith had watched over all afternoon. "It's one of the few things I can leave unattended for long stretches."

Faith was just relieved that the concoction wasn't ruined. She'd stirred it several times over the course of the afternoon, but beyond that, she hadn't known what to do. As a child, she'd always gotten a scolding when she ventured into the kitchen, and as an adult, she'd trespassed on Cook's domain only to discuss the weekly menu. As a result, the goings-on in a kitchen were completely beyond her ken.

At her host's insistence, Faith had taken a seat at the table with her daughter and was waiting to be served. She felt much stronger after resting for several hours. "We quite like Irish stew," she told him. "At home we often had stew for lunch on cold winter days."

He chuckled. "I can't be sayin' if it's Irish or not." With a shrug of his broad shoulders, he added, "Although I suppose that's a good bet. It's my grandmother's recipe, and she was about as Irish as they come." He sent them a twinkling glance. "Straight from the old country, with fiery red hair and a temper to match."

"Ah," Faith said with a smile, "now I know where you got your coloring, Mr. O'Shannessy. Have you her temper as well?"

"I do, I'm afraid. It was a curse in my younger years. Now that I'm older, I've learned to keep a lid on it. For the most part, anyway."

Faith was glad to hear it. A man of Patrick O'Shannessy's
stature would be intimidating in a temper. His hands were
large and calloused from hard work and every inch of his
lofty frame looked to be roped with muscle.

"I threw together some corn bread, too. Nothing fancy,
but at least it'll fill your hollow spots."

"Words cannot express my gratitude for your kind gener-
osity, Mr. O'Shannessy."

"No need to say thank you. As of tomorrow, it looks as if
you'll be taking over as housekeeper. I talked to the preacher
and everyone else I could think of. There are no other positions available."

Faith wasn't surprised to hear that. She folded her hands
tightly in her lap. "Are you certain that you wish to hire me?
In the beginning, you didn't seem to think that I would suit."

As he came to the table with filled bowls for her and
Charity, he said, "Like I said this morning, we'll iron out the
wrinkles somehow." When he returned a moment later with a
dish for himself and a pan of bread piping hot from the oven,
he added, "I'll just be needing to know how many wrinkles
we're likely to encounter."

Faith met his gaze. "Pardon me?"

He propped his elbows on the table, tented his forearms
over his bowl, and rested his chin on his folded hands. His
regard was searching and steady. "I get the impression that
you and Charity come from pretty wealthy folks. That being the case, I can't help but wonder about your experience.
You wouldn't be the first person to stretch the truth a little in
order to land a job."

Faith raised her chin. "Are you accusing me of lying, Mr.
O'Shannessy?"

He arched his burnished brows. "I'm asking if you have,
no insult intended. If you don't know how to do something,
you'd best tell me now."

Faith had every confidence that she could sweep floors,
polish furniture, and change bed linen. "Keeping a house

isn't that difficult. If you'll leave me a list of the tasks you wish done tomorrow, I shall endeavor to complete them to your satisfaction."

He studied her for a long moment. Then he nodded and began eating his meal. Faith had just taken her first bite of stew and was about to compliment him on its fine flavor when he said, "It's glad I'll be to have you take over. I'm damned tired of eating stew and fried chicken. I can make a few other things, but overall, those are my two specialties." Catching Faith's appalled expression, he paused with his spoon halfway to his mouth. "You do know how to cook? That's one of the main reasons I need a housekeeper. During fair weather, I work from dawn 'til dark. Any time I waste in here, trying to rustle up grub, is time I should spend outdoors."

Faith struggled to gulp down the bit of meat and potato in her mouth. She felt her daughter's startled gaze fixed on her face. Cheeks burning, she searched for something to say.

In Brooklyn, there had been a clear delineation between the duties of the cook, who reigned in the kitchen, and the housekeeper, who reigned over the rest of the household. "I'm rather surprised, Mr. O'Shannessy. In my experience, a housekeeper need not be well versed in the culinary arts."

He smiled slightly. "What kind of arts?"

"Cooking, Mr. O'Shannessy. Housekeepers in Brooklyn are not expected to cook."

"You're having me on, right?"

"I am completely serious. When I applied for this position, I did so with the understanding that someone else would do the cooking."

"Does that mean you don't know how to cook?"

Faith's stomach felt as if it had dropped to the region of her ankles. She desperately needed this job. If Patrick O'Shannessy sent them packing, Charity would soon be eating from trash barrels again.

Surely, Faith reasoned, she could learn her way around a kitchen. At home, Cook had kept books filled with recipes in a cupboard. Patrick O'Shannessy must as well. Had he not said that the stew recipe was his Irish grandmother's? That had to mean that the ingredients and instructions for preparing the stew were recorded somewhere.

"Of course I can cook." Even to Faith's ears, her voice sounded strained and high-pitched. "It's a fairly simple thing. Is it not?"

"My sister, Caitlin, makes it look simple." He buttered a square of bread. "She can toss any old thing in a skillet, and it comes out tasting good."

Exactly so, Faith assured herself. Mankind had been preparing food for centuries. If others could master the art, she certainly could. All she needed were some recipe books to guide her.

They finished the meal in silence. Then Faith's new employer said, "I'll tidy up the kitchen. You have a long day ahead of you tomorrow. I normally eat breakfast at four thirty. You'll have to be up before then to get the meal on the table. You should turn in early and rest."

"I'm feeling much stronger tonight," Faith protested.

"Probably because you rested all day." He pushed to his feet, ruffled Charity's hair, and said, "Upstairs with the both of you. There isn't much of a mess. I'll take care of it."

Faith had been taking orders from men all her life. She rose and held out a hand to her daughter. "Will you make out a list of my duties for tomorrow, Mr. O'Shannessy?"

"No problem. I'll leave it here on the table."

Chapter Five

"Maman, why did you tell him you know how to cook?"

Faith tucked the faded quilt in around her daughter and sank onto the edge of the bed with an exhausted sigh. "You heard him, Charity. If he discovers I know nothing about cooking, he may send us away."

The child pursed her bow-shaped mouth. "But, Maman, what will you fix him for breakfast?"

"Eggs and flapjacks," Faith said brightly.

"Do you know how to make flapjacks?"

Faith bent to kiss the child's forehead. "How difficult can they be? There are surely recipe books somewhere in the kitchen. I'm quite capable of reading instructions. I shall manage well enough."

"He didn't look in a book when he made flapjacks this morning. And I saw no books when he was opening the cupboards."

A tingle of alarm raised goose bumps on Faith's skin. "You didn't?"

With a glum expression on her face, Charity shook her head. "Whatever shall you do, Maman?"

Faith thought for a moment. Then she drew a bracing breath, smoothed her daughter's hair, and forced a smile.

"It's not for you to worry about. I shall manage, dear heart. Flapjacks are simple fare. I'm certain that I can throw some flour and milk together with a pleasing enough result."

Charity shook her head. "No, Maman, he put in a lot of other stuff."

"What kind of stuff?"

"An egg." Charity's brows drew together in a frown. "And some drippy stuff in a tin that he keeps on top of the warmer. I think it was grease."

"The warmer? Where, pray tell, is that?"

"The stove shelf above the burner plates. The heat from the oven keeps it warm up there. He heats his bread and stuff there."

Faith filed that information away for later. "Can you recall what else he used to make flapjacks?"

"Sugar. And some white powdery stuff he called saleratus."

"Saleratus?" Faith had never heard of it. "Oh, my. Flapjacks, it would seem, are going to be more difficult to make than I hoped."

Charity sat up and hugged her knees. Her white gown, fashioned of fine lawn, boasted delicate embroidery around the ruched collar and across the bodice. In order to disguise their identities, Faith had been forced to leave all their outer clothing behind, but she had felt it was safe for them to keep their own undergarments and nightgowns.

"I shall help you in the morning, Maman. Perhaps I can remember how he made the flapjacks."

As reluctant as Faith was to involve her daughter in this deception, she could see no alternative. Their survival hung in the balance. Patrick O'Shannessy was expecting a hearty breakfast the next day, and a hearty breakfast he would get. Once the first meal was behind her, she could search for his recipe books. They had to be somewhere. If not, she was in big trouble.

"We shall have to be up and about quite early," Faith mused aloud.

Charity nodded. "I can't imagine eating at four thirty. It'll still be dark."

Faith lifted her palms in a bewildered shrug. "It's a puzzle to me as well. But he was very clear about the time."

Faith slept fitfully and was fully awake at three o'clock in the morning. After she figured out how to light the infernal lantern in her bedchamber, she performed her morning ablutions, shivering in the chill air. Brooklyn summers could be unpleasantly warm at times, but there was seldom such a drastic drop in temperature at night. Here in Colorado, the sun baked the earth all afternoon, but the moment it dipped behind the Rockies, a frigid coldness took hold.

Once downstairs, Faith once again struggled to light a lantern. Then she set herself to the unfamiliar task of building a fire in the horrid old range. When she had finally nursed the flames to life, she was able to search the cupboards for recipe books. She found none.

Trepidation mounting, she advanced on the table to peruse the list of tasks that her employer had left for her. *Milking* headed the lot. Faith frowned. Surely he didn't expect her to milk his cows. She smiled at the absurdity and read on. The second duty was almost as bewildering. *Gather eggs.* Hmm. Any fool knew that chickens laid eggs. But where, precisely, did his domestic fowl deposit their offerings? Undoubtedly in one of the ramshackle outbuildings, she decided. She could surely locate the eggs without much difficulty.

Smiling with renewed confidence, she read on. *Breakfast.* She had already anticipated that edict. The next task set her to frowning, however. *Skim cream.* What exactly did he mean by that? *Make butter.* In parentheses, he'd noted that he liked his butter salted. *Slop hogs.* Faith suddenly felt a bit breathless. The words began to swim, and her head started to hurt.

Feeling cold all over, she sat in stunned disbelief for a full minute. He actually expected her to consort with barnyard beasts. He was out of his mind, she decided. And in her desperation, she was even crazier, because she was actually contemplating the possibility.

"Good morning, Maman."

Faith jumped so violently that she almost fell off the chair. "Charity!" She clamped a hand over her heart. "Don't creep up on me like that."

"I'm sorry, Maman. I heard you get up. I thought I'd come down to help."

Faith had a bad feeling that she was going to need more help than her small daughter could provide.

"What's wrong, Maman?"

As a rule, Faith tried never to burden Charity with adult concerns, but she'd been caught in a decidedly weak moment. "I've been going over Mr. O'Shannessy's list. He expects me to milk the cows and feed the pigs."

Charity's eyes widened. "Surely not. Ladies don't do such things."

"It's different here, I'm afraid. I'm beginning to realize that learning to cook is the least of my concerns."

Charity stood at Faith's elbow and stared at the list. "What else does it say, Maman?"

Faith swallowed, hard. "After I milk the cows, I must skim the cream and make butter."

Charity's eyes grew even rounder. "How does one make butter?"

Faith had only ever just spread the stuff on hot bread. "I believe it's made in a churn."

"Out of what?"

"Cream." Which Patrick O'Shannessy expected her to collect from a cow.

"Perhaps we can find the churn."

First, Faith had to catch the cows and convince the huge beasts to give over their milk. In that moment, she accepted that she didn't have what it took to be Patrick O'Shannessy's housekeeper.

"It's no use, darling." Faith struggled to keep her mouth and chin from trembling. "Your maman is hopelessly inept, I'm afraid. That being the case, we shall have to leave. We cannot expect Mr. O'Shannessy to feed and shelter us out of the goodness of his heart."

"Where will we go, Maman?"

"Back to No Name. I shall apply for a job at the saloon."

"What sort of work will you do there?"

"I shall be a dancing girl," Faith replied shakily.

Charity beamed a smile. "That is *perfect*, Maman. You've always loved to dance."

Patrick half expected to find his housekeeper still abed when he got up the next morning. He was pleasantly surprised when he heard sounds of activity downstairs. He smiled at himself in the shaving mirror as he sloshed water from the pitcher into the bowl. *A housekeeper.* He was going to enjoy having hot meals on the table again. Yet another luxury would be clean clothes.

When Patrick hit the bottom of the stairs, he sniffed the air, expecting to smell breakfast cooking. *Nothing.* Frowning, he entered the kitchen and stopped dead in his tracks. Faith stood by the table. The two satchels that he'd fetched from town yesterday sat at her feet. Charity was nowhere to be seen.

"Mr. O'Shannessy," she said in that hoity-toity way of hers. In the space of twenty-four hours, her strange accent had started to grow on him. "I am tendering my resignation."

Patrick closed the door and leaned against it. Most times, folks in Colorado just threw down their hats and said they were quitting. How like her to find a fancy way to say it.

"What brought this on? As of last night I thought we had agreed that you'd be staying."

"I'm afraid I've misrepresented myself." She held up a hand to stop him from interrupting. "In my defense, I must say it was unintentional. In Brooklyn, housekeeping is a far different undertaking than it is here."

"I see." He had suspected as much. Faith had "fine lady" written all over her.

She pushed at her hair. Black soot streaked her delicate wrist. "I have never milked a cow or slopped hogs, I've never skimmed cream or made butter, and I don't really know how to cook. With recipe books, I'm sure I could learn, but I searched your kitchen, high and low, without finding any."

"I cook from memory, a little of this and a little of that."

She nodded regally. Then with a lift of her hands, she said, "So there you have it. Charity and I must be on our way. I am ever so grateful for your kindness. I only wish I had the experience you require in a housekeeper."

A strange, achy sensation filled Patrick's throat. From the first instant he'd clapped eyes on Faith, he'd felt attracted to her. Now the feeling had intensified and become something more, something that he couldn't readily define. He knew only that she was beautiful and that her sense of fair play touched him deeply.

"You can't leave, Faith. Where will you go? What will you do?"

"That is not your concern, Mr. O'Shannessy. I shall manage somehow."

It was sheer madness, but he couldn't let her go. He knew where she would end up. Five years from now, she'd be old before her time, the innocence in her eyes shattered by one awful experience after another. Even worse, Charity would suffer as well.

"I can't let you do this."

She brushed at her cheek. "You're very generous." Her eyes luminous in the lantern light, she searched his gaze for a moment. "You frightened me when I first saw you. You have the air of a dock ruffian about you."

"Do I, now?"

She smiled. "You do, Mr. O'Shannessy. Having met you and come to know you this little while, I shall never again judge a man's character by the outward trappings."

"Thank you. That's a fine compliment."

"Sincerely meant, I assure you."

Patrick pushed away from the door. "So how's about staying and letting this dock ruffian teach you how to cook and milk a cow?"

She shook her head. "I've far too much to learn. In order to remain here, I need to feel that I'm earning our keep. It wouldn't be fair to you otherwise."

"So you'll go back to No Name and end up at the Golden Slipper? You've no idea what awaits you there, Faith. Men will use you as if you're nothing, and they'll never look back. In exchange for a coin, you'll sell your soul, not once but a dozen times a night. The next morning, the saloon owner will take half your wages. You'll earn just enough to survive, but never enough to leave. And one day soon you'll feel so used up and exhausted you'll no longer care."

Her face drained of color. "Nevertheless, I cannot in good conscience prevail upon your kindness when I've nothing to give in return."

"You've everything to give. If you're going to prostitute yourself, damn it, do it here." Patrick had no idea where that had come from. He only knew that she was about to make the worst mistake of her life, and he couldn't allow it to happen. "I'll pay you a dollar a pop and take half your wages for your room and board. At least here, Charity will be safe."

"Are you asking me to become your paramour, Mr. O'Shannessy?"

That was a fancy term for it, and Patrick had no such intention. But for the moment, it was the only reason he could come up with to keep her there. "In the meantime, I can be teaching you all that you need to know about keeping my house. In time, after you've learned everything, we can renegotiate."

"So I'll only be your paramour temporarily?"

"Trust me, it's a better offer than you'll get at the Golden Slipper. And no one need ever know, either. When it comes time for you to leave, your reputation won't be in complete shreds, only a bit tarnished."

She nodded slightly, which gave Patrick reason to hope. Then, her lovely eyes dark with shadows, she asked, "When you say no one need ever know, will that include Charity?" Her chin came up a notch. "I would very much like to maintain her high regard."

In that moment, Patrick almost leveled with her. She held herself so rigidly that he fancied she might shatter like fragile glass if he touched her. "Of course it will include Charity. She'll never know—or even guess that anything untoward is going on between us."

It was a promise Patrick felt he could keep, not because he considered himself to be the soul of discretion but because nothing untoward ever *would* occur between them. He'd told Faith yesterday morning that he'd never claimed to be a gentleman, and that was true. But he did have standards that he lived by, one of them being to treat women with respect. He'd broken that rule many times in his younger days, the crowning glory being two years ago when he had gotten too cozy with a whiskey jug. Carrying the guilt of that with him to the grave was, in his estimation, burden enough for any man to bear.

"I accept your proposal, Mr. O'Shannessy."

Acutely conscious of how greatly it pained her to say those words, Patrick searched her pale face, nodded, and moved away from the door. In as jovial a voice as he could muster, he rubbed his hands together and said, "Well, then!" She jumped as if he'd poked her with a pin. "Let's begin this arrangement with a cooking lesson, why don't we?"

All that day, Faith's stomach felt like a wet rag that gigantic hands were wringing out. While learning to mix flapjack batter, she could barely attend Patrick's instructions. Later, when he led her to the henhouse, she was so distracted that she barely even noticed the pecks of the chickens or the horrid green yuck on the eggs. When the hogs clambered into their trough as she poured slop from a bucket into their feeding chute, she didn't even flinch. In that moment, she almost wished the horrid beasts would break through the wire and trample her to death.

Faith's employer kindly excused her from the milking that morning, saying she might be overwhelmed if he threw too much at her the first day. As a result, she was left to tidy the kitchen while he went to the barn. She managed to heat water on the stove, and then she and Charity experienced for the first time the joys of washing, rinsing, and drying dishes.

"This isn't so bad, Maman."

Faith had to agree. Under any other circumstances, she might have found the task relaxing. As it was, she could think of little else but the coming night. Once she visited Patrick's bedchamber, there would be no turning back.

What have I done? In her wildest imaginings, Faith had never dreamed she might come to this. She was a *kept* woman now, the lowest of the low. Patrick O'Shannessy would expect her to warm his bed tonight, and rightly so. That was their bargain, after all. And no matter how she circled it, she knew she was extremely fortunate that he'd made the offer. Better to suffer the attentions of one man than dozens.

I'm lucky, she kept telling herself. He was a handsome man, and he kept himself clean, donning fresh clothes each morning and washing up several times a day. His breath wouldn't smell of tobacco and whiskey, there was no grime under his fingernails, and for all his rough manners, he seemed to be a kind man.

In her present circumstances, she should be grateful that he even wanted her in his bed. She had it on good authority from her late husband that she lacked the voluptuous curves that pleased a man's eye. Harold had also given her poor marks as a lover, often chiding her for an unsatisfactory performance. As awful as that had been, she had lived through it.

And she would live through this as well, she assured herself. After Charity fell asleep each night, she would visit her employer's bedchamber, allow him to do his business, and then creep back to her own room. Charity need never know, and perhaps one day, when Faith had put this place far behind her, she herself would be able to forget.

Chapter Six

That evening, after hearing Charity's prayers and reading the child to sleep, Faith crept down the hall to prepare for her last and most distasteful duty of the day. By the soft glow of a lantern and with shaking hands, she ran a cool cloth over her nude body. Waves of sick dread washed through her when she thought of Patrick O'Shannessy's hands following the path of the cloth, touching her in places only a husband should. *Oh, God.* She squeezed her eyes closed and prayed for strength.

It'll be over with quickly, she assured herself repeatedly as she pulled on a nightgown, spent an inordinate amount of time brushing out her hair, and dabbed perfume behind her ears. She would simply tap on his door, slip inside the dark room, and join him in his bed. When he'd grunted his last grunt and collapsed beside her in a pool of sweat, she would be able to return to her own room and hopefully find oblivion in sleep.

She could do this. For her daughter's sake, she *would* do this.

Patrick had just stripped off his shirt and loosened the top button of his Levi's when he heard a light tap on his bedroom door. Bewildered, he stepped across the room and cracked open the portal to find Faith in the hallway. Without a word, she pushed her way inside, cast a disgruntled look at the lighted lantern, and softly closed the door behind her.

In that moment, Patrick knew, beyond a shadow of doubt, that she was the most beautiful creature he'd ever clapped eyes on. Her hair fell almost to her waist in wavy ripples of sable. Her sleeveless shift, though modestly made, revealed just enough flawless ivory skin to make his heart pound like a sledgehammer.

Her lovely eyes almost black with shame, she whispered, "I am here."

For an instant, Patrick was sorely tempted to take what she offered. Only a strong sense of decency forestalled him. He retreated a step to put her beyond easy reach, rubbed a hand over his bare chest, and managed to choke out, "I'm sorry, honey, but I'm flat tuckered." He feigned a yawn. "Maybe tomorrow night."

She fixed him with an incredulous gaze. After staring up at him for several tense seconds, her eyes filled with tears. "It was never your intention to carry through with this, was it?"

"Shh," he countered. "Don't talk so loud. You'll be waking Charity."

Her chin started to quiver, and her mouth twisted. "It was a ruse to keep me here, nothing more."

The way Patrick saw it, he had two choices, either confessing the truth or taking her to bed. "You're not leaving," he warned, his voice still pitched low. "If that's what you're thinking, get it straight out of your head. If I have to tie you to the bedpost, you and that child are staying right here."

She cupped her slender hands over her face, and her shoulders started to jerk. For an instant, Patrick thought she was laughing. Then, to his horror, she dragged in a taut breath, making a sound like the shrill intake of a donkey right before it brayed. Awful sobs followed, the eruptions coming from so deep within her that he feared she would damage her insides.

"Faith," he tried. Then, "Sweetheart?" *Jesus H. Christ,* she was going to wake Charity. "Faith? Hey?"

She made the donkey sound again, more loudly this time.

"Shh," Patrick tried, to no avail. Not knowing what else to do, he gathered her into his arms and pressed her face against his chest to muffle the noise.

To his surprise, she went limp against him and continued to sob her heart out. Patrick had held his sister a few times while she cried, so he was no stranger to the ritual. He ran his hand into Faith's hair, tightened his hold on her, and whispered nonsensical words of comfort while swaying to and fro. She felt right in his arms, he realized, as if she'd been made to fit, her head hitting him at the hollow of his shoulder, her breasts nestling sweetly just under his ribs.

When she finally quieted, she gave an exhausted sigh, turned her head to press her damp cheek over his heart, and closed her eyes.

"You lied to me, Mr. O'Shannessy," she whispered.

"I'm sorry. It seemed like the thing to do at the time."

"No, no, I don't mean about that. You told me"—her voice went thin and shaky again—"that you weren't a gentleman."

Patrick mentally circled that. Before he could collect his thoughts to reply, she added, "You are, without question, a gentleman, sir—the finest that I've ever had the good fortune to meet."

Patrick didn't much care about how he stacked up as a gentleman. "Just say you'll stay here, Faith."

"It's unfair to you," she squeaked. "I'm completely useless, even"—broken sob—"at *this*."

"At *this*?" Patrick wasn't sure what she meant.

"Yes. You know." She flapped a hand at the bed. "I'm not fleshy the way men like, and I am completely inept as a lover. Harold said so."

"Harold?"

"My late husband," she said with a sniff, prompting Patrick to fish in his pocket for a handkerchief.

"Here, sweetheart." When she took the square of cloth and gave it a peering look, he quickly added, "It's clean."

She blew her nose with far more daintiness than she had exhibited while crying, which made him smile. Of all the sounds he might have expected this lady to make, last on the list was the first half of a donkey bray.

After dabbing under her eyes, she hauled in a shaky breath, gulped, and cut him an embarrassed glance with tear-swollen eyes. "You must think me a complete flibbertigibbet."

"Nah." He thought she was far too beautiful for her own good, and possibly his as well. "I think you've been through a hell of a time and finally just sprang a leak. Everybody needs a good cry sometimes."

As he spoke, he led her over to sit on the edge of his bed. To his surprise, she slumped onto the mattress, let her head fall back, and sighed wearily as she closed her eyes. She was so lovely, even with swollen eyes and a puffy mouth, that it took all of his control not to touch her again.

"Everyone should have at least one talent," she whispered. "What is mine?"

Patrick curled his hands over his knees and bit down hard on his back teeth. He could think of several things she might be good at, but he refrained from naming them. "You helped make butter today. And you gathered eggs and slopped the hogs."

She smiled, straightened, and lifted her long, wet lashes to give him a wondering look that made his bones feel like pudding. "I did, didn't I?"

"Before you know it, you'll be a fine housekeeper." Forcing his mind to more practical concerns, Patrick considered the situation. "I'll tell you what. If you're really that concerned about this arrangement being fair to me, you can work without pay until you've learned how to do everything. In the meantime, you'll be helping out enough around here to earn your room and board."

Tears sprang to her eyes again.

"Don't cry." He'd always felt panicky when women cried. Why, he didn't know, but there it was.

She shook her head and blinked. "Normally I'm not given to weeping, Mr. O'Shannessy. It's just that you're such a surprise."

"Not a dock ruffian, after all?"

She smiled tremulously. "No, not a dock ruffian. How will I ever repay you for your kindness?"

Again, he could think of several ways, which he immediately banished from his mind. He had asked her to remain here to save her from lechery, not to subject her to it. "You can start by calling me Patrick. I don't much like my surname."

"Why ever not? It's a lovely surname."

The question sobered him and helped to get his mind off the way her breasts thrust against her shift. "It came from my father, and he was a bastard."

"There's so much pain in your voice when you speak of him. Whatever did he do to make you hate him so?"

Patrick chucked her under the chin and pushed up from the bed. "We can tell each other our life stories another time. It's late." He gave her a slow grin. "When there is time to talk, I'll be particularly interested to hear how you ended up married to a blind man."

"Harold wasn't blind."

"Oh, yes, he was, darlin', stone blind, and stupid to boot."

In the not so distant past, Faith never would have thought it possible for her to become friends with a man like Patrick O'Shannessy. But that was exactly what transpired over the next month. They met before dawn in the kitchen each morning to prepare breakfast, he the teacher, she the student, and always, always, the lessons were fun. Patrick showed her how to crack an egg using only one hand, a feat that she never mastered. He also tried to show her how to flip a flapjack high into the air. When Faith tried to do it, everyone dived for cover.

"Darlin'," he said after retrieving a half-cooked flapjack from the kitchen floor and tossing it into the slop bucket, "the idea is to land it in the skillet."

Faith wondered how he could expect her to learn much of anything when he always looked so distractingly wonderful. Freshly scrubbed and shaven, in clean jeans and a work shirt, with his wavy hair still damp from the washbasin, Patrick O'Shannessy was enough to make any female's heart skip beats. Sometimes when their hands accidentally touched, Faith's fingertips felt electrified. At other times, the husky timbre of his voice near her ear set her heart to pounding so loudly that she felt certain he might hear it.

After breakfast each morning, they adjourned outdoors, where Faith learned about the goings-on in a barnyard. Charity was not excluded during Faith's training.

"Someday, sweetheart, you'll need to know how to milk a cow," Patrick pronounced, and the next thing Faith knew, her little girl was sitting on a tripod. "Excellent!" Patrick said when Charity succeeded at the task. "I'll make a country girl out of you yet."

It was Faith who proved to be a slow learner. Unlike her daughter, city ways had been ingrained in her for a full twenty-two years. She trembled with fright the first few times she went near a cow. Eggs covered with green excrement made her gorge rise. The hogs intimidated her. And, after encountering a snake one afternoon, she ran into the house and refused to come out again.

"Honey, it was only a harmless garden snake," Patrick assured her.

"A snake is a snake is a *snake*!"

Faith couldn't gather the courage to go back outdoors until evening, whereupon Patrick schooled her in identifying serpents while they milked the cows. "The only dangerous snakes we have in these parts are rattlesnakes," he assured her, "and they're real good about warning you before they bite. Also bear in mind that they're more scared of you than you are of them."

Faith seriously doubted that. Even so, she found herself falling in love, not only with the man but with his ranch as well. Living with Patrick was like being released from prison. Back east, she'd had to concern herself with appearances her every waking moment. Ladies dressed in a certain way. Ladies walked in a certain way. Ladies spoke in a certain way. Rules governed every occasion.

In Colorado, Faith could forget all that, and she felt gloriously free for the first time in her life. She could go for long walks with her daughter to pick wildflowers in the heat of the day, unconcerned about the sweat that filmed her brow or the freckles that might appear on her nose. She could snort when she laughed. She could yell when she grew angry. She could even strip off her shoes and stockings to go wading in a stream without fear of reprisal.

To her surprise, she didn't mind the hard work that came with her newfound freedom. She felt a wonderful sense of accomplishment when each day was done. She actually liked to cook, once she got the hang of it. Making butter and cheese proved to be easy. She soon grew relaxed around the barnyard animals. And there was nothing so satisfying as to stand inside Patrick's home, feeling proud as punch because every room was sparkling clean.

That wasn't to say that she never made mistakes. One morning Patrick entered the kitchen in a shirt that hung from his torso in tatters. "Stub your toe when you were putting in the lye?" he asked.

Faith was horrified. She rushed across the kitchen, gathered some of the shirt material in her fingers, and gasped in dismay when it fell apart at her touch. "Oh, Patrick, I'm ever so sorry."

"No matter. I needed new shirts, anyway." He gave her a mischievous grin. "Tomorrow we'll go into town and buy some yardage." He glanced down at her threadbare dress, his gaze lingering overlong on the bodice. "It's high time that you and Charity had some decent dresses, as well."

"But I can't sew!"

"You can learn."

True to his word, Patrick hitched up the wagon the next afternoon, and off the three of them went to town. En route, his arm frequently grazed Faith's, scrambling her thoughts and making her acutely aware of him on the seat beside her. Though she tried to keep her gaze fixed straight ahead, she found herself admiring his muscular forearms, displayed to best advantage by his rolled-back shirtsleeves, his thick, masculine wrists, and his large, capable hands.

What would it be like, she wondered, to have those hands touching her?

"It's a gorgeous day, isn't it?"

Faith jumped with a guilty start and blinked the countryside back into focus. "Yes, it's lovely," she agreed.

He slipped her an amused glance that made her wonder if he could somehow read her mind. The very thought made her cheeks go hot with mortification. Taking herself firmly in hand, she forced her mind onto the shopping trip that lay ahead.

After purchasing the fabric, Patrick took Faith and Charity for ice cream, a treat that Faith had despaired of ever enjoying again.

"Yum!" Charity said as she licked her spoon. "I could eat this all day."

Faith couldn't help but smile. "It is delicious. Thank you, Patrick."

He glanced over just as she touched her tongue to the ice cream perched on her spoon, and his eyes, normally a deep, twinkling azure, went as hot as the blue base of a flame. "You're welcome," he replied in a gravelly voice.

Faith quickly broke visual contact, but not before her hands went suddenly clumsy, causing her to drop her spoon on the floor. When she bent to retrieve it, Patrick did as well, and their heads bumped, making white stars flash before her eyes.

"Oh, damn, I'm sorry." He reached out to steady her, his hand curling over her upper arm. Faith jumped at his touch as if it had burned her. "Are you all right?"

Faith nodded, but in truth she was far from feeling all right. Being around this man wreaked havoc with her common sense. She wasn't a young girl, fresh out of short skirts and her hair still in pigtails. She'd been married for five long years and had hated every minute of it. The last thing she wanted was to be under a man's thumb again.

Only somehow she sensed it would be different with Patrick. The touch of Harold's hand had never set her heart to pounding. And to her recollection, he'd never made her laugh. More important, he never would have thought to buy her ice cream simply because she loved it.

"Let me get you a clean spoon."

Faith shook her head. "No, no. Thank you for offering, but I've had enough."

"But you've hardly touched it," he pointed out.

Faith felt a sudden need to escape the restaurant and get some fresh air. Luckily, Charity had gobbled down her ice cream with unbridled enthusiasm, and they were able to leave.

After paying their bill, Patrick joined them on the boardwalk. Her stomach jittery with nerves, Faith hurried Charity along in front of them, anxious to get back to the ranch where she might find some time alone to get her feelings sorted out. And sort them out she would. Her reactions to this man were beyond silly; they were downright ludicrous.

Up ahead of them, in front of the general store, there sat a large crate. As they drew closer, Faith saw that it contained puppies, darling little things with brown and white splotches and huge, floppy ears. A sign tacked to the side slats of the crate read, FREE TO A GOOD HOME.

"Oh, aren't they sweet?" Faith said.

Charity had long wanted a dog of her own. With a squeal of delight, she dropped to her knees and leaned over the crate.

One of the puppies jumped up to lick the sticky remains of ice cream from the child's face. Charity laughed. "Oh, Maman!" she cried. "Please say I can have one. *Please?*"

"Oh, darling, I'm sorry. Perhaps one day soon."

Patrick gave Faith an inquiring look. "Why can't she have a pup now? There's plenty of running room out at my place. It'll give her a playmate."

Faith was stunned by the offer. "But a puppy must eat."

His lean cheek creased in a grin. "Yeah, I reckon so. Most dogs do."

"No, Patrick. You've already done so much."

Ignoring her protests, Patrick crouched beside Charity. "Which one do you want, sweet pea?"

"This one," Charity cried. "He likes ice cream."

Patrick nodded. "He's the boldest and friendliest, too. If I were doing the choosin', he's the one I'd pick. Gather him up."

"Truly?" Charity's eyes went wide with excitement and incredulity. She hugged the puppy close, beaming an adoring smile. "You mean he's mine?"

Patrick chuckled. "It'll be good to have a dog around the place. He'll be your responsibility, though. You'll have to bathe him and brush him and feed him. Dogs are a lot of work."

"I won't mind."

"Best go put him in the wagon, then," Patrick suggested.

As Charity scampered away, Faith blinked away tears.

"Don't cry," Patrick ordered. "I'd rather take a beating than watch you cry."

Faith gulped and wiped her cheek. "You've already taken on two extra mouths to feed, Patrick." She almost added, *What are you trying to do, make me fall in love with you?* But she caught herself before the words escaped and settled for saying, "This is too much."

"Don't be silly. All kids should have a dog."

*   *   *

Three mornings later, Faith was upstairs putting fresh linen on the beds when she heard a feminine voice call out downstairs. "Hello? Faith? Hello? Is anyone home?"

By the time Faith got downstairs, Charity and her puppy, Spotty, were becoming fast friends with a lovely young woman who held a stack of papers and a wooden box clutched in her arms. The moment Faith saw the woman's red hair, she guessed her to be Patrick's sister, Caitlin.

"Hello," Faith said shyly as she entered the kitchen.

Caitlin set her burdens on the table and came across the room to grasp Faith's hands. "Ah, and now I understand! No wonder Patrick looks like a sick calf whenever he talks about you."

A sick calf? Faith smiled in bewilderment. In another twenty years, maybe she would understand all these people's odd sayings. "You must be Caitlin."

"I am." Placing a palm over her slightly swollen waist, she grinned impishly and added, "And this is Ace Junior. My husband says it's going to be a girl who looks just like me." She laughed and patted her tummy. "But we'll show him."

"Your husband wants a girl?"

"Ace says we need another female around the place," Caitlin said with a laugh. "Even my cat is a male."

After Charity's birth, Harold had entered the birthing chamber, given the baby only a cursory glance, and then informed Faith that she would be expected to do better the next time.

"Well, enough about the baby," Caitlin said with another chuckle. "Given half a chance, that's all I want to talk about. Patrick stopped by after your shopping trip the other day. I'm here to show you how to cut out shirt and dress patterns." She pointed to the stacks of folded paper on the table. "The latest fashions. Later today, my husband, Ace, or my brother-in-law, Joseph, will bring over my sewing machine. I'll teach you how to use it, and you can keep it here until you've replenished your wardrobes."

"Oh, I—" Faith gulped. "I've only ever done needlework. Seamstresses were hired to make our dresses."

Caitlin snapped her fingers. "Simple as pie. You'll see."

Faith wasn't so confident, but she was soon visiting with Caitlin around straight pins clenched between her teeth while they cut out pattern pieces on the kitchen table. It was Charity's job to lay table knives in strategic spots to hold the patterns and material anchored when Faith and Caitlin ran low on pins.

"I brought my recipes, too," Caitlin said as they worked. "I'll leave them here so you can copy them. There are extra cards in the box. Feel free to use as many as you like. When Patrick has a spare moment, you might ask him to make you a box to keep them organized. He made mine for me." Her eyes went soft with affection. "It was his birthday present to me one year. I've treasured it ever since. I never open it without thinking of him."

Faith smiled. "It was kind of you to come, Caitlin."

"Not at all. I've been *dying* to meet you." Caitlin glanced after Charity as the child scampered from the room with Spotty at her heels. "I wanted to see what sort of woman had finally managed to capture my brother's heart."

Faith stopped cutting to glance up. "Pardon me?"

"He's in love with you," Caitlin said simply. Her cheek dimpled in a smile. "Oh, he isn't quite sure about that yet," she said with a shrug. "Men never are, until it hits them square between the eyes."

"In love with me?"

Caitlin sobered and gave Faith a woman-to-woman look that spoke volumes. "My brother has suffered in ways you can't imagine," she said softly. "You can't force yourself to return his affection. I understand that. But I do hope you'll have a care for his feelings. He's seen enough hurt in his life."

Faith was so stunned by this revelation that it took her a moment to reply. "I am indebted to your brother in ways I can't begin to explain. I would never intentionally cause him pain."

Caitlin smiled and returned her attention to the patterns. "That's good enough for me." With a mercurial unpredictability that Faith was fast coming to realize was a part of Caitlin's personality, the pretty redhead launched into the story of how her marriage had come about. "The last man on earth I wanted to marry was Ace Keegan!" she said with a laugh. "It wasn't the best of beginnings."

"But you're happy now?"

"Deliriously happy," Caitlin said with another laugh. "I love him with my whole heart, and he loves me just as much. I honestly believe that Ace would lay his life down for me."

With a shrug, Caitlin changed subjects yet again and began giving Faith a summary on her recipes. "Just *don't,* under any circumstances, try the sauerbraten," she warned. "Right after Ace and I were married, I wanted to impress him and his brothers with something special. I can't remember who it was now, but one of them took a bite and spat the meat out on his plate, telling everyone else not to eat any more because it had gone bad."

Faith loved sauerbraten herself. She laughed until her sides hurt.

"I was crestfallen," Caitlin said with a sigh.

Ace arrived with the sewing machine right after they finished cutting out all the garments. When he entered the kitchen, Faith had cause to wonder if handsome men grew like weeds in Colorado. Keegan was as dark as Caitlin was fair, a tall, imposing figure of a man who wore a nickel-plated pistol on his hip and walked with a slight limp. He was, Faith decided, almost as handsome as Patrick.

"So you're the young woman who has my brother-in-law all moon-eyed," he said as he took Faith's hand in his. After giving her a bold once-over, he winked at his wife and said, "Pretty as a picture. That's one mystery solved."

Faith blushed. "You flatter me, sir."

Ace Keegan threw back his ebony head and laughed. "Not the first time, I'm sure, and it won't be the last." He encircled his wife's narrow shoulders with a strong arm. "How are you feeling, little mother?"

"I'm fine," Caitlin replied with a smile. "You worry too much. Pregnancy isn't a fatal disease, you know."

"I just don't want you to overdo."

"I won't." Caitlin shoved playfully at his chest. "Off with you now. Go pester Patrick while I show Faith how to operate my sewing machine."

That evening, Patrick invited Faith for a walk after supper. While Charity and her puppy raced off to explore, they walked in silence for a while, lost in their own thoughts. Faith's were centered on the man beside her. Was it true that he was developing an affection for her, as Caitlin had implied? And if so, was he thinking of asking her to marry him?

Faith had mixed emotions about the possibility. On the one hand, she was fearful of surrendering her life to someone again. But on the other hand, she had to admit that Patrick was like no other man she'd ever known. He seemed to genuinely enjoy her company, for one thing, and she truly enjoyed his. He had a way of making her laugh when she least expected it, and she looked forward to their suppertime conversations, which usually began over the meal and continued as they cleaned up the kitchen together after Charity was in bed.

"Do you remember that night when you came to my room, and I said we'd have to share the stories of our lives sometime?" he suddenly asked.

Jerked from her reverie, Faith sent him a bewildered look.

"I've grown very fond of you in the time you've been here," he said candidly. "At this point, I don't know where that may lead, or if it will even lead anywhere. But I think it's time for you to know a little more about me."

Faith felt she already knew all the things about Patrick that really mattered—that he was good and kind and generous.

His voice thick with emotion and sometimes taut with anger, he began by telling her about his father. "Wasn't a day went by that Caitlin or I didn't get the back of Connor O'Shannessy's hand," he said gruffly. "And when a cuffing was the worst of it, we felt damned lucky. All during my childhood, he was workin' his way toward the bottom of a bottle. He wasn't a happy drunk, to put it mildly. Mean as a snake, more like."

"Oh, Patrick."

He shrugged and gazed off at the darkening horizon as they walked along. "Many was the time that I crept out from my hiding place when he was tearing hell out of the house in search of Caitlin. For reasons I've never to this day come to understand, he preferred to beat on her rather than me."

"You took the beatings in her stead?"

"Don't go growin' a halo around my head. After he died, I adopted his ways. Started drinking myself stupid and flying into rages. The last time I got drunk, I struck my sister. Slapped her across the face and knocked her clear off her feet."

Faith saw the aching regret in his eyes.

"Caitlin has forgiven me, and I pray that God has, but I'll never forgive myself. All she ever did to deserve it was love me."

Driven by compassion and a need to offer comfort, Faith reached to grasp his hand. "We all do things that we regret," she assured him.

His throat convulsed as he struggled to swallow. Then he hung his head, saying nothing for several paces. "Things went wrong in my head for a while, Faith. That's no excuse, but it's the only way I know to explain so you can understand."

He fell quiet again, as if trying to sort his thoughts. When he finally resumed speaking, his voice had gone hollow.

"When I was only a little tyke, a family named Paxton came west and settled on a tract of land that adjoined ours. The man, Joseph Paxton, Senior, had paid good money for the parcel and had the papers to prove it. My father and others refused to recognize the validity of Paxton's deed and ordered him off the land. Paxton was a peaceful man, not given to fighting. He started packing his family up to leave.

"It was a swindle, plain and simple, perpetrated by my father and his friends. When one of them got shot in the back, they accused Paxton of the murder, and then, without a trial, they hanged him."

Faith's heart twisted at the pain she saw on his face.

"That wasn't the worst of it. I won't get into all the horrible details. Suffice it to say that they hanged the poor man in front of his family. I like to think that my father believed Paxton was guilty." His mouth twisted in a bitter smile. "Why, I don't know. He was a terrible man who did terrible things. But there's still a part of me that wishes there had been a little bit of good in him somewhere. You know what I'm saying?"

Faith understood better than he could realize. She often caught herself making excuses for her father, wanting to believe he had a few saving graces.

"Ace Keegan, Caitlin's husband, was Joseph Paxton's stepson."

She gasped. "And he married the daughter of his stepfather's murderer?"

Patrick sighed. "That's another story. But, yes, in answer to your question. He married the daughter of his stepfather's killer. How he has made his peace with it I'll never know, but somehow he has."

Faith recalled Caitlin's saying that her marriage had had bad beginnings. Now she understood why.

"Ace was only eleven years old the night Joseph Paxton was hanged. I'm sure you noticed the scar on his cheek and the way he limps. That's because my father, Connor

O'Shannessy, bashed him in the face with the butt of a rifle and then shattered his hip with a kick of his boot."

Faith knew she should say something, but words eluded her.

"After my father died, Ace Keegan returned to No Name, hell-bent on clearing his stepfather's name. In the process, he made some terrible accusations, all of them directed at my father in one way or another." Patrick dragged in a shaky breath. "Deep down, I suspected that the accusations were true, but that didn't make the truth any easier to swallow, and I detested Ace Keegan for forcing it down my throat. Came to a point where I was ashamed to hold my head up when I went into town because my last name was O'Shannessy."

"Your father's actions were no reflection on you."

"Oh, yes. You've seen the portrait of him. I'm a dead ringer for my old man. 'Just like your daddy,' people used to say. 'A regular chip off the old block.' You can't know how those words haunted me. I didn't *want* to be like him, but I knew I was. I saw the resemblance when I looked in a mirror, and more times than I wanted to count, I caught myself acting like him. Talking like he did, walking like he did, laughing like he did. As time wore on, and Ace Keegan's accusations became common knowledge, the shame I felt became intolerable. I found numbness in a bottle. I wasn't thinking of Caitlin or how my drinking might affect her. For a while there, I was bent on becoming just like my father and proving everyone right."

"You're *nothing* like him," Faith protested. "Nothing like him, do you hear? There's a physical resemblance, yes. But inside, where it truly counts, you're as different from him as night is from day, Patrick."

"Do you really think so?"

"I know so." Faith gave his hand a hard squeeze. "You're a good man, Patrick, a *fine* man."

He curled his fingers warmly around hers. "So was my father at some point in his life. I don't know what made him turn bad. Maybe the death of our mother. Who knows? But turn he did. When my sister was only sixteen, he sold her favors to a friend for six cases of whiskey."

A picture of Caitlin's lovely countenance moved through Faith's mind. *"No,"* she whispered. "Oh, dear God, Patrick, no."

"It wasn't like he did it when he was crazy drunk and not thinkin' straight. He planned it. Sent me away on a cattle drive to get me out of the way, then sat at his desk, swilling whiskey, while a man brutally raped my sister." Patrick's mouth thinned and drew back from his teeth. "Try living with that," he said tautly. "Knowing a man like that sired you, that his blood flows in your veins."

Faith could only shake her head.

"I needed for you to know," he told her. "Like I said when I started, I've grown very fond of you, Faith, and of your daughter as well. That being the case, it doesn't seem smart to keep secrets. We inherit certain traits from our parents. Bloodlines are the making of a man. Mine are nothing to be proud of."

"And you think mine are?" Faith thought of her father again, and the awful sick feeling returned to her stomach. "Think again, Patrick O'Shannessy. Bloodlines can determine our appearance, but they have nothing to do with who we are inside."

He gave her a searching look. "I'll bet you have a pedigree that would put a champion racehorse to shame."

Faith laughed. "Oh, yes, I come from a long line of Maxwells, all of them very fine and upstanding on the surface. Just don't look too closely."

Patrick leaned around to search her gaze. "You can't tell me that your father ever did anything as despicable as mine did."

"I doubt he's ever killed anyone. That isn't to say he may not have been responsible for someone's wrongful death. He probably just hired it done." She lifted her shoulders in a helpless shrug. "Fathers back east do despicable things to make money, too, Patrick. The swindles are prettied up to make them seem respectable, but they're swindles all the same. They also sell their daughters. The asking price is just a good deal higher, and it's all made legal with marriage."

"Meaning that you were sold to Harold?"

"Essentially."

His jaw muscle started to tick. In that moment, Faith knew that he was in love with her. Not so very long ago, she might have recoiled at the very thought, but she'd come to know Patrick O'Shannessy now. On the outside he appeared to be a rough, common man, but on the inside there was nothing common about him.

"Did the bastard hurt you?" he asked with a dangerous edge to his voice.

Under Harold's tutelage, she had learned that there were many different kinds of pain, but for now, she chose not to go into that. "No, not in the way you mean. Most of the pain in my marriage was more emotional than physical. I was born and raised a Maxwell. From early childhood, I was expected to comport myself with pride and dignity and grace. And then, in marriage, I was stripped of all three." She felt her chin tremble and swallowed hard to steady her voice. "It wasn't a conventional union, if indeed such a thing exists. My father was in textiles. My father-in-law owned a shipping line. When Harold and I married, the two enterprises merged."

Patrick stopped walking and turned to search her expression. "Don't make light of it, Faith. Six cases of whiskey or a fleet of ships, it doesn't matter a damn. You were sold all the same. It must have been bad for you."

Faith seldom let herself recall that period of her life precisely for that reason, because it had been so hurtful.

Peering through the twilight gloom to check on her daughter, she haltingly recounted to Patrick the pertinent details of her life, specifically that her mother had died when she was quite young, leaving her to be raised by a father who resented her because she hadn't been born a boy.

"Shortly after my mother's death, my father remarried. Sadly, his new wife miscarried late in her first pregnancy and then died of childbed fever. My father's hopes for a son seemed to die with her. After living my whole life being virtually ignored by him, I suddenly became the center of his attention."

Patrick gripped her hand more tightly. "Were you glad about that?"

Faith considered the question. "In the beginning, I suppose I was, yes. It was wonderful to be noticed, even when his attention grew obsessive. He began hiring tutors to teach me French and give me music lessons. If I forgot to stand straight or walk like a lady, the punishments he meted out could be quite severe." Faith's throat went thick at the memories. "As I mentioned, I was very young, about ten or so when the worst of it began—and having lost my mother, I was a desperately needy child. In the beginning, I think I mistook my father's absolute focus on me as a sign that he loved me after all. I didn't even suspect his motives when he sent me away to a finishing school at far too young an age."

Patrick gazed solemnly at her. "Why do I get this feeling that Harold is about to enter the picture?"

"Because you're so very astute?" Faith forced another humorless laugh. "If only I had been so intuitive. Perhaps then it wouldn't have hurt so deeply when I figured out my father's plan."

"Tell me," Patrick said simply.

"It truly isn't a very interesting story." Faith turned her hands to stare at the lines on her palms. "Sad, perhaps, but not interesting."

"Humor me."

"When I was polished to my father's satisfaction, he began to seek a suitable husband for me. Harold and his father were invited to supper. I was put through my paces.

They liked what they saw. After the meal, the three men adjourned to the library and began negotiating the marriage contract over cigars and brandy. On my wedding day, I had just barely turned fifteen and had never been alone with my husband."

"Oh, honey."

The understanding in his tone gave Faith the courage to continue. "It wasn't so bad, Patrick. Not that part, anyway. Unbeknownst to me, Harold was gravely ill with consumption and not expected to live out the year. Even with his father pressuring him to get me with child to provide him with another heir, Harold was too weak to bother me on a regular basis, and when he did, more times than not, he failed to accomplish the deed."

"Sweet Christ. And he blamed you for his failures?"

Faith frowned in bewilderment. "How did you—?"

"Never mind. I spoke out of turn. Go on with your tale."

Faith took a deep, cleansing breath. "That's pretty much it, the sordid little story of my life. In the short while we've been here, you've been more of a father to Charity than mine ever was to me."

"I've done precious little for your daughter," he protested.

"Say what you like. Before we came here, it had been months since I'd heard her laugh. Just listen to her now." Her daughter's laughter and the barking of the dog drifted lightly to them on the wind. "Thank you so much for allowing her to have the puppy. She's wanted one for a long while, but neither of her grandfathers would hear of it."

"I'm sorry about your marriage, Faith. It shouldn't happen that way, you know. Two people should love each other when they're joined in holy matrimony."

There had been nothing holy about Faith's marriage.

"It isn't always sordid," he went on. "The physical side of marriage is a beautiful thing when two people love each other."

He spoke with such conviction that Faith could almost believe it. "Perhaps," she settled for saying.

"Trust me. It's beautiful."

She hugged her waist. "I'll have to take your word for it. Nothing between Harold and me was beautiful, not even the birth of our daughter. He was so infuriated when he learned that I'd brought forth a girl that he didn't even look at her when he entered the birthing chamber. He came directly to my bedside and began ranting at me about the fine mess I had made of things. He was growing sicker by the day, time was running out, and his father was absolutely livid that our child was a useless female."

"How old was Charity when Harold died?"

"Four, and it wasn't a day too soon." Faith caught the inside of her cheek between her teeth and bit down until it stung. "Forgive me, Patrick. I shouldn't talk that way. But, God forgive me, it was how I felt. When I wasn't daydreaming about grabbing Charity and running far away, I was wishing the disease might kill him more quickly."

"Don't apologize for being honest. If I had been there, I might have done more than wish him gone. Any man who chastises a woman for giving him a beautiful little girl instead of a son isn't worth the powder it'd take to blow him to hell. You and your daughter are well rid of him."

Faith could only wish that everything else in her life could be so easily resolved. She'd gotten her first taste of freedom here on this ranch, but if her father had anything to say about it, that wouldn't last for long.

"Somehow I have this bad feeling that I haven't heard all of the story," he said gently. "Something prompted you to leave Brooklyn. Charity said your father was trying to make you remarry, but that makes no sense. You're what, twenty-two?" At her nod, he added, "And a widow, to boot. Your father can't pick and choose your husband for you now. You're free to make your own choice."

Faith gazed off through the dimness at her daughter for a long moment. "After Harold died, things were complicated," she confessed. "Considering his wealth, he left me only a paltry sum, but it would have been enough for Charity and me to live in modest comfort, had I ever received the money. Unfortunately, my father convinced Harold that I was financially inept, and the bequeathal was put into a trust, with my father appointed as trustee. After my husband died, I was penniless except for the small monthly stipend Papa allowed me, and even that was conditional. If I behaved and did as I was told, he was generous. If I balked and kicked up a fuss, he withheld all funds and threatened to toss me and my daughter out in the street."

"Surely he never would have done it."

"Perhaps not, but knowing him as I did, I was afraid to put him to the test."

"So he held you in financial bondage."

"More or less. My father is a powerful, ruthless, and relentless man who's accustomed to having his own way. If one tactic fails him, he quickly tries another. He's fond of saying that everyone has an Achilles' heel. At that point in time, Charity was mine, and I didn't protest overmuch when he found me another husband."

Even though Faith had long since come to accept that her father had never loved her, it still hurt to tell Patrick the rest. "His name is Bernard Fielding. He's an old man who may still have it in him to sire a son but will surely die soon after, leaving me to play the bereaved widow again." Tears leaped into her eyes, and she blinked rapidly to chase them away. "When I met Bernard, the truth smacked me right between the eyes. It was no accident that my father had chosen a dying young man to be my first husband. It was never his plan for me to marry happily and raise a family. The plan was for Harold to get me with child and then conveniently die, leaving my father to do the childrearing."

A stricken, horrified look drew Patrick's face taut. "He

deliberately chose husbands for you that had one foot in the grave?"

"That's an interesting way of putting it." Faith's neck had grown so stiff that it hurt to nod her head. "But you're absolutely correct. First Harold, and then Bernard. All Papa cared about—all he has ever cared about—is acquiring a male heir to take over the enterprises and possibly even carry on the Maxwell name if he plays his hand right. I was and still am only a means to that end. He doesn't care if I'm miserably unhappy. He doesn't care if I'm mistreated. He doesn't even care what may happen to Charity because of his evil scheming. We mean nothing to him."

"My God, if he had his way, you'd be nothing but a broodmare."

Again, Faith was momentarily taken aback by his choice of words, but she'd been around Patrick long enough now to shake it off. "A broodmare, yes. That describes it, exactly."

He slowly closed the distance between them, his eyes holding hers with somber intensity. Lifting one hand, he lightly smoothed a tendril of hair from her cheek, his fingertips setting her skin afire wherever they touched. "You deserve more than that, Faith. You deserve a father to love you, and a husband to cherish you."

"We don't always get what we deserve," she whispered.

He bent closer, so close that she could feel the warmth of his breath on her lips, and she realized that he was going to kiss her. Even more surprising, she wanted him to. Oh, how she wanted him to. The air between them went electrical, and an eerie hush seemed to surround them. She leaned toward him, as helpless to resist his lure as a hapless moth diving at a candle flame. Her lips parted. Her breath started coming in shallow, uneven pants that left her lungs aching for oxygen. He slipped his hand under her chin, grasped her jaw, and lifted her face to his.

"Maman!"

Faith jerked, and Patrick stepped quickly away as he turned toward the approaching child. "What have you got there?" he asked, his smile revealing no trace of irritation as he crouched to look into Charity's cupped hands. "Ah, a rock."

Faith almost giggled. She stifled the urge and stepped closer to admire her daughter's grimy treasure. "Oh, my, it has sparkly ribbons all through it that look like gold. You don't suppose it is, do you?"

Patrick lifted the rock in the fading light, turned it this way and that, and then nodded. "You may have something here, sweet pea. Are there any more like this one lying about?"

Charity fairly bubbled over with delight. "Oh, *yes*. Lots and lots of them, Paddy! Are we going to be rich?"

"Maybe so." He cast a glance at the darkening sky. "Run collect as many as you can. When we get back to the house, I'll take a closer look in the light."

Charity was off like a shot. Patrick grinned after her. "Fool's gold," he said softly as he turned back toward Faith. "It's so thick in some parts of this country that Ace Keegan decorated his fireplace with the stuff."

"Too bad. I could do with a windfall."

"Couldn't we all? That isn't to say there isn't gold in this country. No Name was originally a gold rush town that went bust so quickly no one ever got around to christening it."

Faith chuckled at the revelation. "Ah, well."

"Easy for you to say. I've been wanting to steal a kiss from you for over a month, and then when I finally work up my courage, I get interrupted."

A flush crept hotly up her neck.

"It's just as well, I suppose," he added. "I distracted you from your story."

"That's it. When I discovered that Bernard meant to farm Charity out to a boarding school directly after our nuptials, we left Brooklyn. When our money was stolen, we could go no farther and ended up stranded in No Name."

"I, for one, am mighty glad you did."

Faith shared that sentiment. If they hadn't stayed in No Name, she might never have met Patrick.

"All's well that ends well," he observed, his eyes trailing slowly over her face as though he meant to commit each feature to memory. "You're here now. It's time to look forward and put the bad memories behind you."

"I wish it were so simple."

"What's complicated about it? You're over twenty-one. You have a job to support your daughter. Your father's hold on you is broken."

"You don't know my father."

The haunted look in Faith's eyes made Patrick's heart catch.

"If he finds me—and there's strong possibility that he may—he will stop at nothing to have his way. Even more frightening, I know he won't come after me alone. He'll bring a small army of hired guns with him." She toed the weeds that grew between them, then sighed and closed her eyes. "Perhaps we'll be lucky," she whispered, "and he'll never find us."

In an entirely different way, Patrick had experienced the long reach of a powerful man during the early years of his life. On countless occasions, he and Caitlin had tried to run away, only to be caught by well-meaning neighbors or townsfolk and carted back to their father. To this day, he could remember the fear that had nipped at their heels after they made good an escape, how they'd both jumped at shadows and kept looking over their shoulders, terrified of seeing their father towering behind them.

"I honestly don't believe he'll ever think to look for you in Colorado."

"My father might not, but he won't be doing the looking. He'll hire paid bloodhounds, the best investigators in the country. I want to believe they'll never track us down, but realistically, what are the chances that a woman and little girl, traveling so far by themselves, drew no one's attention along the way?"

In that moment, as he searched Faith's eyes, Patrick knew that this was no irrational, feminine fear, but spine-chilling terror based on fact. Her father was searching for her even as they spoke, and eventually he would find her.

Chapter Seven

The following morning, Patrick strapped on his gun. Then he saddled his gelding and rode over to the Paradise Ranch to seek the advice of his brother-in-law, Ace Keegan. Joseph, Ace's younger half brother, joined them out by the corral. Patrick would have preferred to see Ace alone, but he'd long since come to understand that Ace and his brothers were as thick as thieves. When there was trouble, they faced it together, and Patrick had definitely come to them this morning with trouble riding double behind him. He guessed that showed on his face.

"That's a hell of a note," Ace said when Patrick had recounted Faith's story to them.

"Sure is. What kind of father is this Maxwell fellow?" Joseph spat on the ground. He wasn't a tall individual, but for a short man, he packed one hell of a wallop, in Patrick's estimation. Only a fool would tangle with him. "Give me ten minutes alone with the son of a bitch," he said. "Sounds to me like he needs a boot planted up his highfalutin ass."

Patrick had to smile. He and Joseph Paxton talked the same language.

"Jesus, Joseph, get a rein on that temper," Ace inserted. "Patrick's here for advice, not to rally a mob."

Joseph leaned over to spit again. He gave his older brother

a narrow-eyed look. "Time was when you were as quick to get riled as I am. Has marriage turned you soft, big brother?"

"There's nothing soft about me, you cocky little bastard. Any time you get to wonderin', hop on it like a frog."

Patrick couldn't help himself. He had to laugh. He quickly sobered when both men glared at him. He coughed and rubbed his nose. How Caitlin managed to rule her household with such a small fist, he'd never know. There wasn't a man in her new family who dared to enter her home without wiping his boots clean first.

"Back to your problem," Ace said to Patrick, with a warning look at his brother. "And just for the record, I don't think a boot up her father's ass is the answer."

"What is the answer?" Patrick asked.

"Marry her," Joseph said. "Only way I see."

Ace rolled his eyes. "That isn't the answer, Joseph. How do you know if he even has feelings for the woman?"

"By lookin' at him," Joseph replied. "He's got that same sick-calf look that you used to have when you were chasing your tail over Caitlin."

"I never chased my tail over Caitlin."

Joseph chuckled. "You sure as hell did, and had me chasin' mine, too. Snarlin' at everybody, ornery as a badger with a thorn in its paw. Hell, big brother, she's still got you chasin' your tail. You love that girl beyond all reason."

Ace parted his lips to argue, and then snapped his teeth closed. "I'm going to remember this when you finally get hitched."

"Never happen," Joseph replied confidently. "I'm a grazer. Fence me in on one pasture, and first thing you know, I'll be stretchin' my neck to nibble the grass on the far side of the wire."

Ace rolled his eyes again. Then he settled a thoughtful gaze on Patrick. "Is Joseph right? Do you have feelings for this woman?"

Patrick almost said no, but as the word tried to creep up

his throat, he swallowed it back, recognizing it as a lie. He'd been in over his head with Faith almost from the first, and he'd been struggling to stay afloat ever since. He loved the woman; that was the long and short of it. He'd also come to love her daughter as if she were his own. The thought of marriage still sort of alarmed him, but not nearly as much as the thought of losing them did. When he tried to imagine his life without Faith and Charity in it, his blood ran cold and his chest hurt.

"I love her," he confessed. Once the words were out, he wondered why he'd been so reluctant to say them.

"Enough to put your bacon on the plate?" Ace asked.

Patrick straightened his shoulders and nodded.

"Well, marry her, then," Ace said. "That'll put a hitch in Mr. Maxwell's get-along like nothing else will. Man sounds like a bully to me, and bullies only push people around when they can get away with it. Faith won't be so easily intimidated by the arrogant bastard if she has a husband who won't hesitate to push back."

That made sense. Patrick had known a bully personally, and for a goodly number of years. In all that time, he'd never once seen Connor O'Shannessy whale the tar out of a man bigger than he was. His father's victims had always been unable to fight back.

"What about Charity?" Patrick asked. "If I marry Faith, she'll be safe enough, but what of the child? Is there any way Maxwell could get custody?"

Ace scowled thoughtfully. "I think you'll automatically become the child's legal guardian, but to be on the safe side, go straight from the justice of the peace to the courthouse and file for adoption."

Faith was struggling to dismember a plucked chicken when Patrick returned to the house. Charity sat at the table, building a house of cards, the puppy asleep by her chair. Patrick moved in close behind Faith where she stood at the sink and bent to nibble the nape of her neck. She missed her aim with the butcher knife and nearly relieved herself of a thumb.

"What are you about?" she asked breathlessly.

"Trying to get your attention."

He had definitely succeeded. Fiery heat swirled in her belly, and her nipples had gone as hard and sharp as screw shafts. "A simple hello would suffice. I'm trying to make chicken and dumplings."

Patrick latched on to her earlobe and did fascinating things to it with flicks of his tongue. "I love chicken and dumplings. But right now, I've got other things on my mind."

Faith's knees almost buckled. "Like what?"

He glanced at Charity. "Can you tear yourself away from that hen and take a turn around the yard with me?"

"Can I come?" Charity asked.

"May I come," Faith corrected, wondering when her daughter had started to talk like a Coloradoan.

"Not this morning," Patrick told the child. "I need to speak to your ma in private."

Patrick seldom denied Charity anything. Of late, Faith had even begun to worry that her daughter would become spoiled and willful if he had his way. She gave Patrick another wondering look. He only smiled, handed her a towel to wipe her hands, and then grasped her by the arm to lead her outside. Once there, he stalked in a circle around her for a moment, then stopped, planted his hands on his hips, and said, "I love you."

Faith was so startled that she cocked her head. "I beg your pardon?"

"Damn it, Faith, you heard me the first time. Don't make me say it again until you're ready to say it back."

"You love me?"

"That's what I said, isn't it?"

He didn't seem to be very happy about it. In Faith's estimation, it was marvelous news. She started tapping her toe. "May I ask what brought this on?"

"Your father. If he finds you now, he may find a way to make you go home. He could claim you're emotionally unbalanced—or that you abuse your daughter. God only knows. If you marry me, nothing he says or does will hold any sway. I'll be able to tell him to go whistle Dixie."

"That isn't enough reason for us to marry, Patrick."

"I love you. Isn't that reason enough?" He winced and turned his gaze toward the sky. "Damn it. You made me say it twice." He leveled a burning look at her. "Out with it. I want an answer right now. Do you feel the same way or not?"

"You are cursing at me, sir."

He winced again. Then he threw up his hands and turned a full circle. When he faced her again, he leaned forward to get nose to nose with her. " 'Damn' is a byword. It's not a curse word by my definition. All the same, I apologize. I don't reckon I should say it while I'm proposing to you."

"Is that what you're doing, proposing?"

The glint in his eyes intensified. "What? Do you want me on my knees? Is that it?"

"No. It's just that you seem so upset!"

"If you felt like this, you'd be upset, too."

An odd, tight sensation closed around Faith's throat. "How is it that you're feeling, Patrick?"

"Scared."

She searched his sky blue eyes, trying to understand. "Scared of what?"

"Scared to death that you don't love me back."

Tears stung her eyes. The next instant she was in his arms. She wasn't sure if he'd grabbed her, or if she had jumped. And it didn't really matter. She was in his arms, right where she belonged.

"I'm not a good lover," she whispered against his neck.

He laughed and spun in a circle with her clasped against his hard chest. "You will be, darlin'. Leave it to me."

He had taught her so many things, how to milk cows, how to make butter and cheese, how to slop hogs, and how to do laundry. She was also becoming a halfway decent cook. Perhaps he could teach her how to make love as well.

Faith prayed so. She wanted to please this man. She wanted that more than almost anything.

"Oh, Patrick," she whispered fervently, "I love you, too. I love you so very much."

"It's a damned good thing. Otherwise I'd be in a hell of a fix."

At Patrick's insistence, Faith stood at the center of her room an hour later, draped head to toe in ivory silk and lace. To say she was bewildered was an understatement. Patrick was right; the dress that he had stowed in the trunk that first afternoon bore no dirt stains. It was as spotless and perfect as new. There was just no explaining it. Faith clearly remembered dropping the gown in the dirt and despairing afterward that it was ruined. And yet, by some miracle, it wasn't. Even stranger, it fit her like a glove. It was almost as if the dress had been made especially for her.

Faith closed her eyes and ran a hand down the front of the gown, marveling at the tingling warmth that ribboned through her body. She'd felt it the instant she slipped into the dress, and the heat had intensified with each button that she fastened. It was almost as if the dress were imbued with some inexplicable magic. She remembered how she'd felt drawn to it the first time she'd seen it and then how she'd felt when she touched it. Even stranger, directly afterward, she had spotted Patrick's advertisement taped to the door window of the mercantile. How was it that she'd passed that store a fair hundred times and never seen the sign until she'd been holding this dress in her arms?

"Knock, knock. You about ready?"

Patrick shoved his head through the crack of the door. Faith felt suddenly self-conscious as she faced him.

"Dear God," he whispered.

"Is it too fancy?" she asked.

He stepped into the room, his expression stunned. He wore a white shirt and black dress slacks. He was, in Faith's estimation, the handsomest man who'd ever drawn breath.

"Too fancy? No. It's gorgeous. *You're* gorgeous. You look so beautiful, I can't believe you're real."

Faith's stomach was churning with nerves. She wanted to become Patrick's wife more than she'd ever wanted anything, but she couldn't shake the feeling that something terrible might happen to spoil their happiness together.

"Oh, Patrick, I'm scared."

"Of me?"

She gave a startled laugh and then found herself blinking away tears. "No, never that. I'm just—oh, I don't know." She glanced at the window. "It's probably stupid, but ever since you asked me to marry you, I've had this feeling that my father will appear at any moment."

He stepped across the room and drew her into his arms. "All the more reason to get this done. Once you're my wife, you can stop being afraid. If he comes around, I'll draw him a map in the dirt to guide him out of here and give him a boot up the ass to help him on his way."

Faith wanted to believe that. She needed to believe it. But she couldn't shake the feeling that something dark and sinister awaited them just around the corner.

It was to be a simple ceremony before a justice of the peace. And by all rights, it should have been the plainest, simplest wedding on record. The JP performed all nuptial ceremonies in his sitting room, the walls of which were papered in a pattern of ancient roses, long since turned brown from the smoke of his cigars. His wife was a stout, unadorned woman who nodded and seldom spoke. Faith had barely recovered from the shock of finding goats on the people's doorstep when she and Patrick were saying "I do."

Nevertheless, she felt thoroughly and wonderfully married afterward. Caitlin and Ace were there to witness their vows, along with all of Ace's brothers. Charity preceded Faith into the sitting room, sprinkling rose blossoms from Caitlin's flower garden on the worn carpet. All in all, it was, in Faith's opinion, the most beautiful wedding ever.

After the brief ceremony, Faith nearly swooned when Patrick kissed her. It was not only their first kiss but also a startling revelation: She actually *liked* it. He encircled her waist with one strong arm, drew her snugly against him, and tasted her mouth as if she were a succulent piece of fruit.

"My turn," Joseph Paxton said with a laugh. The next thing Faith knew, she was draped over his muscular arm, expecting to feel his mouth on hers at any moment. Instead, he winked at Patrick and bussed her cheek.

After that, Faith received more kisses on the cheek, the first delivered by Ace, the second by Caitlin, followed by quick kisses from the rest of the Paxton men. Esa was a quiet, gentle-mannered man with a kindly smile. David had a tough, wiry look about him, and he wore a silver star on his shirt, leading Faith to believe he must be a lawman.

With congratulations ringing in her ears, Faith signed the necessary papers to record her marriage to Patrick O'Shannessy. When those particulars had been completed, Patrick led her and Charity to the courthouse, where he filed more papers to adopt Faith's daughter. Then Caitlin arrived to collect the child.

"Your daughter and her puppy will be spending the night at our place," she cheerfully informed Faith. "It's your wedding night, after all." Ruffling Charity's hair, Caitlin winked at Patrick and smiled. "Charity has kindly offered to help me make cookies tonight."

Faith had never been apart from her daughter overnight. As though attached to the child by an invisible string, she followed Caitlin and Charity from the courthouse. Never leaving her side, Patrick gave her elbow a reassuring squeeze as Ace swung Charity up into his wagon.

"They'll take good care of her, honey. No need to worry."

Faith was about to agree when she spotted a well-dressed gentleman entering the hotel farther up the street. Her heart gave a nasty lurch.

"What is it?" Patrick asked.

Faith blinked and shook her head. The man had already entered the building. "Nothing. It's just—" She shook her head again and reached blindly for her husband's hand. "Nothing. I just thought for a moment that I saw my father."

Patrick curled an arm around her. "And so what if you did? I told you once how that will go. Do I need to say it again? From this moment forward, the only man you need to worry about is me."

Faith dragged her gaze from the hotel and forced herself to look up at Patrick's dark countenance. His deep blue gaze gave her the strength to dredge up a smile. "You're right. Absolutely right. I'm just being silly."

Faith went up on her tiptoes to kiss her daughter good-bye and then surrendered happily to the circle of Patrick's arm as Ace drove the family wagon away from the boardwalk. When the dust had settled, Patrick bent to kiss her forehead.

"Well, Mrs. O'Shannessy, are you about ready to go home?"

Home. The word had such a lovely, final ring to it. With a last worried glance at the hotel, Faith relaxed and laughed. "I am, sir. Lead the way. I'll follow you anywhere."

"You'll never walk behind me," he whispered huskily. "Only beside me."

In truth, Faith didn't care if she led or trailed behind, only so long as she could spend the rest of her life with him.

It had been a hectic day, packed with varying emotions. By the time Patrick reined in the team of horses in front of his house, Faith was thoroughly drained. After he helped her from the wagon, she went inside and stood at the sink in her wedding dress, wondering stupidly what she should fix for supper. The chicken she'd left in the icebox, she guessed.

"We'll have eggs and bacon," Patrick said when he came in from the barn a few moments later. "It's late. We're both tired. That'll make less mess to clean up after."

Faith jerked back to awareness, wondering how long she had been staring blankly at nothing. "I'm sorry. What did you say?"

He came to wrap her in his strong arms. "Why the worried frown? Are you thinking about your father again?"

Faith wanted to deny it, but when she looked into her husband's eyes, she couldn't bring herself to lie. "That man going into the hotel. He truly did look like Papa. I know it's unlikely, but I can't shake the feeling that it may have been him."

Patrick's embrace tightened. "Given the fact that it's our wedding day, I sincerely hope not. But if he's here, we'll deal with him."

"He isn't easily dealt with."

Patrick's mouth thinned. "You can't live the rest of your life terrified that he may show up, Faith. Have some trust in me. You're my wife now. His hold on you is forever broken. From this moment forward, you have nothing more to fear from him."

She closed her eyes and pressed her face to his shirt. After drawing in the scent of him, she sighed shakily. "You're right. No more worrying." She let her head fall back and smiled. "Eggs and bacon sound lovely."

"I'll cook." He bent to kiss her and set her head to spinning. Then, his voice husky with desire, he gently nipped her lower lip and said, "Why don't you go upstairs and get into something more comfortable while I'm tossing together some grub?"

Faith felt perfectly comfortable in the wedding dress, but she might dribble food on the bodice if she didn't change into something else. She went upstairs, rifled through her armoire, and selected Patrick's favorite, a pale blue dress that had seen better days. After stepping out of the wedding gown, she carefully folded it and laid it at the foot of the bed until she could put it away in the trunk.

When she'd finished dressing, she turned to pick up the wedding gown. It no longer lay on the mattress. Bewildered, she got on her knees to look under the bed. Then she checked inside the trunk, thinking she might have put the gown away without thinking. *Nothing.* It had vanished into thin air.

Patrick found Faith at the foot of the bed. "What's wrong, sweetheart?"

When she told him that the wedding dress had disappeared, he executed a search as well. Finally, he gave up, shrugged in bewilderment, and scratched his head. "I'll be damned. Where on earth could it have gotten off to?"

Faith swallowed, hard. "I think it was charmed," she whispered.

"You think it was what?"

"Charmed." Afraid he might think she was crazy, Faith told him about the tingle of warmth that she'd felt the first time she touched the dress, and how, afterward, she'd seen his advertisement for the first time, even though she'd walked past the mercantile on countless occasions. "When I dropped the gown along the road, I felt sure that it was ruined. But when I got it out of the trunk earlier today, there wasn't a dirt stain to be seen. How could that happen? You didn't clean it, did you?"

"No. I just folded it up and stuffed it in the trunk." He frowned slightly. "I don't remember there being any dirt stains on the skirt, though. I just remember thinking how pretty it was."

"It was ruined, I'm telling you." Faith gave the room another appraisal, half expecting to see the dress somewhere. "I can't help but wonder if it wasn't charmed, Patrick."

He didn't laugh, just gazed wonderingly at the trunk. "Maybe it was charmed," he agreed. "You ended up here, didn't you? That's all I care about, that you found your way to me."

Tears of happiness stung Faith's eyes. "That's what truly matters," she agreed. "That we're together."

He sighed, smiled slightly, and said, "Supper's done. You hungry?"

Faith felt hungry, but not for eggs. "Not really. Are you?"

He moved slowly toward her. "I'm starving."

Moments later, Faith giggled. "I just fastened all these buttons, Patrick O'Shannessy. Now I can only wonder why I bothered."

He nibbled at her throat, sending tingles of heat spilling into her belly. "Beautiful gifts must always be unwrapped," he whispered.

Faith let her head fall back, trusting him as she'd never trusted anyone. "Love me, Patrick," she whispered.

He slipped the sleeves of her dress down her arms, kissed her deeply, and then granted her request, loving her as every woman yearns all her life to be loved. He began with a deep kiss that made her toes curl. Then he lifted her into his arms and carried her to the bed. Her chemise and bloomers soon followed her dress into a puddle on the floor.

"Oh, *yes*," Faith cried when his wonderful mouth trailed to her breasts. "Oh, *yes!*"

Faith floated on a dizzying rush of sensation, surrendering all that she was to him. When at last he entered her, she felt complete as she never had in her life.

Bracing his muscular arms, he suspended himself over her, not moving, barely breathing. "I love you," he whispered raggedly. "Ah, Faith, my sweet, I love you so much."

Before she could respond in kind, he plunged deeply within her and took her with him to paradise.

The next morning, Faith felt content in a way that only a well-loved woman can. She and Patrick had made love several times during the night, each time sweeter and more fulfilling than the last, until they'd collapsed with exhaustion in each other's arms just before dawn. As a result, they had awakened late, and both of them were scrambling to complete their morning chores before the day was half gone. After gathering the eggs, Faith blew her husband a kiss from the back stoop. Then later, just after she finished the milking, he caught her as she exited the stall and led her to the hayloft, where he gave her good reason to wish the day were over so they could make love all night again.

"For a woman who had no taste for this, you're sure warming to the experience mighty fast," he said as he fastened her bodice with deft fingers.

Faith giggled and plucked straw from her hair. "I must look a sight."

"You look beautiful," he whispered and kissed her again.

Before she knew quite how it happened, she was prone in the hay again, her body quivering with yearnings that only he could slake. And, oh, how wonderfully right that felt. For the first time in her life, she felt really and truly loved, just for herself.

That was such a fabulous feeling.

Some time later, Faith was gathering carrots from the kitchen garden for a stew for supper when she heard the sound of horses approaching. She cautiously circled the house, her heart pounding with unreasoning dread. She wasn't really surprised when she reached the front yard and saw her father sitting astride a galloping horse, flanked by at least a dozen riders, all wearing sidearms.

Faith almost bolted, but then she remembered that she was legally married. Legs trembling, she walked resolutely to the front fence and rested a hand on one of the pickets. The men who rode with her father ran hard, glittering gazes over her as they came to a halt in a long line. When Faith looked at them individually, they stared back unflinchingly. The stench of their bodies drifted to her on the warm summer air—a sickening mix of soured sweat, whiskey, and another smell she felt certain was pure meanness. They were mercenaries, the kind of men who regularly sold their souls for a dollar. Faith had seen men like them before in Brooklyn, only there they'd worn suits and postured as gentlemen.

Saddle leather creaked as the men shifted in their seats. A horse snuffled and pawed the dirt, sending up puffs of dust that quickly vanished in the breeze. Faith tried to speak, couldn't, and swallowed hard to find her voice.

"Papa," she finally pushed out by way of greeting. "Whatever are you doing here?"

"I've come to fetch you and my granddaughter home. What do you suppose I'm doing here?"

The harsh clip of his voice propelled her back through time to her childhood, when his every command had been her edict and disobedience had earned her an unpleasant punishment. A shiver of icy fear coursed through her body. She dug her nails into the wood. "I shan't ever return to Brooklyn, Papa. I've remarried. You've no control over me now."

Her father leaned forward in the saddle, his face turning almost purple with rage. "You dare to defy me? Collect your daughter. You shall return home. The marriage can be annulled easily enough."

Faith had no doubt that her father could do it. There was always a way to bend the law if a man was wealthy and determined. "I have the right to make my own choices now, Papa, and I've chosen Patrick O'Shannessy as my husband."

"Don't argue with me, girl. You'll come home if I have to drag you."

Faith feared that her father would try to do just that, his plan undoubtedly to browbeat her into submission once they were back in Brooklyn. There was just one problem; she had a husband now who would object very strongly to her being forcefully removed from the premises.

Fleetingly, Faith wondered where Patrick was. When last she'd seen him, he'd been mending the door of the henhouse. "I'm not going back with you, Papa."

"You will do as you're told!"

One of her father's henchmen wrapped his horse's reins around the saddle horn, as if he meant to dismount and collect her. Faith fell back a step, prepared to run. But before the command from her brain could reach her legs, the smell of smoke surrounded her. Horrified, she glanced over her shoulder. To her dismay, she saw a black cloud billowing up from somewhere behind the house. For an awful moment, her heart froze. Then she rounded on her father.

"What have you *done*?" she cried.

"Nothing!" Her father narrowed his gaze on the sooty plume. "There's a fire, apparently. I didn't start it."

Faith didn't believe him. Her father could be ruthless when he wanted something, and right now, he wanted her married to Bernard Fielding. After being with Patrick, the very thought sickened her. If she ever had a son, and she prayed that she would, the child would be Patrick's, conceived in love.

She ran a frightened gaze over the ruffians her father had hired. They all sat relaxed in the saddle now, their hands close to their guns. They were the sort who could kill without blinking an eye.

"What have you done to my husband?" she cried.

"Nothing," a deep voice said from behind her.

Faith sagged with relief. "Patrick!"

His hand came to rest at the small of her back. His touch soothed her as nothing else could. "Go in the house, sweetheart."

Faith threw him a terrified look. When she saw the tick of his jaw, she cried, "No, Patrick. You're one man against a dozen."

Patrick settled a fiery blue gaze on her father and smiled calmly. "No worries. Your father knows he'll be the first to go down if bullets start to fly. We'll just talk and reach an understanding."

Faith didn't want to leave him. In that moment, as she looked up at his burnished face, she knew that she'd never loved anyone as much as she loved him. She loved her daughter, of course, but that was an entirely different kind of love.

"No, Patrick. Please, if you make me go, come with me."

"Faith, do as you're told," he said evenly. "Go into the house. And don't come out until I say it's all right."

She started to argue. But then Patrick glanced down at her. "Trust me," he whispered. "It's going to be fine."

After sending her father a pleading look, Faith turned to go inside. Leaving the front door ajar so she could monitor the exchanges between her father and husband, she went only as far as the sitting room. There, she stood with her nose flattened against the window glass, whispering disjointed prayers for Patrick's safety. *Foolish man.* Feet planted wide apart, arms held out to his sides, he stood alone against a small army, his right hand poised over his gun. Did he have no sense at all?

Nevertheless, Faith felt proud to be his wife, fiercely proud. By comparison, her father was a pale figure of a man, courageous only when the odds were heavily in his favor.

In the distance, Faith saw a cloud of dust fast approaching. Soon she could make out riders. Her heart lifted with hope. Seconds later, Joseph Paxton brought his stallion skidding to a stop in the yard. He was out of the saddle before the horse had come to a complete stop. Shortly after, Esa and David rode in. They dismounted from their horses and went to flank their older brother.

Faith's father shifted nervously in the saddle. "Don't push me, mister," he warned Patrick. "My men are expert marksmen and fast at the draw. You and your friends here are going to die if you get in my way."

Patrick kept his hand over his gun. "You've got a lot of men riding with you," he agreed, "but sadly for you, Mr. Maxwell, their loyalty is rented." Patrick slowly turned his head to look each hired gun directly in the eye. "I may go down, just like he says, and maybe my friends will go down as well. But we're going to take some of you with us. Which of you falls remains to be seen, but mark my words, at least half of you aren't going to be sitting down for breakfast tomorrow." He looked back at Faith's father. "Are they willing to die for you, Mr. Maxwell? Seems to me that money sort of loses its shine when a man's facing possible death. Can't spend a paycheck from six feet under. Another thought for you to ponder on is that you'll be our first target. No matter how fast your men are, they can't get all of us before one of our bullets finds you."

Joseph flexed his fingers over the butt of his Colt. "You'd best perk up your ears, Mr. Maxwell. Your boys may be fast, but we're faster." Narrowing his eyes against the sun, Joseph scanned the group of hired guns. "If you boys are fast draws, then you've surely heard of Ace Keegan."

"What if we have?" a swarthy man asked.

"Ace is our brother," Joseph replied. "He taught all of us boys how to handle a gun. Maybe we aren't as fast as he is. Maybe we are. Carry on with this madness, and you'll soon find out."

The dark man shifted uneasily in the saddle. He sent Faith's father an angry glare. "You said this would be easy. I didn't bargain on facing fast guns. If I've got to put my life at risk, I want more money."

"He's bluffing," Faith's father cried.

"Am I?" Joseph flashed a dangerous smile. "Proof's in the pudding, boys. Let's slap some leather and see who meets his Maker."

Faith's father had started to sweat. "There's no need for violence. I've just come to collect my daughter and granddaughter."

"You mean my wife and child," Patrick corrected. "Sorry, old man, but that ain't happenin'."

"The marriage is invalid!!" Faith's father shouted. "Faith is betrothed to another man. She cannot be married while she's contractually obligated to someone else."

David stepped forward, thumbing his badge. "By whose law? You're in Colorado now, not Brooklyn, and I'm the marshal hereabouts. Your daughter's marriage to my brother-in-law is legal. Unless you want to ride out of here slung over the back of a horse, I suggest you accept that and make fast tracks."

Carlton Maxwell sent Faith a burning look through the window glass. "This isn't finished, young lady," he called. "Mark my words, this isn't finished by a long shot."

"Oh, it's finished," Patrick corrected evenly. "If I see you on my property again, the time for talking will be over. I'll shoot you on sight."

"Do you hear that, Faith? This no-account piece of trash that you married just threatened to shoot me." Her father jabbed a finger in her direction. "You'll rue the day you formed this alliance. When the time comes that you realize your mistake, don't come whining to me. From this moment on, I don't have a daughter. Do you hear me?"

Faith was still trembling when her father and his men wheeled their horses and rode from sight. She raced from the house. Patrick held out an arm to encircle her shoulders and draw her close to his side. He bent to kiss her hair. "Hey, darlin', you're shakin' like a leaf."

Faith turned her face against his shirt. "Oh, Patrick, never in my life have I been so sick with fright."

"All's well that ends well." Patrick drew his wife closer and met Joseph Paxton's gaze over the top of her dark head. "I owe you one."

Joseph dusted his hat on his trouser leg. "You don't owe us nothin'. If the tables were turned, you'd do the same for one of us."

"That may be, but I still appreciate that you came so fast."

Joseph's cheeks creased in a grin. "Of course we came fast. You're family now. We Paxtons look after our own. Besides, it appeared to me like you were handlin' them well enough on your own." He clamped a hand on Esa's shoulder. "We just evened up the odds a bit. Right, little brother?"

Esa nodded. "Ace is gonna be flat pissed that he missed out on all the fun."

David spat in the dirt, then toed away the evidence. "Nah. He's got more important fish to fry this morning." With a twinkling look at Faith, he added, "He took Caitlin and Charity into town to shop for baby stuff."

Joseph settled his tan Stetson back on his blond head. The wind kicked up just then, lifting golden hair straight as a bullet to trail the strands across his chiseled face. "Well, boys?" He narrowed an eye at the sun. "Looks to me like it's near about noon, and my belly's sayin' it's lunchtime."

"Won't you stay and have the noonday meal with us?" Faith asked. "We've plenty, and we'd love to have you."

"What're you fixin'?" Esa asked with a hungry glint in his eyes.

Joseph gave his brother a sharp jab in the ribs. "Thanks for the invite, but we'd best mosey on home. Chores to do, and all that."

"What chores?" Esa asked.

"Afternoon chores." Joseph grasped his younger brother's elbow and turned him toward their horses. "Do I need to make out a damned list?"

As the three brothers mounted up, Patrick could hear Esa muttering under his breath that all the chores were done. Joseph and David ignored his protests, waved farewell, and herded the youngest Paxton's horse from the yard.

"I think they refused the invitation to lunch because we were married only yesterday," Faith observed.

Patrick nodded. "I think you're right."

When the Paxton brothers had ridden out of sight, he tightened his hold on his bride and turned her into his arms. "Are you all right?"

She nodded and went up on her tiptoes to hug his neck. "Just a little rattled. When I came around the house and saw my father, my heart almost stopped beating." She leaned her head back to look up at him. "Whatever will we do if he comes back?"

"He won't," Patrick assured her. "I got my message across to him, loud and clear, and Joseph let him know that I'll always have their backing. Men like your father are too fond of their hides to risk getting shot. They only throw their weight around if they think they can get away with it. I can almost guarantee that we've seen the last of him, and good riddance."

A troubled expression entered her eyes. "That bothers you, doesn't it?"

"That men like your father are too fond of their hides to risk getting shot?"

"No, that you'll always have the Paxton brothers' backing."

Patrick bent his head to rest his forehead against hers. "I suppose it does in a way. I reckon it always will."

"Why, Patrick? Your sister is married to Ace. Soon she'll have a child, binding your families together. It's time to put the past behind you."

His throat went tight. "My father killed theirs. Two years ago, we all buried the hatchet, and on the surface it's all but forgotten. But down deep, I can't believe they don't still hate me, at least a little."

"Why? Because down deep, you'll always hate yourself?" Faith leaned back to take his face between her hands. "Oh, Patrick. You aren't your father. You're a kind, wonderful man, and I love you with all my heart. I'm so proud to bear the O'Shannessy name. Don't you think it's time that you felt proud of it again yourself?"

"My father—"

"Enough about your father. It isn't about him anymore, Patrick. It's about *you*. It's about *us*. We can spend the rest of our lives looking back, but to what end? I don't want our future to be tainted by bad memories, neither yours nor mine. I want Charity and our other children to hold their heads high when they go into town, proud to be O'Shannessys."

Faith held her breath as she waited for Patrick's response. When his eyes went suspiciously bright, she knew that she had reached him.

"You're right," he whispered huskily. Then, grabbing her hand, he led her to the barn. "Stand right here," he ordered.

Faith did as he asked, frowning in bewilderment as he rummaged around inside the building. After a few minutes, he emerged into the sunlight, dragging a huge wooden sign behind him. Faith stepped around to read the carved letters. Then she laughed.

"Will you help me hang it back up?" he asked.

"I'd love to."

And so it was that Faith stood on the tailgate of Patrick's decrepit old wagon, holding up one end of the sign while Patrick nailed the other end to the side of the barn. When the task was completed, they linked arms and stood back to admire their work.

The sign read, THE O'SHANNESSY RANCH. Faith nodded in approval, and in that moment, she knew she would never again yearn for all that she'd left behind in Brooklyn. Everything that she'd ever wanted or needed was right here. She turned to hug Patrick's waist with a deep sense of rightness and belonging.

As their lips met, she thought of the wedding dress, wondering once again where it might be. After making the bed that morning, she'd searched the room a final time and found nothing, which had convinced her, for once and for all, that the gown had vanished. She had no explanation for that, other than the one she'd whispered to Patrick last evening, that the dress was magical.

It was a fanciful, crazy answer, Faith knew. Or was it? As her husband deepened their kiss and her blood began thrumming with desire, she couldn't deny that sometimes, when a woman least expected it, truly magical things could happen to forever change her life.

Read on for an excerpt from
Catherine Anderson's next heartwarming
contemporary Harrigan family story

HERE TO STAY

Available from Signet in February 2011.

Prologue

Music blared from the barroom stage where the Bush-whackers, Crystal Falls' top country-western band, pounded out rhythms that kept the dance floor packed. The lead singer—a tall dude in Wranglers, a spangled Western shirt, shiny cowboy boots that had never met up with cow shit, and a Stetson studded around the crown with silver conchos—offered a fervent rendition of John Michael Montgomery's dated hit "Be My Baby Tonight." The fast beat throbbed in the air, inspiring couples to pick up the pace as they executed the intricate heel-and-toe steps of a country line dance on the well-waxed plank floor surrounded by small tables.

Zach Harrigan lounged in a far corner of the room, his chair tipped precariously onto its rear legs and his arms folded loosely over his chest as he studied babes with the ease of long practice. Bronco Bart's was his favorite hunting ground, a popular watering hole that normally attracted a lot of gorgeous women. Problem was, tonight they all looked the same: tall, slender bleached blondes in skintight jeans and figure-hugging knit tops that left little to the imagination. As he took measure of their cookie-cutter bodies, Zack wondered if a terrorist had spiked the Oregon water reservoirs with a virus that made women want big boobs. A large percentage of the females within his line of sight looked as if they'd gone under the knife. Hell, a lot of the women he'd slept with over the last six months—and that was no small number—had paid thousands for breast augmentation. Some had even suffered nerve damage during surgery. What man in his right mind wanted to suckle a numb tit? In Zach's opinion, a guy could have almost as much fun nibbling on an overfilled water balloon.

Feeling oddly irritated, Zach reached for his bottle of beer. Empty. Zach glared at it with dark suspicion. Maybe he was drinking too much, but what the hell? He lifted an arm and signaled the new waitress. She wasn't hard on the eyes, and getting another beer would give him an excuse for a closer inspection.

She nodded, dealt with another customer, and approached Zach's tiny table. "What's for you, mister?"

Noting automatically that while she had magnificent breasts, she was also wearing a wedding ring. Zach placed his order. She gave him a knowing smile, stepped away from the table, and soon reappeared with a fresh bottle.

Zach snatched it up and took a long pull. Condensation beaded on the glass, wet and icy under his fingers. The ale had a brassy edge that puckered his tongue and left his throat feeling as if he'd just swallowed a piece of chalk. *What the hell's wrong with me?* Zach usually loved beer and women. Okay, he always loved beer and women. That was why he was a steady at Bart's, where the taps ran cold and the babes ran hot. He'd come here to pick out a squeeze, cozy her up in a Texas Two-Step, and sweet-talk her into bed, preferably at her place so he wouldn't have to deal with her little mating calls in the morning when he had a hangover. Then he'd scat before two so he could catch a little shut-eye before starting a long day of hard work at his ranch before dawn. As a bachelor, that was his modus operandi. It had worked nicely for years. So why did he suddenly feel bored, disgruntled, and at loose ends?

Maybe, he decided with a vague sense of panic, he was getting too old for this shit. The thought no sooner took root in his mind than he shoved it away. *Old, my ass.* He was only thirty-one. He could still work circles around his hired hands, and the women still went for him. Just why they did, Zach wasn't sure, but they did. Always had. He'd studied himself in a mirror many times, trying to figure it out, and all he saw was a carbon copy of his dad, Frank— trim, well-muscled build, skin that had turned permanently dark from too much sun, black hair, brown eyes, and the Harrigan nose, which was more along the order of a beak. *You sure couldn't call either of us handsome,* he decided. Nevertheless, females seemed to be attracted to the package. So, he couldn't be over-the-hill yet. He was just having an off night.

Just then the dance ended, and a blond sexpot left the floor to undulate between the tables toward him. Zach narrowed his eyes on her face. *Wake-up call.* He knew her. He'd slept with her last Saturday night, an experience he didn't care to repeat. A year ago, some bozo had gotten too rough with her during sex and ruptured her right breast implant, leaving her with serious hang-ups about any kind of pressure on her chest. She didn't want to be hugged. She couldn't lie on her stomach. When Zach so much as bumped against her breast accidentally, she'd gone ballistic. He didn't mind being gentle with his partners. It was the way his dad had raised him to be. But to his way of thinking, sex should be spontaneous and fun, not a lesson on the proper handling of saline sacs.

"Hey," he said, knuckling up the brim of his hat, a cowboy's casual gesture of respect when a lady approached. "How's it going?"

Without an invitation, she perched her world-class ass on a chair across from him, flashed a smile of pearly white overlays, and batted her mascara-coated eyelashes. For the life of him, Zach couldn't recall her name. Mary, Sherry, Terry?

Something like that. _Shit_. She'd feel insulted, and rightly so, if he couldn't think of her moniker.

"I'm feeling sad," she said. "The best dancer in the place is sitting on his duff." The eyelashes did another spider dance. Her baby blues locked on his. "I thought you might at least come over to my table and say hi."

Zach forced his lips into a curve that he hoped would pass for a grin. _Terry_. That was her name. "It's crowded in here. A pretty little gal like you gets lost in the maze of bodies. I didn't see you when I came in."

She pursed her lips in a well-practiced pout. "So I don't stand out in a crowd? Thanks. I had no problem spotting you."

Zach took another swallow of beer, making a mental note to switch brands the next time the barmaid made table rounds. Maybe it was just a bad batch, but the stuff tasted nasty. As he set the bottle back down, he studied Terry's face, then dropped his gaze to her deep cleavage, which was seductively exposed by the low scoop of her cherry pink top. _Not interested_. She could hassle some other poor bastard tonight about hugging her. He wanted no part of it.

"So . . . are you with someone?" she asked. "I'm pretty much free for the evening."

Probably because every man in the bar had slept with her and knew she was about as much fun as a bad case of the clap. "I'm on hiatus tonight. Hurt my back yesterday picking up a foal."

"Oh, no." She flashed her dental work again. "I'm a fabulous masseuse. Come to my place, and I'll make it all better."

Zach shifted on the chair and pretended to wince. "Give me a week, and maybe I'll take you up on that. Not tonight, though. A pretty little thing like you deserves a cowboy who can deliver, and I'm out of commission."

Her eyes darkened, and Zach knew she saw right through him. He hated hurting someone's feelings. He and Terry hadn't really connected on a personal level last weekend. It had been only about sex, two consenting adults scratching each other's itch, only he had come away from the experience feeling unsatisfied. Not her fault. Some guys probably didn't mind the "don't touch" routine, but for Zach, it had been a turnoff.

He was about to flip on the cowboy charm and convince her that he truly was interested in seconds some other night. He always began that routine by asking for a woman's phone number. But just as he opened his mouth to speak, a ruckus erupted on the opposite side of the room. Always on guard, Zach zeroed in on the commotion. A thin brunette was arguing heatedly with some rhinestone cowboy, waving her hands and yelling. Behind her stood a lanky redheaded man who wore dark glasses and carried a white cane. _Blind?_ Zach had never seen a sight-impaired guy in a place like Bart's, but he guessed there was a first time for everything. And, hello, even the disabled had a right to patronize a bar and listen to a local-yokel band.

The woman turned to take the redheaded man's arm. As she tried to guide him forward, the cowboy dude grinned broadly, stuck out his boot, and deliberately tripped the blind fellow, sending him into a staggering sprawl that ended with what had to be a painful face plant on the planks. Zach rocked forward on his chair, bringing the front legs down so fast they emitted a loud popping sound.

Zach didn't feel himself move, but he could hear Terry calling out from behind him as he pushed his way through the couples who stood frozen on the dance floor. "Don't interfere, Zach! Someone will call the cops. Let them handle it!"

Yeah, right. Even through the maze of bodies, Zach could see the blind guy regain his feet, right his dark glasses on his bloody nose, and try to step forward again, only to be tripped a second time by that stupid excuse for a cowboy.

"Pardon me," Zach said as he squeezed past a woman. "Sorry," he said to her partner.

When he reached the edge of the dance floor, he grabbed hold of the blind man's arm to help him stand up. "Hey, man. Are you okay?"

The frames of the guy's dark glasses were now broken, and his bottom lip was streaming blood. Zach's own blood went from hot to boiling. His father had taught him never to start a fistfight. The only exception to that rule was when a bully was harming another person or an animal. Zach figured deliberately tripping a blind man was an offense that fell into that gray area his father so often talked about. _Sometimes, son, you got no choice but to man up and kick ass._

Even so, Zach had no desire to get cuffed and stuffed by Crystal Falls' finest, or to spend a sleepless night in the local hoosegow. He turned to the grinning idiot who'd just tripped a blind man for the hell of it. Nudging back the brim of his hat, Zach squarely met the dumb fuck's gaze and said, "Partner, you're either a little too drunk to be in a public place, or your daddy failed to teach you any manners. Which is it?"

Zach never saw the blow coming. The other man's fist landed like a wrecking ball right between his eyes. Everything went star bright and then pitch-black. Zach felt his body going airborne and his muscles turning limp. Someone screamed. And then he landed on his back, his spine striking something flat and hard. The next instant the surface broke under his weight, and he tumbled to the floor in a splintering pile of wood. A table, he determined as his vision spun blurrily back into focus.

Dumb Fuck stood over Zach, smirking as he sucked his bruised knuckles. Somehow Zach doubted the man's hand was hurting as badly as Zach's face was, but the mean-hearted asshole was about to find out he'd made a helluva mistake by laying into a Harrigan. When Frank Harrigan read about this fracas in the _Crystal Falls Daily_, Zach wanted him to laugh and say, "That's my boy. He kicks ass first and takes names later."

Zach tried to break free of the debris to sit up. As he did, he saw Dumb Fuck lean forward with one fist knotted to deliver another blow. Zach fell back into the pile of wood, knifed up with one knee, and planted his foot dead center on the other man's chest. With one hard shove, the bastard reeled into fast reverse, staggering to keep his balance, flailing wildly with his arms, and then sprawling across a table. Zach scrambled to his feet, swiped at his eyes to clear his vision, and then leaped on the guy. The combined weight of two grown men sent the second table into a joint-shattering meltdown.

Zach didn't have a clear thought in his head after that. Vaguely he realized there was a lot of commotion and screaming, and he felt someone grab his arm from behind. He jerked free and let the creep have it again. His mind came clear only when two other men dragged him off his opponent, saying, "That's enough. He's had enough."

Zach shook his arms free and wiped his mouth with his shirtsleeve. Blood came away on the cuff. No matter. Dumb Fuck lay on the floor in a fetal position, holding his middle and whining that his jaw was broken.

"Police! Break it up! Step aside. Police!"

Shit. Hoosegow, here I come. Zach was a little unsteady on his feet and sidestepped to remain standing. A second later, his balance, or lack thereof, didn't matter. His wrists were cuffed behind him, and a cop held him erect by one arm as he was led from the bar to an awaiting police car.

"He hit me first!" Zach protested.

"Tell it to your lawyer, buster. You have the right to remain silent. Anything you say—"

"I know my rights," Zach interrupted. "I've heard them a few times."

"We know, Harrigan," the cop said as he cupped a palm over the top of Zach's head and shoved him down onto the backseat of the vehicle. Zach squinted hard to focus. This same guy had taken him in a few months back for jumping in to defend a mistreated bull at the rodeo. He seemed like a decent sort for a cop.

"Wait a minute! Where the hell's my Stetson?" Zach yelled.

The slamming of the door was the only answer he got.

Three hours later, Zach, still minus his hat, sat on the edge of a jail cot, knees spread, his aching head compressed between his swollen hands. Dumb Fuck hadn't been brought in yet. He'd been taken to the ER for some stitches before lockup time. Zach had learned minutes ago that the idiot was filing charges against him for assault with intent to kill, or some damned fool thing like that.

Yeah, right. Zach couldn't believe this. He was in the clinker, faced with serious charges, and all he'd done was step in to defend some blind guy he didn't even know.

No real worries, though. Zach had used his one phone call to contact his dad. Frank Harrigan had money and connections. He'd have Zach out on bail in a matter of hours. It was the wait between now and then that had Zach's nerves jangling. He was a little claustrophobic, and being locked up gave him the cold sweats. Of course, he wasn't looking forward to another chewing out from his dad on the subject of his nightlife, either.

Man. He couldn't believe this, just couldn't believe it. Only when Zach rewound the scene at Bart's and replayed it in his mind, he knew he had no regrets and never would, even if he cooled his jets in this hellhole for a week. There were some things to which a man couldn't turn a blind eye. For Zach, the abuse of a disabled person was one of them. Kick a dog, and Zach was there. Beat a horse, and he was there. No man who called himself a man stood aside with his thumb up his ass while some jerk made sport of an animal or person who couldn't fight back.

Maybe, he decided, he'd reacted so angrily because of the article about guide horses that he'd read at the dentist's office last week. The mini horses being trained to guide the sight-impaired were amazing, and as a horse trainer, Zach had found the entire feature fascinating. So fascinating that he'd torn the pages from the magazine for future reference, thinking he might try his hand at training a mini himself. The thought had remained with him for a couple of hours, and then he'd forgotten all about it until now. *Typical.* He was so busy with his horse ranch and barhopping that he had little time for anything else. Zach couldn't even remember where he'd stuck the article. In a drawer, he guessed.

Staring blearily at the floor, he decided a hangover would have been preferable to the headache he had right now. At least then he would have had some fun earning his misery. The thought made him wince. *Yeah, right, like my life is fun? I'm so sick of this.* What would next Saturday night bring, another woman like Terry to his table? Another boring round of sweaty sex with him hurrying away before the semen dried on his dick?

There has to be something more than this to look forward to.

His father and a couple of his brothers had found love and happiness, but it hadn't happened for Zach yet. Maybe it never would. So where did that leave him? Was he destined to spend the rest of this time on earth working his ass off by day and taking up space on a barstool at night? The thought made him feel almost as claustrophobic as the cell bars did. *Okay, fine.* Maybe he wasn't cut out to be a family man. Maybe that simply wasn't in God's plan for him. But surely the Old Man in the Sky had something in mind for him to do that would be meaningful, something that would make a difference.

Zach's thoughts circled back to the article he'd read about guide horses and the blind man he'd fought to defend in the bar tonight. Was God tapping Zach on the shoulder? *Maybe.* The blind guy's dilemma in the bar could have been God's way of yanking Zach's chain to remind him of that magazine feature.

Zach straightened from a slump. *Tiny horses?* Oh, man, if he decided to train them, he'd have to keep it under wraps. Zach was renowned for his work with world-class cutting horses, not toy equines that slept in the bedroom and accompanied you to the grocery store. His brothers would laugh themselves sick and never let him hear the end of it.

Besides, Zach knew squat about training a service animal. Hell, he didn't know anything about disabled people, period. Even so, Zach had this weird feeling, way deep inside, that he'd been meant to read that article and that the incident tonight had been a reminder to him that there were better things to do with his time than to have less than satisfying sexual encounters with women whose names he couldn't remember.

When his dad got here, and after they went through the familiar bailout crap, and after he'd listened to his dad fulminate about his son wasting his life, Zach was going to go home and find that article. He'd careened through young adulthood thinking mostly about himself. Maybe it was time he gave a little something back. He knew horses. And if they could be trained to guide a blind person, he could learn how to do it, even if he had to be mentored for a couple of years by a Seeing Eye dog trainer.

What did he have to lose by giving it a try? *Nothing.* A mini horse would cost him some money, but Zach had plenty in the bank. His biggest investment in an experiment like that would be time, and at the moment, with the inside of his mouth still bleeding from a barroom brawl, keeping busy with something worthwhile seemed like a plus.

An odd feeling welled within Zach's chest. He realized that he felt excited, really excited, and he couldn't remember the last time that had happened. There had to be more to life than sex and beer, and maybe, just *maybe*, he'd found it—something he could do that would make a real difference in the world.

Chapter One

Two Years Later

Mandy Pajeck sat down beside her brother, Luke, on their old tweed sofa and balled her hands into fists. She had to talk to him again. She'd been stalling for days because she knew how he'd react. But she had no choice. Luke's entire future was at stake.

Pulling in a breath, she surveyed his sullen face, biting her lip as she searched his sightless gaze. Right now, he was focused on music blasting through headphones that pushed his chestnut hair into a rooster tail. His backbone slumped against the worn cushions. His long, slender fingers tapped his knees in time with the rhythm.

Sunlight slanted into the living room through the wood-framed windows, illuminating the scars on his handsome face and emphasizing the opacity of his hazel eyes, once so very like her own. At his feet, candy wrappers peppered the burnt orange carpet. Mandy kept a basket at his end of the couch, but he still tossed the papers on the floor. She didn't know if he found it difficult to locate the basket or if he was just thoughtless. For her, it was a minor irritation, so she'd never taken him to task for it. She'd learned over the years to choose her battles, focusing on things that really mattered.

"Luke?" When he didn't acknowledge her, she touched his arm. "Can we talk?"

He jumped with a start. Then, brows snapping together, he jerked off the headphones. "Dang it, Mands. Give me some warning. You scared the crap out of me."

"I'm sorry. With the music so loud, you couldn't hear me."

"Next time, jiggle the cushion or something to let me know you're there."

"I'll do that," Mandy assured him. "I just didn't think."

Luke nodded, and the scowl melted into a reluctant grin. "No big. My heart has started beating again. So, what's up? Is it time for afternoon snacks?"

Mandy moistened her lips. "We already had them. It's just— We need to talk."

The stony look that settled over his face told her he knew what the topic would be. "We've had a great day so far, and you're not going to change my mind, so just drop it."

Mandy wished she *could* drop it. It would be lovely to float along, pretending all was well. "Can't we just talk like two adults? You're nineteen now, not a little boy anymore."

"That's right, nineteen, old enough to make my own decisions. Just let it go."

"Sweeping problems under the rug doesn't make them go away." She kept her tone nonaccusing. "It's February. You passed the tests and got your high school diploma last June."

"And all I've done since then is take up space. Got it. You can skip the demoralizing details and get right to the point."

Mandy lifted her hands. "You've got no life! *That's* the point. No friends, no activities. All you do is sit in this house! I love you. How am I supposed to deal with that?"

"The same way I do, by accepting it." His voice rose in anger. "What do you want from me? It's not as if I can go out and get a job!"

Why can't you? she yearned to ask. Luke's counselors said there was no reason her brother couldn't do everything other blind people did. He was intelligent and able-bodied. Unfortunately, as a child, Luke had refused to use a cane and resisted rehabilitation, and when Mandy was awarded custody of him seven years ago, he'd insisted on being homeschooled, an option in Oregon that allowed kids to get a real diploma through the local education service district. Mandy had even hired tutors when her workload interfered with Luke's lessons. Luke had excelled academically, but the seclusion had left him socially inept.

Mandy knew her brother's negative attitude was mostly her fault. She'd been barely thirteen when their mother left. Their father should have hired household help to look after his four-year-old son. But Tobin Pajeck had been a tightwad, and those tasks had fallen to Mandy instead. Traumatized by the loss of his mother, Luke had clung to his big sister for reassurance, and Mandy, who'd felt lost herself, hadn't discouraged him. Over time, Luke's neediness had worsened, peaking at age six when he lost his sight.

A burning sensation washed over Mandy's eyes as she recalled that time in their lives. Riddled with guilt because she'd caused the accident that blinded Luke, she had made every mistake in the book: doing things for him, giving in when he threw tantrums, and never correcting his behavior. What Luke wanted, he got. If only she could turn back the clock. But life didn't work that way, and now her brother was paying the price.

She pressed a fingertip to her throbbing temple. "I don't expect you to get a job right now, Luke. You need some kind of training first."

"Here it comes," he muttered. "The college pitch again."

"You need to get an education."

"Why? I'm happy the way things are." He switched off the CD player. "Besides, what would I study to become? It takes no training to sell pencils on a street corner."

"There are people at the college who would help you pick a major. They'd give you aptitude tests to see what you're good at. You could find something that you really love to do."

"And how would I make my way around the campus?"

"You know how to use the cane. All you need is practice." At the moment, Luke wouldn't even move from one room to the next without Mandy's help. "You'll be running footraces around here in nothing flat."

"Finding my way around a house is different than moving around a big campus. Get real, why don't you?"

"I admit that it might be challenging for you the first few days. Maybe I could attend your classes with you for a while. I'm sure I can get special permission to do that."

"And have everybody think I'm a big baby who needs his sister to hold his hand?"

In truth, Luke was a big baby—a spoiled, demanding young man who was frozen in place—and, God help her, she didn't know how to help him reverse that.

"Sometimes," she said carefully, "the things we fear turn out to be no big deal once we force ourselves to face them."

"Easy for you to say."

Pinching the bridge of her nose, Mandy replied, "I know you get upset when I bring it up, but maybe a guide dog is the answer. We could get you on a waiting list and—"

"_No!_ We've been over this a hundred times. I'm terrified of dogs."

As a child, Luke had been bitten by the family Doberman, and an irrational fear of canines had bedeviled him ever since. "Guide dogs aren't your average, run-of-the-mill animal. They're very well trained and trustworthy. Why not at least give it a try?"

"End of subject!" He flipped on the CD player, clearly intending to block her out again. "Not one more word." He pushed the headphone muffs firmly over his ears. "Get off my back and leave me alone."

Mandy shot up and grabbed the headset, feeling a brief stab of satisfaction at her brother's startled expression.

"What if something happens to me? You have no one else. Mama had no family. Dad's in prison. His parents hung up on me the one time I called them for help. Name one other person you can count on besides me!"

Luke parted his lips but then sank back against the cushions without speaking.

"I'm it, Luke! What if I get hit by a bus or die of cancer? Who'll take care of you? Do you think our grandparents will have a change of heart? They don't give a damn about us. You need to get your head on straight and start acting like an adult instead of a spoiled brat!"

"You haven't seen *brat* yet, and you aren't going to die. You're only nine years older than me. Don't be melodramatic."

"Just because I'm only twenty-eight is no guarantee I'll be around forever. I need to know you can take care of yourself. It's not just about a job. It's about your being able to do simple things, like make a sandwich! If something happens to me, what will you do, sit in this house and starve?"

Luke groped the air for the headset. Determined to get through to him, Mandy held the apparatus just beyond his reach. "Will you please listen to me?"

"All I hear is white noise." He made a lucky grab and wrested the headphones away from her. "Leave me alone, I said."

Mandy trembled so violently, her legs almost buckled. Luke put the headphones back on and turned up the volume so far she feared the mirror behind the sofa might crack. "If you don't stop that, you'll end up deaf!" she yelled, but Luke couldn't hear her. His closed eyes, crossed arms, and hunched shoulders signaled total shutout.

Scalding tears pooled in Mandy's eyes. From dawn until well after midnight, she devoted nearly every minute of her day to Luke—helping him bathe and dress, cooking his meals, doing laundry, cleaning, and then working long hours as a medical transcriptionist in the tiny bedroom she'd converted into an office. And this was the gratitude she got?

Whirling away, she cut through the dining room to the adjoining kitchen. When she reached the chipped sink, she curled her fingers over the edge of the counter and stared out the window at the huge backyard, which was fenced and perfect for a dog. Her brother was such a blockhead. She hated to see him wasting his life this way.

Her knuckles throbbed from the force of her grip on the Formica, the ache in her temples had shifted behind her eyes, and her chest felt as if it might explode from frustration. *Take deep breaths. Don't let him get to you.* It was easier said than done.

To calm down, Mandy concentrated on the yard, which always lifted her spirits. One of her passions was gardening, and seeing the tidy flower beds, all mulched under a thick crust of snow, filled her with a sense of accomplishment. The peony she'd planted last spring was clipped to the ground now. She hoped it would snuggle under the layer of icy white and push up fresh green shoots again next summer.

Central Oregon was experiencing a cold snap, the temperatures so low that the air sparkled. Condensation blurred the window glass. Before long, it would be Valentine's Day. With a quivering fingertip, Mandy drew a heart in the film of moisture, wishing the holiday were already here. She could make old-fashioned chocolates and applesauce bread. The smell of loaves hot from the oven always made her feel festive.

My fault. She always came back to that after a quarrel with her brother. It didn't ease her conscience to remember that she'd been a child herself when she'd been raising Luke and only twenty-one when she'd finally gotten custody. Her brother had been her responsibility, and she'd made countless mistakes, end of story. Now he was a mess, and unless she could somehow get through to him, he would remain a mess.

She wouldn't think about it now. She needed to focus instead on salvaging the rest of the evening. To that end, she turned to her baking cupboard. She had no applesauce for bread, but chocolate-chip cookies would fill the house with lovely smells. Even better, Luke would be forced to call a truce if he wanted some. Not that he'd give in that easily. Unlike her, he was a brilliant strategist when it came to cold war.

Each evening before dinner, Mandy treated herself to an hour of television, her program of choice the local five o'clock news. She wouldn't forgo that today because Luke was in a snit. She made a cup of hot chocolate dotted with marshmallows, filled a plate with fresh-from-the-oven cookies, and snuggled under a throw at her end of the couch. Holding the mug close to her chin, she breathed in the sweet scent, enjoying that almost as much as the drink itself. It gave her a wicked satisfaction to bite into one of the cookies when she knew Luke smelled them. Well, he could either politely ask for some or do without.

Grabbing the remote, she turned on the television. Her brother's sulky expression told her he was still pouting. Tough. This was her only downtime of the day, and she would *not* let him ruin it. A talk show was ending, and the drone of voices started to soothe her. With the blinds drawn, the play of multihued light coming off the screen danced over the off-white walls. Mandy waited through several commercials for the news to come on. She didn't really care that much about what was happening in her hometown of Crystal Falls. It was the ritual she needed. Vegetating for an hour restored her energy before she had to start dinner.

Sometimes Luke listened to the news, but tonight he seemed bent on maintaining a frigid silence. That suited Mandy fine. College was important, and the longer he stewed about it, the better her chance to impress that upon him.

As if he read her mind, Luke balled up a candy wrapper and sent it flying with a flick of his finger. Mandy knew he did it to tick her off, his way of getting back at her for bringing up the guide dog again. Well, he could throw paper wads as far as the dining room. She'd just vacuum them up in the morning, like she always did.

Another wrapper went flying. This one struck the television, which she knew was accidental. Luke couldn't see to take aim. She tapped a toe on the cushion. He could be *such* an ingrate.

"I have to use the toilet," he informed her.

Luke had perfect timing; she'd give him that. The news was starting. She hit the RECORD button. No matter what, she would enjoy her hour of TV. If he played the interruption game, he'd get a late dinner. She wasn't hungry yet because she'd eaten cookies. Luke, on the other hand, couldn't even heat up a can of soup to tide him over.

Having that thought made Mandy feel terrible. She had no idea what it was like to be blind. It was wrong to be judgmental and have so little sympathy. Still, his cane, a tool he could have used to enhance his motility, remained in the closet. It was absurd that she had to guide him through this small house to the bathroom.

While Luke went inside to do his business, Mandy remained near the closed door, waiting to lead him back to the sofa. Seconds later when Luke emerged, he said, "I missed the bowl when I peed."

Mandy clenched her teeth; she knew he'd done it on purpose. *Fine.* She'd have to clean it up, making dinner even later. Saying nothing, she led him back to the living room, got him situated on the couch, and then went to get rags and disinfectant.

It was twenty after five before she could sit down again. Luke scowled, but she ignored him. He put his headphones back on and cranked up the volume until the sound reached her. She responded by turning up the television.

Setting thoughts of Luke aside, Mandy focused on the screen to see a cowboy leading a tiny palomino horse along a sidewalk in downtown Crystal Falls, only a half mile from her house. He didn't seem thrilled to be caught on camera, but when he tipped his black Stetson low over his eyes and quickened his pace, the news team hurried to keep up. The animal wore a harness with a handle that lifted over its back and a looped leash attached just below the chin. Interest piqued, Mandy curled both hands around the now cold mug and shifted to get more comfortable.

A slender blonde wearing an expensive-looking gray trench coat said, "This is Zach Harrigan, a renowned local quarter horse trainer."

Mandy recognized the name. The Harrigans were well-known, not only in Crystal Falls but all across the nation, for breeding and training world-class cutting champions.

"Mr. Harrigan has been spotted here on Main with this tiny horse at about the same time each afternoon for nearly a week," the reporter continued. "That sparked our interest, so we did some investigating. To our delight, we've discovered that he has recently embarked upon an incredible journey, training a guide horse for the blind."

Mandy jerked upright. Shooting a glance at her brother, she turned down the volume on the TV and leaned closer to the set. A guide horse? Was this for real?

"Recently is right," said the cowboy. Clearly annoyed, he kept walking. "Rosebud's in the early-training stages, not yet ready for the public eye. Why not wait until she's trained before you feature her on the news? The future of guide horses is on the line."

The blonde scurried to keep pace. "Can you tell us about the training process?"

Harrigan tugged his hat lower and declined to comment. The reporter stepped in front of him, leaving him no choice but to halt or cannon into her on camera.

"Please, Mr. Harrigan. Surely you understand what a novelty this is. People have seen you working with Rosebud. We're curious. Won't you talk with us briefly? We're not here to catch her making a mistake. We merely hope to educate the public about these wonderful horses, the assistance they offer sight-impaired individuals, and the fact that the Department of Justice and the ADA might ban them as service animals." The reporter smiled into the camera. "For viewers who don't know, ADA is an acronym for the Americans with Disabilities Act, and the Department of Justice is the agency in charge of enforcing it."

"You've done your homework," Harrigan observed.

"Yes, and by running this footage, we may inspire the public to begin writing letters in support of guide horses to our senators and congressmen."

Tension easing from his shoulders, the cowboy turned toward the camera. Though the brim of his hat shadowed the upper planes of his face, Mandy could see that he had jet-black hair, a sun-burnished complexion, a strong jaw, and a firm but mobile mouth. From his broad shoulders down, he was pure cowboy, trim but well muscled, dressed simply in a blue work shirt, faded jeans, and dusty riding boots. He wore no jacket. Maybe, Mandy decided, working outside so much had made him immune to the cold.

He settled a hand on the little horse's head. "Letters of support would be wonderful, but they should probably be sent to the Department of Justice and the ADA."

The reporter switched the mike from her right hand to her left. "You've taken on a big challenge. How did you prepare yourself to train Rosebud, Mr. Harrigan?"

"I've been training horses most of my life. I also worked for two years with a guide dog trainer to learn what blind people need a service animal to do."

"And that was all?"

Harrigan smiled. "Not by half. Training Rosebud is different than training a dog in some ways, and she must learn stuff big horses don't, so a lot of this is new to me. I don't want viewers to get a bad impression of guide horses if I make a stupid mistake."

The reporter was pretty, with golden hair and large blue eyes. She settled a solemn gaze on the mini. "It appears you're doing a marvelous job. I saw Rosebud lead you around a planter and signal you to step up at a curb. Watching her is fascinating. She seems as accomplished as any guide dog. What else must she learn?"

Harrigan's mouth tipped into a halfhearted grin. "Right now I'm trying to teach her how to deal with stairs. We're working on that at home."

"Are stairs difficult for her?"

He rubbed his angular jaw. "They're tricky. Stairs intimidate her. It's challenging for her—and for me."

"Will you be able to teach her how to do it?"

"We'll get there. She's very smart and catches on pretty fast."

The reporter nodded. "Can you tell us what led you to purchase Rosebud and embark on this journey?"

"I've done well with cutting horses, but there's more to life than making money. I wanted to do something more, something that would make a real difference. When I found out about guide horses, I knew I wanted to try my hand at training one."

The reporter glanced down at a black notebook in her hand. "With guide dogs already in use, why is it necessary for horses to be trained to perform the same job?"

"Not all blind people are candidates for a guide dog. Some are allergic to canine dandruff. Others are prohibited because of religious beliefs. Mini horses are a great alternative. The guide dog has an average life span of twelve years. A horse can live to be thirty and sometimes even forty, which means they can be of service much longer."

"Was it difficult to find Rosebud?" the reporter asked.

"It was. There are several things to look for in a guide horse—size, temperament, intelligence, good conformation, and health. Rosebud was perfect on every count. For a time, she performed in a circus. Then she went on to become a champion many times over in halter performance and other Division A classes. She's accustomed to large crowds and a lot of noise, yet she's only three, with plenty of years ahead of her."

The camera lens widened to show the newswoman grinning broadly as she leaned forward to pet the animal. Harrigan blocked her reach. "I'm sorry," he said, "but no contact is allowed. Rosebud is very affectionate and enjoys the attention of strangers a little too much. When we're working, she needs to stay focused on her job."

"I see." The reporter withdrew her hand. "She's darling!"

Mandy had to agree. With a stocky golden body and a fluffy white mane and tail, the mini was one of the cutest creatures she had ever seen. Rosebud's cowboy sidekick wasn't half bad, either. He had a deep, rich voice and an easy grin. Even on-screen, he exuded strength and had an air about him that commanded respect.

A guide horse. Glancing at Luke, who was still lost in his music, Mandy set aside her chocolate and pushed to her feet. Hurrying to the kitchen, she jotted down the cowboy's first name so she wouldn't forget it.

The latest Harrigan Family novel from

New York Times **bestselling author**
Catherine Anderson

Here to Stay

Mandy Pajeck had a tough childhood—an abusive father, a mother who left, and a younger brother, Luke, who depended on her when she was just a child herself. Now 28, Mandy remains devoted to Luke, and feels responsible for the accident that took his sight. But his complete reliance on her care is making them both miserable. When she meets handsome Zach Harrigan and his mini guide horse, she thinks she's found the ticket to her brother's happiness—and maybe her own.

Of the five Harrigan siblings, Zach was the hellion who partied hard and took nothing seriously. But lately his life has felt empty. So, employing his skills as a horseman, he begins training a mini guide horse for the blind—never expecting the project will lead him to beautiful, tender-hearted Mandy. She's everything he's ever wanted in a woman. But though she's charmed by Zach's patience and compassion, she can't bring herself to fully trust him. And when Zach urges her to confront the truth about her mother's disappearance, the secrets they uncover are so shocking that even Zach's steadfast devotion may not be enough to win Mandy's heart...

Available wherever books are sold or at
penguin.com

New York Times **bestselling author**

Catherine Anderson

"Her stories make you believe in the power of love." —Debbie Macomber

Available wherever books are sold or at
penguin.com

O. 0004968576 20201012